On Tilt

An Alexis Parker novel

G.K. Parks

Copyright © 2018 G.K. Parks

A Modus Operandi imprint

All rights reserved.

ISBN-13: 9781942710110

For my mom and dad

BOOKS IN THE ALEXIS PARKER SERIES:

BOOKS IN THE JULIAN MERCER SERIES:

ONE

I stared out the windshield, watching the hookers work their territory. It was no secret this was gang turf. Wearing the wrong colors in this neighborhood could get a person killed, but that wasn't going to stop me from asking questions. I had a girl to find.

According to the dated police reports, the lead detective suspected a gang connection but never investigated for lack of evidence. From my perspective, it appeared to be shoddy work, but not many privileged debutantes ended up in neighborhoods like this. Plus, the cops had come under pressure from the family to keep any potential ties to such pedestrian crimes off the media's radar for fear it would sully their daughter's good name. Now it was five years later, the girl was never found, and answers had become more important than image.

Stepping out of the shiny new luxury sedan, I hit the locks, wondering if the vehicle would end up stripped and on blocks by the time I returned. At least it was the company car. My ride wouldn't get a second glance, but I was playing in the majors now, even if it might be temporary. My employment status was contingent on solving this case, and given the track record of over a dozen investigators who already tackled it, the odds weren't in my favor.

The working girls glanced up as I made my approach. I didn't exactly blend in with their typical clientele. It was also a little early in the day for a good time, unless the businessmen liked to score blow or get blown before arriving to work for their early morning meetings. Maybe smack was in and coffee was out. I wasn't exactly up on the latest trends. Caffeine was about the only drug I could handle most days, and sometimes, even that was iffy.

"Morning," I greeted, squinting against the bright sunshine. "I'm curious. Are you just now starting your workday or getting ready to call it quits?"

"What's it to you?" the woman with neon orange boots asked. The color made her legs look like two shapely traffic cones. Perhaps that's how she stopped johns who were driving high-end sports cars. Was that how Julia Roberts did it? "You a cop or something?"

"Something," I replied.

"What?" Traffic Cones asked.

"Out of those two options, I'm something since I'm not a cop." I shook my head. "Never mind." Explaining my wit was always a bad way to start a conversation. It was also possible I actually wasn't witty, but I doubted it. I removed the photograph of the missing girl from my jacket pocket and held it out. "I'm trying to find this girl. The photo's a bit dated. I don't think she looks exactly like this anymore."

Traffic Cones turned away, not even bothering to look at the photograph. "Figures you're a cop."

"I'm not a cop," I retorted, exasperated. I turned to the other hooker who hadn't said a word since I approached. She continued to puff on her cigarette while she leaned against the brick wall. "I'm just looking for this kid. I thought there was a chance she might be working around here. Have you seen her?"

She dropped the butt to the ground and smushed it out with the toe of her shoe. "You think she's turning tricks?"

"It's a possibility."

"Why do you care?" She studied me and then the picture. "She's too old to be your kid. Is she your sister or something?"

Resisting the urge to offer the same reply that made her friend walk away, I took a deep breath. "Her mom and dad asked me to look for her."

"I can tell you one thing. If her folks sent someone after her, then you're probably in the wrong neighborhood. We don't end up doing this because we like the work. Sometimes, it ain't bad, but it ain't good either." Her eyes glanced up the block. "Fancy school uniforms don't exactly kick it in the 'hood." She sniffed, taking a step backward toward the alleyway. "So if someone dressed like that did show up one day, a person might remember. Maybe that kind of information is worth something."

"It might be." I knew how this was about to go. "Do you know something?"

She shrugged. "It'll cost you. And sweetie, I need the money upfront."

Unsure if this was a shakedown or legit intel, I reached into my pocket for the fifty dollars I earmarked for this particular reason. My wallet contained extra cash should I need to buy off a few hookers, but it was best to keep that kind of information on a need to know basis or else the price would skyrocket.

Peeling off a twenty, I held the bill firmly before she could snatch it away. "Were you doing this five years ago?"

She tugged on the end of the bill. "Five years ago I was doing a lot more than this. I remember seeing some fresh blood coming around, thinking my life was gonna get a lot harder. The less of us there are, the easier it is to get by. Some fresh-faced nubile could make attracting johns more difficult."

"So she worked these streets?" I let go of the twenty.

"Nope." The hooker tucked the cash into her brassiere. "I told you girls like that don't come into these neighborhoods." She grinned wickedly. "Have a nice day."

Instead of cutting my losses and walking away, I held my ground. "You know something. You recognized her. Tell me what you remember."

She reached into the pocket of her cutoff denim skirt and pulled out another cigarette and a lighter. Inhaling, she held it for a moment before blowing the smoke in my face. "I suggest you stop looking. You have no idea who you're messing with."

Before I could say another word, someone yanked my arm from behind. I spun, shifting into a fighting stance. My nine millimeter rested in my shoulder holster. Pulling a gun would escalate the situation. In neighborhoods like this, firepower was met with heavier firepower. And I didn't want to get any holes in my new jacket.

"Whatcha want?" a man asked. He wore a wife beater over low slung jeans. The piece tucked in the front of his waistband was meant to intimidate. It was a large caliber, silver handgun with a pearl handle. Perhaps I should have been impressed or frightened. Instead, I couldn't help but think placing the business end of a firearm against his junk was a bad idea. "You hasslin' my girls?"

"Not at all. We were just having a conversation."

"They don't get paid to talk." His eyes raked over my body. "I could put a tight ass like yours to work in a second. How's that sound, babe?" It was supposed to be a threat. He stepped back, expecting me to scurry away.

Instead, I smiled at him. "Really?" I took a small step closer, hoping he'd interpret it as flirtatious rather than insane, which is what it was. "I might be looking to make a few bucks if my current gig doesn't pan out. Do you think you can help me out?"

His instincts took over, and he gave me a wary look. His eyes darted to the slight bulge at the side of my jacket. "What do you want?" He took a step away, and I moved with him, aware my previous lead fled in the same direction as Traffic Cones.

"I'm looking for a girl." I held out the photo. "Is she one of yours?"

He assessed me for a long moment, searching for a badge. "Who's asking?"

"Her parents just want to know where she is. That's it."

Plucking the photo out of my hand, he glanced at it. For a moment, the faintest hint of recognition crossed his eyes, and then it was gone. He crumpled up the photo and tossed it aside. "Get the fuck off my street."

"That's not an answer."

He placed his palm on the handle of the gun. "Bitch, I'm not saying it again."

I stepped back, holding up my palms. "Fine, I'm leaving."

His eyes remained fixed on me, and I refused to turn my back on him. Unfortunately, that made it nearly impossible to notice the two men approaching from behind. They had come from the direction the hookers had gone. They must have been alerted to the potential situation. One thing was clear; interlopers were not welcome here. With any luck, my departure would make them back off.

My car was parked a block away. It wouldn't take long to clear that distance, but when the men started firing, I knew I couldn't remain in the open. I pulled my piece and darted across the street. Thinking the shots might have been a warning or one of the thugs trying to prove himself, I waited to return fire and ducked down the nearest alleyway, hoping they'd stop shooting once they were convinced they scared me away.

A bullet whizzed past, and I dove to the ground. Shit. Using the side of the building for cover, I aimed around the corner and blindly returned fire in their direction. Since there weren't any pedestrians a moment ago, I wasn't too worried about shooting an innocent bystander. The incoming barrage of bullets clued me in that I did nothing more than piss off my pursuers.

With few cover positions and even fewer places to hide, I moved deeper into the alley and slid behind a dumpster. The clip in my nine millimeter was nearly empty. Four bullets remained. Another three shots impacted against the dumpster, echoing against the rattling metal. Taking a breath, I reached for my phone.

One of the men crept closer. He fired, and I ducked behind cover, squeezing off a round in his direction. The resounding cry let me know I hit my target, and I peered around the dumpster, watching as he clutched his shoulder and skittered behind a derelict car.

"The police are on their way. I suggest you run while you can," I bellowed. I heard whispers but couldn't make out the words from this distance. Not waiting for them to make a decision on how they ought to proceed, I dialed 911 and gave my location. "Assault in progress. At least two active shooters." Not counting yours truly. "Both male, roughly twenty to twenty-five years of age, medium height, slim builds. Possibly members of the Seven Rooks, should be considered armed and dangerous." I went flat on the ground when one of their bullets pierced the dumpster and punched a hole next to my chest. "Roll units to this location. Now."

Dropping the phone, I pressed my toes against the wall and inched outward, remaining on the ground. When I was far enough past the dumpster to see out, I noticed the man with the pearl handled gun was nowhere to be seen. The two men who tried to get the jump on me were now huddled together behind the car. I had no idea how much firepower they had, but with the amount of lead they already expelled, I hoped they were out of ammo.

"Come on, fellas," I called, "I just wanted to know if you'd seen a girl. Should I take your gunfire as a yes?"

"Bitch," one of them hissed, firing again. Luckily, the bullet sailed over me and impacted against the brick.

"Okay. Thanks for cooperating. You can go now." Sirens wailed in the distance, and I said a quick prayer of thanks. "And for the record, I've been called worse. I'm guessing if you don't take off right now, your cellmates are going to have a lot of ugly names for you."

"Shit, man, let's go." The uninjured one took off, firing blindly behind him as he ran.

The one I hit was slower, but he didn't waste his time or effort firing at me. Instead, he dashed down the street in the opposite direction, tucking his side arm underneath his jersey to conceal it. Clutching his shoulder, he continued at a slow gallop.

"I'm sure no one will notice the blood oozing beneath your fingertips," I remarked.

Glancing around, I took a deep breath and brought myself to my feet. If I was smart, I'd get the hell out of here too. The last thing I needed was to explain to the cops what I was doing. My new boss strongly suggested our investigations shouldn't require police interventions, but here I was less than forty-eight hours after being hired and already breaking the rules. Oh well, I'd find another gig. I could always go back to work for a different federal agency if need be. The offers had come in; I just didn't want to take them. Maybe I didn't have much of a choice.

"Freeze," a police officer ordered, "drop your weapon and put your hands on your head."

"Okay." I let my nine millimeter dangle from my pointer finger before crouching down and placing it on the ground. Then I knelt, placing my hands on top of my head and lacing my fingers together. "I made the 911 call. You can check. That's my phone right there." I nodded at the device near my feet. "The shooters ran when they heard sirens. They split up. The one who went to his right was shot in the shoulder. He'll need medical attention. If he shows up at the hospital, you'll hear about it. A third guy was across the street, but I can't be certain if he opened fire."

"On the ground," the officer said, edging closer while his partner took up a position near the mouth of the alley. She was on the radio, requesting additional units and relaying what I just said to dispatch.

My hands shook as I lowered myself face first to the ground. Damn nerves. "My identification is in my back pocket. I'm a private investigator."

I could practically hear the contempt in the officer's voice when he told his partner to run my name. He placed a firm hand on top of both of mine and did a quick pat down. Then he reached for my discarded weapon. He checked the clip, finding it almost empty. "Do you have a carry permit?"

"In my wallet." Slowly, I sat up. "It's in my jacket pocket. I'm going to reach for it very slowly." He nodded, and I removed my wallet and handed it to him. "Like I said, they attacked me. I came to the neighborhood to ask if they'd seen a runaway girl, and things turned violent."

While I was providing my statement, a town car pulled to a stop, and my new boss stepped out of the vehicle with one of the city's best defense attorneys in tow.

"Is Miss Parker under arrest?" the attorney asked.

"No." The cop glanced up, the question clear on his face. "Who the hell are you?" His eyes flicked from the attorney to my boss.

"Lucien Cross," my boss replied, "and I'm sure you know Mr. Almeada by reputation." He jerked his chin at me. "Are you done here?"

"She needs to come down to the station to give a statement," the police officer insisted. "We need her to provide descriptions of the shooters."

"My client is frazzled. She was attacked by street thugs and nearly killed. She needs a moment to process. I assure you, she will stop by the precinct at her earliest convenience," the attorney said. He handed the cop his card. "You already have her information. In case you have any other questions, I'd be happy to answer them."

I gave the officer a contrite smile. If I walked away, he'd probably end up in a lot of trouble, but it was obvious I didn't have much say in the matter. I wasn't under arrest, so he technically couldn't force me to cooperate. "Start at the hospitals. One of the men has a hole in his shoulder. He'll need to be patched up."

My weapon was confiscated until ballistics could verify my story. Technically, I probably should have been brought in for questioning, but Cross had a lot of pull. Perhaps too much.

"Let's go," Cross said. He took the car keys from my hand and tossed them to Almeada. "I don't want to get ticketed if the meter runs out. Take her car." He held the rear door open, and I slid inside, aware of my scraped palms as soon as they came into contact with the cold leather seats. Cross climbed in after me. Once the door shut, he signaled the driver who pulled away from the curb, leaving the flashing lights of the police car in our wake. "What the hell were you thinking? My people monitor police frequencies. We heard the call. Why did you involve the authorities? You were given strict instructions this investigation was to remain private."

"What the hell was I supposed to do?" I glared at him, adrenaline fueling my rage. "Two heavily armed men decided to shoot first in order to keep me from asking questions later."

"Jeez." He scratched his head and assessed me. "I knew you'd be trouble. I just didn't realize how much."

"So why did you hire me? More importantly, why did you give me this case? You must have known what it would entail. Since you don't like problems, you should have found someone else to handle it."

His jaw muscles bunched while he worked out whatever he was thinking, and then he laughed. "It needed fresh eyes. Yours are the freshest. And clearly, you've made more headway on this in less than a day than any of my other investigators have in a month. You do things messy. We'll clean them up, but you should know, I don't like messy."

"Is that why you have Almeada in your back pocket?"

He smirked. "He's a friend. We keep him on retainer just to rattle the police and prevent them from harassing us. Most of our clients don't want police involvement. The sooner you learn this, the better off we'll be."

"Yes, sir." The sarcasm dripped from my words, but Cross ignored it.

He nodded to himself and settled back in the seat, watching me from the corner of his eye as I fought off the jitters and shakes. When the car stopped in front of the building, we got out. After an elevator ride to the thirtieth floor, I returned to my brand new office while Cross went up another level. Cross Security took up three stories in the high-rise. One floor was dedicated entirely to evidence collection. The second was conference rooms and offices for his employees. And the third was his space, along with whatever high-tech toys, assistants, and attorneys he felt were useful at the moment.

Basically, Lucien Cross privatized the police department. His clients were wealthy, occasionally criminal, and willing to pay through the nose for his services. The investigators he hired weren't that dissimilar from me. Most were decorated former federal agents, police officers, or military personnel. They were proficient in hand-to-hand combat, firearms training, and investigative techniques.

After my forced resignation from the Office of

International Operations, a headhunter got me an immediate interview with Lucien Cross. I'd only been out of work a week when I was hired. It was fast. Maybe too fast. I didn't even have time to catch my breath. After losing my job, James Martin, my boyfriend, and I spent five days at his villa in Spain. Frankly, the jetlag didn't even wear off yet, and gangbangers were already shooting at me.

Cross called this my audition period and handed me a case the previous P.I. couldn't seem to crack. Five years ago, a girl disappeared during a flash mob performance at her school's pep rally. Her parents reported her missing, and the police investigated. They found no signs of foul play. She was sixteen at the time, making her twenty-one now. Every few months her parents would check back with the police, hire a private eye, and continue to wait. Eventually, they stumbled upon Cross Security, paid the exorbitant retainer, and were promised results. That was four months ago.

During that time period, three of Cross's top guys looked into the disappearance, but they didn't find anything. So Cross made me a deal. I was hired on a temporary basis, and if I located the girl within a month's time, I would get to keep the fancy office, the abundant resources, access to high-powered defense attorneys, the company car, and the six figure salary that went along with it. And if I couldn't find the girl, I'd be looking for my next job. At the time, it seemed fair. But after this morning, I was reconsidering.

What the hell did I get myself into? Shaking off the self-doubt that plagued me since I became an investigator, I went to the coffeemaker and filled a mug, dumping in several heaping spoonfuls of sugar. I returned to my office, hoping the sugar and caffeine would prevent my body from crashing when the adrenaline wore off.

Taking a sip of the too sweet sludge, I went behind my desk and keyed in the number assigned to my missing persons case. Jessika Wellington, light brown hair, thin, hazel eyes, freckles, and a perfect smile. The photo Cross Security had was Jessika's last school photo. She sat with her hands folded neatly on her knee in her school uniform.

Copies of the relevant police reports were included, as were the photographs and screenshots the police compiled at the time of her disappearance. Hard copies of her e-mails and text messages filled an entire drawer in the filing cabinet. We had everything except her.

I just started reading through the statements her friends had given for the third time when someone knocked on my open door. I glanced up to see Kellan Dey entering with a bottle of scotch or maybe it was whiskey. At this distance, I couldn't tell one amber liquor from another.

"I heard about your morning. You okay, Alexis?"

"I prefer Alex." I gave him a reassuring smile. "I'm fine." I reached for the coffee cup. "Sugar and caffeine work miracles." I eyed the bottle in his hand curiously.

"If that fails, I brought you a welcome gift." He strolled across the room and placed it on the tiny bar cart in the corner. He turned around, reconsidering the gift momentarily. "You aren't an alcoholic?"

"Not yet. Maybe if I play my cards right."

He laughed. "A couple of the guys are recovering. I imagine that's how they ended up in the private sector." He was poking around for my background history, but I wasn't in a sharing mood. Getting shot at can do that to a person. "Anyway, I'll let you get back to it. If you need anything, I'm just across the hall. This place can be a bit intimidating at first, but you seem to be adjusting."

"Seven days ago, I was behind a desk inside the federal building basically doing the same thing. As long as the computer recognizes me and I can access the Cross database and the government databases, I'm good."

He nodded, ducking back into the hallway.

Truthfully, it was weird I didn't require an adjustment period. I interviewed Wednesday for the position. Cross signed me on the spot. Thursday, I was outfitted with computer access, given security clearance, and shown the ropes. I took copies of the Wellington files home, familiarized myself with the attempts previously made to determine Jessika's whereabouts, made a few phone calls, and started my day by following up on a lead given by one of my friends in the major crimes division.

"Damn, Nick," I muttered, "maybe you sent me sniffing through the Seven Rooks' territory just so I'd stop asking you for favors." Detective Nick O'Connell turned me on to the fact the local gang had a reputation for preying on runaways, turning them into junkies, and turning them out for a profit in order to pay for their habit. Since Jessika grew up with a privileged background, where drugs were often readily available, it seemed like the perfect avenue to explore and one that was never thoroughly investigated.

Grabbing a pen, I jotted down a few notes concerning my encounter this morning. I got the message loud and clear; fuck off. Too bad that just made me want to dig deeper. Making a list of Jessika's closest friends, I cross-referenced the notations the authorities made concerning their potential involvement in her disappearance. When I ran out of notes, I went down the hall, reading the placards on the doors as I went. My first stop was the Cross investigator who originally caught the case, Bennett Renner.

TWO

Renner was a former homicide detective with a decorated past. His career ended abruptly when he was severely injured on the job, but he made a miraculous recovery. He walked with a slight limp, but even that didn't make him appear any less formidable. He knew the streets, which made the way he conducted the investigation seem odd.

"Cross assigned you the Wellington case four months ago," I said. We met briefly yesterday, so no introduction was necessary. "I've been reading through your notes. You must have racked up quite a few frequent flyer miles. It looks like you traveled across the country to talk to Jessika's friends in person."

"Friends, her boyfriend, a few of her favorite teachers, and the volleyball coach." He sighed. "It's been five years. The kids are in college now, and a lot of the adults in her life have moved on to bigger and better things. I just wanted to see for myself what they were doing. It was a long shot, but I thought perhaps someone might be in contact with her now. It's conceivable she ran away and reconnected with someone from her past after the authorities stopped snooping around. From the texts and photos we found on her phone, she and the boyfriend were pretty hot and heavy. If he was involved, he should have known something."

"But he didn't?"

"None of 'em did."

"If you say so."

He scratched at the patch of gray at his temple. "I get you're new here, but a word of advice, don't treat your colleagues like suspects. I understand the instinct. Hell, I practically had to have someone beat it out of me, but I'm not your enemy." He jerked his chin at the notepad I was holding. "What do you really want to know?"

"You were still a cop when she went missing."

"I didn't work the case."

"But you knew about it. Heard about it. Probably knew some of the guys who worked it."

"You need some practice being direct."

I shrugged. "Did they think she ran away?"

"Like I said, I didn't work the case. I don't know what the lead detective thought. I can tell you when I reviewed everything that went into finding that girl from day one, I realized there was never any indication she was taken against her will." He quirked an eyebrow, looking smug. "If it was an abduction, I imagine you would have heard about it, being FBI and all. You were FBI five years ago, right?"

"Yes, but not that kind of FBI." I rubbed a hand down my face. When I looked up, I knew Renner saw the tremor. "Okay, so your theory is she ran away."

"That's everyone's theory. Have you finished reading the reports and going through the evidence?"

"Now who's being hostile?" I tossed him a playful smile.

He smiled back. "It's not much fun, is it? Now answer the question."

"I read everything, and I made a couple of calls. Two hours ago, I was pinned down while members of the Seven Rooks took potshots at me because I walked up to two prostitutes and asked if they ever saw Jessika, which brings me to my next question. What kind of investigating did you do locally in order to find her?"

He didn't speak for a full minute, mulling over the facts

I just provided. "When I caught the case, the police had hit nothing but dead ends. The cops were thorough. I'm guessing the Rooks shot at you because you were on their turf and you look like a cop. The lack of badge makes you fair game, or have your years inside the federal building killed any sense of street smarts you might have had?"

"My street smarts are intact, and they're telling me someone missed something. A girl like Jessika doesn't just disappear in the middle of the day without leaving a trace. Something went down, and if she ran, she was running from someone."

"I agree. I just don't know what happened. And it happened too long ago to determine now. Her friends don't remember much. Her parents have a skewed perspective on things. I tried to find the truth, but every rock's been overturned. Unless her body surfaces somewhere or she decides to come back, we're not going to find her."

"Is that what you told Cross?"

"That's what everyone tells Cross. You can talk to Lancaster and Darwin, the two guys who investigated after I did, and they'll tell you the same thing. It's why Cross hired you. No one else will take this assignment."

"And if I don't find Jessika, I'm fired."

He pressed his lips together. "In that case, it was nice meeting you."

"I'm not giving up that easily." I stood, giving him another glance. "I didn't imagine a man with a record like yours would either."

An incredulous smile painted his lips. "Talk to me at the end of the month when you've memorized every report, photo, and text message from Wellington's file and none of them add up to a workable lead."

I went to the door, knowing my attitude was a result of my crappy morning. No wonder my colleagues and I tended not to get along. "I'm sorry I bothered you."

Before I could duck back into the hallway, Renner spoke. "What made you think the Seven Rooks had anything to do with her disappearance? I never explored that connection. As far as I know, no one else did either. Was a new report added to the file?"

"No." I turned around to watch his expression. "A friend in the major crimes unit did some digging. He told me the lead detective had some suspicions but never found enough evidence to dig too deeply into it."

"If that's true, there wasn't enough evidence to make it into any official report either. Have you spoken to the detective?"

"Not yet. I'll probably pay her a visit when I go to the precinct to give my statement concerning the shooting."

"Do you mind if I tag along?" His lip twitched slightly. "I'd like to know if there's something I overlooked."

"No problem. I'll let you know when I'm heading out."

*   *   *

Giving my statement didn't take long. Since I didn't get a good look at the shooters, my descriptions were vague. I did provide a better description of possible witnesses who were in the area, namely the two whores and their pimp. I stuck with my story, even though Mr. Cross would not appreciate I was disclosing key facts of our investigation to the police department. Oh well, he would have to get over it.

After some cajoling, my weapon was returned. It had been in police evidence enough times in the past to have been properly catalogued. But since no one was pressing charges for my involvement in the shooting and the police weren't going to cite me for public endangerment or illegally discharging a weapon within city limits, I was free to go.

Taking a detour, I went upstairs to the major crimes division to see if I could grab a hold of Detective Nick O'Connell. I needed an introduction to the detective assigned to the missing persons case. Renner followed me, not saying a word. When I stepped through the second set of double doors, I spotted Nick at his desk.

"You owe me," I said in lieu of a greeting, dropping into his partner's empty chair.

"You have it wrong. I did you a favor, so you owe me." O'Connell's gaze left the computer, noticing the hulking man standing uncomfortably off to the side. "Are you aware you're being followed?"

"Yep."

Nick nodded at Renner. "You have an uncanny resemblance to a real detective. We might have to arrest you for impersonating a cop."

Renner grinned. "Shut your fucking mouth, O'Connell."

I blinked. "You two know each other?"

"Unfortunately," Renner said. He took a few steps forward and held out his hand, and they shook. "It's good to see you again, Nicky. How's Jen?"

"She's fine. I heard about you and Susan. I'm sorry."

Renner shrugged. "It happens. At least she left before the money started rolling in." He cleared his throat. "So you gave Parker a tip to check out the Seven Rooks' territory? Where'd you get your intel? The funny pages?"

O'Connell's eyes darted to mine, silently asking what he was allowed to say in front of Renner. I shrugged. I didn't think it was worth keeping secrets from my co-workers, and if it was, I was too new to know.

"When Alex asked about Jessika Wellington, I made a call upstairs. That was a high profile case. I remember Sparrow was lead, so I asked her about it. She kept meticulous notes and remembered the GPS on Wellington's phone pinged in that neighborhood several times during the previous few weeks leading to her disappearance. It wasn't solid, but it was the one thing that was never really investigated. Some uniforms canvassed the neighborhood, but no one saw the girl," O'Connell said.

"And without any other leads, it was dropped." Renner practically rolled his eyes. "Wellington's phone could have pinged in the vicinity because she was using it while driving or taking a train or bus through the area to get elsewhere. That's less than nothing."

O'Connell shrugged. "Hey, I'm just the messenger." His gaze hardened on Renner. "And the message wasn't meant for you."

Renner snorted. "I knew this was a waste of time. I told ya I checked into everything relevant."

"Good for you," I replied, glancing up at him. "Why

don't you give us a minute? Maybe see if you can get a hold of Det. Sparrow. I'd like to have a word with her."

"Okay." Renner nodded at O'Connell. "We should grab a beer sometime."

"Sure." Nick waited for him to leave before speaking. "What's that about?"

I shook my head. "The lead you gave me was good. At least, I think it was. Two guys chased me out of the neighborhood this morning. I had to call the police for back-up. No one said anything damning, but Jessika Wellington was there at some point. Someone knows what happened to her." Biting my lip, I looked back at the stairwell. "Do you think you can introduce me to Sparrow?"

Nick chuckled. "It might be a couple of days. Sparrow's out of town."

"Then why didn't you stop Renner from going upstairs to look for her?"

"He's a hotshot. I'm sure he'll figure it out." O'Connell assessed me. "So you're really back to the private investigator schtick? Is this permanent or just the flavor of the week?"

"Cross Security might be the flavor of the week, but I think the P.I. gig is going to stick this time."

"Okay. If you get your ass in hot water, I'm just a phone call away."

"I knew there was a reason I liked you. Give me a call when Sparrow's back in town. We have some things to discuss."

"Will do." His eyes darted back to the stairwell. "Hey, Parker, be careful around Renner."

THREE

During the ride back, Renner spoke at length about some sort of bet he and O'Connell made a few years ago concerning the outcome of the World Series. It was supposed to be a comical tale, but my mind was elsewhere. Perhaps I was finally feeling the effects of the adrenaline crash. Glancing at my new colleague, I couldn't help but think of Nick's warning. As soon as I had time to catch my breath, I'd have to ask him about it.

"Miss Parker, Mr. Almeada's assistant dropped off your company car. It's parked in the garage." The receptionist held out the keys as I moved past the desk. I stuffed them into my pocket and thanked her.

Renner gave me a curious look as we continued down the hallway. "Isn't today your first official day on the job?"

"Yeah."

"And Almeada already had to save your ass, and you misplaced your work vehicle. No wonder you were so bitchy when you barged into my office this morning." He stopped at his door. "I really do hope your day gets better. If you want to chew my ear about the Wellington case, I'll be around. I'm sorry the afternoon at the precinct turned out to be a bust."

"Thanks." But I didn't believe it was.

I opened the cabinet and pulled out Wellington's phone records. Aside from the numbers and texts, the relevant metadata was written at the top. After determining which locations corresponded to the gang-controlled neighborhood, I sifted through the thousands of pages, removing the messages and calls placed from that location.

None of the numbers were out of the ordinary, and the text messages were of a similar nature to the rest I read. Still, I was certain there was something here. Lifting the desk phone, I dialed the one number that popped up more than any other — the boyfriend.

When the call went to voicemail, I left my name and number and asked for a call back. The police ruled Dylan Hart out almost immediately. And from the previous Cross investigator files, none of my colleagues believed he was involved. Assuming everyone was right, he would be the most likely to help and one of the few people who might still possess relevant materials from the time of Jessika's disappearance.

The next phone call I placed was to Jessika's parents. Cross wanted us to meet in order to reassure his clients someone from the office was actively searching for their daughter. Janet Wellington answered the phone on the second ring, sounding out of breath.

"Hello, Mrs. Wellington. This is Alex Parker from Cross Security. I've been reviewing your daughter's case file and was hoping we could meet in person to discuss her disappearance."

"Have you made any progress?" she asked.

"Nothing substantial." False hope could be devastating, but I didn't like mincing my words either. "Would it be okay if I dropped by to speak to you and your husband?"

"Fine. That's fine," she stammered. "I'll be home all evening, but Bill isn't here."

"That's okay. I appreciate you taking the time." Once I verified her home address, I told her to expect me within the hour.

After hanging up, I grabbed my jacket and checked my appearance in the washroom. I didn't want to make a bad first impression. I already did that once today. And given what Mrs. Wellington had been going through over the last five years, it might help ease her nerves to believe her daughter's case was in the hands of a competent investigator, even if that point might be debatable.

When I arrived at the townhouse, I glanced around. The complex was large, filled with seven figure homes and condos. The area was family-oriented. The lawns were well maintained; the hedges were professionally manicured. At the end of the row of townhouses was a designated playground area, and I passed a neighborhood pool and tennis courts on my way in. Signs boasted the area was under surveillance by a neighborhood watch, but I didn't see anything that appeared particularly intimidating. Maybe the sign was enough.

A tall, slender woman answered the door. Her eyes were dull and gray, but her appearance was immaculate. Her clothes were neat, her hair and makeup perfectly in place. She smiled slightly, the expression not making it any higher than the curved corners of her lips.

"Miss Parker?" she asked, and I nodded. "Please make yourself at home." I followed her through the foyer and into the living room. The house was just as tidy as its owner's appearance. Expensive crystal accents dotted the dark wood furnishings. I spotted a few photographs. Three were of Jessika at various ages taken by a professional photographer. A family photo hung on the opposite wall, next to a wedding photo. "May I offer you something to drink?"

"No, thank you." I took an uneasy seat on the cream colored sofa, hoping my pants wouldn't leave remnants of my morning in the alleyway on the expensive fabric. "I hope my visit isn't an inconvenience."

She shook her head, moving to the bar and pouring a gin and tonic. After placing it on a coaster, she took a seat in the chair across from me. "This happens periodically. You're not the first P.I. to come here." Sadness filled her eyes. "I do hope you will be the last."

"Yes, ma'am." I took a deep breath, feeling her inscrutable gaze analyze everything about me. Unsure of where to begin, I looked around the room. "Did Jessika grow up in this house?"

She nodded. "The police and some of the other investigators have searched her room for clues. I imagine you probably want to do the same."

"In a few minutes, if you don't mind. First, I'd just like you to tell me about your daughter."

Mrs. Wellington's confusion was evident. Apparently, this question wasn't normally asked, and she didn't have an immediate answer. She reached for her drink and took a slight sip. "She's smart, driven, so beautiful. She had it all together. At sixteen, she had her life figured out. Who does that? I'm forty-four, and I don't know which way is up half the time. I just hate this. It's not fair."

"No, it isn't."

She inhaled, her gaze finding its way to the row of photos. "Jess never lets things get her down. She's very resilient. Always with a plan. Always with a back-up." She bit her lip. "I just don't see how this could have happened."

"Were there any problems at home? Fights? Disagreements?"

Those gray eyes snapped fiercely to me. "No." Despite her svelte form, she'd take down a Sumo wrestler if he questioned her ability as a parent. "I'm sure we must have fought about typical teenage dramas, like curfew or clothing choices, but we didn't have problems, Miss Parker. I want you to know that. I need you to understand that. Jessika didn't run away. Someone took her."

"Any idea who?"

I could see the scornful expression in her eyes. That question just demoted me from the great white hope to gum stuck to the bottom of a shoe. "If I knew that, don't you think I would have told the police?"

"Of course, I just wanted to make certain there were never any ransom demands or anything like that."

"No."

"Did anyone close to the family sever ties around the time of Jessika's disappearance?" Typically, abductions were personal, and even if this wasn't an abduction, Jessika might have run to a trusted friend or family member if things in her house weren't as quintessentially perfect as her mother believed they were.

"Not that I remember. Everyone was supportive. If anything, we bonded together in the search to find Jess." She took another sip of her drink, but her eyes went to the wedding photo.

Sensing there was something to it, I asked, "Where is your husband?"

She let out a bitter laugh and took another sip. "At the hotel, I imagine." Her eyes left the photo, and she looked at me. "We're estranged. Have been for three years now. He used to sleep in the guestroom to keep up appearances, but our therapist said we should commit to a trial separation. That was eight months ago. I'm not entirely sure when this trial is supposed to end."

"I'm sorry."

She nodded. "If you'd like to meet with us both, that can be arranged. He wants to get Jess back as much as I do. That's something we agree on."

"That won't be necessary." My words saddened her, and I felt like I was doing nothing but pouring salt on the wound. "Mrs. Wellington, you said your daughter had everything planned out. What do you mean by that?"

"Life. She figured it out. She was dating a nice boy. She already knew where she wanted to go to college and what she wanted to do. She had a ten year plan." Remaining silent, I waited for her to elaborate. "Jess wanted to be a pediatrician. She wanted to go to USC with Dylan and major in biology with a minor in child psychology. After graduation, she planned to move back and go to medical school."

"Wow, that's impressive." And insane. "I don't even know what I'm going to eat for dinner."

"I know." For the first time, Mrs. Wellington smiled, proud of her daughter.

"But she was only sixteen. How in the world did she know she wanted to do all of those things?" More importantly, how could she predict those things would happen? I didn't think pointing out the obvious flaws in her daughter's plan was a good place to start.

Mrs. Wellington laughed. "Dylan was her first love. I'm

not completely naïve. I'm certain Jess would go through plenty of men in her life, but she was driven, goal-oriented, and a hard worker. The only thing she ever wanted to be was a pediatrician. Her math and science scores have always been wonderful. She aced her SAT. I'm certain the rest of it would have fallen into place, if she had the chance." She stood. "Let me show you her room."

Jessika's bedroom fit in perfectly with the rest of the house. It was tastefully furnished with a minimal amount of clutter. A few framed photos stood on her dresser, family, friends, and her boyfriend. Her bookcase was filled with a collection of YA novels, chick lit, and required reading. After getting permission to check the drawers and closet, Mrs. Wellington excused herself, not wanting to watch another stranger tear through her daughter's personal belongings.

I took a seat on the bed and looked around the room. I knew the usual places had been checked. The police probably went through everything, but I didn't know if any of them had ever been a teenage girl. She would have things she wanted to keep secret. So where would she hide them?

I checked under the bed and the mattress. I knocked on the floorboards, determining none were loose. Inside the closet, I checked her purses and inside her shoeboxes. Aside from a few expired condoms, I didn't find anything particularly scandalous. At least she and Dylan were responsible.

Inside one of the dresser drawers, I found several pairs of scrubs and a photo ID. Removing the ID, I completed my search, not finding anything else particularly useful. When I went downstairs, I found Mrs. Wellington in the living room with a fresh gin and tonic. In her hand was a framed photo. When she heard me coming, she wiped her eyes and put the photo down on the table.

"I'm sorry," I said sincerely.

"Did you find anything?" She was resigned to a perfunctory answer, probably one she already heard a dozen times.

"Actually," I held out the ID, "can you tell me about

this?"

She ran her thumb over the photo. "Like I told you, my daughter was prepared for anything. Not only did she want to make certain she had plenty of community service for her college applications, but she also wanted to have a leg up for the pre-med program. As you can see, she made sure to incorporate that into her extracurriculars. Her high school advisor...crap." She looked up at me. "I can't remember her name."

"I'm sure it's in the files we have." I nodded reassuringly. "Go on."

"Well, the advisor helped set her up. It was a school program. Prospective Doctors of the Future or something like. There were fifteen or twenty students involved. Wait right here. This might help." Mrs. Wellington crossed the room, opening another door and stepping into what appeared to be an office or library. She returned a minute later with a yearbook. "This was Jessika's sophomore year." She flipped through the pages. "There's the advisor, and here's the club."

I studied the photos and the detailed information on the page. "May I take this with me? I promise I'll take very good care of it and get it back to you soon."

She clutched the book against her chest for a moment, weighing the pros and cons. Holding it out, she said, "Of course." She must have seen something in my eyes because she cocked her head to the side. "This means something, doesn't it?"

"I don't know yet." I looked down at the photo she had been holding. "Your daughter was in the hospital?"

"When she was little. It's why she's always been determined to be a pediatrician. She used to say, *Mommy, I want to help other little girls, just like me.* It was sweet. I thought it was something she'd outgrow, but she never did."

"Do you mind if I ask what was wrong with her?"

"She fell off the monkey bars and broke her arm. It was a bad break. They had to do surgery, which was a bit problematic because she has a rare blood type. Needless to say, she stayed in the hospital for a few days, but it made a lasting impression." She closed her eyes. "At the time, it seemed like the worst thing in the world. Now I wish getting her back was as simple." Her eyes shot open, and she stared at me. "Promise you'll find my daughter."

"I'll try."

"Don't try. Promise." She grabbed my arm, desperate. "Promise."

I nodded, immediately feeling terrible for agreeing. This was a mess.

FOUR

I never worked a missing persons case, at least not that I recalled. The only missing people I ever found were criminals, which meant they weren't exactly missing. This was different. Jessika Wellington vanished five years ago. No leads ever surfaced. Possible suspects were quickly eliminated. A sixteen year old girl simply disappeared off the face of the earth, never to be heard from again. Things like that weren't supposed to happen.

"Dammit." I looked at the list of names I scribbled down. Before I went any further, I needed updated backgrounds on several individuals. William Wellington III was at the top of my list. I hated to think it, but sexual abuse occurred too frequently between parents and children not to consider the possibility. Her advisor, Carla Cleese, was next on my list. She appeared to be an influential person in Jessika's life. That meant she might have been a trusted confidant or someone who exploited a young girl. Aside from that, I wanted an update on Dylan Hart's whereabouts, and it wouldn't hurt to run Janet Wellington's name either.

Obviously, the police did this, but time passed. Circumstances might have changed. Secret payoffs might have appeared in bank accounts. Frankly, I didn't know what I'd find, but I had to find something. Lifting my desk phone, I waited for the assistant to patch me through to the people upstairs. Cross spared no expense, and his techs were trained in everything from DNA and fingerprints to the fastest and most reliable methods of performing background checks. I passed the names along and was told the reports would be on my desk by the morning.

For the next several hours, I read through the signatures and messages written in Jessika's yearbook, cross-referencing them to the texts and e-mails recovered from her phone and laptop. As I went through the signatures, I keyed in the names, searching social media and scouring profiles for a clue as to what became of Jessika.

The desk phone rang, and I pressed the speaker button. "Miss Parker, I'll be leaving for the night. Should you require assistance, someone from upstairs will help you." The secretary gave me the extension. "Did Mr. Cross inform you evidence collection is staffed twenty-four hours and professionals are always available? Building security can help should you encounter any problems."

"Yep. Thanks." I reached for the speaker, adding a quick, "Good night."

"Good night, Miss Parker."

That was something I didn't think I'd ever get used to. I glanced at the clock. It was a little after eight on a Friday night. I could put in a few more hours before calling it quits. After all, Cross didn't seem to care if I spent all night in the office or if I never bothered to come in. I had a month to solve the case. It didn't matter where or how it occurred, just as long as it didn't involve the police.

Rolling my eyes at the thought, I picked up my empty coffee mug, decided against a refill, and went back to my analysis. When I couldn't take sitting behind a desk any longer, I took a seat on the floor, leaning against the bend in the L-shaped couch, and placed my notes on the coffee table. Most offices didn't have glass coffee tables and modern furniture; at least they didn't in the federal building. This was nice.

I dropped my head against the seat and stared at the

ceiling. At sixteen, I was driven and goal-oriented. My goal was figuring out how to fend for myself. My adopted parents weren't cruel or abusive. They provided. They even covered my college expenses. They just wanted to have nothing to do with me, and I couldn't say the feeling wasn't mutual. But even I didn't run away. You learn to make the best out of a bad situation. So if Jessika ran, her life must have been hell. But there was no indication of that in her file.

Grabbing her school schedule, I attempted to reconstruct her typical week. The classes she took, the teachers she had, the clubs she participated in, and her after-school activities. To be thorough, I'd have to run through every classmate, teacher, bus driver, and coach, but it had already been done. Hell, Renner did it less than four months ago. I leafed through his notes, but it was another dead end.

The abrupt sound of a man clearing his throat echoed in my office. I turned to find Cross standing in the doorway, his expensive suit looking freshly pressed even after twelve hours at work.

Standing up, I nodded to my new boss. "Sir?"

He eyed the scattering of paperwork on the table and desk. "Are you hoping to get a larger office?" His tone was without a hint of amusement or teasing.

"Not unless it comes with a view. A window or two would be nice."

He remained in place, ignoring my glibness. "How did your meeting with Mrs. Wellington fare?"

"She believes someone took her daughter. Nothing supports that theory, but it can't be disproven either." I licked my lips. "Men shot at me this morning because I asked if they saw Jessika. I believe that leads some credence to her claim."

He stepped into my office and closed the door. Folding his arms over his chest, he asked, "What led you to those men and that particular neighborhood?"

"Gossip around the police station and an unexplored avenue the lead detective didn't get a chance to examine due to lack of evidence."

"And because of pressure to maintain appearances exuded by Mr. Wellington." Cross wasn't just a fancy suit. He knew his shit. "He won't like that we're running another check on him when we just conducted one four months ago. Is there a particular reason you made that request?"

"It's been four months. Things might have changed." I was already in hot water, but I wasn't good at holding my tongue. "I'm curious. Do you micromanage all of your company's investigations?"

His eyes narrowed slightly. "This is your trial period. I need to make sure you don't do anything to harm my reputation."

"In that case, you probably shouldn't have hired me."

"That can be corrected if necessary." He turned to the door and reached for the handle. "I'm rarely wrong, Miss Parker. Let upstairs know if you require any additional information. I'll smooth things over with Mr. Wellington should the need arise."

Once again alone, I thought about the morning and my conversation with Smokey, the second hooker. She knew something, even if she denied it by playing it off as an easy way to score a twenty. There was recognition in her eyes when she looked at the photo. Her description and tone when describing new talent moving into the area made me question a lot of things.

I went through Jessika's phone records again, checking the times her cell used the towers that corresponded with that neighborhood. After about an hour of recording the time intervals, a pattern emerged. Jessika was there between the hours of six and seven on Tuesdays and Thursdays. Leafing through her schedule, I didn't see anything penciled in for those times. It was possible she might have been there longer, but I could only gauge the times and locations based on her cell phone activity. If she wasn't talking or texting, we couldn't pinpoint her location.

Over ninety percent of the communications she made during that time were to Dylan. They were typically flirty or fun texts. Nothing out of the ordinary. Nothing that indicated she was in any type of distress. His responses were equally lighthearted. It wouldn't make sense they'd be chatting if she was working the corner. Frankly, I couldn't picture the girl in the photos selling her body to those creeps. A high-end call service, perhaps. But not as a sex worker in the trenches. So what was she doing there at those specific times? I needed to talk to Dylan, but since I couldn't get a hold of him, I went with plan B.

"Really?" I said to Renner's locked office door. The lights were out. He must have gone home hours earlier. Frankly, almost every office I passed was locked. Apparently, it didn't matter where you worked; everyone wanted to start the weekend as soon as possible.

I thought about calling Janet Wellington, but I didn't want to cause more damage. Besides, if Jessika was doing something illicit, her mom wouldn't know about it anyway. Letting out a sigh, I decided I needed to identify the hookers, their pimp, and the shooters from this morning. Finding out those details could provide leverage, and in order to get answers, I'd need to twist a few arms.

After returning the files to the cabinet in the corner, I grabbed my belongings and called a cab to the precinct. The last thing I planned to do was take the company car to the police station. I was positive Cross had the vehicle rigged with GPS trackers, and I didn't need another lecture from the uptight suit. I also didn't particularly want to take the car home, especially on the weekend when I wouldn't exactly be at my address. That might raise a few red flags at the security firm.

Since I'd been inside the police station a little over a week ago with FBI credentials, most of the cops thought I was still on the job. Seeing no need to correct them, I asked if they apprehended the shooters from this morning. The beat cops were on the lookout, but as of yet, they had nothing. The desk sergeant assigned an officer to assist, and we settled behind a computer and flipped through the digitized mug books.

"That one." I pointed to Portia Russo. Multiple arrests for possession, solicitation, and intent to distribute. "She was the first hooker I approached. She walked away, presumably to get her pimp to scare me off."

The officer nodded, jotting down a note. Reaching for

the radio, he passed along her name, address, and description. Someone would pick her up for questioning in relation to this morning's shooting.

We flipped through more photos, but I didn't get a good look at the shooters. Several screens later, I pointed to Jorge Toald, the pimp. But no matter how many photos I scanned, I didn't see Smokey.

"We'll bring them both in for questioning, but if I were you, I wouldn't hold my breath. They probably won't talk," the cop said. "Do you want to press charges against Toald?"

"Not yet. He had a pearl handled, large caliber handgun. It was probably a forty-five. If you pulled any of those slugs out of the dumpster or walls, then let's go for it, but if not, he'll walk."

The cop looked at me oddly. "Shouldn't you be a little less indifferent about this? These men tried to kill you."

"They aren't the problem. They're just a symptom of the problem."

"Which is?"

"For my purposes, they're preventing me from figuring out what a girl from the other side of the tracks was doing in a neighborhood like that. In a much more general sense, society's fucked."

The cop thought for a moment. "Kids from good neighborhoods only venture into gang turf for one reason. They're looking to score."

"Nothing indicates that."

"Then look harder."

Hoping his cynicism was merely due to years on the job, I thanked the officer for his time and asked him to inform me if anything else developed in regards to the shooting. Catching another cab, I stared out the window and thought. Jessika was a regular in that neighborhood for at least a month prior to her disappearance. If her presence was such a common occurrence, someone must have known. So why didn't it surface during the initial investigation or any subsequent investigations? Did someone bury it?

The driver pulled to a stop outside the high-rise apartment building. I paid him with the money left in my pocket, just as the doorman opened the car door.

"Good evening, Miss Parker."

Tired, I barely managed a smile. It was after midnight as I made my way to the elevator. My head was pounding. I didn't remember eating today, but even now, I wasn't hungry. I wanted to figure out what Jessika was doing in that neighborhood and why after five years some streetwalkers and bangers thought it was imperative to keep a lid on things. An unsettling thought entered my mind. There was no statute of limitations on murder. Honestly, even though every investigator insisted she ran away, I didn't think any of us believed she was still alive, which probably meant someone killed her.

I pushed open the front door, locking it behind me. Moving into the kitchen, I dropped my purse and jacket on the nearest stool and put my gun and phone on the counter. Resting my elbows on the countertop, I put my head in my hands. I needed to figure this out.

"Hey, gorgeous," James Martin called from the chair in the living room. He was working on his laptop. "How was your first day?"

"Fine." I pushed away from the counter. "I need a shower." I glanced at him. He looked like he just stepped foot inside. His tie and jacket were strewn across the coffee table, and his sleeves were rolled up. A barely touched glass of scotch was on the side table. He was still working, even though he wasn't in the office. "When did you get here?"

"Less than an hour ago." His eyes remained fixed on the computer screen. "I just need to finish reviewing this presentation. It won't take long."

"Take your time." I disappeared into the bathroom, relieved something else had his interest. I didn't want to talk about my day.

After washing off, I changed into one of his shirts and returned to the kitchen. I needed to eat before my skull exploded. Oddly, the fridge was stocked with unfamiliar leftovers. I made a plate with meatloaf, mashed potatoes, steamed spinach, and baby carrots. After gulping it down at the counter, I stretched out on the grey suede sofa. It was the first piece of furniture we bought together.

I closed my eyes and turned on my side. Thoughts raced through my head. She was dead. Someone took her. She was in that neighborhood. Why? I sighed loudly.

The cubes in Martin's glass clinked. "Alex, I know this is supposed to be a work-free zone. This is our weekend getaway. It's meant for the two of us to spend time together, but after we jetted off to Spain last week, I'm really behind."

"Don't apologize."

"You might want to hold that thought until I give you the rest of the bad news. I'm leaving Sunday. I'll be gone ten days. Work conference."

"It happens." His words barely registered, not that I'd ever begrudge him his career anyway.

"Hey," he put the computer down on the side table, "how was your day?" He studied me in that annoying way of his. "Has Mark called to check on you?"

"Of course, he has. I have six voicemails from him."

"He's worried." That concerned expression didn't leave his face. "These last seven days have been a whirlwind. It's okay if you're feeling a bit overwhelmed."

"You have no idea." I sat up. "I don't think things are going to work out at Cross Security. I'm already in hot water, and I only have a month to solve a cold case. Do me a favor and keep your headhunter friend on speed dial."

"What happened?"

I shook my head. "You don't want to know." He opened his mouth to protest, but I cut him off. "Trust me, you don't want to hear about my day."

Deciding not to argue, he went back to work, and I went back to being motionless on the couch. At some point, he picked me up and carried me to bed.

FIVE

A cool breeze danced across my skin, and my eyes slowly opened to the sight of the sheer white curtains billowing in the wind. For a second, I thought we were at Martin's villa in Spain before I ever heard the name Jessika Wellington. Too bad we were home, and work was beckoning. Reluctantly, I climbed out of bed and went to the doorway. Martin was on the terrace. His laptop was on the table next to a cup of coffee. A Bluetooth was clipped to his ear. But despite all that, he looked peaceful in the oversized patio chair. The door creaked, giving away my position, and he glanced up and smiled.

"I'll call you back," he said, pressing a button on his phone and unclipping the Bluetooth. "Did I wake you?"

"The breeze did." I stepped outside, and he pulled me onto his lap. "Is there a reason you didn't close the door?"

"I wanted to make sure I heard you get up." He kissed me, playing with the hem of my shirt.

"I am capable of taking care of myself."

"That's debatable. If it weren't for me, you would have skipped dinner and slept on the couch."

My eyebrow quirked up. "What's wrong with that?" I jerked my chin at his computer screen. "How long have you been at it today?"

"Since seven." He rubbed a hand down his face.

"Did you even sleep?"

"About three hours."

"Martin, don't you realize I'm the one who stays awake and works crazy hours? You only run a multimillion dollar company. It's not like you have any reason to work past four."

He chuckled. "But you make it look like so much fun."

We both knew he was a workaholic, but the reason for this was due more to our impromptu vacation last week. After I was fired, he thought we could use the break. Instead, he spent half the time working, and our trip was cut short when I was given an interview at Cross Security. This was actually my fault. Hell, most things were.

"I'll let you get back to it." I glanced through the doorway and into our apartment. "You shouldn't leave the door open. We'll end up with pigeons."

"I don't think there are pigeons at this height."

I gave him a mock serious expression. "Yes, there are. Haven't you seen those aviaries people keep on the roof? That's where the pigeons live."

"Okay, smart ass," he teased, "how many times have you seen these aviaries?" He pressed his finger to my lips before I could respond. "And I don't want a list of movies. How many actual roofs have you been on that house pigeons?"

"None, but we aren't on the roof. We're twenty-one stories up. They could fly this high. And when we have an infestation, what are you going to do about it?"

He smirked. "We could move. I could call building security and have them handle it. Or I could let you use them as target practice." I slapped his arm, and he rubbed the sting away. "Fine, I'm the man of the house. I'll take care of them."

"Are you going to club me over the head and drag me back into the bedroom too, Mr. Man?"

"What if I carry you back to the bedroom instead?" His eyes lit up.

"I'd probably sleep for another," I reached for his wrist

and checked the time, "ten hours. Damn jetlag. Spain was beautiful. Your villa was gorgeous, but I'm not doing a great job bouncing back."

Martin's expression turned somber. "From the trip or from the sucker-punch you received before we left?" He ran his thumb across my cheek. "I know you said you were okay with the forced resignation, but..."

"But nothing." I climbed off his lap. "The OIO was hurting us. Hell, it was hurting me." I glanced at his computer screen. "If you're going to start this, I'll have to remind you our weekend place is a work-free zone, and you're in violation of the terms of our agreement."

"I know, sweetheart. The timing isn't great." His eyes flicked from the computer to me and back again, silently asking permission. "I need to play catch-up."

"Okay," I took a step inside, "but you owe me. You can do this all day if I can run to the office and pick up some files, deal?"

"Just for today. I want to take you out tonight. We need to celebrate your new job, and I want to remind you how much you'll miss me these next ten days."

"So you're not going to call every night to tell me I should miss you, like you usually do?"

"You're remembering wrong. You're the one who calls to tell me what you're wearing and the things you want to do to me when I get home."

"That's not how I remember it."

"The loneliness must have been so excruciating you blocked it out."

I swallowed. "I guess so." We recently weathered a three month break-up. It was agonizing and caused a lot to change in our relationship, including our need for a shared apartment. This was neutral territory, and the only place we would meet until our relationship was appropriately rebuilt and Martin trusted me enough to allow me to return to his house. I kissed him. "You can come inside to work, just make sure you leave the pigeons out here."

"Okay."

After dressing in something casual and grabbing my Cross Security access card, I went downstairs and asked the doorman to hail a cab. I wasn't used to these fancy buildings. My apartment was a sixth floor walk-up. The hallways always smelled like cooked cabbage, and there was mold in the stairwells. That was home. Sometimes, I felt like I was just pretending when I was with Martin. His life was elegant and catered. I was an imposter. Cinderella before the stroke of midnight. Unfortunately, as the cab pulled to a stop in front of the office building, I realized I felt like a fraud in my professional life too. Well, just another twenty-nine days until I was out on my ass. Oddly enough, I found that reassuring.

Shaking off the wayward thoughts that were starting to delve into the psychology behind those feelings, I went through building security and made my way to the bank of elevators. For a Saturday, the building remained busy. I found a manila folder on my desk containing the updated background checks.

While I scanned through the sheets for a solid lead, I noticed the red blinking light. I had a missed call from Dylan Hart. Phone tag could be a bitch, but he only phoned a few minutes ago. I dialed him back, relieved when he answered.

"Mr. Hart, this is Alexis Parker with Cross Security. I've been tasked with looking into the disappearance of Jessika Wellington," I said, feeling as if I were reading from a script. "I'd like to ask you a few questions, if that's okay."

I could hear him inhale and exhale. "Have you made any progress finding her?"

"Not yet. That's why I need your help."

"Anything." His tone was desperate and anxious. He could be a great actor, or he really wanted to find out what happened to his high school sweetheart.

"Do you remember the last time you saw or spoke to Jessika?"

"It was that morning at school. Y'know, before she vanished. It was Wednesday. We had chemistry together and lunch. It was so stupid. I spent the entire time trying to convince her we should go to the movies on Friday. They were having a marathon showing of some superhero franchise. It started at seven and would go until two a.m.

She didn't want to go."

"Did she seem anxious or afraid?"

He laughed bitterly. "Do you know how many times someone has asked me that?"

"I'm sorry."

"I've thought about that question every day since the first time I was asked. And I don't know. Maybe she seemed off, but I just thought she was stressed about school. We had exams coming up, and she was always freaking out they could ruin her perfect GPA. That seems really stupid now, y'know?"

"Yeah." I waited to see if he wanted to volunteer anything else, but he didn't. "Can you tell me about her routine? What did she do after school? Did she work?"

"Jess was always busy. During the fall, she ran cross-country. They had meets on weekends and practices during the week before school started. During the spring, it was volleyball. She was on the debate team, but they only met on Mondays. She was really big into Prospective Doctors of the Future or whatever the fuck it's called."

"Obviously, you weren't a fan."

He let out a huff. "It took up so much damn time. Every time I wanted to go do something, it's like she was volunteering at a clinic or taking some kind of CPR class with the club. Sure, she wanted to be a doctor, but she didn't have to be Doogie Howser."

No one mentioned any of this to me. I went to the filing cabinet and pulled out her schedule and the police reports. Why didn't anyone make note of this?

"Do you remember where she worked? Or when? Days? Times? Anything?" I looked at her financial records, but the only deposits were around holidays and her birthday. Nothing correlated with a steady job.

"It changed. She bounced around a lot. It was always Tuesdays and Thursdays after school. That's how she decided on her other extracurriculars. She wanted to make certain she prioritized that."

The bitterness was obvious. He hated she chose to spend more time focused on her future than on him. That might have been motive, but he did have an airtight alibi. It also sounded like he missed her a lot. And he was angry instead of regretful or guilty. So I pushed on.

"Do you remember what faculty member was in charge of that organization?" I asked.

"Yeah, Mrs. Cheese," he spat. "That's what we called her. Her speeches about saving the world were downright cheesy."

"Carla Cleese?" I asked.

"Yeah."

I looked down at the notations I made. "You and Jessika texted and spoke frequently. I noticed she texted you between six and seven on Tuesdays and Thursdays. Any particular reason why?"

He snorted. "That's when she had a break at the clinic or whatever."

"Do you know where the clinic was or what it was called?"

"I'm sorry. I don't. I'm not sure she ever said. She bounced around from the hospital to doctors' offices to clinics. It changed all the time. I remember she talked a lot about helping at a free clinic toward the end, but I didn't always pay attention."

"That's okay." I thought for a moment. "I have one last question, and it's rather personal. Were you sleeping with Jessika?"

He swallowed. "We messed around a bit. We were always responsible and careful though." For a moment, he sounded like a scared sixteen year old who just got busted.

"All right. That's all the questions I have for now. If you remember anything else, regardless of how minor, please get in touch."

"I will." He waited a moment. "Why are you looking into her extracurriculars? She disappeared during a flash mob performance. It was part of some pep rally thing, but no one saw her after that. Shouldn't you be looking there?"

"Is that where the other investigators focused their attention?"

"Yes," he replied.

"Since that didn't work, I'm hoping we'll find answers elsewhere."

"Let me know if you do. I just...I miss her. I don't even know if we'd still be together, but I wonder about that a lot. I wish we had the chance to find out."

Hanging up, I jotted down some notes from the conversation. I needed a meeting with Cleese and to figure out what this organization was all about. Grabbing Jessika's yearbook, I flipped back to the page and read the headline. *Prospective Doctors of the Future.* What a name for a club. The faculty advisor was Carla Cleese. No credentials were listed. She probably had the requisite teaching degree. She could have just as easily been the volleyball coach. Her background check came back clean. There was nothing suspicious in her finances. On paper, she was just another underpaid and overworked teacher.

Returning to the filing cabinet, I dug through the dozens of folders until I found the police reports. I wasn't entirely certain how Cross obtained transcripts from police interviews, but it was best not to ask. More than likely, I didn't want to know. Detective Sparrow interviewed Mrs. Cleese on three separate occasions.

Cleese praised Jessika's work ethic, spoke of her high grades, and said she was one of the most active members of the club. The club volunteered at the local hospital, shadowed some health care providers at their offices, and helped out at a clinic. Given that Jess was a minor with no formal training, her duties included things like taking inventory, running errands, and helping out in reception.

"Why the hell isn't there a list of locations with dates and times?" I continued searching the filing cabinet, checking Renner's investigation notes and the notes made by the two Cross investigators who took the case after him, but no one bothered to determine where Jessika was working at the time of her disappearance. Muttering to myself about incompetence, I grabbed the phone off my desk and dialed Renner, but he wasn't in his office. So I left a voicemail requesting his help and leaving my cell number.

I stared at the pages, waiting for answers to materialize. When they didn't, I did a search for free clinics in the city, narrowed it down to the gang-controlled neighborhood where her texts originated, and found one in the area. Writing down the name and address, I searched through the files again. Not a single person ever mentioned that specific clinic.

Calling upstairs, I asked someone to run the location. Apparently, this request would take a bit more time and work than the one I made yesterday. Unsure of how I wanted to proceed in the interim, I dialed O'Connell. The major crimes detective might be able to get the intel faster than Cross's resident techs.

"Hey, Nick. I need another favor."

"I think I'm going to start charging for these favors," he said. "What do you want now?"

I read off the name and address. "This might be what connects Jessika Wellington to that neighborhood. Can you see what you can find out about the free clinic?"

"I'll look. A lot of poor neighborhoods have free clinics. It might be a necessity in the community, or it could be a place to score. I'll let you know what I dig up."

"Maybe the guy I shot went there to get his shoulder patched up. Perhaps you could have some uniforms check it out and ask some questions."

"You do realize I'm a cop. I probably would have thought of that on my own." His chair squeaked, and I figured he was leaning forward at his desk. "By the way, no one's been brought in yet for the shooting. Officers checked the addresses on file, but no one was home. It's like they disappeared."

"Maybe that's a side effect of hanging out in that neighborhood."

"Just be careful, Parker. I don't want to have to send units to look for you."

SIX

My mind was buzzing. I didn't exactly have a lead, but I had something that might turn into a lead. Before going back to the apartment and Martin, I picked up my car from outside my apartment and drove around the neighborhood in question. It was a Saturday afternoon. Several men, barely old enough to drive, lingered on the street corners and around the apartment buildings. I didn't spot any hookers working near the businesses, but it was early in the afternoon. I was just lucky to catch them the other morning before they clocked out.

Pulling to a stop across the street from the free clinic, I snapped a few photos. The hours were posted on the door, and not surprisingly, they were closed Saturday and Sunday. They had regular office hours from noon to nine, Monday through Thursday. Fridays they closed at four. Obviously, there were some professionals in this world who didn't work weekends. Martin just wasn't one of them, and neither was I.

After meandering through the streets for another twenty minutes, I knew I'd have to come back during peak hours. Saturday afternoon wasn't the best time to conduct recon. I needed the cover of nightfall. That's when things would get interesting.

The other points of interest in the Wellington case would require setting up interviews, and since everyone on my list previously cooperated with one investigator or another, I had no reason to doubt that wouldn't be the case now. Besides, I imagined my new boss would like things done properly. He had a reputation to uphold.

When I made it back to our weekend getaway, I parked my car in Martin's reserved space. His driver dropped him off last night, so the spot was empty. There was no reason to let it go to waste. After grabbing a large stack of files, I went across the street to the building, pleased the doorman was on duty before I dropped everything in a messy heap.

"Thanks," I said.

He followed me to the elevator, stuck the key inside, and pressed the proper floor. "Do you need help upstairs?"

"No, I'm okay."

When the elevator car stopped on the twenty-first floor, I stepped out, knocking against the apartment door with my knee. After a minute, Martin opened the door, stepping out of the way as I moved past to put my work on the counter. The Bluetooth remained in his ear, and when he spoke, it wasn't to me.

Since he claimed the coffee table and living room as his workspace, I took the island counter in the kitchen as mine. After sorting through the files, I climbed onto one of the stools and sat on my knees, leaning over the countertop. The notes I made after speaking to Dylan were guiding my thoughts.

Jessika Wellington must have been working at the free clinic. Reaching for the phone, I dialed Renner again, but he didn't answer. Didn't anyone ever check their office messages from home? Realizing I had to do things myself, I grabbed my laptop to gather some preliminary information about the clinic. The list of medical staff filled my screen, and I wrote down every name. Unfortunately, I had no idea if any of them worked at the clinic five years ago or if they'd even remember Jessika. Why didn't the police do their due diligence?

Out of options, I phoned Mrs. Wellington. "I'm sorry to

interrupt your weekend," I said, "but I wanted to ask about Jessika's work schedule."

"Jessika didn't work," she replied.

"Work might be the wrong word. She volunteered at clinics and the hospital. Would you happen to remember Jessika's schedule or where she volunteered?"

After a long, unsteady pause, Mrs. Wellington cleared her throat. Her voice was tight when she said, "It's my understanding the entire club would take classes or assist at medical offices during the club meeting times. They went in a group and left in a group. I don't know the specifics. As far as I know, Jessika didn't do these things on her own."

"Okay, thanks."

Gnawing on this new piece of information, I wrote down the list of club members and began to pace. I didn't think to bring those files home. Instead of going back to the office, I opened another browser window and began a social media search. After matching the yearbook photos to profile pictures, I scrolled through posts and photos from around the time of Jessika's disappearance. I found a few photos of the group at various events, along with some comments.

Taking a chance, I sent private messages to Jessika's classmates, identifying myself and asking if anyone remembered the kinds of places the club met or how long these meetings lasted. Within forty minutes, I received eight responses. Almost everyone was dialed in and actually wanted to help. That was unexpected. From what they said, the club met after school and was bused to various locations. The destination changed every few weeks. Sometimes it was the local city college where they learned CPR or how to take blood pressure, or they went to a hospital, clinic, or nursing home to shadow the workers. They were always finished before five.

Staring at the screen, I couldn't decide if they each played a part in Jessika's disappearance and subsequent cover-up or if no one had any idea what she was actually doing after these club meetings. I needed to speak to Cleese and Jessika's father. Each was a huge part of Jessika's life, and I hoped one of them knew something. I read through the reports given by her few close friends, along with her text messages and e-mails, but I didn't think any of them would be helpful. Like most teenage girls, she spent the majority of her time with her boyfriend or her family. The boyfriend was a bust, and so was the mom. I was running out of options.

"Alex," Martin's hand ran gently down my spine, "are you almost finished?"

"I've barely started." Shaking my head, I climbed off the stool. "How is it already this late?"

He smiled sadly. "We were working."

"Yeah."

"Tell me where you want to go. I'll pull some strings and get us a reservation."

"Can we just stay here? We have leftovers. I'm not sure how that happened when I don't remember making meatloaf."

"That came from my fridge. I thought you might want a home-cooked meal instead of takeout." He winked. "Are you sure you want to stay in?"

"Absolutely. Everything I need is inside this apartment."

"Damn, that's a good answer." He kissed me, looking down at my notes while I started to clear off the counter. "What are you working on?"

"Missing person." While he heated dinner, I filled him in on the case, leaving out the shooting from yesterday morning and concluding with, "Needless to say, Cross expects answers, and if I don't have them in the next month, I'll get canned. Again."

"Bastard." Martin's eyes flamed for a moment. "If your new boss is going to be such a prick, you're better off without him."

"I know."

He eyed me. "Except now the only thing you want to do is find out what happened to the girl."

"Pretty much." I sighed. "I also need to put in some serious time and effort on Julian Mercer's case. I owe him. Before I left the OIO, I called in every favor to get as much information as possible. And the resources at Cross

Security are beyond anything I ever imagined. They'll come in handy, so I don't want to let the opportunity slip through my fingers. I just need to make some real progress on this first, and hopefully, I'll be able to slip the murder investigation in under the radar. The next twenty-eight days are going to be busy."

"For me too." He came around the counter and hugged me. "We'll figure out how to make this work, but we have to make time for each other. We'll carve out a day here or there, even if it can't be an entire weekend. Agreed?"

"Yes." I kissed along his jaw. "Does this mean you've given up searching for a new couples counselor?"

He snorted. "For now. You have to admit, the last guy we went to had an unhealthy infatuation with our sex life." Martin stepped back behind the counter, adjusting the dial on the oven. "And I didn't like the way he leered at you. He wanted details to get off on later."

I smiled. "And what was wrong with the one before that?"

He turned and gave me an annoyed look. "I don't see how my mother has anything to do with our issues."

"Maybe you should ask Freud to explain it to you."

Martin's mom was a painful topic. Her death devastated him, and it led to some odd break with his father. He lost both parents not too far apart, and it was something we rarely spoke about, like the relationship I had with my adopted parents. These things happened over a decade ago. They weren't a part of our shared history, and therefore, out of bounds.

"And the one before that?" Martin looked at me expectantly. "You didn't even make it twenty minutes into the session before you told him to fuck off and walked out."

"He was clearly a quack, believing I self-sabotage because I don't feel I deserve to be loved. If that were true, I wouldn't have fought so hard for us."

"It takes two to fight."

I laughed. "And to scare off a few therapists. Face it, we aren't good at this therapy thing, but we gave it a fair shake. That counts."

"Two and a half sessions with three different therapists

probably proves how unstable we are. But I agree. I don't want to waste our limited time listening to some moron with a degree tell us what we're doing wrong." The oven beeped, and Martin removed the leftovers and searched the cabinets for plates. "I made a copy of my travel itinerary and left it on the coffee table for you. It's just meeting after meeting. We're basically working our way across the country to get these conferences and business deals handled."

"Don't apologize. That's just part of the CEO package."

"You've always been rather fond of my package." He grinned. "Personally, I do have quite an affinity for it, as well. And it'll be put to good use this evening."

I rolled my eyes. "Do you want to know what my favorite part of your package is?"

His green eyes danced. "Do tell."

"The fact that I'll have the next ten days distraction free. The time apart might be just what I need to make some headway on this case."

He clutched his chest. "You wound me." His teasing eyes flicked to mine. "You know, you aren't as heartless as you pretend to be. I'm not falling for that badass bitch routine. You're gonna miss me." He moved closer, snaking his arms around my back and pulling me against him.

"Every damn day." I put my cheek against his chest. "You better have a safe trip because when you get back, I'm all yours, handsome."

"I'm holding you to that."

We spent the rest of the evening laughing, talking, and connecting. That was the point of having this apartment and spending the weekends together, even though our time was cut short. Despite the fact Martin barely slept, we spent hours in bed, talking and not talking.

It was a little after four a.m. when the phone rang. He kissed my shoulder as I leaned over to grab it from the bedside table. Recognizing the precinct number, I hit answer.

"I thought you'd like to know we just brought in one of the shooters and the prostitute you identified," the desk sergeant said.

Martin had to leave in three hours, and neither of us had slept much, not that we were planning on it. He intended to sleep on the plane, and I figured I'd sleep after he left. But fate had other plans. Unperturbed by the phone call, Martin kissed along my clavicle, ignoring the phone in my hand as best he could.

"It's the middle of the night. Can you keep them on ice until morning? I'll be there by eight."

"Like you said, it's the middle of the night. We'll toss the girl downstairs in the tank, and we'll put the shooter in an interrogation room. They're smart. They already asked for lawyers, and you know the public defender's office doesn't want to get a four a.m. phone call."

Neither do private eyes. "Thanks." Hanging up, I ran my hand through Martin's hair, tugging slightly at the dark brown locks until he tore his lips off my skin and looked up at me. "You're not even going to ask?"

"You're not leaving, so the rest is inconsequential."

SEVEN

After Martin left, I brewed a strong cup of coffee and went to the precinct. O'Connell was behind his desk, reading reports. I crouched down next to him.

"What's so interesting?" I asked.

He looked over his shoulder, surprised to see me. "What the hell are you doing here?"

"I got a four a.m. phone call from the sergeant on duty. Apparently, officers arrested the shooter and prostitute I identified." Moving away from his desk, I filled my now empty travel mug with coffee. "I'm surprised they notified me immediately."

"They must think you're still on the job."

"Probably." I rolled my neck and took a sip of the burnt coffee. "The shooter's in interrogation. The hooker's downstairs. I'm not certain exactly what I want to ask, so I figured I'd come see you first."

He chuckled. "So you need help coming up with questions. Damn, I didn't realize I had to do my job and yours."

"Smart ass." I sighed and lowered my voice. "Actually, I wanted to ask you about the other day. What's the deal with Renner?" The bastard never called back, but it was Sunday. If he didn't go to the office on Saturday, he sure as hell wouldn't be stopping by on Sunday.

Nick glanced around to make certain no one was in earshot. Aside from his partner, Thompson, who was pretending I didn't exist, the rest of the bullpen was fairly empty. "Bennett's a tool. He has a reputation for being a hothead. Did some asinine things, kinda like you. When he was hurt on the job, it raised a few questions. He didn't exactly follow protocol, and maybe he went in without waiting for back-up. He wasn't exactly a team player."

"Just like Parker," Thompson mumbled, finally glancing at me.

"But he's not a bad guy?" I asked, needing to reaffirm this.

Nick shrugged. "Not really. He wasn't dirty or anything like that. He's just..."

"Only concerned with covering his own ass," Thompson said, his focus on his computer screen. "He doesn't give a shit about what happens to anyone else."

"Was that before or after he was hurt?"

"Before." O'Connell swallowed. "I don't know what he's like now, but you should know not to trust him in the field. That's all I meant by be careful."

I nodded. "So any word from Detective Sparrow? Did she get back from her trip yet?"

"I think I saw her this morning," Thompson volunteered. "I'll see if I can track her down for you." Being uncharacteristically helpful, he got up from his desk and went out the double doors.

Laughing quietly to himself, O'Connell swiveled to face me. "He'll be gone awhile. You might as well take care of matters downstairs. When you're done, come back and I'll take you up to missing persons."

"Thanks, Nick. Have I mentioned you're my favorite detective?"

"All the damn time. Now stop stalling." He jerked his head at the door.

Downstairs, I recognized the arresting officer as the one who took my statement in the alleyway. He nodded, leading the way into the adjoining observation room. Through the two-way mirror, I recognized the man as one of the shooters. The sling and bandage on his arm were telling of the bullet wound.

"He stopped by the ER last night. The hospital alerted us. We matched the bullet they removed to the ballistics we have on record for your piece," the officer affirmed. "Right now, it's basically his word against yours, but he says he was hit during a drive-by. He didn't see who shot him."

"Convenient."

The cop looked at me. "Seeing you might make him reconsider his story. Is there anything you haven't told me that might be of use?"

I shook my head. "I don't know why he opened fire. I'm working a cold case. I asked the hookers if they recognized Jessika Wellington, and this guy and one of his friends came out in force. I'm guessing they wanted to scare me off."

"From the number of casings we found, they wanted to do more than scare you. Are you sure you didn't say or do anything else to upset them?"

"No."

"Fine. We're going inside. You wanted to ask about the girl, so ask about the girl. Maybe he'll tell us what's going on."

I followed the officer into the room. The banger looked up, lips pressed together in a tight line. His head dipped down, almost as if he were nodding, and his brown eyes blazed. The public defender sat in a chair beside him. She looked worse than I did, and I hadn't slept yet. I had a feeling she wasn't going to bother wasting her breath in the interview room, so I decided to pretend she wasn't there.

"What's your name?" I asked.

The banger didn't speak, so the cop answered. "Rodney Jefferson. Twenty-two. Four priors for assault. One attempted murder. And two possession with intent."

I whistled. "I'd think by now you would have known better than to go to the ER."

Rodney glared at me. "Didn't have a choice. Someone shot me." His eyes went to the cop. "I didn't do nothing. I was minding my own damn business. I don't give a shit what this bitch says."

"Bitch hasn't said anything yet," I retorted. "You part of the Seven Rooks?"

"What if I am? Whatcha gonna do about it?" Rodney asked.

The lawyer glanced up. "For the record, my client did not confirm that detail."

I snorted. "I don't give a shit. I want to know what the Rooks had to do with Jessika Wellington's disappearance five years ago."

"Who?" Rodney asked.

I turned my attention to the cop as if to say, *can't we hit him with a phonebook now*, but the cop just shook his head. "Answer the lady," the officer said, but Rodney remained tight-lipped.

"She was sixteen. Light brown hair. Pretty. Came from a rich family. When she went missing, people went looking for her," I said.

Rodney licked his lip, opening his mouth in a half smile. "Five years ago, I was seventeen. I don't know what you're talking about. The only time rich bitches step foot in the 'hood is to score. And I wouldn't know nothing about that."

"Listen, things could go one of two ways. I press charges; you go to jail. Or maybe I forget what happened Friday morning. You give this nice officer a statement saying how you were a victim of a drive-by, and you walk out those doors in a couple of hours." Bargaining with a banger wasn't how I wanted to start my day, but I'd be damned if I didn't try to make lemonade from these lemons.

The lawyer looked up. "Are you serious?"

"Sure, why not?"

She gave her client a hard look, encouraging him to open up, but he just shrugged. His cold stare focused on me. "I don't know her. I don't know you. And I don't know what the hell you're talking about."

Realizing this was a waste of time, I left the interrogation room. The cop followed.

"You know how this goes. There isn't much we can do.

Without a corroborating witness, things will get jumbled. I'm guessing he'll get bounced. He'll probably be back on the street by tomorrow night."

"What about the hooker?" I asked.

"Another revolving door. Vice scooped her up, along with another half a dozen prostitutes. If you want to talk to her, she's in the tank."

Sighing, I went down the stairs to holding. After some cajoling, I convinced the officer on duty to take a break while I went to check on the prisoners. Portia "Traffic Cones" Russo was seated near the bars. Her neon orange boots were practically blinding under the fluorescent lights. At the sound of my footsteps, she looked up.

"I knew you were a cop."

"Not a cop." I scanned the other uninterested faces in the holding cells, but I didn't recognize any of the working girls. "How old are you?"

Her eyes hardened. "That's none of your damn business."

"The girl I'm looking for would be twenty-one now. She was sixteen when she vanished. Jessika Wellington. Her face was all over the TV and in every newspaper at the time. I think it might have even gone national. Her phone records indicate she spent some time in your neighborhood. Do you remember seeing her?"

She tapped her matching orange nails on the bench. "Nope."

"C'mon, she's just a kid."

"We're all just kids trying to scrape by. Five years ago is ancient history. Why the hell do you even care anymore?"

"Her mom wants to know what happened. Can you imagine having a loved one disappear and never knowing why? Do you think anyone deserves that?" Pulling at her heartstrings might be pointless, but I didn't know what other cards to play.

She licked her lips. "It's been five years. Tell the old bat her kid's dead and to get over it."

The cop returned before I could say anything else. "Time's up," he said.

"Is she dead?" I asked.

Portia shrugged. "If she's been on the street that long, probably. Shit, she'd be older than me, and I'm not sure I'll make it to twenty-one."

The cop came closer, prepared to physically drag me away, but I threw up my hands in surrender and walked back to the stairwell. My two leads remained ice cold. Dejected, I returned to the major crimes division. Hopefully, Detective Sparrow would salvage my morning.

O'Connell took one long look before dragging me back into the stairwell. "Didn't get the answers you wanted?"

"The banger won't talk, and I don't think the hooker knows anything. She's just a kid herself. She can't even legally buy alcohol, and she's working the corner. This is so screwed up."

"Cross Security really has you in a tight spot, don't they?"

"It isn't about keeping the job. Honestly, I'm prepared to start the job search again in a month. Landing this one in a matter of days was unexpected. And truth be told, I'm a bit unprepared for it."

"That's why you look like you're burning the candle at both ends?"

"Martin and I pulled an all-nighter. He's out of town for the next ten days, so we tried to work in some time together before he left. We're supposed to be on solid ground, but who knows. Anyway, as soon as I'm done here, I'm going home to sleep."

"Don't count on it until you speak to Sparrow."

After spending the last four days reading through five years worth of reports, there wasn't much Detective Brooke Sparrow could tell me that I didn't already know. However, when she pulled out her notepad, we hit pay dirt. Her notes from the time of Jessika's disappearance were meticulous. She traced the phone records, and after exhausting all the normal avenues regarding the school, the flash mob, and the usual suspects, she determined Jessika spent part of her time in the wrong neighborhood.

"I told my captain," Sparrow said, "and we sent a squad of uniforms into the area. They did a thorough canvass. No one remembered seeing the girl."

"From the interview notes I read, her after-school activities involved volunteering at clinics and other medical facilities. Did you check with them?"

"We asked the staff and instructors at those locations about Jessika. They had such kind things to say, none of which was helpful to the investigation." She searched through the files in her desk drawer until she found an old folder. Inside was a map, yellowed and curling at the corners. She laid it on her desk. "We triangulated the area that would feed off those two cell towers. As you can see, it's pretty big."

"And you checked everywhere?"

"Conceivably everywhere a sixteen year old runaway might end up. We went to the bars, the clubs, and the strip joints." She took a breath. "We raided crack dens and stash houses. We checked the shelters and skid row. We hauled in every prostitute and pimp we could find. Nothing ever shook loose. After two weeks, the captain called off the search. Her cell signal could have bounced off those towers while she was taking the train home or something. We don't know. All I remember is her mom and dad saying she never made it home before ten on Tuesdays and Thursdays."

"And they weren't worried?"

She raised her palms in a *who knows* gesture. "The girl's curfew was ten on school nights. She never broke it. Everyone I spoke to said she was a good kid. Studious. They didn't have reason to worry or think she was up to no good. Her parents probably figured she was at the library or with that boy."

"Dylan Hart?"

"Yeah." Something flicked across her face. "He was a jock. Not good enough to play college sports, but good enough to be a big shot in high school. He was the type to go to house parties and get drunk on the weekends. But he was too sheltered to go into a neighborhood like that to score weed or ecstasy. I wanted to like him for her disappearance, but the kid fell apart in interrogation the second time we brought him in. I wish I didn't waste so much time thinking he knew something. Maybe then we would have found her."

"What about the parents?" I asked. "I've spoken to the mother. I have yet to meet the father."

"Before this shit went down, they were too wrapped up in their own lives to pay much attention. They probably figured they were lucky enough to have a good kid they didn't have to worry about. The mom's the typical suburban housewife. She has a weekly appointment for her hair and nails, plays tennis at the club with the other ladies, and works for a lot of local charities. The father spends his days at the office, golfs on the weekends, and maybe does the secretary on the side."

"Any truth behind that?"

Sparrow shrugged. "Nothing substantiated, but it fit the profile."

"Profiles are rarely accurate."

She studied me for a moment. "Hey, that's just what the FBI cranked out when I asked for assistance. Bitch to them about it." She jerked her chin up. "So you went into the Seven Rooks' neighborhood Friday morning, asked about Jessika, and were almost capped for your trouble. Sound about right?"

I nodded.

A large grin popped onto her face, and she smacked her palm down on the map. "Then I was right about Jessika being there. It has to connect to her disappearance."

"Did you check out the free clinic? She was adamant about becoming a doctor. I imagine a place like that would welcome volunteers, and it would put her in the neighborhood at the right time."

"I thought about it. I asked Mrs. Cleese about it, but she said the school never authorized the club to go there. They thought it was too dangerous. But I asked around anyway. One of the doctors who worked at the clinic after his normal office hours knew Jessika. He'd seen her and the rest of her classmates at the hospital a time or two, but he didn't remember if any of them volunteered at the clinic."

"Do you remember his name?"

She flipped through her notepad, finally coming to the proper page. "Here."

I copied down the name, Dr. Ridley Dalton. The file contained an entire list of medical personnel, but there weren't any notations next to the other names. "Who are they?"

"The rest of the clinic staff."

"I don't remember seeing any of this in Jessika's file."

"This didn't make it into the files. It was unofficial. By the time I finished running down everything else and discovered the possible connection to the free clinic, Jessika had been missing a month. We wasted a lot of time and resources on locating her, and truthfully, anything beyond the first forty-eight is pretty slim pickins'." She frowned, her eyes falling to the table. "Ninety percent of the cases that cross my desk are never solved, at least not until a body washes up, and that's typically years later. By then, other cases were piling up, and while we were still following fresh leads, this didn't look promising. Dr. Dalton didn't remember her from the clinic, and the canvassing we did in that neighborhood never turned up anything. We didn't have enough to get a search warrant or subpoena for their records or security footage, so that was that. Medical privacy rights trump police investigations almost every time." Her eyes met mine. "That's why the Wellingtons have been hiring private investigators to do the tracking. From the lack of progress they've made, I guess I shouldn't kick myself too hard for not finding her. If you ever figure out what happened or if you think you have a solid hunch, let me know. This one's always bothered me."

"Sure." I stood. "Thanks for your time, Detective. I'll be in touch."

EIGHT

After returning to our apartment, I crashed for the rest of the day. Waking up with creases across my cheek, I frowned at Martin's pillow and dragged myself out of bed. When I finished showering and straightening up, I collected my files, tossed some of the leftovers into a bag to take home, and left a note for Rosemarie, the cleaning lady. She worked for Martin and now had two places to keep clean on account of our relationship turmoil, so I thought it might be nice to let her know she was appreciated.

By the time I made it back to my place, the sun was setting. Sunday nights were usually quiet. It wasn't a particularly popular time for illegal activity on account of most people staying home in preparation for another work week. I checked my office inbox, but I didn't have any messages. Deciding I needed to get some meetings on the books, I left a request with one of the assistants to arrange a face-to-face with Dr. Ridley Dalton and the current administrator at the free clinic. Since I already asked for a sitdown with Mr. Wellington and Mrs. Cleese, there wasn't much left to do. Or was there?

There was no denying Jessika's disappearance was linked to that neighborhood. Perhaps she was working at the free clinic or hanging out with some yet to be identified third party. It was no secret good girls liked bad boys, and that neighborhood was full of some very bad boys. Perhaps she was seeing someone on the side. It would explain her late Tuesdays and Thursdays and the condoms in her purse.

Pulling out a copy of Sparrow's map, I studied the several square blocks those two cell towers covered. The entire area wasn't controlled by the Seven Rooks, but I'd be foolish to think they didn't have some influence on the neighboring streets and businesses. Since I wanted to see what else was in the vicinity, I decided to risk it and changed into something that didn't scream investigator.

Making a point to avoid the gang's stronghold, I found some bars and shops near the edges of the search area. Sparrow said officers canvassed the bars and clubs, but it yielded no results. The five years would only make the problem worse. Still, one nagging thought remained in the back of my mind — the Rooks didn't want the truth of Jessika's disappearance to surface. That meant whatever became of her might be happening to other girls. Perhaps more people had gone missing. I needed to know what scams the Rooks were running and if anyone noticed.

I parked on a side street and entered the busiest bar I found. It was a few streets over from where the firefight occurred, and I hoped with my hair down, the makeup slathered on, and dressed like someone looking for a hookup I wouldn't be recognized should anyone familiar be inside. Although, I didn't think this was a gang bar. I just wasn't sure.

As I walked inside, my eyes adjusted to the haze. Four pool tables took up the back half of the room. Some pinball and video poker machines were grouped together in the other corner. A dartboard was on the side, near the hallway that presumably led to the bathrooms. The bar itself was nothing special. Old, cracked, and stained, like the bartender. He was a brawny guy, pushing fifty, with a thick beard and mustache. The faded ink on his forearm told me he'd done a stint in prison at some point.

A few eyes watched as I moved toward the bar. The bartender continued to wipe off the glass in his hand, his expression unreadable. I leaned over one of the stools, pretending to be fascinated by the bottles behind him. My gun was in my crossbody bag, resting reassuringly at my hip, but I also had a knife tucked at my ankle. One could never be too careful in these situations.

"Haven't seen you around here before," he said. "Are you sure you're in the right place?"

"This is a bar, isn't it?" I turned and surveyed the room, seeing a few eyes divert. "Looks like a fun place."

He put the glass down, placing his hands on the edge of the bar. "You might want to try somewhere else."

"Is there a problem?"

He searched my face for a moment. "What'll it be?"

"What do you have on tap?"

He read off the choices while I took a seat on the closest stool. After I made a selection, he grabbed the glass. His eyes didn't waver from mine, even as he filled my order. "You new to the neighborhood?"

"Just passing through." I placed some bills on the counter. "I take it fresh blood doesn't come around often."

His eyes glanced down at the money, but I wasn't buying information. Not yet, anyway. "What brings you by?" he asked.

"Like I said, I was passing through, decided I wanted to grab a drink, and saw the lights and tables from outside. Figured I'd step in and maybe play some darts or pinball. Y'know, just another wild Sunday night."

The look on his face told me he didn't believe a word I said. He wiped down the counter, his eyes moving to someone behind me, but I didn't dare turn around. I focused on the reflections in the mirror behind the liquor bottles. No one was approaching, so I relaxed and took a sip of my drink.

"I don't think this is your kind of place."

"No?"

He didn't respond.

"Is this the kind of place where a girl's given a hard time? Maybe she shows up a few times and never comes back, almost like she just disappeared."

He scowled. "You trying to ask me something? Because I don't have any answers for you." He leaned down, so his face was just inches from mine. "This isn't the kind of place where you should ask questions. People around here don't like that. I suggest you finish your drink and skedaddle."

"Can I get some quarters?" I needed an excuse to hang around for a bit, and the fact that the bartender wanted to throw me out wasn't conducive to my plan.

He took the cash, placed it in the register, and provided change in quarters, like I requested. "I don't want there to be trouble. Got it?"

I smiled innocently. "Do I look like trouble?"

His eyes narrowed slightly. "We'll see."

Taking my pint and the quarters, I maneuvered around the tables and took a spot in front of one of the pinball machines. The sound was turned off, but the game was plugged in. Placing the pint on top of the glass, I glanced behind me. At last count, six men were at the pool tables, two at the dartboard, three at the bar, plus the bartender, and seated in the back corner were three women. From the way they cackled and called to the guys at the nearest pool table and dartboard, I was certain they were together.

Since I walked in, six of the men started paying attention. Maybe they thought I was cute, but something told me that wasn't it. Hopefully, they weren't with the Rooks. If they were, they might realize who I was. Or perhaps they were just naturally leery of strangers.

I wondered what the place was like five years ago. Would a sixteen year old have come here with some muscled, tattooed bad boy to shoot pool and drink beer? Probably. If it weren't for the uncomfortable stares, this place might have seemed fun.

With no real way to determine the men's interest in me, I slid the quarter into the slot and turned back to the game. After a few rounds, I would make an approach. It would seem less suspicious, and hopefully one of the patrons would be more willing to talk than the bartender. I needed to know if anyone else disappeared or heard about people being abducted. If I was really lucky, one of these guys had been around five years ago and would remember seeing Jessika in the area. The bartender must have been here, but he shut down my questioning quickly.

My pinball skills sucked since I was watching the reflections in the top portion of the game to make sure no one planned to shoot me in the back. After spending most of the quarters, two men approached. They were around my age, in their late twenties or early thirties. They smelled like beer and sweat. One came up on my right side, leaning his elbow against the pinball machine. The other remained at my seven o'clock, just skirting my peripheral vision.

"'Sup?" The one on the right jerked his chin up, even as his body sunk lower against the table to try to distract me from the metal ball intent on slipping past the flippers.

"Hey." I lost another ball and reached for my glass, aware I needed to actually make a pretense of drinking. "Did you want to play?"

"Nah. I like watching. I'm Josh. What's your name, babe?"

"Alex."

"This is my friend, Victor." He jerked his chin at the man at my flank, waiting for me to acknowledge him. So I turned and nodded at Victor. "Y'see, we were wondering exactly what it is you think you're doing here."

"Sorry?" Play dumb, my mind screamed.

Victor stepped uncomfortably close. "You heard him."

"Look, guys, I don't know what your problem is, but I just stepped inside to grab a beer and blow off some steam. That's it." I edged to my right, feeling boxed in. Lifting my beer off the pinball machine, I spun around, my eye catching a glimpse of the bartender who was wiping down the counter, his focus on us. "I'm not looking for trouble."

"No?" Josh asked. Casually, he brushed the back of his fingers against my arm. "How come we've never seen you around here before?"

"I'm just passing through."

"From where?" Victor asked.

I moved away from the pinball machine in the direction of the pool tables, hoping to put some distance between us, but Josh and Victor remained glued to my flanks. "It doesn't matter." I placed my beer on one of the empty tables. I let my hand drop to my bag. It'd take less than two seconds to clear my weapon. That wasn't a lot of time, but in close quarters like this, even the slightest delay could be substantial.

"So," Josh said, "are you visiting friends? Family, maybe? Is anyone missing you tonight?"

"Why?" I decided to play this off as flirty despite the warning bells going off in my brain. "Are you going to ask me to spend the night?"

"What if I did?" Josh asked. Something dark was just behind his eyes. He thought he was playing me. Unfortunately, I wasn't certain what he wanted, but I was positive it wasn't a random hookup.

"What if you did?" I maneuvered farther away from the men. Two of the couples decided to clear out. That left four men near the pool tables, not counting Josh and Victor. "Let me guess, your place is just around the corner."

He flashed a devious smile. "The bartender's a friend. We could find a cozy spot in the back."

"Do you take a lot of girls into the back?" I raised an eyebrow, hoping for flirty.

"Just the special ones."

"Oh, yeah?" I smiled. "You think I'm special?"

"You could be."

"So you're friends with the bartender. You must come here a lot. Is this your hangout?" I tilted my head toward Victor. "The two of you look like professional pool players."

"We've been coming here since before we could drink," Victor said. "This is our place." The way he said it sounded more like he was asserting dominance than supplying an answer. He wanted me gone. Truthfully, they both did, but Josh was just smoother.

Asking about Jessika was a bad idea, but I did it anyway. "Either of you remember a girl who used to come around here." I looked up, smacking my lips as if trying to remember. "God, it must be like five years now. Her name was Jess or Jessika. I think she might have been seeing that guy." I snapped my fingers repeatedly. "What was his name? You know, that guy."

"I've known a lot of Jessikas," Josh said. "Right now, the only person I'm interested in knowing is an Alex." He edged closer. "Why are you asking about some chick? You into that?"

Something dark passed over Victor's eyes. "Anyone here know a Jessika?" His voice boomed throughout the room, and the bartender tensed, moving closer to the register.

My eyes scanned the area for weaknesses and escape routes. The front door was the only guaranteed exit. As if reading my mind, two of the men cashed out their tabs and went outside, lingering near the front door. The only other woman seemed to sense the sudden shift in atmosphere and dug her nails into her boyfriend's arm. Within moments, they were gone.

Victor went to the recently vacated pool table and racked the billiards. "Since you're doing nothing but being a cock tease to my boy, show us what you've got."

I glanced at Josh while I sized up the situation. Seven people remained. The man drinking at the bar seemed so committed to that task I wasn't certain he was aware of anything around him. The bartender's eyes continued to take everything in. Did he signal these two clowns to harass me? The other three guys remained clustered together at the table farthest from us. They placed their glasses on the felt and spoke in hushed tones that didn't carry. From the constant looks they tossed in our direction, I couldn't determine if they were with Josh and Victor or if they were planning to intervene on my behalf. One thing was for sure, Jessika's name cleared the room. Or maybe it had more to do with the person asking.

"Pool's not really my game." I took another step backward. "I should call it a night."

"Not so fast." Josh grabbed my arm. "You shouldn't be walking around alone."

"Why?" I challenged, meeting his eyes. "What happens to people in this neighborhood?"

His eye twitched ever so slightly. "It's not safe. You don't want to find out."

"I'll be fine." I tried to pull my arm free, but he held tight.

"I can't let you do that." He yanked me closer.

Pressing my free hand against the table to keep my balance, I reached for the beer glass and smashed it into the side of his face. Surprised, he loosened his grip, and I broke free. The breaking glass drew the attention of the rest of the room. I darted through the tables, hoping to get out without finding myself in another altercation. Two of the men surrounded me, closing in from opposite ends of the table.

I unzipped my purse, grasping my nine millimeter just as the third man struck my wrist with the heavy end of a wooden cue stick. The sting automatically made my hand recoil, and Victor grabbed me from behind. He hooked the carbon fiber pole of another pool cue around my chest, grabbing both ends and pulling backward until I was flush against him. I jerked forward, and he moved the stick higher until it was crushing my windpipe.

I rammed my body backward, blindly clawing at his face and neck. Bringing my left leg up, I grabbed the knife from my ankle strap and in one swift motion buried the blade in his side. He howled, throwing me into the pool table. My hand immediately went back to my bag, but something solid cracked down against the soft spot between my spine and jaw.

Numbness shot through my right arm as the world pitched forward. I landed hard on the ground, dazed. Before I could recover, a strong kick to the gut sent my body sliding across the floor. Spotting the knife, I stretched my fingers for it, clasping the handle as several more kicks pounded into me. Victor leaned down, grabbed my hair in his fist, and threw a punch that made stars explode behind my eyelids and my ears ring.

Black bubbles clouded my vision, and I wasn't sure how strong my hold on consciousness was. I stabbed the blade into the toe of someone's shoe, hearing an unexpected scream. For a moment, the kicking stopped. Rolling underneath the nearest table, I reached across my body with my left hand, yanking my nine millimeter out. My right was worthless at the moment, full of painful tingles, just like most of my body.

"Stop," the bartender commanded, followed by the loud ratchet of a shotgun being loaded. "Get the fuck out of my bar before I call the cops."

Josh crouched down, and I swallowed, aiming at him. I blinked through the impeding darkness, my breath shallow.

"Back off," I hissed.

"Leave her be," the bartender growled. "I'll deal with her." He stared at the men. "Out. Now."

Footsteps echoed against the hardwood floors as most of the men piled out of the bar. From what I could see, they remained just outside. I struggled to get up, but I was woozy from the hit to the back of the head. The floor pitched, and I found myself sprawled on the ground. The bartender came closer, and I pointed the gun at him. My aim was unsteady. I tried to blink my vision clear, but it didn't help.

"Put that down," he said, not bothering to wait for compliance before taking hold of my collar and dragging me across the floor.

I clung to the corner of the wall, clutching my gun with all my might. He yanked harder, my grip slipping as I struggled to decide what was more important, holding my ground or maintaining control of my firearm. In the end, the usefulness of my nine millimeter won out, but that choice proved pointless when I started to black out and the drunk from the bar approached, took my weapon from my hand, and followed us into the back office.

NINE

I blinked back to reality a few moments later. The bartender was standing over me, the barrel of the shotgun resting against his shoulder. He didn't take his eyes off me while the drunk rifled through my bag. I noticed my nine millimeter tucked in the back of his waistband. Bastard.

"Who is she?" the bartender asked.

The other man searched through my wallet, finding my license and Cross Security card. "Alexis Parker. She's a private eye."

The bartender nodded. "Make sure the front door is locked and turn the lights off. We want those assholes to realize the show's over so they'll go home."

"Right, boss."

The bartender crouched down, grabbing my chin roughly in his hand as he turned my head side to side. "I need you to pay attention. What you say will determine what I do with you." He let go of my chin. "Why did you come here?"

He was too close for me to get a good look at the room, but if he clocked me with the shotgun, it'd be lights out. And at the present, I wasn't in any condition to put up a fight.

"I'm looking into the disappearance of Jessika Wellington."

"Wellington?" he repeated the name uncertainly. "That was years ago. What the hell are you doing snooping around now?"

"I don't know. That's the gig."

He searched my eyes. "Yo, bring me some ice in a towel," he called to the other man. He held out his hand, offering to help me up. "I won't hurt you. Just don't try anything stupid."

I grasped his forearm, grunting as every muscle and bone in my torso let me know it was bruised from the assault. He eased me into a tattered leather chair and grabbed the ice from his friend.

"Why are you helping me?" I winced, pressing the ice against the knot at the back of my neck. The son of a bitch who hit me got lucky and landed the perfect strike. If he didn't, the bar brawl would have turned out a lot differently.

"I'm not." He stepped into the hallway and spoke briefly to the other man, their voices too soft for me to hear. "I'm helping myself." He leaned against the wall, studying me. "How's your vision? Can you see out of that eye? Is everything blurry?"

"It's getting there."

"Good. As soon as those jerks leave, I want you out of here." Before I could speak, he held up his palm. "My business is none of yours. I don't know what happened to the Wellington kid. I can tell you the population around here tends to get smaller as time goes on, and it isn't entirely due to murders and arrests. But I know to keep my head down and not ask questions."

"Tell me what you know."

He scrubbed a hand down his face. "Shit, how hard did you get hit? I just told you I don't know anything. I can't help you. More importantly, I won't." He swung the shotgun off his shoulder, placing the barrel against the floor to remind me he was in charge. "If I let you go, there are two things you need to remember. One, I know your name, your address, and where you work. So if you fuck with me or my business, I'll end you. Two, the shit that goes on with the gangs has nothing to do with me. Those guys who roughed you up aren't my guys. I think they are part of the Seven Rooks. A few days ago, you made quite the impression, and the neighborhood was told to report any strangers showing up and asking questions. You obviously have a beef with someone. It's them, not me. I imagine what you're doing will eventually lead to the cops flooding this neighborhood. I don't care if they dismantle the gang, but they better not step foot in my bar. Or we'll have a problem. And I don't like problems."

I stared at him, realizing he had his own agenda. "Did you ever see Jessika around the neighborhood? What was she doing? Was she with someone?"

He swore. "Damn, you're dense. Do you understand I'm giving you a freebie? I could have let those guys drag you out of here and do god knows what with you. I could have let them kill you."

I adjusted in the chair, bringing about an onslaught of pain in my head and abdomen. Squeezing my eyes shut, I took a breath. "Someone would have ended up dead. It might have been me, or it might have been a few of them. Either way, it would have led to the police banging down your door, and you don't want that. So just answer my question, and I promise to never darken your doorstep again."

He chewed on the inside of his cheek for a moment. "Anyone ever tell you you're annoying?"

"Yep."

He sighed. "Back in the day, I might have noticed someone calling for a cab from the free clinic fairly regularly. After a while, the cab stopped showing up. I guess no one needed to call for a ride out of this hellhole anymore." He looked back into the hallway. "Is it clear?"

"Yeah," his friend responded. He handed my bag and gun to the bartender.

After removing the magazine from my weapon, the bartender emptied the cartridge into my purse and ejected the bullet from the chamber. Then he opened my wallet and pocketed the cash. "That's to cover the damages." He grabbed my swollen wrist and yanked me out of the chair. A few feet from the office was a side door, and he opened it and tossed me into the alleyway, dropping my purse and gun next to me. "Remember what I said. I don't want to see you again. If I do, I'll let the Rooks have you, and maybe then you'll find out what happened to that kid firsthand." The door slammed shut.

With shaking hands, I reloaded my weapon. Every sound and flash of light made me think someone was behind me to the point I was a paranoid mess. Frankly, the bartender might have posed a greater risk than the punks. Palming my keys, I kept my gun at my side as I limped back to the car. I needed help.

In too much pain to think clearly, I drove to the one place I imagined was safe. Building security watched with wary eyes as I scanned my card and hobbled to the elevators. On the thirtieth floor, I made my way to my office. Grabbing the bottle of whiskey from the cart, I twisted off the cap and took a few swigs. Collapsing on the couch, I hissed in pain. Perhaps a trip to the hospital would have been a better idea, but it would have resulted in the assault being reported. The police would have questions, and they'd go to the bar to ask them. Until I knew how serious the bartender's threat was, I couldn't risk it. I needed to find out who he was and what he knew.

The thought of getting off the couch wasn't pleasant. I gulped down more booze, ignoring the way it burned the back of my throat. I just needed something to take the edge off; then I'd figure out how to proceed.

After twenty minutes, the pain dulled and I dragged myself to the computer. Despite the warning, I needed to learn some things about the bartender and his bar. I didn't doubt his threat. I'd been in a bad situation with a crime boss before, and I needed to make sure this wasn't about to turn into the same type of predicament.

From a quick glance at the property records, I discovered his name — Jared Prince. That led to his arrest record. He'd been imprisoned for trafficking contraband cigarettes. He served a nickel but was clean ever since. Figuring the bar might be a front to move product, I assumed that's why he didn't want the police poking around, even though he threatened to call them if my assailants refused to vacate. Perhaps he was bluffing, but it worked. Either way, I didn't want to think about it.

Cigarette trafficking was big business, just ask any ATF agent. Due to differing taxes, a person could make a killing off the resale. Perhaps Jessika saw something, and he made her disappear. However, no matter how I manipulated the facts, I couldn't get them to fit with the assault, the people involved, or the brief conversation with the bartender in the back room. It just didn't coalesce.

It was almost two a.m. I needed to call O'Connell, but it was late. He was probably asleep. Ringing him now would indicate an emergency. And this wasn't an emergency. Not anymore.

Deciding it could wait until the morning, I struggled to get out of the chair and grabbed the large first aid kit I stuffed in my drawer. It was the only thing I bothered to move into my new office, and unfortunately, it was already being put to use. After a trip to the washroom to assess the damage, I wrapped an elastic bandage tightly around my middle to hold in the heat, dull the pain, and limit movement to prevent further injury. I really needed ice for my face and neck, but I couldn't be bothered going to the break room to check the freezer. Instead, I went back to the couch.

"That's one screwed up neighborhood," I murmured, lifting the bottle of whiskey and swallowing another mouthful.

*   *   *

The overhead light came on, and I blinked a few times. I hurt all over, but the focus of the throbbing was centered just behind my ear. I slept on the couch in my office and had no idea what time it was.

"You told me you weren't an alcoholic," Kellan chided, barging loudly into the room and putting the cap on the bottle. "If I knew you had a problem, I would have brought you a geranium instead." My muffled moan made him turn. "Shit." He edged closer. "When did this happen?"

"Last night."

"Where? Did someone get inside the building? Did you call security?"

"It didn't happen here." I struggled to sit up, even as he gently took my face in his hands and assessed the bruising. "I was looking for leads and ended up on the losing side of a bar brawl."

He lowered his voice. "Did you report it to the police?"

"Not yet."

"How about getting checked out at the hospital?" He poked at my cheekbone. "Your eye's a mess. How's the rest of you?" He watched the way I cradled my middle. "Broken ribs?"

"I think they're just bruised." I turned to look for a clock, but I didn't have one on the wall.

"Hence the hospital." He saw the knot on the back of my neck. "What about a concussion?" He held up his hand. "Follow my finger."

"I'm fine." I pushed his hand away. Shit, I stabbed Victor. My knife was gone, probably stuck in the shoe of another assailant. I needed to call Nick and give him the heads up. "Cross said not to involve the authorities in our investigations. I was just following company policy."

"That doesn't apply when it comes to getting the daylights beaten out of you. Your safety comes first. Did you at least have medical check you out?"

"Medical?"

Kellan practically rolled his eyes. "Upstairs. Do you want me to get someone to take a look at you?"

"No."

The abrupt sound of someone clearing his throat echoed in the room, and I closed my eyes, dreading what was about to happen. "Mr. Dey, I believe you have a client meeting scheduled in twenty minutes. Shouldn't you be preparing?" Cross asked.

"I'll get right on that, sir." Kellan gave me an uncertain look. "Is there anything I can do, Alex?"

I pulled my car keys out of my pocket. "Can you grab the bag out of my trunk? It's my personal vehicle, so I parked it in a visitor space."

"No problem." Kellan mumbled a good morning to our boss and disappeared out the door.

I didn't turn around, but I didn't need to. Lucien strode into my office and came to a stop in front of me. I looked up, prepared for another ass-chewing. Instead, his voice took on a slightly less commanding tone.

"Tell me what happened." When I was finished, he licked his lips. "I will accompany you today. You should clean up and change. We are meeting Mr. Wellington in two hours." He gestured at me. "This is not what he expects from Cross Security."

"Right away, sir."

Moving behind my desk, I checked my messages. The assistants set meetings for the entire day, starting with Mr. Wellington and ending with Dr. Dalton. I had a long day ahead, and Cross was likely to stay with me every step of the way. As I turned to leave my office, I spotted Renner lingering just outside the doorway.

He wouldn't look me in the eye when he asked, "Is everything okay? I heard something happened last night."

"Yep." I stalked past him, taking my bag from Kellan who was returning from the elevator. At least I was smart enough to keep a change of clothes in my car. That was one useful thing I learned to do at the OIO. "When you offered to help, you might have bothered to mention you don't check your messages on the weekend, so I decided to improvise. It wasn't the best plan."

"I was busy. I have my own investigations to conduct." He watched as I opened the locker room door. "Are you okay?"

I didn't bother to respond.

TEN

"William," Cross greeted, firmly shaking hands with Mr. Wellington, "thank you for making the time. This is Alexis Parker. We just snatched her away from the FBI, and I asked her to look into your daughter's disappearance."

I shook hands with William and took a seat in the offered chair. We were inside a conference room at an investment bank. William took a seat across the table, making an effort not to stare at the ruptured blood vessels in my eye. On the bright side, that kept him distracted from the barely concealed bruises on my face.

"Miss Parker," he asked, "do you have previous experience with missing persons cases?"

"No, sir. But I am aware of the situation. I've spent the last few days reviewing your daughter's file. I just have a few questions."

"This won't take long," Cross assured him.

William nodded. "Whatever I can do to help." Despite his words, he checked the time.

"Tell me about Jessika," I said.

William looked disinterested, and I could practically feel Cross's gaze burn into the side of my face. It didn't seem like a complicated question, but it surprised Jessika's parents.

"What do you mean?" Wellington asked.

"What were your daughter's interests? Her goals? How was your family life? Did you spend time together? Go to ballgames or concerts? Was she a good student? Did she come home for dinner every night? Tell me about her."

Cross stiffened, but I resisted the urge to glance at him. He made it clear he didn't like the way I did things. Frankly, I wasn't sure I liked the way he conducted himself either.

William scrubbed a hand down his face. "She was a teenage girl. She went to high school. She planned to go to college. She had a boyfriend, Dylan Hart. When she was younger, she wanted a pony. Instead, we let her take riding lessons." He blinked. "What does this have to do with anything?"

"Was she seeing anyone besides Dylan?"

His eyes went even harder. "What are you implying?"

"I'm not implying anything. I just asked a question. It's high school. From what I remember, most girls had a new boyfriend every other week."

"I wouldn't know."

"It sounds like the two of you were really close," I said.

William reddened. "Lucien, I'm a busy man. I don't have time to waste on such trivial matters."

Before Cross could respond or put an end to this meeting, I pushed on. "Mr. Wellington, you seem to have done very well for yourself. I imagine a man in your position might have made a few enemies. Did anyone ever threaten you or your family?"

"No."

The police already looked into the possibility, but they might have missed something. "You never received a ransom demand or a blackmail letter?"

His Adam's apple bobbed, and a slight sheen developed on his upper lip. "Nothing like that. Jessika wasn't kidnapped. If she was, we would have gotten her back."

"So what do you think happened to her?"

He shrugged.

"Do you think she ran away?"

He sucked on his bottom lip and stared out the

conference room door, not seeing anything. After a moment, he said, "I don't know."

"Did your daughter have a reason to abandon her life and take off? Your wife said Jessika had plans to become a doctor. She had excellent test scores. She seemed to have a ten year plan. Why would she just pick up and leave it all behind? Were there problems at home? Problems at school? Anything out of the ordinary? Was she bullied or picked on?"

Wellington's gaze settled on me. "Honestly, Miss Parker, I don't know." He stood. "That's all the time I have. You can see yourselves out."

As soon as Wellington cleared the conference room, his assistant stepped inside. "Is there anything else?" she asked, a professional smile glued to her angular features.

"That was all," Cross replied, leading the way out of the building. He didn't speak again until we were in his town car. "We're meeting with Mrs. Cleese at noon, but we have some time to kill. Take the long way around," he said to the driver. Turning to face me, he put his knee on the seat and rolled up the privacy window. "What was that?"

"You tell me. The guy couldn't wait to get the hell out of there. If this is his priority, he has an odd way of showing it."

"I meant you," he hissed. "Is that how you think an interview should be conducted?"

"Not exactly."

Cross inhaled audibly. "At least you realize your mistake."

I shook the demeaning condemnation away. The only mistake was letting him accompany me, but after last night, Cross was tightening the reins. I just wasn't certain if it was for my safety or to preserve his company's image.

"William referred to his daughter in the past tense." I'd been replaying the entire meeting since Wellington walked out of the conference room. "He's given up hope. Maybe he knows she's dead."

"Or he's a realist." Cross sneered. "He's also the one paying our fee. Do you find it necessary to alienate our client?"

"He's hiding something. Did anyone look into his personal dealings?" I read his statement and the threat assessment law enforcement performed, but nothing surfaced. The man said no one ever blackmailed or threatened him, but I didn't believe it. In his business, death threats should be a common occurrence. If he did his job right, he made money while others lost money, and if he did his job wrong, he lost money for his clients and firm.

"William was ruled out as a suspect."

"I don't care. He's hiding something. The police went through his phone records and work e-mails. Did anyone ever look through his personal computer or internet history? I didn't see it in the files."

"I doubt the police had the balls to ask permission, and even if they did, Mr. Wellington values his privacy," Cross responded. "He wouldn't have granted them access."

We fell silent for a time. My mind ran through the possibilities. I didn't exactly get to ask the questions I wanted due to my boss shadowing me. But from the answers I received, I didn't trust William Wellington III. He had secrets. I just didn't know if they had anything to do with his daughter's disappearance.

"I need access to his internet history. I need to know who this man is and what he does in his spare time." I glanced at Cross. "Allegations have been made he's screwing his secretary."

Cross cleared his throat; something he seemed to do frequently. I suspected it was a measure he took to buy time to think before he spoke, perhaps to curb his yelling. "I thought you believed Jessika's disappearance has to do with the Seven Rooks. Now you think she ran away because of family problems. Are you planning to pick a theory or simply run with all of them simultaneously?"

"They might not be mutually exclusive, and until something solid surfaces, everything is conjecture. It wouldn't be wise to rule anything out." I glared at him. "If you don't like the way I work, you can wait in the car. I don't need a babysitter while I conduct my investigation."

"It's my investigation. My name is on the line. My firm is on the line. And I've been warned about you, my dear.

You lack finesse, and you aren't much of a team player. After what happened last night, I believe it's best that you have a chaperone."

"Whatever you say, Mr. Cross." I gave him a fake smile. "I'll attempt to do better in the future."

"See that you do."

For the duration of the ride, my thoughts flip-flopped between William and creative curses to call Lucien. Obviously, the hit to the head didn't impact my ability to multitask. The back of the car felt oppressive, and Cross maintained his hard glare.

Finally, I couldn't take it anymore. "You've looked into the Wellingtons' financials. Did you see any ties to anything that links to the Seven Rooks or businesses in that neighborhood?"

"No."

"What about payouts?"

He snorted. "William didn't pay a ransom or blackmail." He glanced out the window, realizing we stopped. He pressed the intercom button. "Give us another minute," he said to the driver, "circle around the block." As if it pained him to admit it, he said, "I saw the same thing you did in the conference room. Mr. Wellington has skeletons in the closet someone has tried to exploit. I'll look into it."

"I can."

But with a single look and a raised palm, he shut down my argument. I knew better than to protest. Someone else would handle it. Apparently, I lacked finesse.

When the car stopped a second time, Cross opened the car door and stepped out. I scanned the area. Apparently, we were meeting Mrs. Cleese for lunch. Cross strode into the high school. He stopped briefly to speak to the security guard at the door, smiled, shook hands, just like any other businessman, and grabbed two visitor badges from the table. He held one out while he clipped his to the lapel of his suit. Then with a perfect sense of direction, he led the way down a corridor, took a right, turned left, went up the stairs, and rapped gently against a classroom door. He'd been here before.

A squat, round woman opened the door. She wore neon

green scrubs that made her look like an oversized lime. Smiling warmly, she grasped both of Lucien's hands in hers. "Mr. Cross, it's good to see you again. Have you made any progress finding Jessika?"

"We're doing our best, Carla," he said, his voice smooth and almost sweet. The sudden change was a shock to my system, and I stepped backward, trying to keep a cautious distance out of fear the alien that crawled into his ear and took over his brain might attempt to possess me next. "This is one of my newest hires, Alexis Parker." He freed himself from Carla's grip and put his hand on the small of my back, practically shoving me between them.

Biting back a wince at the unexpected contact with my bruises, I shook her hand. "It's nice to meet you. From what I've read, you played a significant role in Jessika's life."

Mrs. Cleese sniffed, nodding sadly as she led me deeper into the empty classroom. "Please take a seat." She gestured to one of the nearest student desks as she sank into a chair. "What can I do to help?"

I glanced back at Cross, who was studying the posters tacked to the walls. For once, I was in charge. "For starters, how did you know Jessika?"

For the next forty minutes, Cleese rambled on about Jessika being one of her most promising students in freshman biology. After midterms, Jessika asked to join the Prospective Doctors club and played an active role for the next two years until her disappearance. "She never missed a meeting. Some of the other kids would blow it off, but Jessika loved it. She wanted to do more. We talked about ways she could volunteer, classes and programs she could take during the summer, and some of the best ways to pad a college application. She wanted to be pre-med so badly she could taste it. I just can't imagine what happened to her. Everyone loved Jess. She was the sweetest girl you'd ever want to meet. She had the biggest heart. She actually cared about helping others. That's why she was doing this. A lot of my other students join the club because their parents want them to become doctors or because they want to go into the medical field for job security. But not Jess."

She dabbed at her eyes. "I always thought she'd be a crusader."

"How's that?"

For a moment, Cleese looked embarrassed. "I figured she'd join the Peace Corps or Doctors Without Borders or some organization like that. I remember her mentioning something about wanting to volunteer for the Red Cross over the summer and help in disaster areas. I guess she never got to do it though."

"What kinds of things did she do with the club? How often and how long did meetings last?" This could link Jessika to the neighborhood and clinic, and although it still wouldn't explain her disappearance, it would be a solid lead we could focus on. It might explain why the Rooks fired on me and why I was targeted inside the bar.

"We met Tuesdays and Thursdays from 3:30 to five. If we weren't staying on campus, a bus would take us to whatever location we were visiting. Usually, it was an area hospital, the nearest nursing home, or the city college."

"Did you ever have your students assist at free clinics?" I asked.

"We volunteered at the health clinic at the university and some private practices." Her eyes grew angry, and she wrung her hands together. "Volunteering at free clinics was something I tried to champion with the school board, but for insurance purposes, we couldn't get approval. Free clinics do wonderful things, but the school board felt it would expose the children to too much and possibly open the school up to a lawsuit."

"Did you ever encourage Jessika to help at one of these clinics on her own?"

"I encourage all my students to help at the clinics. It's about as close to the trenches as they can get at a young age and without any formal training. Free clinics need people and would be more likely to let them be hands-on rather than the hospital or nursing home that simply has them shadow the workers, take inventory, clean up, or visit with the residents. Not to say those tasks aren't important, but that's just a tiny portion of what medical professionals actually do. Of course, there are privacy rights and medical licensure issues to consider, but handing out band-aids is more exciting than organizing files or counting cotton swabs."

"But the school board doesn't agree?"

"Of course not." Her eyes darted around the room to make sure we were alone. "This place is too snobby to even consider assisting in most of those neighborhoods."

Cross loomed closer, his hands buried in his pockets. "Do you know if Jessika ever volunteered at any clinic?"

"She never mentioned it to me, so I doubt it." She wiped some crumbs off her desk. "Did you ask her mom and dad? They would know for sure."

"Her boyfriend was under the impression that's what she was doing a couple nights a week," I said, hoping Cleese might reconsider her answer.

The woman frowned. "Like I said, we shadowed the staff at the university clinic, hospital, nursing home, and some private practices. He might have gotten it wrong. But her parents would know for sure."

"We'll check with them," Cross said before I could say another word. "We've taken up enough of your time. Thank you for meeting us during your planning period."

"No, no. It's more than fine. I was so proud of Jessika. I'm glad people still care enough to look. Drop by again if there's anything else I can do." She led us to the door, grasping Cross in a hug while I darted into the hallway.

"Thank you, ma'am. We'll be in touch." I took another step backward, doing my best not to laugh as Cross righted himself, straightening his tie.

He didn't speak as we went back to the staircase. At the front, we returned the visitor passes and went back to the car. Two meetings down. Two to go.

ELEVEN

"Here." My boss removed several folded sheets from his pocket and shoved them onto my lap. "That should answer whatever remaining questions you have about the club."

I read the brightly colored papers. One was the yearly schedule of events, including meeting times and locations. Another was a list of past skills and achievements the Prospective Doctors completed in the past five years, and the last was a collage of photographs from five years ago. Several of the shots were in Jessika's yearbook, but these included captions with dates and locations listed.

"You ripped these off the wall of her classroom?" I asked.

He shrugged, staring out the window. "She won't notice. And if she does, she'll blame one of her students."

"Given her affinity for you, I would imagine all you'd have to do is ask, and she would give you anything your heart desires."

He squirmed slightly, and I found I rather enjoyed making him uncomfortable. He'd been nothing but domineering and robotic since we met.

"That would have wasted time. She'd have to take the flyers off the wall, go downstairs to the photocopier, and spend twenty minutes chatting with Nancy or Debra or one of the other office secretaries. We do not have that kind of time." He glanced at me. "At least I don't."

No matter how hard I tried, I couldn't wipe the grin off my face.

"What the hell are you smiling about?" he barked.

"Nothing. I take it you've been through this process with Mrs. Cleese before."

"Several times. It is not something I want to repeat." He went back to staring out the window.

After jotting a few notes, I placed the pilfered flyers in my purse. "You know, I've read through the files. I read Renner's report and Darwin's and Lancaster's. I was under the impression they were the only Cross Security employees to have worked on the case. How come your notes and files weren't included?"

He continued to stare out the window.

"Mr. Cross?" I asked, wondering if he heard me. Even though I'd only been at the company a short time, we both knew he couldn't pretend he wasn't a micromanaging prick. "Your files?"

He cleared his throat but refused to turn toward me. "Why do you think the men at the bar attacked you?"

"I don't know. According to the bartender, word spread that I was asking questions and the Seven Rooks wanted it stopped. The gang is probably offering some sort of incentive to anyone who extinguishes the problem."

"So the men were part of the gang?"

I thought for a moment. "That's what I was told, but I didn't get that impression. My guess is they are just some area lowlifes who want to get in good with the Rooks. They weren't armed. Bangers would be."

Cross nodded, finally turning to face me. "They probably wanted to please their dealer or garner some favor with a pimp. It's a barter system. It's hard to manipulate the economics of such a small microcosm when an entire system is already established. Having standing as an outsider makes it harder to comprehend what is already owed and expected. They have a lot to lose. It puts you at an obvious disadvantage. You're a stranger asking questions. Anyone who steps foot on their turf with ulterior motives will probably meet similar resistance. That is, of course, dependent on a single key factor." He met my eyes. "Do you believe the bartender? He could have just as easily orchestrated the assault. It might have nothing to do with the Seven Rooks or the Friday morning shooting."

"It's simple, really. If he made Jessika disappear, he would have made me disappear too. He had a shotgun. I was dazed. He could have killed me if he wanted."

"Are you sure?"

"No, but I don't want to piss him off and find out."

"So there's actually someone on this planet you don't want to piss off? I'd like to know more about this man." He reached into his pocket and removed his phone. "What's his name?"

I shook my head.

"Fine." His eyes narrowed. "I imagine you've already conducted your own search. I can look through your computer history, if you want to make this difficult, but I will get an answer to my question."

"Is this really how you conduct business? When I signed on to Cross Security, I was promised autonomy when conducting an investigation."

He sighed. "Miss Parker, are you aware we are on the same side? I am attempting to assist you."

"Then how come I haven't seen your name on any of the investigation files? After these last two interviews, it's apparent you've spent a great deal of time looking into this matter. I want your notes."

"Is that how you play things? Need I remind you I'm your boss?"

"I don't give a damn who you are. I care about finding out what happened to a sixteen year old girl. If that means I do or say things you don't approve of, oh well. I can't worry about that right now."

His dark eyes scanned my face. "That's why you were let go from the OIO. I know the truth behind your resignation. You had a choice to make, and instead of saving your own skin, you took the blame. Mark Jablonsky was lucky to have such a loyal protégé. Most people in this world are rather cutthroat."

The mention of Mark's name surprised me. "You know Jablonsky?"

Cross tilted his chin just slightly, an amused glint in his eye. "The son of a bitch trained me." My mind was still reeling when the car came to an abrupt halt. Cross opened the door, glancing back at me. "I hope one day you'll show me the same kind of loyalty, but for now, I don't care. I don't require it. The only thing I require is an answer to my question and for you to do your job. I expect a report concerning last night's incident on my desk by the morning. If we didn't have such a full day, I'd expect it this afternoon." He turned and looked over his shoulder. "I'm making concessions. You need to do the same."

The next meeting was with the current administrator of the free clinic. Instead of meeting inside the clinic, we were meeting inside a medical office building. From the architectural design and modern artwork that filled the lobby, I knew this was a prestigious place. It was not what I expected from someone who ran a free clinic.

"Tell Henry Brandt that Lucien Cross is here," he said to someone in reception. "We have a meeting."

"One moment." She pressed a button on the phone and spoke quickly. "He'll be down shortly."

"Thank you." Cross stepped away, his eyes scanning the area.

I should have been paying more attention to my surroundings, but now I was focused on my boss. The way he moved. The things he saw. He didn't move like a federal agent. He didn't act like one. Sure, I'd run up against several pompous pricks inside the federal building, but they were usually ex-military with small dick syndrome. Cross didn't act like he had something to prove; he acted like he was waiting for the world to prove something to him. I guess that's why he was in charge.

The meeting with Mr. Brandt was short and to the point. Cross introduced me as an associate, asked direct questions about the clinic, its daily operations, and the staff and volunteers. Brandt had several clinics. He wasn't a doctor. He was a businessman. This was his business. Or rather, the free clinics provided some form of tax write-off or incentive which bolstered his business. They made up the bulk of the nonprofit portion of his medical empire, and somehow that led to government grants, aid, research money, and all sorts of wonderful things. There was no mention of actually helping the people in the community, and when the meeting was concluded, I realized Cross didn't even mention the name Jessika Wellington.

When I opened my mouth to speak, his cold eyes warned me not to, and I swallowed down the question. By the time we made it back to the car, Cross's phone was glued to his ear. He spoke quietly, keeping his body turned away for privacy. So much for being on the same side.

"I expect it on my desk by the time I return." He clicked off the call and spoke to the driver. "Drop Miss Parker off for her next appointment. I'll be going back to the office." He looked at me. "Can you handle an interview on your own?"

My expression read contempt. "Give me a break," I spat. "Are you going to tell me what that was about?" My gaze traveled to his phone.

"I'm exploring a new angle."

"On my case?"

"Our case."

I wanted to hit him. "This was my assignment. I don't need your help."

"That black eye says otherwise." He lifted his phone and typed out a few messages, refusing to acknowledge me until the car pulled to a stop. "I'll see you tomorrow. I want that report first thing in the morning."

"Only if you share your Wellington files and whatever leads you're exploring."

"You really don't understand how this works. You do as I say. You report to me. Every Cross Security investigation is mine. You are simply assisting."

Don't say it, Parker. But I couldn't hold my tongue. I had enough of his attitude. Maybe he'd fire me on the spot. At this point, I didn't care. "No. This is my case. You handed it to me, implied it was hopeless, and said when I failed I'd be back in the unemployment line. That's fine.

But my failure will not be because of your interference."

"Careful," he warned, but I was on a roll.

"If you expect a proper investigation with a chance in hell of figuring out what happened to the girl, then you disclose everything you have. If not, neither of us will get very far. And it's obvious that before I arrived, you were at a dead end." I opened the car door. "I want your notes moved to my office immediately. And I'll see you tomorrow morning, assuming you agree to my terms and I still have a job. If not, well, I can't say it's been fun because it hasn't." I wasn't foolish enough to think he couldn't toss me out on my ass. Frankly, I wasn't being particularly subordinate, but this wasn't about me or him or his stupid company. This was about Jessika. So we'd work together, or this wouldn't work at all.

"I don't tolerate threats." Something crossed his eyes.

"Good. For the record, that wasn't a threat." I tried to slam the door shut, but he leaned across the seat and put his palm against it.

"Given the last few days, I'm starting to think you're more trouble than you're worth." He looked calm, as if he were enjoying this in some twisted manner. "The report. My desk. By morning." He yanked the door closed. Obviously, he thought it imperative to have the last word.

Despite my better judgment, I flipped off the car as it drove away. The prick probably didn't even notice. This was why I asked about case autonomy when I was hired. And despite the fact I was assured it was my investigation to conduct as I saw fit, Cross changed the rules. Would there always be this level of interference or was I unaware of something that occurred behind the scenes?

After making a note to call Jablonsky later, I marched into the hospital. Dr. Ridley Dalton had an office on the ninth floor, and we needed to talk. This man might be able to shed some light on Jessika's disappearance or connect her to the neighborhood. I just needed to make damn sure I played my cards right.

Unlike the last appointment, there was no receptionist or secretary, just a door with a faded nameplate. I knocked, waiting for a muffled acknowledgement before twisting the knob and entering. The man before me was probably around forty-five, white lab coat, blond hair dusted with gray, and hazel eyes. He had a warm, tender smile which brightened his face. He gestured to an empty chair after I introduced myself. His desk was neatly organized, and the shelves behind him were just as orderly.

"How can I help you?" he asked, sitting up straight and placing a silver framed pair of reading glasses on top of his desk. One of the stems had a permanent blue ink smudge near the temple. That was the only sign of imperfection in the entire office.

"Five years ago, you volunteered your time and services at a free clinic." I provided the location and waited for confirmation. "I'm just curious what you remember from back then."

His face scrunched as he considered the question. "It wasn't that different from how it is now."

"You still volunteer?"

"Yes. Why would I stop?"

"Are you at the same location?"

"I split my time among three clinics." He frowned. "What is this about?"

"Cross Security is looking into the disappearance of Jessika Wellington. She vanished five years ago. At the time, she was only sixteen." I took a photo of her from my bag and slid it across the desk. "Do you recognize her?"

He lifted the photo, pursing his lips as he studied it. Handing it back, he said, "I'm not sure. What does this have to do with my work at the clinic? Do you believe she was a patient?"

"Do you see a lot of private school girls at the clinic?"

He blinked, unperturbed by the question. "On occasion. If you believe she might have been a patient, we can discuss the matter with legal and perhaps check the records."

Maybe it was true what they say; doctors don't remember their patients, just their charts. "Is it possible she might have volunteered at the clinic?"

"It is. I don't remember everyone's name or face. Most of our volunteers are fulfilling a requirement, whether it's court mandated or part of a training program. You said she was sixteen. That's a little young to be working at a clinic. Wouldn't she have been more apt to work at the mall?"

That comment irked me. "She was special. Her goal was to become a doctor, and she wanted to get a jump on that."

Something about my statement registered behind his eyes. "That sounds familiar." His brow scrunched. "That's right." He bit his lip, his eyes darting back and forth as he thought. "The police asked me about her when she vanished. I remember she was involved in some kind of after-school program at the hospital."

"Uh-huh." I didn't want to remind him of his previous statement to Detective Sparrow in the event he lied. "Do you remember anything else?"

"Let me ask some of my colleagues if they recognize the name." He picked up a pen, jotting a note for himself on a pad. "Do you have a card so I can get in touch with you?"

I wrote my office number on the back of one of Cross's cards and handed it to him. "Anything you can tell me will be much appreciated."

He chuckled politely. "Honestly, it's been a long time. The name is just vaguely familiar. I doubt I'll be much help."

"It doesn't hurt to check, right?"

"Not at all." He smiled again, standing when I did. His eyes took me in, and he looked concerned. "Are you okay?"

"I'm fine."

He noted the covered bruises and broken veins in my eye. "Broken ribs?" His eyes went to my middle.

"They're just bruised."

"How did it happen?"

Even though he was trained to notice a person in distress, I didn't like the curious questions. I also didn't want him to think my investigation could be dangerous or else he might not be willing to help. "I fell down the stairs."

"Try to be more careful." He winked. "Doctor's orders."

TWELVE

The last place I wanted to be was back in the office. I didn't want to see Cross again. There was a good chance my big mouth would result in my termination, so if he didn't see me, he couldn't fire me. Or so I thought. Grabbing a cab to the precinct, I figured I'd update Nick on the situation and fill out the paperwork on a misplaced knife.

As usual, the precinct was busy. Not wanting to waste anyone's time, I went up the stairs to the major crimes division and found Nick working on his current caseload. It looked like he could use a distraction, so I filled him in on my day.

"Let me get this straight, until last week you were a federal agent. And this week you're shooting bangers and stabbing people," O'Connell said.

"Well, it sounds bad when you say it like that."

"That's because it is bad." He sighed, exasperated. "It sounds like you've gone off the reservation."

"You're the one who sent me into that neighborhood in the first place."

"I didn't tell you to shoot anyone, did I?"

After a calming breath, I said, "No, you didn't. But they shot at me first."

"Excuses, excuses." He typed something into the computer. "And now you're telling me you misplaced a knife. Where did you last see it?"

"That's complicated."

His eyes went hard. "Uncomplicate it."

I winced. "That's not really possible. Can we speak off the record in hypotheticals for a moment?"

He let out a huff. "Fine, but I'm not an idiot. I know these hypotheticals are anything but."

Choosing to ignore that statement, I told him about the run-in with the bartender, leaving out the rest of the details. "I don't know much about Jared Prince, but I don't want to get into another situation like I did with Vincenzo."

"No one wants that," he grimaced, "which is why this guy needs to be investigated." He held up a hand before I could voice the obvious protest. "I will do it quietly, below the radar. For all you know, he could run the Seven Rooks or be responsible for Wellington's disappearance. Someone needs to look into him, and given what you said about your overbearing boss, I understand why you don't want him to open a can of worms." He went back to typing on the keyboard. "Now let's get back to the issue of your lost knife. Tell me about it."

"Four inch blade, folding, military construction. Probably has my prints on it, unless someone wiped it clean." I leaned over, hoping to see if there were any reported stabbings, but the screen he was on was for reporting stolen property.

"Any blood on it?" he asked, eyeing me.

"Not mine."

"Hypothetically, where did you last see it?"

"In the toe of some asshole's shoe."

"And before that?"

"Jabbed in the side of a guy who was trying to take my head off with a cue stick."

O'Connell exhaled. "So since the bar brawl is entirely hypothetical, shall I say it went missing sometime Friday morning during your altercation with the Seven Rooks?"

"That sounds about right."

He practically rolled his eyes. "Do you want it back if we

locate it?"

"No. I just wanted to make sure I wasn't going to get blamed for any fatal stabbings." I leaned over again, studying the screen. "There haven't been any fatal stabbings reported in the last eighteen hours, have there?"

"No."

"Good." I smiled and climbed out of the chair. "Do I need to sign anything?"

He shook his head. "Do you want to file a report on the assault? Your eye could use a touch-up."

I gestured to my bruise. "This? I fell down the stairs."

"Sure, you did." Nick's face read concern. "Listen, I gave you that tip, so I feel responsible. Also, if anything were to happen to you, I can think of several people who would be mighty pissed at me for not covering your ass. The next time you're in a jam, call me. I'll be there."

"Does that mean you'll go to my office and run interference so I don't get fired?"

"That one's all you. Good luck, Parker."

"Thanks. I might need it."

When I returned to work, I was relieved building security didn't revoke my access cards or show me out. In fact, things appeared quiet. It was almost five. Several of my colleagues were in a conference room, discussing a corporate espionage case. Kellan spotted me and offered a friendly smile.

"Hey, Alex," Renner called, jogging down the hallway to catch up, "do you have a minute? I listened to your messages. What happened this weekend?"

Opening my office door, I looked around the room, expecting to find a pink slip on the desk. It wasn't there. However, a single manila folder was carefully centered in the middle with a sticky note. I lifted the note and read: *Tit for tat. It's your move.*

"Asshole," I muttered.

Renner's brow furrowed. "Excuse me?"

I crumpled the sticky note into a ball and tossed it in the trash. "Not you. Actually," I dropped into the chair and gave him an icy stare, "I'm not sure yet." I jerked my chin at the sofa, suggesting he take a seat. Grabbing a legal pad and a pen, I pulled myself up and stood in front of him. "You said you did your due diligence on Wellington's case. What do you know about her involvement in school activities?"

He scratched his chin. "She ran cross-country, played volleyball, was a member of debate team, and was in some kind of science club. So what? I spoke to the coach, her teammates, her teachers, and that lady mentor of hers. None of them knew what happened, and they were cleared by the police."

"It seems there might be something there. That science club volunteered at different places. I thought one of them might have been the free clinic in the Seven Rooks' territory, but when I asked her parents about it, they were oblivious."

"Shocking." His sarcasm might just rival mine. "What'd you think of her old man?"

He was arrogant and disconnected with something to hide. "He is technically our client," I said, remembering O'Connell's warning to watch my back around Renner.

"Yeah. That doesn't mean I have to like him."

Deciding to play with fire, I asked, "But do you like him for her disappearance?"

"Airtight alibi, just like everyone else. His was better than most. He was at a corporate retreat. A dozen people can place him there." Before I could think to say anything else, Renner asked, "What happened to you last night? I heard security gabbing to the receptionist this morning. Getting hurt on the job is a given, but the new girl stumbling through the lobby in the middle of the night looking like she just went a round or two with a prizefighter isn't really common."

"Well, like you said, I'm new. They'll get used to it."

He snickered. "Okay, don't tell me. But I'm guessing it has something to do with whatever happened to Jessika. And that's probably why Cross is taking such an interest."

"Did he work the case?" I hoped the question was innocuous enough that Renner wouldn't think too hard about it.

"He sussed it out to determine if it had any merit. The

client's checkbook also plays a part in those decisions, I'd imagine." Renner shrugged and stood. "All I can tell you is he never spent the day following me around. Make of that what you will." He went to the door. "If you need anything else, let me know. I will get back to you at some point."

"Thanks for the addendum. I could have used it yesterday."

He winked and flipped me off before walking out.

The only thing I learned from Renner was he didn't find the same link. He never explored the clinic avenue, and regardless of whether or not I could prove Jessika volunteered, I was positive she'd been in that neighborhood. I was shot at and beaten for lurking around and asking about her. That meant whatever happened to her linked to the Seven Rooks and maybe the clinic. If Dr. Dalton couldn't provide answers, I'd find someone who could.

Perhaps there was a way to connect the Seven Rooks to the clinic. The obvious overlap would be drugs, patching up injured bangers, and treating the working girls. Other than that, the gang could be using the clinic as a front for something, but that was too cerebral a thought to have at this point. The simple solution was usually the right one.

Before getting myself too worked up, I flipped open the manila folder. Inside were four typed sheets of paper. One was a profile on Jessika. The next was a page with nothing but names and short descriptions of where the possible suspects were at the time of Jessika's disappearance. The third page was an abbreviated version of her permanent record, including test scores and extracurriculars, and the last sheet was nearly blank. From what I gathered from the headings, it was a list of leads to explore. All of which resulted in dead ends. And I was to believe these were Cross's notes? It was nothing but a concise version of the files I spent dozens of hours reading.

"Yep, definitely an asshole," I muttered. However, that asshole was my boss. And he wanted a report, so I wrote a report. With any luck, he wouldn't decide to poke around and piss anyone else off. I didn't want the bartender and the drunk to show up at my apartment and put the shotgun to use. At least Detective O'Connell would be able to tell me how serious the matter was. I wasn't much for blind faith, but Nick was clever and skilled. He knew how to handle things and read between the lines, and he was one of the few people on this planet I trusted implicitly.

When I was finished, I grabbed my cell phone and dialed Mark Jablonsky. He was my mentor at the OIO. He taught me everything there was to know about being a federal agent and how to conduct an investigation. And no matter how hard I tried, I couldn't reconcile Cross's proclamation with the fact that I didn't see anything even remotely related to Jablonsky in the way my new boss conducted business.

"Shit, Parker," Jablonsky said in lieu of a greeting, "it's not the early morning or the middle of the workday. Have you finally put an end to our game of phone tag?"

"I have a question. Do you know Lucien Cross?"

"Yeah, I know him. Why?"

I shrugged, even though he couldn't see it. "He said you trained him."

Jablonsky practically choked. "I wouldn't call it that. I'd call it trying to teach him to pull his head out of his own ass. And it didn't take. What the hell are you doing talking to Lucien Cross?" Before I could say anything, he cursed, "Fuck, Alex. Is he the reason you haven't returned any of the calls from the other federal agencies that offered you a position? Don't tell me Cross Security is your new gig. You're too good for them."

"Okay."

"Okay what?"

"I won't tell you. So you trained Cross?"

He cursed again. "No. Yes." He was frustrated and flustered. "It was a multi-agency training program. Director Kendall made me go. Some corporate security types were invited to attend. It was a two week intensive program in training and tactics and the usual hoopla. Y'know, just a bunch of bullshit. And here was this punk kid, thinking he was the shit. Needless to say, it didn't go well." I heard knocking over the line, and Mark barking at someone that he'd be there in a minute. "Did you call for a reason or was it just to send my blood pressure through the roof? Are you doing okay? I've been concerned. Obviously, if I knew how seriously screwed up you were over resigning, I would have intervened before you sold your soul to the devil."

"I'm okay. We'll talk soon."

I hung up, feeling a mix of emotions. For some reason, saying those words hurt. Until now, I didn't give any thought to exactly how different my life was. I was in denial, pretending this was just another OIO case, even though it was far from it. I knew all the reasons another job with law enforcement wouldn't work, but until now, I didn't realize I was also a little bit afraid this wouldn't work either.

What I needed to do was work smarter. Act smarter. No one had my back here. We didn't have partners or access to emergency services. Perhaps that's why Cross didn't want us to rely on police involvement. Aside from the bullshit reasons he gave, we were on our own. And that was one thing I understood, even if the past year made me forget some of that.

Marching up the stairs to Cross's office, I left my report with his assistant. His door was closed, and I was certain he left for the day. If he had a lead, maybe he'd share it, and if not, I'd find it on my own. Since there was no reason to stay here to get my work done, I grabbed whatever files and intel I thought I might need, took my car from the visitor's space, and drove home. Since I was on my own, I'd work best in seclusion, free to express my thoughts and theories however I liked without a colleague stumbling into my work area and fearing I might be a serial killer or schizophrenic. Buck up, Parker, the fun is just beginning.

THIRTEEN

Everything was connected — Jessika Wellington, the clinic, the Seven Rooks. As of yet, no one could place Jessika at the clinic. She disappeared from school. I watched the surveillance tapes. I studied the still photos until the images were burned into my retinas. One minute she was there; the next, she was gone. No strange vehicles were spotted in the vicinity. No one remembered seeing anything. Damn flash mob. They were all the rage, and then they disappeared, just like every other trend, but not before taking Jessika with them.

Someone from the Seven Rooks' neighborhood must have seen Jessika five years ago. The prostitute who took my money was a good starting place. The pimp, Jorge Toald, would be a close second. But going back would be risky, especially after last night's debacle. Unfortunately, the answers were there. Someone needed to find them, and at the moment, it looked like that person should be me. Dressing for war, I strapped on a vest, concealing it beneath a black hoodie. I tied my hair back and wore dark pants and dark shoes. I didn't want to be seen.

It was after midnight when I stepped foot in the neighborhood. The streets were quiet. The hookers were working their usual spots. Portia Russo, a.k.a. Traffic Cones, was back to work, having been released from lockup. Some people would never learn. I wanted to speak to Smokey, but I didn't spot her. Lowering my binoculars, I stared down at the street beneath me. I was on the roof of a parking garage. It provided the best view, and with the wide open space, it limited the chance of anyone sneaking up on me. With only one way in or out, it could be a tactical stronghold or a kill box; it just depended on which side brought the most firepower. The nine millimeter on the seat beside me dictated this ought to be a stealth mission, as did the constant ache in my torso.

Stepping out of the car, I slipped into the shadows and crept down the ramps and out of the garage. Silently, I made my way onto the sidewalk. My target was the pimp. Perhaps he didn't know anything, but sending that much firepower to deal with a problem was overkill. He had to be protecting some kind of secret.

The streetlights were spread out. Most of the businesses were closed. With the exception of the neon signs of a convenience store, the majority of light came from the vehicles that cruised by. I saw the dealers making exchanges with drivers, shoving small packages into car windows for cash which was then couriered to someone else. The more players and steps involved in a single exchange, the harder it was for a proper arrest to be made. The Seven Rooks weren't stupid. They'd been in business for some time. They knew how to keep a low profile. So whatever happened to Jessika must be significant enough to blow their operation out of the water should anyone find out. Even after five years, my simple questions threw them into a tizzy.

Three men were approaching from the far end of the street, and I turned onto the first cross street to avoid them. I wasn't positive they saw me. And even if they did, there wasn't much to see. A dark figure in dark clothing. Everything about me at the moment was nondescript, including my gender. I was just a shadow. Nothing more than a trick of the lights.

Crouching down, I removed my gun and waited for

them to pass. I wasn't taking any chances. They continued at the same pace, talking about last night's game. When I could no longer hear their voices, I stood, shoving my hands in my pockets before stepping onto the sidewalk. The prostitutes were working the next few streets, and from the occasional stopped car, I knew they were open for business. That meant upper management would be close.

I continued moving down the block, past the spot where I spoke to the girls on Friday morning. The sound of someone getting their rocks off echoed, and I glanced to the right. It was a dead end street with apartments on both sides. Ignoring the otherwise occupied couple, I moved toward the blue glow coming from an open side door.

The nearest interior door was ajar, and from what I could tell, that was the Seven Rooks' base of operations. Money and small plastic bags were on a table, and three men were standing around talking. The light glinted off the pearl handle of a large caliber handgun. I found the pimp. Now I just needed to get him away from his friends.

Ducking behind a dumpster, I remained in the dark, listening as the man finished and paid for the service. The sound of heels clacking across the concrete grew louder, and then his date for the evening went up the steps to the apartment. After exchanging a few harsh words, she went back outside to trawl for a new client.

"I gotta make sure they ain't slacking off," someone said.

The sound of heavy footsteps thundered through the hallway, changing to a scuffing scraping noise when he emerged on the stoop. Pressing myself against the dumpster, I waited. Blind to my presence, he strutted past, struggling to keep his pants up while exuding authoritarian superiority. That was some feat. After making certain no one else was planning to leave the stash house, I silently moved away from the dumpster. Let's see how he liked being cornered.

That swagger was hard to miss, so I kept my distance. He yelled at a few of the girls. Some cowered and blindly obeyed. A few of the others gave him dirty looks, but no one mouthed off. They knew their place. That fueled the fire in my belly.

Once I was past the hookers, I sent a text to O'Connell with the address and location of the stash house. I didn't want the police to show up too quickly, but I might need a distraction to ensure an easy escape. He responded immediately, giving an approximate ETA of seven minutes. That didn't leave much time for an interrogation, but it would have to do.

At the end of the block, the pimp stopped in the perfect location to survey his domain and keep an eye on the employees. It was also close enough to a side street that I could drag him away for a bit of privacy. Tightening the grip on my nine millimeter, I took a deep breath, glanced behind me, and made my approach.

With the hood up and my face tilted downward, he didn't recognize me. He actually didn't pay much attention. This was his turf. He had no reason to fear anyone. At least not yet.

As soon as I was within striking distance, I shoulder-checked him. He wasn't particularly tall, and he had the twitchy muscles of an addict. The hard bump spun him slightly, and before he could do anything else, I shoved the muzzle of my nine millimeter beneath his chin, forcing his head skyward. With my other hand, I pushed him backward against the wall.

"You yell for help, I'll kill you," I warned.

"You don't know who you're messing with." His voice sounded like a cross between a cartoon villain's laugh and a smoker's cough. Even now, he didn't lose the swagger. He wanted to intimidate me, but unless he possessed ninja skills or combat training, I could hold my own.

"Enlighten me," I hissed.

A car drove down the street, the lights catching a portion of my face despite the building behind us. "Shit. You, again?"

I kept my head on a swivel. If things went south, it would happen fast. "Let's make this simple. Answer my questions, and I'll go away."

"I'll give you simple." He tried to push away from the wall, and I shoved him back, jamming the muzzle hard against the hollow of his chin.

"Or we'll do this the other way. I blow your brains out and ask someone else my questions. It's your choice."

"What do you want?"

"Five years ago, Jessika Wellington vanished. Prior to that, she was in this neighborhood. Why?"

"I don't know."

"Did you ever see her?" In that instant, I saw something in his eyes. "What did you do to her?"

"Bitch was in the wrong place at the wrong time. Thought she was a crusader. Gonna save us all. Instead, she saw some things she shouldn't have."

"What did she see?"

He didn't answer. "Maybe she ran away." His eyebrows twitched, as if he thought he was clever. "Or maybe she just tried to." Without warning, he batted my forearm away with his left and reached across with his right to grab at the gun.

Instead of struggling, I dropped my left hand to the weapon in his waistband. The sound of the gun being cocked made him freeze. "You might want to reconsider before you become a soprano."

He let go of my wrist and put his hands up. His eyes darted from my face to my hand on his gun. "I didn't do anything to her."

"Who did?"

He swallowed, trying to push farther back against the wall in the hopes of saving as much of his third appendage as possible in the event I gave the trigger a squeeze. "I don't know."

"What was she doing here?"

He licked his lips, and I noticed he was sweating. "Helping out. I saw her handing out blankets at the shelter and working at the clinic. Girl probably got community service for crashing her daddy's sports car or something. But no one ever taught her to mind her business."

This was taking too long. "What did she see?"

Another exaggerated shrug. "All I know is she saw something she wasn't 'spose to. The next thing I knew the problem was taken care of. Don't know more than that."

I didn't believe him, but I didn't have time to break him either. The sound of stiletto heels approaching indicated we were about to have company. It was time to disappear. Yanking the gun from his waistband, I stepped backward. The sudden relief of not having to worry about his johnson being blown off made the pimp braver, and he lurched forward, fists swinging. I deflected the first two punches but underestimated the timing on the third. It was a solid hit beneath my sternum. Despite the vest, I stumbled backward, clutching my nine millimeter but dropping his gun. He darted toward the dropped .45, and I aimed at him.

"Step back," I said, just as the hooker rounded the corner. She screamed, and I knew the enforcers would be arriving shortly. "Back," I barked.

This should be the part where the cavalry rode in to save the day and clinked bracelets on the crooks. Sirens sounded in the distance, and when they turned toward the noise, I slipped into the darkness and moved within the shadows until I made it safely back to my car.

A few seconds later, a police truck turned a corner and came to a stop in front of the dead end street. Several men in full tactical gear stepped out of the armored vehicle, shouting at the people nearby. Patrol cars moved in next, but I didn't wait to see how many of them would be arrested. Instead, I drove out of the garage and away from the raid before flipping my headlights on.

I took the long way home, checking constantly for a tail. I even stopped a few blocks from my house at the twenty-four hour pharmacy to pick up some bandages. No one was following, and with the exception of the bartender and his drunk friend, no one from the neighborhood ought to have any idea who I was. Still, it was better to be safe than sorry. No one came into the store or waited for me outside. It was safe to go home.

I checked my apartment, locked and bolted the door, and updated my intel. Even now, I lacked hard facts. But I knew Jessika had been there. So what the hell did she see? Did she run away? Did they leave her no choice? I didn't know, and now I had more questions than before.

FOURTEEN

A knock sounded at my office door, and I looked up just in time to see Cross step inside. Obviously, he didn't think he needed to wait for an invitation. He cleared his throat and took a seat in one of the two client chairs.

"Miss Parker," his voice lacked the harsh clip it usually had, "we need to speak for a moment. Whatever you're working on can wait."

I dropped my pen, sensing something was wrong. "Did you read my report?"

"Yes. That's not why I'm here." He chewed on his bottom lip, clearly uncomfortable which made me uncomfortable. "Mr. Wellington expressed some concern over your involvement in his daughter's case. He wants you immediately removed from the investigation. He feels you are muddying the waters and hindering any progress that might be made."

"Like he gives a shit about progress. He's already lost hope." I let out a huff. "Did you ask someone to dig into his internet history?" Cross watched me closely, not responding to my question. "Oh, I'm sorry. Is this the part where you hand me my walking papers and security escorts me out of the building?"

Without a word, Cross put his elbows on the edge of the desk and leaned forward, resting his chin in his hands while he stared at me. The scrutiny was wholly unwelcome, and for a moment, I saw the tiniest bit of Jablonsky's training tactics. When I failed to break, he straightened and adjusted his tie.

"Don't pack your things just yet. But until further notice, you're off the Wellington case. I'll reassign you when I get a chance, but for now, find something to work on that doesn't involve screwing around in a police investigation or pissing off our current clientele. By the way, you should be aware of how complicated and illegal it is to obtain someone's browser history without their consent or a warrant."

"Does that mean you can't get the information?"

"It means it'll take time and resources, and it'd be best to wait and see what the police unveil before we violate an already disgruntled client's privacy."

I snorted. "Isn't rule number one to avoid the authorities at all costs?"

An amused glint streaked across his face. "Last night the police conducted a raid and arrested twenty-one people connected to the Seven Rooks. From what I understand, Detective Sparrow has been questioning each of them in regards to what happened five years ago. She's under the impression one of them might know something about Jessika's disappearance, and since she didn't have the backing or support needed to make these arrests at the time, she's taking advantage of the bust now. Would you happen to know anything about that?"

"It sounds like you know more than I do."

"In this instance, I doubt it." He glanced at the filing cabinets on the way to the door. "If you like, I can have these removed from your office. I don't want you to be tempted."

"They're fine where they are," I mumbled, unsure exactly how to read this situation. Was Cross playing a game? Did he want plausible deniability in case William Wellington turned out to be a vindictive bastard? Or was I really supposed to just sit around and twiddle my thumbs until my trial month ran out? "You can have your notes back." I held up the manila folder just as he made it to the doorway.

"Keep them. Shred them. Whatever you want. I have no use for them."

"Neither do I." I stared down at my notepad. "What about the lead you were exploring yesterday afternoon?" I asked, but he was gone.

Unsure how to proceed, I tapped my fingers impatiently on the desk. I barely slept last night. I didn't feel safe at home, not when I didn't have any hard facts about Jared Prince. The arrests last night would result in a lot of new enemies. The bangers were already gunning for me, and without the backing of Cross Security, regardless of how minimal it might be, I needed to keep my distance. Detective Sparrow would do her job. Maybe that's also what Cross figured.

I wasn't sure how long I'd been staring at my notes when my cell phone rang. A glance at the display indicated it was O'Connell, and I hit answer. "Do you have good news?" I asked. "If not, I'm hanging up."

"Well, the gangs unit is taking me out for drinks tonight. That anonymous tip really paid off. They made sweeping arrests and recovered almost sixty grand in cash, drugs, and illegal weapons. I'm a fucking hero."

"Does that mean you're going to wear tights and spandex underneath your clothing?"

"Ha ha." He exhaled. "I ran through the bartender's background and spoke to some people. He doesn't have a history of violence, and nothing links him to the Seven Rooks. However, he's definitely into something. Whatever it is hasn't hit our radar yet, so you might need to ask around. Given his history, ATF is probably keeping an eye on him. They'd know more than I would."

"He's been in that neighborhood for six years." I ran his background too, even though Nick seemed to forget at times I wasn't completely helpless. "You speculated he could have been involved in Jessika's disappearance. Do you still think that?"

"It's a possibility, but Sparrow didn't recognize his name

or the bar. Either she never got that far in the investigation, or what he said is true. To be on the safe side, I suggest you avoid him and be careful. Are you planning any more late night trips into the Rooks' territory?"

"Nope. Cross pulled the plug right before you called. Apparently, William Wellington doesn't like the way I do business."

He laughed. "Since when does that stop you?"

"I'd like to have a chat with a few of the gangbangers."

"You and I both know that's a bad idea. I'll handle it. Just tell me what you want."

"Wow, service with a smile. This is new." I told him about Jorge Toald and the intel he provided the previous night. "Someone else might know something. I just don't know who."

"I'll let Sparrow know, but if you're off the Wellington case, you should keep your distance. These bangers aren't a joke, and you just blew up their entire operation. They'll want revenge." I didn't say anything, and his voice took on a resigned tone. "Watch yourself, Parker."

For the rest of the morning, I remained at my desk and fielded a few calls. Sparrow offered to loop me in if something solid surfaced, but none of the perps answered her questions. The gangs unit wasn't concerned with a five year old case, so she wasn't getting much support from the arresting officers or the lead detective. On the bright side, it looked like a good chunk of the gang was now incarcerated. With dwindling numbers, maybe the neighborhood had a fighting chance of cleaning itself up.

Around noon, Kellan knocked on the door. His office was directly across the hall, and he made it his mission to make me feel welcome. I wasn't used to co-workers taking such an interest. In fact, I might have been a little suspicious.

"Are you busy?" he asked.

"Not exactly."

"Good, let's go to lunch."

Since there was no use in protesting, I stuck my notes in a drawer and grabbed my things. We went to a Mexican place down the street. After asking what I wanted, he spoke perfect Spanish to the waiter, who grinned. I noticed a slight shoulder rub before the server disappeared, but I didn't comment. It wasn't my business. But if Kellan was a regular, it had nothing to do with the food.

We made small talk about the weather and traffic before the conversation turned to work. I was reluctant to divulge much on the Wellington case, particularly since it was no longer mine, but it wouldn't hurt to get someone else's perspective on Cross. Kellan had been with the security firm for seven years. Prior to that, he worked for the DEA. I wasn't sure why he left or why he was forced out, but it was probably for one of the usual reasons. It also explained his slight obsession with identifying which of our colleagues had addiction issues. Regardless, he knew Cross a hell of a lot better than I did.

"Shit," he rubbed his eyes, "if I knew you were taken off the case, we would be drinking our lunch instead."

I laughed. "Didn't you accuse me of having a substance abuse problem yesterday? Now today, you want to make that accusation true."

He looked sheepish. "How are you?"

"Bruised. The body and the ego." I put my fork down. "Is this the kind of thing Cross does often?"

"Sometimes. For that case in particular, the investigation changes hands just as often as a person changes clothes. So I wouldn't worry about it. In a day or two, he'll have you on something new."

"So when he says back off, is that a hard and fast rule?"

He grinned. "You're a stubborn one. He must love that." He tried to shake off the amusement, but it didn't take. "Here's some friendly advice, the boss man is a bit stiff, but if you get the work done without screwing the company over in the process, he won't mind. That being said, you better be damn sure you know what you're doing before you do it. He doesn't like surprises or confrontation."

"Confrontation?" I practically choked. "Since the day he hired me, he's been nothing but confrontational."

Kellan snickered. "Oh, that's okay. He doesn't like to deal with confrontation unless he provoked it."

"Great." I checked the time, figuring at least one of us

G.K. Parks

needed to get back to work. "Only another twenty-something days of dealing with the madman."

He paid the tab, despite my protests to split the bill. "I wouldn't be so sure. In case you can't tell, Lucien likes you."

"Now I know you're full of shit."

Once we were back at the office, I checked the time and made a call. Cross Security possessed what felt like infinite resources and connections, but Mr. Cross's priorities were geared toward appeasing his clients. It was good business practice, but I wasn't sure how far down the rabbit hole he was willing to travel when our client was adamantly opposed to being investigated. I also wasn't sure how far I was supposed to go. However, since he gave me some extra rope, I might as well use it to swing from the rafters. My days were numbered, so anything I did at this point couldn't hurt. But to be on the safe side, I'd remain under the radar until his highness decided to issue another edict. That's what Kellan suggested, and it didn't sound like bad advice.

"Love," even with that single term of endearment, the British accent was evident, "is everything all right?"

"Hey, Bastian. I need a favor." I crossed paths with a group of former SAS mercenaries turned K&R specialists on two separate occasions. The first time, I clashed with their leader, Julian Mercer, over how to recover a group of kidnapped girls, one of which was O'Connell's niece. The second time, Mercer's team saved my life. As payment, I vowed to find a lead in Julian's wife's murder, but life got busy with deep cover assignments, bombers, and getting fired. Apparently now that I was taken off the Wellington case, I had some time, but that wasn't the reason for the overseas call. "I need someone with amazing computer acumen to check into a man's internet history from roughly five years ago to the present."

"And I'm the only bloke you know who can do it?" He made a tsk noise. "What will your government think about an agent so willing to violate one's privacy?"

"About that." Swallowing, I filled him in on the happenings in my life since the last time we spoke. "You deal with blackmail and extortion all the time. You'll know if William Wellington issued a payoff, if there was a ransom, or if he was blackmailed. Honestly, he might be involved in his daughter's disappearance, but I can't fathom how he connects to a local gang. But there's definitely something slimy about him."

"I'll see what I can do. Did you get the data packet I sent with the security cam footage you requested?"

"I did. I gave it a preliminary viewing, but I need more time with it and the crime scene photos. How is Mercer?"

"Jules is managing. Most nights, I have to drag him out of the pub. Being sequestered in London is ripping him apart, but he won't leave, not until Hans has recovered. He can be a stubborn git, but he'll get there."

"Julian or Hans?"

Bastian laughed. "Both, I suppose." I heard the telltale gnawing. Bastian was probably chewing on a pen while he booted up his computer. "Let me see how extensive Wellington's firewall and ISP security is. That will determine how quickly I can dig through it. Do you think the girl was kidnapped and things went tits up with the ransom?"

"It's possible, but if someone took her, only her father knows. The mother is oblivious."

"Mums are never oblivious." The clatter of lightning-fast typing echoed in the earpiece. "I'll be in touch."

Just as I was about to give up on the Wellington case for the time being, my office phone rang. It was Dr. Dalton.

FIFTEEN

"I spoke to my associates," Dalton said. "It turns out Jessika volunteered at the free clinic. She didn't work there long, just a little over a month. It's probably why I don't remember her being there."

"Okay." Finally, we could place her in the neighborhood. "Do you have the dates of her employment? The hours she worked? Her duties?" We needed patient lists and a warrant. Actually, Parker, you're not a federal agent; you're a private detective. You don't need a warrant. Bribe money, maybe. Warrant, no.

"Hold your horses. I'm sure human resources has some paperwork concerning her work schedule, application, and whatever required records we needed. I haven't had a chance to look into it. I just wanted to let you know I didn't forget to ask around. I'm busy the next few days, but I will put in a request and get back to you."

"I appreciate it." My mind was already ten steps ahead. I had a choice to make. I could tell Cross and Sparrow about this, or I could keep it to myself.

"Um, full disclosure, I'm not entirely certain what we can actually give you," Dalton said. "Legal takes matters of employee privacy almost as seriously as patient privacy.

However, since the girl has been missing for such a long time, I'll see what I can do. Would it be fair to say she is presumed dead?"

I didn't want to admit it, but privacy didn't always extend to the deceased. "That's a common assumption in missing persons cases."

"Good. Well, it isn't, but it might make things easier. Honestly, it's been so long, I can't remember for certain, but I feel like I must have spoken to the police about this. I'm sure a detective questioned me. I just can't remember much about it or Jessika. Have you checked to see if they have a record of this?"

"I'm not sure. We're a private security firm. The police aren't always inclined to cooperate."

"I see." I heard the sound of the intercom through the earpiece. "I'm being paged. I'll be in touch, Miss Parker. When I get a hold of the records, should I have them sent to your office?"

"That works."

After a few moments, I began pacing. If I told Cross what I found, he'd intercept the package, and I'd never see it. This was my lead, and I wanted to look through Jessika's employee file. I didn't believe Sparrow withheld information, which meant someone withheld it from her.

After closing my door, I dug out my cell phone and called the detective. After disclosing what I deemed to be the most important breakthrough in Jessika's disappearance, Sparrow was elated.

"That's amazing. When I interviewed Dalton five years ago, he said he didn't remember any high school students at the clinic. That's the reason I didn't bother to question the rest of the staff. This changes everything. If we can get documented proof of Jessika's presence, it'll open everyone up to investigation. Maybe we'll actually find out what happened to her. When are you getting the paperwork?"

"I'm not sure. The doctor is supposed to pull some strings in order to gain access to the employee file. I will have a copy sent to you as soon as I receive it."

"If you receive it," she said, mulling over the possibilities. "He didn't remember her the first time I asked. I don't understand why he never checked before now. Do you have any proof besides his word that Jessika actually worked in the clinic? The sooner we can move on this, the better. With most of the Seven Rooks in custody, now's the time."

I told her what Jorge said the previous night, leaving out the fact he was under duress at the time. "It isn't much to go on, but if it's true, he can't be the only one who noticed Jessika. Most of the Seven Rooks are around her age, so they might have spoken to her or paid more attention than most. Have you considered the possibility she could have been in a relationship with one of them? That might be why she wanted to help out and why she didn't get home before ten on Tuesdays and Thursdays."

"You think she was sending flirty texts to Dylan while screwing someone else?" Sparrow asked.

That didn't exactly fit either. "I don't know. Perhaps she made some friends in the neighborhood. From what everyone says about Jess, she had a big heart. She wanted to help people. A lot of people around there need help. Maybe someone took advantage." I sighed. "It's been five years, but I'm guessing a prep school girl might stick out in someone's mind."

"She'd be an obvious target," Sparrow agreed. "Let me do some asking. More specific questions tend to get better responses. Assuming what you've been told is true, I can use that to convince one of these knuckleheads someone else talked, and who knows, maybe they'll all talk. I'd like to subpoena the clinic's records, but that'll be a tough sell without substantial corroboration. I need that file."

"It's yours, assuming I get it." A few thoughts crossed my mind. "Any walk-in, clinic worker, or patient could have fixated on her, followed her home or to school, and devised a foolproof plan to grab her."

"It sounds like you believe Jessika was being stalked."

"Considering how completely she disappeared, she might have been taken. You've already run through the usual suspects. I'm just scraping the bottom of the barrel for ideas, even if they might be farfetched."

"You're sure the clinic is solid?" she asked, needing to

double-check this fact.

"As solid as anything else. Dr. Dalton said a record exists, and the pimp said he remembered seeing her there. That's two for two. And an unidentified witness said he remembered a cab pulling up to the clinic on the nights Jessika allegedly volunteered. That might have been her way home."

"Then you might be right. We've looked everywhere else. Too bad no one came forward sooner."

My gaze fell on the filing cabinets. Leafing through the records, I went through everything again. Any time I spotted the slightest mention to volunteer work, school clubs, college, or healthcare, I removed the correspondence. I never bothered to call most of Jessika's friends, and doing so now would fly in the face of Cross's orders. So I did it the hard way.

I examined their social media profiles, but none of them ever checked in or posted from anywhere near the clinic. The texts and e-mails Jessika exchanged with them never gave specifics. Volunteering was basically her go-to excuse for not being able to see a movie or hang out at the mall. Honestly, it might not have even been true. Jessika might have been shy or awkward in social situations. After all, Mrs. Wellington made her daughter sound like a bookworm.

"Mums are never oblivious," I repeated Bastian's words, snorting. I'm sure he worked enough cases to disprove his own theory, but I couldn't help thinking maybe Janet did know more than she let on. Maybe she even knew the kinds of things in which her husband was involved.

"What are you doing?"

I spun on my heel, realizing I was caught with my hand in the cookie jar. Cross leaned against the doorjamb. Even though his hands were in his pockets, the lines of his suit remained pristine. Someone invested a few pennies in fine tailoring. Hell, he probably went to the same designers Martin did.

"Just making sure I put everything back where I found it. I wouldn't want whoever gets the case next to be unable to locate some of the files," I lied, "even though I'm certain

I never saw all of them."

He narrowed his eyes, sweeping his gaze to the computer. He already made a point of telling me the company computer was monitored. Apparently, he wasn't joking. "Uh-huh."

"Is there something I can help you with, sir?"

Stepping away, he shook his head. So that's how we were going to play this game. If he thought I would be deterred by his presence in my doorway, he was mistaken. I'd just be more careful in the future.

* * *

The next couple of days were a blur. Cross didn't reassign me, so I spent my time surreptitiously reviewing the Wellington files. Sparrow phoned to say she spoke to Jorge Toald, but he denied having ever said anything to me about Jessika Wellington. His story dramatically changed, and no one else remembered seeing anyone matching Jessika's description in the area. When asked specifically about her involvement at the clinic, soup kitchen, and shelter, Sparrow was met with nothing but blank stares and apathy. Until she received irrefutable proof, the police couldn't move on that angle. Instead, they were happy to process evidence from the bust and line up an endless string of indictments against the gang members.

While I was stuck in limbo, I had a feeling Cross wasn't facing the same difficulty. Something told me he was investigating his own leads. I thought about our meeting, knowing whatever piqued his interest had to do with Henry Brandt, the clinic's administrator. I just had no idea in what regard Brandt might be involved, and I couldn't use company resources to check for fear Cross would find out and cut me off entirely. My new work environment was an oppressive dictatorship, and it was no secret I had a problem with authority. Eventually, something would ignite and cause a massive chain reaction explosion. So I tried to behave in order to postpone the inevitable. But anyone who knew me knew I didn't handle boredom particularly well.

Drumming my fingers against the edge of the table, I stared at my laptop, watching uploaded videos of the flash mob performance. Since Cross's ominous appearance in my doorway, I barely touched the company computer. He shouldn't track my activity, particularly when he was opposed to tracking Mr. Wellington's.

Hitting pause, I copied down yet another license plate and vehicle description. The only good thing about the number of videos was the various camera angles they provided. Most were taken from a distance and focused on the performers. Very few even caught a glimpse of Jessika, and none saw her disappear.

"The police looked through those, and so did I," Renner said. He glanced down at my notepad. "Water cooler gossip says you were reassigned."

"Still waiting on that."

"So you're looking for missed clues in the meantime?"

"No, I'm trying to learn some new dance moves. I fired my last choreographer. He had no rhythm." Saving the file list so I could continue when there wasn't an audience, I lowered the cover on my computer. "Do you need something?"

Renner held out an envelope. "This came for you."

"Why didn't the assistant deliver it?" I raised an eyebrow and reached for the envelope.

He tapped his watch. "It's lunchtime. There's only one person at the desk. She couldn't get away."

"She could have phoned."

"You want to be a hardass when I did you a favor? Sheesh." He shook his head. "By the way, I hope you plan to run this upstairs to Cross."

I swallowed the apology from the tip of my tongue. "This is none of your business."

"It's none of yours either," he lowered his voice, "but that doesn't mean I'm not curious to find out why no one ever mentioned Jessika working at the clinic before now."

"You opened it?"

He shrugged. "I am a private detective."

"Or maybe just a dick."

He grinned and locked us inside my office. "So tell me,"

he rubbed his palms together, "what the hell have you discovered? Do you know what happened to the girl?"

"Not yet. We can place her in the neighborhood. The cell towers used for some of those texts and calls now make sense. From what I can tell, her involvement at the clinic was encouraged by Mrs. Cleese, but the teacher said she didn't know anything about it. The parents don't know anything about it. Even the doctor who sent this didn't remember Jessika volunteering at the clinic, so we still have a long way to go." I gave him a hard look. "Correction, Mr. Cross has a long way to go. This is his case. Now if you don't mind, I need to run this upstairs."

Renner checked his watch. "Just so you know, Lucien has a lunch meeting. He won't be back until two. That gives you an hour and ten minutes to figure out if there's anything else in the file."

"Thanks."

He nodded. "I'm not sure what O'Connell might have said, but I just want to know what happened to the girl. My intention isn't to screw you over. I really was just helping out by delivering the mail."

"And helping yourself to my lead."

"Call it curiosity."

"Haven't you heard? Curiosity killed the cat."

"It's a good thing I'm not a pussy."

My eyes narrowed, and he took that as his cue to leave. As soon as he was gone, I dumped the contents of the envelope on my desk. Everything inside might be useful. It contained Jessika's volunteer schedule, a record of her vaccinations, and her application. Since she was a minor, the clinic required parental permission. I stared at the name scrawled on the paper — Janet Wellington. Shit.

Taking out my phone, I photographed every document inside the envelope. Then I crossed the hallway to the photocopier, glanced nervously around to make sure no one was nearby, and made a copy for Detective Sparrow. I stuffed the sheets back inside, went up the stairs to Cross's office, and slid the envelope beneath his door.

My next stop was the precinct. On my way to missing persons, I almost ran into Detective Thompson who was on his way down. He rolled his eyes and said, "Back so soon?"

"I have something Sparrow wants to see."

"Brooke's not here. She's out on a call. I can give that to her, if you'd like." He nodded at the stapled papers in my hand.

Handing them to him, I narrowed my eyes. "Is there any particular reason you're being so nice lately?"

He frowned. "I'm not."

I glanced around, but we were alone. "Something going on with you and Sparrow? I mean, Brooke."

He grumbled under his breath. "Last time I offer to do you a favor."

I grinned, enjoying tormenting him. "Didn't anyone ever tell you not to shit where you eat?"

"Says the woman who's shacking up with the man who originally hired her to protect him. What happened to your qualms about dating someone from work?"

"Things change."

"Yeah." He blew out a breath. "The only people I have time to meet are cops and crooks. It doesn't take a genius to figure out it's a very limited dating pool."

"I remember you taking home a badge bunny or two."

"If you have the need to discuss personal matters, talk to O'Connell because you and I do not have that kind of relationship." He looked down at the pages, skimming through them. "I'll give these to Brooke. Is there anything you wanted to tell her?"

"Just ask her to check out the application and let me know what she makes of the signature." I noticed the time. "I need to get back to the office. If she wants to discuss it, have her call my cell. My boss doesn't know about this, and I want to keep it that way." I waved on my way down the stairs. "Thanks, Thompson. You're a sweetheart."

"Screw you, Parker."

SIXTEEN

Did Janet Wellington lie? That's what I couldn't figure out. When asked about her daughter volunteering, she made it sound like it was entirely school related. But according to the application, she granted Jessika permission to volunteer at the clinic. There was no mention of the school anywhere on the application. Something about Janet's story was beginning to bother me. It was possible she was involved in her daughter's disappearance. Hell, maybe the tears were part of the act. Perhaps she was jealous, or maybe she thought she was helping her daughter reach her goals, only to feel responsible for placing the kid in jeopardy. Whatever her motivation, I didn't appreciate the misdirection. It was either an unnecessary denial, or Janet had something to hide.

My desk phone rang, and I picked it up. "I received the envelope you left. I'll look into the matter," Cross said.

"Okay. I can—"

But he cut me off. "That will be all, Miss Parker."

I listened to the dead airspace for a moment before lowering the receiver. Now what the hell was I supposed to do? Before I could rush over to Janet Wellington's house to confront her, my cell rang. Damn, I was popular.

It was Sparrow. "You really are as good as they say."

"Not at all. I'm just lucky. And a pain in the ass."

She chuckled. "That's funny. Thompson might have used those exact words." She shook it off. "Anyway, I just spoke to Mrs. Wellington. She insists she knows nothing about this. She's on her way to the precinct to examine the papers in question. But in the meantime, I pulled the police reports she and her husband filed. And there's a hitch. The signatures don't match."

"Dammit."

"I'm no expert. I actually asked one of the handwriting experts for a quick assessment. He doesn't believe they were produced by the same person. It's possible Mr. Wellington signed the police report for his wife or he signed his wife's name on the application. We'll know more once Janet gets here." She sighed. "There is another possibility."

"Jessika forged her mom's signature," I concluded.

"Yeah, unless someone else did."

I wanted to slam my head into the wall. Why was everything so circuitous? The girl was gone. The investigation should lead from point A to point B and inevitably the truth. "So much for my helpfulness."

"At least we have proof Jessika volunteered. This might be a cold case, but this is the hottest lead I've had in years. Nothing panned out with the arrests we made, but now I should have enough to get the clinic's records. We'll go from there. Any idea what Cross Security's next move is? Mr. Cross just phoned in the same tip you delivered. He's acting like he's helping, but that would be a first."

Wonders never cease. "Your guess is as good as mine. His priority is the client."

Disconnecting, I decided it was best to think outside the box and act outside the confines of Cross Security's best interest. It was time to set my sights on a new mark. The police would deal with the gang and the clinic. That just left Jessika's parents. In the event one or both of them were involved, the recent accusations would be enough to make them nervous. And nervous people would act suspiciously and possibly compromise themselves. It was time to conduct some surveillance. I just wasn't certain who I wanted to shadow.

Janet Wellington was the easy choice. I knew where she lived, what she drove, and where she would be in the next few minutes. Her husband was more of a mystery. Sure, I'd been to his office, and I had his plate number. But he lived in a hotel. He may or may not have a mistress, and his internet history was being researched from across the pond. At this precise moment, I had no idea where he was or what he was doing.

"Janet it is," I declared.

After grabbing my things, I ducked into Kellan's office to tell him I was going home. I didn't want Cross to get suspicious about my early departure. Maybe a part of me wanted to do well at this job, even if I mouthed off to my boss, upset the client, and failed to follow orders at every turn. The reason I did those things was because I wanted to act in Jessika's best interest. She wasn't here, so someone needed to stand up for her.

I detoured home, trading the company car for my car. I didn't want Janet Wellington to recognize the vehicle, and I didn't want Cross to track the GPS. He tracked the car once before, so I wasn't just being paranoid.

As I drove to the precinct to begin my surveillance, I wondered how long I'd stick with this case. It had been ongoing for five years. It might never be solved. Sure, I dealt with other unsolved cases at the Bureau, but inevitably another priority would replace them. That was the nature of crime. However, if I never had another priority, what would make me walk away?

My thoughts went to Julian Mercer. His wife's murder would always be his priority. His main focus. The thorn in his side. And if I were being honest with myself, the reason I was avoiding working on it was because I feared I couldn't help him. When I first agreed to trade my skills for his, I spent nearly a month immersed in the case. Everything I thought to look into had already been examined, leaving me with nothing but straws to grasp. I didn't want to let him down, so instead, I avoided it and came up with excuses. Being forced to resign took away every excuse, so I found new ones. I signed with Cross Security without giving it too much consideration, and now I was chasing another hopeless endeavor.

Vowing to pace myself and work equally on both cases, I parked near the squad cars and waited. I spotted Janet's luxury sedan in a reserved space, and the surveillance began. Forty minutes later, she exited, and I started my car. Thirty seconds after she drove away, I pulled into traffic. The game was afoot.

*　　*　　*

The buzzing headache was enough to force the coffee cup out of my hand. I placed it in the cup holder and rubbed my eyes. How long had I been at this? A quick glance at the clock told me it was time to call it a night. I'd been tailing Janet Wellington for nearly a week. I knew her routine better than my own.

Her life was structured. She woke up every morning at seven. By eight, she was out the door. After picking up breakfast, she spent the morning at a nonprofit, presumably doing something charitable. Like mother, like daughter. Around noon, she'd leave and meet friends for lunch.

Depending on the day, she'd spend an hour with her support group, shop, or log some time at the salon or spa. I did some checking and knew she had a standing appointment every Thursday. The service changed weekly, but the appointment time did not.

Afterward, she'd hit the gym. She always arrived by four. I watched her take a yoga class one afternoon and spin class another. Other times, she worked with a trainer. Despite what she did at the gym, she always stayed two hours.

Wednesday, she went to dinner with her husband. Their interaction seemed forced, as if neither of them wanted to be there. Aside from that, he had little visibility in her life. They really were estranged. The rest of the week, she stayed in every night. No one came to the house. Nothing suspicious was delivered. She watched TV, puttered around, and went to bed. It was about time I did the same. When I got home, I looked at the wall of my apartment. Whenever this was settled, I'd have to paint again. I papered every surface with notes, documents, and surveillance photos. But despite my best efforts, I still didn't know much. Janet Wellington never stepped foot on the Seven Rooks' turf. She didn't meet with any shady characters. She didn't have a drug dealer drop by with a bag of painkillers and uppers. For all intents and purposes, she didn't act any differently than I expected. She didn't sign the permission form, and until a few days ago, she had no idea her daughter volunteered solo at a free clinic.

"Maybe the husband knows something," I said to my empty apartment.

Bastian finished digging through his internet history, and the things he found were unsettling. William Wellington III never paid a ransom or blackmail, at least not that we could tell from his internet history and bank records. That didn't mean he didn't have an untraceable account in the Cayman's or other hidden assets at his disposal, but second guessing everything wasn't going to get me anywhere. So assuming he didn't pay someone off, his daughter wasn't kidnapped for ransom. If she was taken, it was for other reasons. None of which were good.

Like his wife, he didn't have any interactions with anyone in the Seven Rooks. However, his internet history wasn't exactly spotless either. William had a pornography habit, which wasn't uncommon, but his preferences involved simulated violence and women who were barely legal. That might not mean anything, but it didn't sit right. He also spent a lot of money purchasing expensive jewelry, perfume, and lingerie. Perhaps those were bribes to keep his mistress happy while catering to his baser desires. That was entirely speculation on my part, but William rubbed me the wrong way. After all, it was his fault I was conducting an off the books investigation from my apartment while running myself ragged at work. So yeah, I was biased.

Too tired to think, I made sure the door was locked and

went to bed. I hadn't exactly been sleeping well, and tonight was no different. Too much caffeine. Too many questions. And admittedly, the slight fear Jared Prince might decide to do what he didn't in the back room of his bar crept into my thoughts every time I closed my eyes. I considered staying at Martin's apartment — correction, our apartment. But I didn't feel right about that either.

After an hour of tossing and turning, my phone vibrated against the charger, and I rolled over and grabbed it. It was almost five a.m. As soon as my fingers touched the device, the annoying sound stopped.

It was a text message. *Miss me, yet?*

Smiling, I dialed Martin's number and sat up in bed, brushing my hair out of my face. "Why are you texting this early?"

"Good morning, beautiful. I didn't mean to wake you."

"You didn't."

Even though I couldn't see him, I knew he was grinning. "Can't sleep?"

"Nope." Climbing out of bed, I went to the kitchen. It was going to be a four cup morning and maybe an eight cup day. "How's your trip?"

"Eh." He didn't say much, which either meant someone was in earshot or things could be better. "Is everything okay?"

"More or less." I blew out a breath. "I just need to figure out a few things, and until I do, I don't imagine I'll be getting much sleep."

"I don't buy it. The reason you can't sleep is because you can't stop thinking about me."

"Actually I can't stop thinking about William Wellington."

"Is he your type?"

"Ugh. Not in the least." Feeling playful, I asked, "I'm just curious, what is my type?"

"Devastatingly handsome, intelligent, witty, and hung like a horse."

I laughed. "You might have just described my new boss."

"Lucien Cross is not devastatingly handsome, and I

doubt he's hung like a horse."

"When I find out, I'll let you know."

"Alex," he scolded.

"What?" I feigned innocence.

"You know what." He sighed, and his voice sounded sad when he said, "I wish I was there."

"In that case, finish your conferences and get on a plane. I miss you."

"I knew it." He went quiet for a moment. "Stay safe. I love you."

"Ditto."

Since sleeping was overrated, I pressed the button on the coffeemaker and went to shower. By 6:30, I was nestled in my office. Cross finally assigned me to assist Kellan on the corporate espionage case. But it was mostly paperwork and technical jargon. There wasn't much left to do with the actual investigation, and since Kellan said he had it covered, I spent the early morning working on Mercer's case.

His wife, Michelle, was murdered in the middle of the afternoon inside their home while Julian went to the market. From the crime scene photos and what Julian said, his wife was cooking in the kitchen. He came home to find her on the kitchen floor, bleeding profusely from multiple stab wounds.

My jaw clenched, and I swallowed. From the photos and his words, the attack and loss were devastating. I nearly lost Martin to an assassin's bullet, and I knew that helpless feeling. The silent begging, the anger, the pain. Pushing those thoughts aside, I needed to do something, and since it didn't appear I was going to bring closure to the Wellingtons, I had to do something for Julian. He needed this, and I owed him. Maybe I wouldn't bother tailing Janet today. I was tired of beating a dead horse. Hell, I was just tired.

"Miss Parker," Cross's voice caught my attention, and I looked up from the scattering of crime scene photos and police reports, "this doesn't look like the assignment I gave you."

"It isn't."

He looked down at the bloody photographs. "Did you find a new client for the firm?"

"Not exactly. This is personal."

He leafed through the pages. "We don't take murder investigations. Those fall entirely within police jurisdiction. Since there is no statute of limitations, anything we do could be construed as obstruction of justice. We stay away from things like that."

"Like I said, it's personal." I leaned back and sighed. "You told me to find something to occupy my time. There's nothing here for me to do. Kellan said he has the corporate case handled. And I'm off the Wellington case, right? Unless you feel like sharing whatever lead you've been working." He remained tight-lipped, and I shook my head. "Fine. Why don't you just say it?"

"Say what?"

"That you don't need me, and you wish me luck on my future endeavors."

Cross snorted. "You signed a contract for thirty days with the option for renewal based on performance. Time's not up yet."

I wasn't going to sue him for breach, but when I opened my mouth to say as much, there was something disconcerting in his eyes. He leaned down, flipping through the rest of the police report. Picking up an enlarged image of the stab wounds, he frowned.

"Where's the murder weapon?"

The wound tracks matched one of the knives found in Mercer's closet, but there was no blood evidence on it. The only thing the police found were his fingerprints on the grip and residue from where it had been cleaned. I handed Cross the photograph of the knife.

"Is that a joke?"

"That's what the police concluded."

"Do you believe their assumption is correct?"

I didn't need to see the photo again or read the report. "No, I don't. But the stab wounds match the blade. The lack of defensive wounds indicates she knew the killer. So the police had no problem cherry-picking their prime suspect, even though he didn't do it."

"You sound certain."

"I am." I flipped to another page. "They liked Julian for the crime, but the evidence was circumstantial at best. This happened over two years ago, and since then, New Scotland Yard has made no progress."

He smirked, placing the papers neatly on the table. "After that amount of carnage, there would be physical evidence on the blade. Even a thorough cleaning wouldn't have eradicated it. The murder weapon was a different knife but the same make." He went to the door. "I'm assuming that's also the case for the knife the police recovered from a stabbing involving Mr. Wellington's assistant which took place late last night. It was the same type of blade you reported stolen, but what're the chances it's actually yours?" Without waiting for any type of follow-up, he went out the door.

How did Cross know about my police report? I caught up to him at the elevator. "Is the assistant dead?" I swallowed, not believing this was a coincidence.

"You should head to the precinct and find out."

Narrowing my eyes, I wondered if this meant I was back on the Wellington case. "I guess I should. How did you hear about this? I thought you avoided interacting with the authorities."

"That doesn't mean I don't have friends in the department. That's why I'm here so early. William is on his way. Perhaps you should make yourself scarce." The implication shone in his eyes, but he didn't voice it. I was bad for business. "And Parker, you should consider taking that file upstairs. It's amazing what our people are capable of doing. They could recreate the entire crime scene. It might help you figure out what you're missing."

"Thank you, sir."

SEVENTEEN

"She'll have some nasty scars, but she'll live," O'Connell declared. He pushed the sealed evidence bag toward me. "Is that yours?"

I looked down; the serial number was etched off. Most people didn't even know some knives had serial numbers. Mine did. "It looks the same. I can't be positive. It's not like I carved my initials in the handle."

"The lab hasn't had a chance to run it yet, but if we find your prints, I'll just assume it's yours."

"Smart thinking."

He scowled, letting me know the sarcasm wasn't appreciated. "How'd you find out about this?"

"Cross."

O'Connell's eyebrows went skyward. "That man doesn't miss a trick. Since someone looped him in, I'm guessing this has to do with Jessika Wellington's disappearance."

"That's what I'm here to find out."

"As you know, I can't discuss an ongoing investigation." He stretched. "Do you want a cup of coffee? You look tired."

"Please."

He stood, sliding a folder to the edge of his desk. "I'll

make a fresh pot. Whatever's here has been for hours."

As soon as he turned his back, I picked up the file. Samantha Capshaw, twenty-seven, worked as Mr. Wellington's assistant for the last three years. She had a degree in accounting, so she probably planned to be an investment banker instead of the assistant to one. The next page contained photographs from the hospital and the crime scene.

She was assaulted in the parking garage beneath the office building. I didn't know why she was at work at three a.m., but since William provided a statement to the police when they arrived on scene, I had a good idea what she might have been doing. The description of the perpetrator was broad, practically generic. Male, early twenties, average height, thin, dressed in dark clothing. He was waiting in the garage, and when she approached her car, he came up behind her. He intended to cut her throat but was startled by William. Instead, he cut her from the side of the neck to the tip of her shoulder.

According to the report, Wellington intervened and tackled the assailant, knocking him against the side of the car. The broken rear window indicated it was a hard hit. The assailant dropped the knife and fled the scene while William tried to stop the bleeding and phoned the police. Or at least that's what the report said.

The garage used the same security system as the rest of the office building, but there was no indication whether the footage would be helpful. From what the investigators saw, it was impossible to identify anyone in the video. I closed the folder and put it back on the edge of O'Connell's desk, picking up the evidence bag and examining the knife through the plastic. This was my knife, which meant whoever did this was sending a message.

O'Connell put down a steaming mug. "Just to save time in the event there are questions, where were you at three this morning?"

"Outside Janet Wellington's house."

"I don't suppose anyone can corroborate that?"

"There's a neighborhood watch. If they were paying attention, they might have seen my car. Worst case, you could probably pick me up on some traffic cams. If I'd been following William instead of Janet, I might have been able to prevent this from happening."

"Don't put that on yourself. You shouldn't be following Janet around either, but I guess it's nice to know the wife has an alibi too." He flipped through the sheets, but nothing new popped out. "So how long do you think it'll take before Capshaw or Wellington admits why they were really inside the building late at night?"

"He's married. A divorce is looming. I doubt he wants anything like this to go public." I took a sip of the coffee. It wasn't good. Someone needed to clean the pot one of these days, but I drank it anyway. "You didn't hear this from me, but William has a fetish for young girls and rough sex."

O'Connell thought for a moment. "Do you think that's an anger thing stemming from his daughter's disappearance?"

"Don't know. But I like that theory better than the other one."

"You think he was messing around with his own kid? That's sick." He blew out a breath. "This most recent attack might provide some leeway. Any place else I should be digging?"

"Financials show expensive lingerie and perfume purchases. Nothing indicative of ransom payouts or blackmail. No strange transfers in or out either. He might have hidden accounts, but if he does, I don't know about them."

"He is an investment banker. He'd know how to move money around without us noticing, but our focus should be on his connection to that neighborhood. Jessika was connected to the clinic. It's about time we see if he is too." He wrote on a sticky note and put it on top of the file. "I'll have this sent up to Sparrow. Thompson will be thrilled we're going to work with missing persons."

I jerked my chin at his partner's empty desk. "How long has that been going on?"

"What?" O'Connell asked innocently. He met my eyes, hiding his amused grin. "Not too long. Less than a month. It's how I was able to procure the information you wanted, so don't jinx it. Plus, it's about time he dated someone who doesn't spin around a pole for a living."

"Don't knock it 'til you try it."

He chuckled. "I don't think my wife would agree."

"Jen's a fox. I bet she dated plenty of pretty boy strippers before she settled for a cop." I winked. "Don't forget, the last time she invited me over, she showed me the photos from her bachelorette party. Maybe the cop thing is actually why she married you. That seems to be a common theme in the stripper-verse."

"Don't you need to be somewhere? Preferably, anywhere but here."

"Yeah, yeah." I headed for the door, calling over my shoulder, "I owe you."

After driving back to the office, I took a moment in the elevator to collect my thoughts. O'Connell was tasked with finding the assailant, and Sparrow's cold case turned hot. Regardless of these facts, Jessika Wellington was missing, and I was the reason everything else was happening. Whatever I set into motion led to the attack last night, and the one glaringly obvious thread connecting them was William Wellington III.

The elevator doors opened, and I moved past the reception desk. But Cross's personal assistant blocked my path. "Miss Parker," he said, "Mr. Cross wants to speak to you."

"Okay." I tried to sidestep, but the man held his ground. "Now."

He led the way back to the elevators, and we stepped out of the car on the thirty-second floor. I followed him to the large corner office. The door was open, and Cross was seated behind his mahogany desk, searching through a stack of papers.

I cleared my throat. "You summoned?"

"How did things go at the precinct?" He went back to his search as I dropped into the chair across from him. "Was it your knife?"

"It's undetermined, but yes." I opened my mouth to say what was on my mind but abruptly closed it. Lucien made it clear this wasn't my case.

"Out with it." He glanced up for the briefest moment, and I wondered how he knew I had something else to say.

"The client knows something. Somehow, William's involved."

"I agree."

Caught off guard, I waited for elaboration that never came. "Did you confront him?"

Cross stopped his search and focused his attention entirely on me. "Attacking the problem head-on is not advisable, particularly when we're suspicious of the person financing the investigation." Finally, he located a hefty folder, flipping through the pages. "I presume you haven't actually followed my instructions in regards to this investigation."

I shrugged. "Is that a problem?"

He blinked. "Do you know who attacked Samantha Capshaw?"

"No. I wasn't there."

"Your knife was." His eyes went back to the file, and he didn't speak for several minutes. Eventually, he glanced up. "You can go."

I stood, but something held me in place. "Actually, we're not done yet. I have something to say. I don't know how William Wellington is involved, but he is. He has to be. Why would someone attack his mistress after we started poking around into his daughter's disappearance?"

"We already established this. Do you have an answer to that question?" The smug arrogance displayed across his face. "I didn't think so."

"You know something. Ever since our meeting with Henry Brandt, you've been working on something. What is it?"

He removed several glossy photos from inside the folder and spread them out on the desk. "Capshaw isn't William's only mistress. She's no one special. William speculated the assailant was waiting for him, but she exited the building first. Over the years, he's kept several women on the side. His infidelity isn't his only secret, but he swears he doesn't have a connection to the Seven Rooks or the free clinic. I have yet to disprove those claims."

"You spied on him? I thought you were concerned about his privacy."

Cross snorted. "When he first approached me about taking his daughter's case, I made sure to vet him properly. We don't protect murderers or rapists. That isn't what Cross Security does. And William is neither of those things. It's possible he might have catered to the criminal element at some point, money laundering, hiding assets, tax evasion, things of that nature. It's also possible one of his investors could have retaliated by abducting Jessika." He leaned back in his chair. "He denies it, and I've never found anything to the contrary. William might not be a good man, but until last night, nothing ever connected him to his daughter's disappearance. I plan to dig deeper."

"Okay." The wheels started turning in my head. Henry Brandt was the clinic administrator and a businessman. He used the free clinics to boost his image and establish a nonprofit status. "Does William have a connection to Henry Brandt?"

Something in Cross's eyes told me he did. "That possibility is being explored. It has to be done carefully. Angering men like William and Henry isn't advisable. I won't risk my business by making enemies for no reason. So you need to stay away from them. I don't want William to realize he's being investigated. If he spots us, we'll never find whatever he's hiding."

"Okay," I repeated.

"However, I'm putting you back on the case. William Wellington and his mistresses aren't to be touched. If you find something that leads to them, I will handle it. Everything else, the police investigation, the clinic, Jessika's routine, her friends, her mom, play it how you see fit."

"What if Janet tells her husband I stopped by?"

"It doesn't matter. I already told William your involvement is the only reason we've made any progress and he'd be a fool to bar you from assisting. As long as you stay away from him and his private life, he won't have a problem."

"Great," I deadpanned.

My boss quirked an eyebrow. This was the job. Complaining was neither professional nor appreciated, and he wanted to make sure I knew it. He continued flipping through the file, removing several pages as he went. He held them out, and I took them from his hand. "Those are the skeletons I've found in William's closet. The wife didn't have any, and neither did Jessika. It isn't exactly his browser history or financial records, but it should tell you enough. I've thoroughly explored every possible avenue. They were dead ends. But you have a knack for livening up otherwise stalled investigations, so it is possible that in my haste I might have missed something. Let me know what you find, but do it quietly. You screw this up, you're gone. No thirty days. Nothing. Do you understand?"

"Yep."

He smiled. "Good." He jerked his head toward the door. "Get back to work."

EIGHTEEN

I wasn't surprised Cross kept secrets, but I was surprised he was more than an expensive suit and Italian shoes. Everything about him screamed business tycoon. I'd been around the type long enough to know how they looked, smelled, and acted. Honestly, I didn't know a thing about the man's past, and I didn't bother to ask. But he had a file on his client. Hell, he probably had a file on everyone — client, employee, random passerby on the street. Choosing not to let this disconcerting fact get in the way, I took a breath and plowed through the files again.

Every part of the investigation seemed to rest on William Wellington, which meant Cross was handling it. I tapped my nails impatiently on the desk while I scrolled through the same data I already analyzed. Maybe whoever I pissed off would go after Janet next. I checked the time. I missed her morning departure. She was probably at the nonprofit or eating an early lunch. I'd catch up with her at the gym.

Lifting the phone, I dialed Dylan Hart. He didn't answer, so I left a message. I didn't know if he knew any more than what he already said, but out of everyone in Jessika's life, he had the best chance of knowing the truth. I asked if the name Dr. Dalton sounded familiar. After imploring him to return my call, I hung up. There was one other thing I wanted to ask, but questioning his girlfriend's fidelity in a voicemail wasn't the way to go.

"I thought sorority girls were the only ones who begged college boys to do things," Kellan said from my doorway, having heard the tail-end of my message.

"You mean to tell me you wouldn't beg a college boy to do things?"

He grinned. "I wouldn't be the one begging." He crossed the room and dropped into a client chair. "Cross just phoned, read me in on what happened to William Wellington last night, and said I should make myself available to assist. So what do you need?"

"Did he mention any specifics?"

"Only that you might need a secondary surveillance unit. Who are we following?"

"I've been keeping watch on Janet Wellington, but I could use a set of eyes on William, assuming Cross clears it. Under no uncertain terms am I supposed to go near him or his girlfriends." I lifted my phone, asking the receptionist to patch me through to the big boss. Once he answered, I put the call on speaker. "Mr. Dey offered his assistance. I'd like to have him maintain eyes on William. Any objections?"

"None. Why do you think I tasked another investigator to the case?" Cross asked, clearly pissed about the interruption. "Mr. Dey has never worked on the Wellington case. He won't be recognized. He's a safe choice."

"No problem," Kellan said.

"I thought you were handling it." I glared at the phone.

"I am. This is how I chose to handle it. They call it delegation. Is there anything else?" Cross asked.

"Nope." I disconnected and pointed a finger at Kellan. "I guess you have your marching orders. He probably could have given you the specifics without involving me."

"You'll get used to it. This is your investigation, so he wants you to feel like you're in charge."

"I doubt it. He's made it very clear he's pulling the strings." This was his show. We were just the puppets.

Kellan shrugged. "I imagine the exciting world of investment banking doesn't allow someone a day off just because they were nearly assaulted the previous evening. I'll see if he's at work and keep an eye on him. How often should I check in, boss?"

"Ask Cross. But if something occurs, let me know."

"Will do."

I'd been here a week, and my co-worker was already at my beck and call. At this rate, I'd be moving into Cross's office by the end of the month. Internally laughing at the ludicrous notion, I went to get another cup of coffee and work my way through the rest of Cross's notes. The information concerning Henry Brandt and William Wellington was circumstantial at best. They attended similar charity functions. They golfed at the same club, and that was about it. After going over William's financials again, looking for a connection between him and one of Brandt's businesses, I gave up and returned to analyzing the list of clinic employees. Since the Seven Rooks weren't talking, I needed to find a clinic employee who would.

Of the dozen people the clinic employed at the same time Jessika volunteered, nine still worked there. Half of them didn't remember her. And the rest only had a vague recollection of some teenager who reorganized the supply room, took inventory, and filled out order forms. It had been too long to get much out of them, especially over the phone. Perhaps the other three who were no longer employed by the clinic would be more helpful.

Before I left to conduct surveillance, I requested the current addresses and phone numbers for those three former clinic workers. It was nice having support staff to do the tedious things. Cross should be proud. I was delegating.

On my way across town, my phone rang. I hit answer, holding it against my ear and hoping the cops were too busy to pull me over for talking while driving. It was Dylan. He didn't know any specifics about the clinic and sounded rather irritated that I would accuse him of withholding facts in Jessika's disappearance. Even after five years, the kid was still heartbroken. Matters only got worse when I asked if he knew if Jess had any friends in that neighborhood. He said she didn't. He knew all her friends. They traveled in the same circles.

"Did you guys ever break-up?" I asked.

"What? No." His vehement response let me know this wasn't the time to ask, but I didn't know when I'd speak to him again.

"Do you know if Jess had any ex-boyfriends?"

"I was her first. Her only." Dylan's breath hitched. "Are you telling me she was cheating?"

"No. I just wanted to make sure she didn't have any other reason to hang out in that neighborhood besides volunteering at the clinic."

"That would have been enough for Jess." He swallowed. "I have to go."

Spotting Janet Wellington's luxury sedan parked in a spot near the gym, I was glad to see she was right on schedule. After spending fifteen minutes scoping out the area, I stepped out of the car. Since I had another hour and a half to kill, I might as well do it inside my new favorite haunt. Frankly, I just didn't want to sit in the solitude of my car and think I broke some kid's heart with baseless accusations.

The bell above the diner door chimed, but no one was in sight. The place was always empty at this time. Normally, I'd see the cook or one of the two waitresses. Today, I didn't see anyone. I took a seat near the window, keeping my back against the wall.

Noises traveled from the kitchen, and someone called out, "She'll be with you in a sec."

Ignoring the voice, I stared across the street. After a few minutes, I located the proper window for spin class and found Janet on a bike near the back. At least no one tried to cut her throat. It was a good thing I only lost one knife, and no one took my nine millimeter. The last thing anyone needed was a string of homicides that linked back to me.

An annoyed huff sounded, and I turned to see one of the waitresses. She picked up a menu and crossed the room. Her jet black hair reflected the sunlight almost as much as the numerous piercings which covered various parts of her face and ears. "You're back again?"

"I didn't want you to get lonely."

She rolled her eyes. "Taking up a table for two hours every day isn't exactly doing me any favors."

"At least I let you break up the monotony by refilling my coffee."

She crossed her arms over her chest. "That isn't exactly making me rich either."

I looked around the empty diner. "I'll make you a deal. If this place gets crowded and you have to turn over some tables quickly, I'll take a hike. But if that doesn't happen, I'll sit here, drink this stuff you call coffee, and hang out."

"You need a life. Don't you have a job? Haven't you heard it's not very healthy to remain stationary?"

"I like to people watch. It's how I meditate."

"Yeah, right." She held out the plastic coated menu. "Do you need a minute? Or do you want the usual?"

"Let's start with an iced tea instead, and I'll see if the mood strikes to try something else." I took the menu from her hand. "Thanks," I glanced at her name tag, "Skye."

She walked away, probably muttering curses under her breath. Returning a minute later with a glass of iced tea, she put it down and gave me a death glare. I wasn't sure if she was tough or just pretending to be tough, but I ignored it. "Do you know what you want?"

"What's good?" Admittedly, annoying her was a great way to kill a couple of hours. She looked young, but pinpointing an age with the amount of ghost white makeup contrasted with blood red lipstick and smoky eyes made that nearly impossible.

"I don't know. I'm partial to the grilled cheese." She glanced across the street in the same direction I was looking. "Do you workout at the gym?"

"No."

"Do you work around here?"

"Nope."

"Then why did you just start popping up all of a sudden?" Her inquisition wasn't normal diner conversation. She was suspicious. Maybe they were selling pot out of the back. With the lack of customers, they must be doing something to keep this place running.

"How do you know I'm not a regular?"

She snorted. "I've worked here for three years. I've never seen you before this week."

"I'm new to the neighborhood."

"Yeah, well, there are better places to hang out. Have you tried the coffee shop on the corner? They have free wi-fi."

I put down the menu. "I'll have a Cobb salad, no bacon." I fished a twenty out of my pocket, hoping that offering a tip up front would prevent her from spitting in my food. "Just in case you get bogged down with customers, I'll save you the trouble of bringing the check." I offered my friendliest smile. "Keep the change."

Pocketing the money, she picked up the menu and shouted my order to the cook. While she waited, she took to wiping down the counter and playing with the cash register. Someone else walked in, and she looked up. "Hey, Paul. You eating here or taking it with you?"

"With me. I told Tori I'd bring dinner home."

He went to the counter, and I watched the friendly chitchat. Apparently, the waitress just didn't like me. After calling in his order to the cook, she picked up my salad and brought it to the table. She put it down and dared me to ask for something else. I thanked her, and she went back to the counter to talk to Paul.

My eyes scanned the street. Traffic was picking up on account of rush hour. I didn't see anyone lurking outside the gym, at least not on foot. My eyes went to the parked cars. Most were empty. I looked for the usual suspects, older, beat-up models or brand new luxury rides. Several high-end SUVs dotted the street. And with their tinted windows, I'd need to get closer to see if anyone else was waiting for Mrs. Wellington.

While I finished my salad, some of the SUVs pulled away. Two remained parked on the corner. I'd give them another fifteen minutes before making my approach. Janet had another thirty minutes of spin class, so I didn't think anyone would make a move on her until she left the building. No one suspicious entered the gym, but one of the prostitutes could have donned workout clothes and snuck inside without my noticing. Still, it seemed unlikely. Most gyms had staff and cameras, and they took security seriously. Not to mention, it required a membership. Honestly, it might be one of the safest places Janet could be, assuming someone intended to harm her. I wasn't sure if she was even a target since I had no idea why anyone wanted to harm William or his side piece.

"Is this some kind of voyeurism thing?" Skye asked, moving to clear away my plate. "You sit here and eat while you watch people exercise." She assessed me. "I'm guessing you are no stranger to a gym, so why the obsession? Stalking someone?"

"Like I said, I'm new around here. I'm deciding if I want to join."

"That place is too expensive. You wouldn't like it."

"How do you know?"

"You order the cheapest things on the menu, and you don't have a job from what I gather. That place is probably too rich for your blood."

"Do you know anyone who is a member?"

"Nope. Most people aren't going to duck into a greasy spoon after sweating it out." She cleared the table, indicating it was time I leave.

I went to the door. "I'll see you tomorrow."

She glanced up from the register. "I don't work weekends."

"Monday then."

She let out a frustrated sigh, and I waved goodbye. Perhaps I made a new friend. She just didn't know it yet.

I moved down the street, placing my hand inside my purse and clutching my weapon. I was tired of being caught by surprise, and since I didn't know if anyone might be inside the SUVs, it was best not to take any chances. The first was empty, and I continued strolling down the sidewalk to the next one. Someone was inside, talking animatedly on her cell phone. The woman looked like a harried soccer mom, and I had issues imagining the Seven Rooks sent this lady to threaten Janet Wellington. However, a dark blue sedan parked on a side street caught my attention.

I knocked on the side window and waited for the man to unlock the door. I climbed inside. "What the hell are you doing here, Nick?"

He continued to stare out the windshield. "The same as you, I'd imagine." He picked up his travel cup and took a sip. "How many hours a day does a woman really need to exercise anyway?" He gave me a sideways glance. "Never mind, I'm asking the wrong person."

"What's that supposed to mean?"

Even though I couldn't see his face, I knew he rolled his eyes. "Has anyone ever mentioned you have an obsessive personality?"

Ignoring the jab, I answered his previous question. "Two hours. Janet spends two hours at the gym every day."

"Not every day. Monday thru Friday. Her weekend itinerary changes. This weekend the charity she works for is hosting a function. She has reservations at a hotel. Apparently, it's quite the event." He leaned back in his seat and checked the time. "After her husband's secretary was attacked last night, the captain assigned a detail to him and his wife."

"What about bodyguards?"

"Wellington probably hired out, but he didn't inform us. Hell, we didn't inform him either. We're keeping this on the DL. Detective Sparrow thinks the assault might have something to do with Jessika's disappearance, and we don't want to miss the boat on this a second time."

"You think whoever abducted Jessika is planning to take another member of the Wellington family? That seems unlikely."

"That doesn't mean whoever took Jessika isn't making new threats. Perhaps Jessika's disappearance was the result of failing to comply with an initial demand. Like you said, William never paid a blackmail or ransom, so maybe they've decided to try again. After all, you have been poking around. Stirring the pot probably pissed them off."

That would explain why William didn't want me anywhere near him. It could also be the same reason Cross didn't want me invading the Seven Rooks' turf again.

Perhaps my boss already knew what was going on. Maybe he just didn't know what happened to Jessika.

"And no one else could run surveillance on the Wellingtons?" I gave him a pointed look. Rubbing at his cheek, he glanced at me. "Thompson volunteered."

"Then shouldn't he be here?"

"One would think." O'Connell took another sip from his cup. "But he's staking out the investment bank with the pretty missing persons detective."

"Don't feel bad. I'm sure he thinks you're pretty too." I watched as Janet exited the gym and went to her car. "That's my cue." I opened the door. "How long are you shadowing her?"

"Until eight, then another team will take over."

"Great, you just cleared the rest of my day."

NINETEEN

The police didn't know what motivated the assault on Samantha Capshaw, and they had no leads on identifying her attacker. Missing persons and a few of the guys from major crimes were sitting on the Wellingtons in the event a second attempt was made. Seeing as how the police were following the Wellingtons, I decided I should do something more productive with my time.

"Did William say anything else when you met with him?" I spent the last twenty minutes grilling Cross. He was on his way out of the building when I was coming in.

"No." Cross continued at a brisk pace, maneuvering around whatever obstacles he encountered in an attempt to lose me, but it wasn't working.

"What about bodyguards?"

"What about them?"

"Does he have any? Is he hiring some?"

Lucien let out a huff, impatiently waiting for the light to change so he could cross. "We are a security firm. If he wanted protection, he would have asked about it."

I gnawed on my bottom lip. "So he's not worried they'll come back. Are you sure he doesn't know who attacked his mistress?"

"Assistant," Cross hissed, but he showed me the photographs this morning. We both knew she was more than that. "Since the police are maintaining eyes on William and Janet, there's no reason you or Mr. Dey should continue with that endeavor. Let me know if they identify the attacker. In the meantime, I'm late for an appointment."

The light changed, and he darted across the street. I didn't follow. Instead, I trudged back to the office and called Kellan. Taking the initiative, he said he would tail Capshaw since the authorities didn't seem interested in protecting the actual victim. Frankly, I was surprised the woman reported to work today. Either she loved her job or her boss. Truthfully, she'd probably be better off without them.

I ran her background, but she didn't have a record. And as far as I could tell, she didn't have a presence on social media either. That was refreshing but not particularly helpful. After spinning my wheels for another hour, I realized the most recent attack didn't put me any closer to finding out what happened to Jessika. It just made things complicated, and I was tired of complicated.

Regardless of how selfish such thoughts might seem, the attacker used my knife to conduct the assault. The police didn't find any prints on it, so that ruled out the possibility someone was trying to pin a crime on me. But I couldn't help but think it was a warning. William and Janet hired Cross Security to find their daughter. I was attacked and threatened because I asked one too many questions, so the attack on Samantha Capshaw seemed blatantly obvious. Whoever was responsible for Jessika's disappearance wanted William to call off the hounds. That's probably why William spoke to my boss this morning, but Cross convinced him otherwise. We were on to something, and William would have to be a complete idiot not to realize it.

I contemplated ways of determining who the attacker was, but I had nothing to go on. The description was vague. Most of the Seven Rooks were in custody. I glanced through the profiles of clinic workers. Most didn't have photos, and none matched the description. Jared Prince might know who was behind the attack, but that was just a guess. Unless it was a certainty, I wasn't stepping foot inside the bar, even if it was where I lost the knife.

Again, I found myself muddling through Prince's record. The databases provided a list of known associates and mug shots, but they were all a decade older than the man who reportedly attacked Capshaw. I called an old contact at the ATF and asked about Prince. I was told he wasn't involved in Jessika's disappearance and wouldn't have orchestrated an attack like that. I suspected the ATF was watching him, but when I asked what else they might have seen in the neighborhood, my questions were shut down immediately and the call concluded.

Tired and frustrated, I started to pace. I needed to do something to clear my head. Then maybe I'd be able to figure out what I was missing.

Mercer's file remained dissected on the coffee table. Moving to the couch, I realized how appreciative I was to have a spacious office. At the OIO, I had a desk in the bullpen. No privacy. No space. If I had something massive to work on, I always had to relocate to one of the conference rooms. Here, I could spread everything out with room to spare.

A disconcerting thought crossed my mind. I could see this working long-term. Stifling the commitment-phobe inside of me, I took a breath and focused on the other complicated case, rather than my own complicated life. Maybe it could distract my conscious mind while my subconscious figured out a solution to finding the truth behind Jessika's disappearance.

The murder weapon was key. The police assumed the military issued knife found in Mercer's closet was used to kill Michelle, but it wasn't possible. The timeframe alone made that obvious. When Julian returned home, his wife was gasping for breath. She died in his arms. If he stabbed her, he wouldn't have had time to call for help, clean the weapon so thoroughly not a drop of blood existed anywhere on it, and stow it in the closet before the authorities arrived to find him clutching her to his chest in the middle of their kitchen.

Sure, anyone could buy a knife, but how many people knew precisely which blade Mercer kept at home? Scribbling a note, I ran through the database. It wasn't the typical blade issued to the Special Air Service. This one was different. It was custom-made. Only a limited number were forged. And given that Julian kept most of his gear off-site, away from his home, how did the killer know what was in his closet?

The lack of defensive wounds indicated Michelle knew the killer, or so the police claimed. It was also possible whoever did this snuck silently into the house and attacked with stealth. Anyone highly trained in close quarters combat would know how to strike swiftly and cleanly, leaving no evidence behind. A gun would have been loud, but a knife was silent. I narrowed my eyes at the crime scene photos. It was possible the attacker left footprints, but the way the cops and first responders tromped through the house made recognizing them impossible.

Reaching for my laptop, I clicked a few keys and scanned through the footage. Bastian sent CCTV footage from the immediate vicinity surrounding Mercer's house for the two weeks prior to Michelle's murder and up to a week after. Needless to say, there was a lot to watch. I only glanced at it briefly, but Bastian ran everyone's mug through facial recognition. Nothing pinged in the databases, so whoever killed Mercer's wife was a ghost.

To execute a plan that perfect, the killer must have been watching the house from somewhere. Mercer's trip to the market was unplanned. The assassin couldn't have known when or if Julian would leave Michelle home alone. And if the goal was simply to kill Michelle, it would have been smarter and easier to do it while Julian was away on a mission. If the timing wasn't precise, Julian would have been at home, and the body on his kitchen floor would have been his wife's killer.

Bastian floated another possibility, one that Julian spent many sleepless nights battling. Maybe Julian was the target, but the killer found Michelle instead. I had problems believing that. It was possible I just didn't want to believe it. I didn't want to fuel my own nightmares concerning Martin's safety by analyzing a real life example of worst case scenarios. But more importantly, it didn't make a lot of sense. Attempting to murder a highly trained soldier would take a lot of planning and probably a high-powered rifle from several hundred feet or a silenced gun on a crowded street, not a home invasion planned so perfectly the killer was never caught.

Whoever did this wanted Julian Mercer to suffer. And since that day, Mercer had been suffering. He was forced out of the Special Air Service due to mental instability. He left his home and his life because he couldn't bear to be there without the woman he loved. The pain he was in was excruciating and real. Frankly, it was unimaginable, and I almost wondered if the only thing that kept him from putting an end to the misery was his desire for revenge. That was a great motivator to keep going.

Determined to figure out who might have been surveilling Mercer's home, their daily routines, and everything else about him and his wife, I flipped my notepad to the sheet I started this morning and continued recording vehicle descriptions and license plate numbers parked in and around the area. Since we didn't get this bastard's face on tape, there had to be some other record of his presence. Of course, the voice in my head reminded me facial rec would only get a ping if the person responsible had a record. Given the givens, I was positive whoever did this was exceptionally good. It was unlikely he'd ever been caught.

Just as I was scribbling down more of my musings concerning possible motives and potential ways to determine a probable suspect list, my desk phone rang. Figuring it was someone from Cross Security, I lifted the handset while I continued to write. After I finished my thought, I realized whoever phoned hadn't said a word.

"Hello?" I asked.

"Hi. This is Ridley."

I searched my mind, trying to match the name to a face. "Dr. Dalton?"

He chuckled. "Yes, sorry. I should have realized that's how you'd remember me. I was just wondering if you were free to meet."

"When?" I asked, wondering what this was about.

"Um, sometime tonight. I'm just about to leave the hospital and thought I'd get a drink. Want to join me?"

"I can do that." I checked the time. "Is everything okay? What's going on?"

His laugh sounded a bit nervous. "Nothing really. I didn't get a chance to call after sending Jessika's records, but after looking at them, I remember a bit more about her. I thought we could talk about it over drinks."

It sounded suspiciously like a date. "Just tell me when and where."

"Let's say the Apple Top in an hour. Do you know the place?"

"I'll find it."

* * *

The Apple Top was a microbrewery hidden in an out of the way place. The owners tried to recreate the atmosphere of a speakeasy, and they did a decent job. Dr. Ridley Dalton sat in a thick plush leather chair that could have easily fit two. He lifted his drink, an amber liquid that reflected in the dark gleaming wood of the table.

"You don't drink?" he mused, eyeing the seltzer and lime.

"Sometimes."

The place was crowded. From the expensive watches and Ivy League class rings, this was a hangout for the affluent. No one from the Seven Rooks would show up in a place like this, but William Wellington might. Just to be on the safe side, I kept my head on a swivel.

Dalton sipped his drink, placing the glass back on the table. "They're famous for their hard cider. They brew it themselves. You should try it."

"Another time." The dim lighting and the dark interior made me realize just how tired I was. I'd been running on caffeine for days, and if I wasn't careful, I'd probably crash, perhaps face first onto the polished tabletop. "You mentioned Jessika." It was time we move this conversation along.

Dalton nodded. "Yes. I saw her photo attached to her employee documentation. I remember her now. She was so serious and so young. The police still haven't found out what happened to her?"

I stared at him. "If we knew what happened, I wouldn't be bothering you with this."

He shook his head. "I misspoke. Do they have any ideas or theories on what might have happened to her or where she might have gone?"

"No."

He took another sip. "Is she really presumed dead?"

"Generally speaking, if a missing person isn't recovered within the first few days, it's unlikely she ever will be."

"Such a shame." He finished his drink and glanced around, catching the eye of a waitress and motioning for another one. "Are you sure you haven't changed your mind?" He glanced down at my sparkling water. "I hear they make amazing apple martinis."

"This is fine." I studied him. His hazel eyes seemed to glow gold in the dark atmosphere. He wore his watch on his right hand, an expensive Piaget I could probably hock for a new car, but that was the only ostentatious thing about him. "What else do you remember about Jessika?"

He leaned back. "Like I said, she was serious. A lot of the volunteers we get at the clinic don't really want to be there. We get the usual court mandated group every once in a while, but most are students looking to make hours for their respective programs. CNAs, LPNs, RNs, you get the point. Jessika was different. She was only in high school, but she wanted to learn everything. See everything. It was fascinating to her."

"What did she see?"

"Not much, I'm afraid. Most of our patients show up with common infections or basic injuries. We have several who can't afford healthcare and are hoping the clinic can offer them some method of managing chronic illness and disease progression, but without the right meds, that's a difficult feat."

"And Jessika saw these things?"

"Occasionally. I remember one time this little boy came in for stitches. He was freaking out and crying because his leg was cut up from getting caught in his bike chain, so the nurse went looking for something to distract him. And Jessika comes into the room with a sock and a marker, makes a puppet, and performs a show while I stitched up his leg. The entire time she was entertaining him, she was watching how the stitches were done. It was the craziest thing. The kid loved it. I don't even think he realized what was happening. And after they left, she had a million questions about stitches and the chances of infection and scarring."

"Was it always like that?"

"Unfortunately, no. She probably spent more time organizing the stockroom and taking inventory than watching actual exams or procedures." He smiled at the waitress when she replaced his empty glass with a new one. "Jess ran a lot of errands for us. We'd send her down to the soup kitchen and the homeless shelter to bring them supplies or ask for some basic things." He laughed bitterly. "One day, we ran out of tongue depressors. The city doesn't allocate much funding for the clinic, and we had to ask the soup kitchen if we could borrow a box of plastic knives to substitute."

"I thought the clinic was privately funded." Henry Brandt cut the checks or asked donors to cut the checks.

"It is, but given the location and dedication to public service, we still receive government grants. Healthcare is expensive. No matter how much money we receive, it's never enough." My eyes darted to the expensive timepiece on his wrist, and he tugged on his sleeve. "That's why I try to help as much as I can. It feels good to give back."

"Jessika came from money. Did she ever offer to donate to the clinic or suggest her family could help?" That might be motive for a kidnapping, if a patient or clinic worker became desperate enough.

"Not that I recall. She might have mentioned her mom working for a charity or something, but she wanted to do this on her own. She was already giving so much of her time and energy. She really wanted to help, but I don't think she wanted her family involved. I got the impression she wanted something that was just hers."

"Interesting you should say that. She was a minor. I've been made to understand due to her work schedule and the nature of the clinic she was required to have parental permission to volunteer. Did you ever meet either of her parents?"

His brow furrowed. "I don't remember. I just remember the helpful young lady who showed up a few times a week with a smile on her face." He looked out the window. "It's a shame she just vanished. She would have been something."

"Like you said, she was a pretty girl. That's a rough neighborhood. Did anyone ever take a particular interest in her?"

"Not that I remember."

"How often do you treat gang members?"

He almost spit out the sip he was taking. "I wouldn't know."

I smiled. "Sure, you would. That area is controlled by the Seven Rooks. Shootings and stabbings are common. I'm guessing ODs probably are too. You must see them frequently."

His eyes narrowed. "We are required by law to report violent crimes. We have treated gunshot wounds and victims of muggings, but we've always notified the police. What are you implying?"

"I'm not implying anything. I'm asking if it's possible Jessika could have seen something she wasn't supposed to or caught the attention of someone dangerous."

"Anything's possible." He checked the time and finished his drink. "It's getting late. I have early morning rounds."

"Just one last question," I said, resisting the urge to mention he was the one who invited me here. "When she went missing, her face was everywhere. How come no one from the clinic ever informed the police she volunteered?"

"I don't know."

"Why didn't you? You remembered the sock puppet story five years later. Why didn't you remember it when the cops questioned you a week later?"

"I don't have an answer. I work long hours. My job is

stressful. Even science doesn't fully understand how the mind works. Maybe I just thought those occurrences happened at the hospital instead of the clinic. I was bouncing from place to place. I had no idea where I was or what I was doing half the time."

"And yet you were treating sick people. That doesn't seem particularly wise."

"Free clinics get bad reputations. We didn't need to risk losing additional funding with bad publicity. And we didn't have anything to do with her disappearance. There was nothing for us to report. She just stopped showing up one day. That was it. It's been five years. Since you care so much, why did it take you this long to find us?"

I held up my palms and leaned back. "I'm not the one who called and asked you to drinks to talk about this. Obviously, you must have wanted to say something. Maybe you were hoping to clear your guilty conscience."

"This was a mistake. I didn't have anything to do with her disappearance. Why would I have given you her file if I did? The fact that it happened makes me sick. I hope you find her. I really do. I'm sorry I didn't remember sooner or tell the police Jessika volunteered at the clinic, but I can guarantee you're looking in the wrong place. The clinic and the people there had nothing to do with it."

TWENTY

After leaving Apple Top, I couldn't shake the thought the doctor doth protest too much. Sure, I was butchering Shakespeare, but Dr. Dalton was caught in a lie. And his excuse was he didn't remember. It might have been the truth, but his reasoning that her disappearance would have hurt the clinic might be motive to conceal some key facts, like the dangers of being in proximity to that neighborhood.

Determined to find out what really went on at the clinic, I went back to the office and checked to see if the support staff ever tracked down the three clinic employees who no longer volunteered there. One of them died in a car accident a year and a half ago. Another was working for Doctors Without Borders and couldn't be reached in the middle of the jungle, and the third was MIA.

Out of ideas, I called O'Connell, hoping he'd have a suggestion. The next thing I knew, I was sitting beside him in an unmarked car. Going back into gang territory alone wasn't ideal, but as long as I had a police escort, it would be fine. Maybe there was something going on near or around the clinic I missed.

"With the way you make friends, it's no wonder the majority of the people in this neighborhood want you dead," Nick mused.

I sighed. It was a little after one in the morning. After the police raid on Friday, the remaining hookers were taking precautions in how they approached potential clients. The dealers were equally subdued, sticking to the porches and stoops. They weren't conducting the usual handoffs due to the more frequent patrols. Plus, they were low on manpower. Their ranks had been severely decimated.

"What the hell are we even doing here?" he asked.

"Waiting."

"No shit." A low growl rumbled through his chest.

I stared out the window at the clinic. Several people passed by, but no one lingered near it. "I'm trying to figure out why Dr. Dalton wanted to meet for drinks."

"Sparrow ran him and everyone from the clinic as soon as she received confirmation Jessika volunteered there. Everyone came out clean. The worst violation we found was a DUI."

"I know." The exhaustion was starting to show. I was tired and cranky. And since I dragged Nick along, he was a bit cranky too. "Something tracks back to this neighborhood. I was attacked twice. Samantha Capshaw was targeted probably for being too close to William Wellington, and none of those things happened until I started asking about Jessika. The clinic is her only tie to this place, so there's something to it."

He scratched his head and fiddled with the radio. "That's why I agreed to this pathetic stakeout. But I don't think we're going to accomplish anything, unless someone gets shot."

I thought for a moment. "Someone did get shot. Actually, a few people were injured. I put a bullet in that one guy's shoulder, remember?"

"Yeah, and he went to the emergency room. They gave us a call, and that's when we arrested him. He didn't go to the clinic."

My mind went back to the bar brawl which happened a

couple of blocks from here. "What about reported stabbings?"

O'Connell shook his head. "It's easier to lie about that than a GSW."

"How? My knife went through a guy's side. It would be pretty damn obvious." I bit my lip, thinking. "That was the same knife used in the attack against Capshaw. You can't tell me it's a coincidence."

"Well, it's not like someone went to the ER with the blade sticking out. You said you stabbed a second guy in the foot. Maybe they picked up some band-aids or a needle and thread and figured that was good enough."

"You ran the knife for prints. And it didn't have any."

"Not even a smudge."

I rubbed a hand down my face and stared at the sign on the door. "Those guys could have been patched up right here. The bartender might know something. He seems to have a good grasp on the local happenings."

"I thought he told you not to come back."

"I'm running out of ideas. What do you think we should do?"

"We should call it a night. It's been a long day, and I'm damn tired. We've already looked through the clinic's records and spoke to the staff. Everyone and everything appears as it should, but I'll see about dropping by during the day for a surprise visit."

"Did you ask the staff about Jessika?"

"They vaguely remember her. They didn't remember if she had any friends or if anyone took a special interest in her. It's been five years. We don't have a snowball's chance in hell of a recovery. The brass doesn't want to waste the manpower, so they denied Sparrow's request to have a surveillance unit sit on the clinic. I'm hoping narcotics or gangs might have a more persuasive argument. Several members of the Seven Rooks were in possession of pharmaceutical grade narcotics. The free clinic is my best guess on where they obtained them. But as of yet, no one's willing to cooperate."

"Big surprise. What about William Wellington and Samantha Capshaw? Did either of them remember anything useful?"

"When we floated the theory that the attacker might have some connection to his daughter's disappearance, William got pretty upset. He said this was different and warned us not to conflate issues."

"Someone's trying to scare him off. He met with Cross this morning. I bet my boss knows more than he's saying."

O'Connell rubbed a hand down his face. "You should ask him. In the meantime, we'll do what we can. My guess is one of the corner boys will get antsy and freak out. Once he does, he'll give up the supplier, and with any luck, that will lead straight to the clinic. We'll find the connection between the clinic and Jessika's disappearance. It'll just take some time. Be patient."

I curled up on the seat and rested my forehead against the window. "You're convinced something went down at the clinic which led to Jessika vanishing?"

"Yep. The same as you. But we're not solving this one tonight. How about I drop you off at home?"

"Thanks." This felt like giving up, but there was nothing else to be done. It was time to sit back and wait, at least for another day or two.

* * *

It was the weekend. I slept most of the day, went for a run, videochatted with Martin, and checked my office voicemail. There were no messages. I checked in with the precinct to see if they made any progress. Apparently, word got around I was no longer a federal agent which meant my questions were met with unhelpfulness and hostility instead of just hostility. Oh well, at least my friends in blue were still willing to toss me a bone every now and again.

Around seven, Mark Jablonsky showed up at my doorstep. Arriving with dinner in hand, he made himself comfortable in my apartment and grilled me for most of the evening about my new job. He felt responsible for my resignation. Our last case together got us into hot water, and I fell on my sword to save his career. If I didn't, we'd both be facing unemployment and possibly a criminal investigation. At least I might have, and that was something I couldn't afford. My checkered past needed to remain in the past.

"You're sure you had nothing to do with Cross hiring me?" I asked skeptically. A few years ago, I walked away from the OIO after an op went south and two agents were killed. My guilt and depression left me paralyzed on the couch for weeks on end. So any time I faced a life-altering hiccup, Mark became concerned. "I was still in Spain when he set up the interview. We had to fly back early on account of it, and he hired me on the spot. Things like that don't normally happen."

Mark held up his hands innocently. "It wasn't me. I bent over backward to get you those four job offers from other government agencies, and you didn't even have the courtesy to call anyone back." He looked annoyed. "Hell, you didn't even have the courtesy to call me back. And then I find out you're working for that shark. Unbelievable. I thought you hated corporate work."

"I'm not doing corporate work."

He gave me a pointed look. "Give it time." He spooned another helping onto his plate. "So what are you doing?"

"Missing persons case." I told him everything I uncovered. "Her disappearance has to be linked to the clinic."

"Or the neighborhood," he surmised. "Without a ransom, the motive wasn't monetary. Someone needed Jessika Wellington to disappear. If they wanted her as a sex worker, she would have been picked up for solicitation by now. The Seven Rooks aren't entrepreneurial enough to be involved in human trafficking. They deal in the usual things, drugs, guns, and whores. What about the bartender? Prince, was it? His record would indicate he has out-of-state connections. He could have made her disappear."

"We looked into him. He already established his presence in the neighborhood by then, but he wasn't around at the time of her abduction. He actually has an alibi for the entire month, and the ATF agents who keep tabs on his movements can vouch for him."

"Is that what the ATF told you?"

"Yeah."

Mark wiped his mouth with a napkin. "At this point, it's best to assume she's dead. Whoever killed her doesn't want anyone else poking around, which is probably why the dad's girlfriend was attacked. It probably also means Jessika's father knows something about what happened and the killer wants him to keep quiet."

"If he knew something, why wouldn't he have come forward when Jessika was taken? We are talking about his daughter. His own flesh and blood."

"You said he has something to hide. Maybe he's implicated somehow. We don't know what types of illegal things he might be involved in, but money laundering or insider trading is probably a given. The threat of his crimes coming to light might be enough to keep him quiet." He brushed at his upper lip. "I can do some checking."

"No. OPR was sniffing around two weeks ago. You don't need to call in any favors at the moment, especially on my account."

"Alex," he dragged out my name, making it apparent he felt guilty about the situation, "I can do this."

"I already had someone look into it. William Wellington did a good job of hiding his tracks, assuming we're correct. It'll take more than the OIO and a few forensic accountants to figure out what's going on. We need records of everything and lots of man hours. You can't commit those types of resources. If Cross decides he wants to do it, he can."

"I never thought I'd see the day you would defer an investigation to the ruling of your boss."

"He wants to keep the client happy. Apparently, that's necessary in order to get paid."

"What about concealing crimes?"

"We don't do that."

He cocked an eyebrow. "Are you sure?"

"I guess we'll find out." I blew out a breath. "In the meantime, I'm working on this, and the police are working on this. If there's something to find, we will. And if there isn't," I shrugged, "I still have a few job offers waiting in the wings."

"Just don't wait too long. You don't want to forget all your training."

After Mark left, I slumped on the couch. I didn't have any room left in my brain to reconsider the facts again. Not tonight. I'd been living and breathing this for the last week and a half. Instead, I went back to Mercer's case, needing a change of pace in the hopes of gaining a new perspective and fresh eyes when I tackled Jessika's disappearance again on Monday.

I spent the rest of the weekend parsing through the surveillance footage. By the end, I had a list of vehicles and plate numbers. I was collecting pieces. If I did it right, they'd fit together and point to the killer. It would just take time and energy, but my gut said this was progress. I needed a win, preferably two. And by Monday morning, I was ready to dive back in on all fronts.

Knocking on Kellan's door, I smiled and held out the bribe – a cappuccino from the coffee cart out front. I put the paper cup on his desk before speaking.

"How was your weekend?" I asked.

He snorted and lifted the lid off the cup. "No one made a move on Capshaw. She went to a wine bar with friends Saturday and spent time with her parents on Sunday. No one paid a damn bit of attention to her, not even William. I don't believe she was the intended target. I think she became the target of opportunity. I spoke to Lucien. He agrees. He also thinks we need to back off the surveillance and not interfere in the police investigation. Once the cops back off, you can go back to doing what you like."

"Great." My thoughts went to the clinic and drinks with Dr. Dalton. "Do you think we're going to figure this out?"

Kellan looked up. "Honestly, I don't. That doesn't mean you should throw in the towel. I hear Alex Parker is a stubborn bitch. Plus, it's fun having you across the hallway. I'd like to see you stick around."

"Well, that's contingent on this case." I moved to the doorway. "Thanks for helping."

He nodded. "One of us should do what we're told. Next time, I want to break the rules."

"You got it."

Returning to my office, I went through the updated files. There was absolutely nothing there I didn't read or see before. The things Cross chose to share about William were things Bastian and the police department previously provided. The third clinic worker remained MIA, and there wasn't a damn thing I could do about it.

Picking up the ringing phone, I wasn't surprised to hear Cross's gruff voice. "How did Friday evening with Dr. Dalton go?"

"How?" I shook the question from my lips, knowing the office calls were probably monitored. "I'm not sure." Seeing no reason to conceal anything, I gave Cross the play-by-play. "We need more on the clinic. The police have court orders for their records, but those are unlikely to shed light on whatever illegal activities are going on behind closed doors."

Cross took a moment before responding. "I'll check into it. You're probably correct to assume the clinic caters to the gang. They'd have to in order to survive without their drugs being stolen or the waiting room turning into a war zone. But you're probably barking up the wrong tree. I'll focus my efforts on the nurses or any doctor who grew up in a poor neighborhood. They'd understand the gang's plight better than an outsider and would be more likely to bend the rules. I'll keep you apprised."

"Sure, you will," I said to the dial tone.

I had to find someone who knew what went on inside the clinic. It was only logical to assume Jessika saw or heard something she wasn't supposed to, and someone made her disappear because of it. That was precisely what Jorge Toald said until he clammed up.

Biting my lip, I couldn't figure out how that connected to William or his mistress. Another thought went through my head. This time it involved hookers. Maybe daddy dearest picked up a working girl. Jessika might have seen him or heard about it. Perhaps he never told the authorities about his daughter working in the clinic because he was afraid of the dirt they'd find on him. It was speculation, but it was my best guess. Hell, it was my only guess.

TWENTY-ONE

Nick and I were huddled at a booth in the diner. Today the place was crowded. An older guy with a beer gut was eating scrambled eggs and pancakes at the counter, and a woman was feeding a toddler who sat in a booster seat at a table in the middle of the room. The two waitresses, Skye and Delores, were on shift to cover this bustling Monday afternoon.

I just finished telling him my theories, taking care to keep my voice low for fear someone might overhear. He stabbed the prongs of his fork into a slice of pumpkin pie, jerking his chin up slightly. I stopped speaking while Skye refilled our coffee cups.

She gave me a quizzical look. "Did you pay this guy to sit with you so you wouldn't look like a pathetic loner?" O'Connell snickered around a mouthful of pie, and I jabbed him with my spoon. "At least this means I don't have to waste my time talking to you," she quipped, an evil grin on her face.

"I'm sure your other customers will appreciate that. Run along now. This place is hoppin'."

She rolled her eyes. "No one says hoppin'. That went out with Richie Cunningham and poodle skirts."

"Aren't you too young for *Happy Days*?"

"And you aren't?" She raised a challenging eyebrow. "It's called streaming. But then again, I'm sure no one has ever asked you to Netflix and chill." She eyed O'Connell for a moment, but he focused his attention on the pie. "Would you like another piece, mister? Maybe something on the side?"

He checked the time and glanced out the window. "I'll give the blueberry a try." He looked at my lonely coffee mug. "You feeling okay, Alex?"

"Yeah, why?"

In a stage whisper, he said, "They have pie." I shook my head, and he dismissed the waitress. "How long have you been coming here?"

"Since I started tailing Janet. It has the best view, even though the food's questionable and the waitress is difficult."

O'Connell studied Skye for a long moment as she went to the counter and spoke to the man. Her black hair was tied in braided pigtails today. It made her face look a little rounder, or maybe it was just a trick of the heavy makeup. Today she wore silver and black eyeliner which made her unnaturally blue eyes pop, completing the effect with glossy black lipstick.

Delores returned to the kitchen with an empty plate she grabbed off a table. On her way back, she cut a slice of pie and brought it to O'Connell at Skye's request. Unlike her counterpart, Delores was a sweet, middle-aged woman who talked while she worked and tended to hum as she bused the tables. "How's the pie?" she inquired.

"Excellent," O'Connell said, but I had a feeling he was lying to spare her feelings. "I'm surprised to find pumpkin on the menu. Isn't that a seasonal thing?"

"Everyone loves pumpkin pie." She wiped down a nearby table and went back to the kitchen.

"Pumpkin pie and a girl with zombie makeup, this place is Halloween year round," O'Connell murmured as he scraped some crust away from the blueberries, deciding the filling might be better on its own. "Is that why you come here so often?"

"Perhaps it is." My gaze turned to Skye who remained behind the counter, but she was staring out the window. I turned to see what caught her attention and watched Janet Wellington and three other women leave the gym. "Your mark's on the move."

"Yeah, I'm on it." O'Connell stood, grabbing his jacket. "I'll meet you tonight." He darted out the door, leaving me to cover the check.

Deciding not to waste the rest of the day, I went to the counter to pay, but Skye was gone. Delores ambled over, and I paid for the coffee and pie, dropping a twenty in the tip jar for the two of them to split. Then I walked out of the diner and back to my car, catching a glimpse of those jet black pigtails near the dumpster. Obviously, someone had to take out the trash, and tonight, O'Connell and I would hopefully be picking up some trash of our own.

The late afternoon crept into evening while I analyzed the last five years of arrest records involving prostitution. William Wellington's name never surfaced, but I finally found a name and address for the woman I dubbed Smokey. Her name was Ivy Greene. I suspected it was an alias. She lived in the apartment building across from the clinic and had priors for prostitution and possession.

After performing another search, I found she filed a report concerning an assault. It was dated two days before Jessika's disappearance. The photos in the police file were brutal. Ivy's face was swollen and bruised, and the rest of her didn't look much better. It sounded like some john roughed her up, and the police never did much about it. I blew out a breath and printed a copy of the file. Did William Wellington do this to her? Or did the same man do something worse to Jessika?

Filing the thought away, I grabbed my things and left the office. O'Connell's shift was about to end, and we had a date with a hooker. If luck was on our side, tonight would be a threesome.

*   *   *

We cruised the neighborhood for the better part of an

hour. Patrols had lessened, so the dealers and hookers were out in force to make up for the nights of lost revenue. In this capitalistic society, no one wanted to operate in the red, and being out of business for a few nights might mean customers would find a new place to shop. I pointed to a group of women huddled near the pharmacy. A few of them were smoking and watching traffic patterns as if they were on the prowl.

"Ivy's wearing the purple sequined halter and the leather miniskirt," I said.

O'Connell nodded, continuing in the opposite direction. He turned at the first opening and stopped the car. Removing his cell phone, he dialed my number. I answered, and he put his on speaker while I muted mine. Then he tucked it above the visor. "Can you hear me?"

"You might want to wait until I get out of the car before you ask." I opened the door. "Be careful."

"Not a problem."

I closed the door and found an out of the way spot near the liquor store. Sliding to the ground, I pulled the bill of the baseball cap lower and held the phone to my ear, listening to O'Connell conduct a sound check. I gave him a thumbs up, and he backed the car away and headed down the street.

He found a parking space near the pharmacy and idled. Now we just had to wait. I observed enough to know this was how deals were done. Since the girls were being extra careful who they approached on account of their pimps and protection being in custody, O'Connell thought approaching a dealer would be unexpected and arouse less suspicion. I didn't disagree, but it posed a bit more risk. And the last thing I wanted was to explain to his wife or his partner how something went wrong.

"Trust me," O'Connell said, "I know what I'm doing." That made one of us.

It took nearly twenty minutes before someone approached the car. From this distance, I couldn't see a face. After two soft taps, Nick rolled down the window. I pressed my phone closer to my ear, holding my breath while I waited. My other hand inched toward the nine millimeter at my side, but I didn't grasp it. Forcing my eyes to scan the surrounding area, no one was paying the car any attention. So far, so good.

"Hey, man," Nick said, his voice sounding a bit breathy and frantic. He was probably twitching a bit, trying to come off nervous or in desperate need of something. "What's going on? I've been having one long ass night, you feel me?"

"Yo. Whatcha need, baby?" The guy outside the car checked the area and the back seat before leaning down and opening his jacket. "I got smoke, coke, uppers, downers. Whichever way you want to go, I can make that happen."

O'Connell swallowed. "Yeah, um, that's not exactly what I was looking for, y'know what I'm saying?"

"Oh, you want to go sideways, baby. I can make that happen too. What flavor you looking for tonight? I got some Asian, some Ethiopian, a bit of fusion." The dealer chuckled. "A boy like you probably wants some white bread, huh?"

After a few moments, O'Connell spoke again. "That glittering plum looks tasty."

A shrill whistle sounded through the speaker, but I resisted pulling the phone away. "Ivy, get yo' ass over here, girl. I got a new friend for you to meet," the dealer yelled. "How freaky do you want to get?"

O'Connell shrugged, waiting for Ivy to open the door. "Like you said, I just want to get sideways." He turned toward her. "Is the back seat okay?"

I couldn't hear what she responded or if she responded, but the man asked for the money upfront. O'Connell passed him a wad of cash through the open window, and the dealer directed him to move the party to the parking garage half a block away. The system set up didn't take into account the hooker's safety, but no one ever said hooking was a safe profession. But since it was the oldest, someone should have come up with something better by now.

As soon as the car began moving, I did too. Given that the garage was positioned between O'Connell and myself, I actually made it inside before he did. We planned everything out earlier after watching a few other transactions occur. I knew where Nick would park, so I ducked into the shadows and waited.

"At least wait until I put it in park," Nick said, and I figured Ivy must be getting handsy. The car pulled into the space, and O'Connell killed the lights and the engine. I waited a beat. "What's your name, gorgeous?"

"Ivy," she purred. "How do you want to start? My hands, my mouth, or my pussy?"

"Get in the back," he commanded.

She made an ooh sound and slid between the two seats, spreading out on the back. "Is this how you want me?"

"About that," O'Connell said, hitting the locks the moment I opened the door, "it turns out I'm not in the mood." He glanced at me, seeing my gun aimed at the hooker. That wasn't exactly by the book, but I was a private investigator. We didn't have books. "I believe you know my friend."

"Bitch," she hissed, sitting up and tugging her skirt back into place. "What the hell do you want? Haven't you learned your lesson yet? If anyone from the Seven Rooks spots you, you're as good as dead." Her glare turned to O'Connell. "Both of you."

He removed his badge from the center console and held it up. "Did you know it's illegal to threaten a police officer?"

"Shit." She gave the rear door handle a tug, but it didn't budge on account of the child safety locks. Whoever invented those was a genius. "What the fuck do you want from me?"

I slipped my gun back into the holster, knowing she didn't have anywhere to conceal a weapon. "I want to know what happened to Jessika Wellington. And I'm not going away until I find out. Make this easy on yourself and your gangbanger buddies and just tell me the truth. I know Jessika volunteered at the free clinic. That puts her in this neighborhood and on gang turf. What happened?"

"The Rooks didn't do nothing to her," Ivy spat. "Nothing. And I don't know nothing either."

"Yes, you do. You said as much the first time we spoke."

Her face scrunched in annoyance. "I did not. I played

you, fool. I got twenty bucks, and you got chased off by Rodney and Dario. That's all that happened." Her eyes betrayed the lie, and when she couldn't take my stare any longer, she looked out the window. "You want to arrest me, go ahead. This is entrapment. I know my rights."

"I don't want to arrest you," Nick said. "We need your help." Removing a copy of the photographs from Ivy's reported assault, Nick passed the paper back to her. "I'm sorry that happened to you."

She glanced at the photograph before crinkling it in her lap. She tongued the inside of her lip. "Yeah, right. Not a single cop gave a damn. Whore got what she deserved."

"Do you know who did that to you?" I asked.

She shook her head. "That was a long time ago. I've been more careful since. The Rooks protect me now. Well, they did until you had them arrested. Now I'm just trying to get enough cash together to get the hell out of here. Shit's getting real."

"What's going on?" O'Connell asked.

She shrugged one shoulder and played with her hair. O'Connell tossed a concerned glance in my direction. That wasn't good news, but the gangs unit suspected someone would move into the territory if the remaining Seven Rooks didn't solidify their control fast enough. She stared out the window, swallowing.

"Why didn't the Rooks protect you when this happened?" I asked, flicking the end of the photo and drawing her attention back to us.

"Back then, this was a solo act. I needed cash, and I did what had to be done. Whatever had to be done." She swallowed again. "After that night, I knew I needed protection. They've taken good care of me. Jorge and Rodney, they watch out for me. They keep me safe. And they wouldn't like me talking to either of you."

I scrolled through my phone, finding a photo of William Wellington and holding it up. "Is this the man who hurt you?"

She glanced at it. "I don't remember. It's been years. All those rich, white guys look the same."

"From the report, you refused to go to the hospital. Did

you go to the clinic?" I asked. She blinked, tapping her nails on her thigh. She probably wanted to smoke but didn't have a cigarette handy. "They do a lot for this community, right? They patch up whoever gets hurt. They deal with ODs. They help everyone, including the bangers and whores."

Her shoulders shot up half an inch, but she continued to stare out the window.

"Is that when you met Jessika Wellington?" O'Connell asked.

She turned her head from side to side, struggling to find a way out, but we had her trapped. "The girl was at the front desk when Dario brought me there. The things I'd done didn't matter. She didn't make me wait out front with the sick people. She took me straight back to a room and called the doctor. That was the first and last time I ever saw her."

"That was it?" I asked. It didn't coincide with what she alluded to during our first encounter.

She shrugged. "Yeah."

"Anyone else ever mention her afterward?" O'Connell asked. "Maybe Dario thought he'd recruit some new talent."

She flushed slightly. "How'd you know that?"

He snorted. "I didn't. Now I do. Did the gang take her?"

"No. They took me instead. That's when I went to work for them instead of myself. I needed a pimp to protect me from the johns. That's how I hooked up with Jorge." Her eyes went to the dashboard clock, and I saw the slightest bemused smile dot her lips.

"He's out of the picture now," I said. "So is Rodney. Which one's Dario? Is he still around?"

"You already met him," she said, suddenly looking confident.

"We're running out of time," I said to O'Connell, figuring we had another ten minutes before someone came looking.

"What about Jessika? Did Jorge or Dario mention her again? Did you hear whispers they sold her?" O'Connell asked.

Ivy laughed. "You're talking about some small time dealers and pimps. No one gets sold around here. And when the girl stopped showing up at the clinic, they lost interest. Out of sight, out of mind."

"Did you tell her to stay away?" I asked.

Ivy snorted derisively. "I had enough of my own problems. I didn't have time to worry about anyone else."

"What about the other people at the clinic?" O'Connell asked.

"What about them?" she retorted.

"Did any of them have a problem with Jessika? Take a special liking to her?"

She snickered. "How the hell would I know? I was beaten half to death. I had more important things on my mind than some stupid girl."

"Does anyone at the clinic work for the gang on the side?" O'Connell asked. "The bangers probably need to get patched up from time to time, and they can't afford the police getting in the way. I just need a name."

She laughed. "Damn, you people really don't understand how this works, do you?"

"Enlighten us," I urged.

"That clinic does what the fuck it wants. They have an understanding with the Rooks, and the Rooks own everyone and everything that steps foot on their turf," her eyes went to mine, "including you. You just don't know it yet. No one's going to tell you anything because they know what will happen." She looked out the window. "Your time's up. You better let me out unless you want to bring World War III down on your asses."

I glanced at Nick. We knew she'd be released from custody within a day, and it wouldn't get us anywhere. She was more afraid of the gang than the cops, and even from jail, they could still reach her. This life was about self-preservation, and she did whatever she needed in order to survive. Nothing we said or did would change that.

"Are you going to tell anyone we spoke?" I asked.

She shook her head. "No fucking way. They have trust issues. If they even think I talked to you, I'll be feeling it for weeks. Now open this car door." She turned to Nick. "And I need another fifty. You ran over your time." I threw two twenties and a ten into her lap while Nick stepped out and opened the rear door. "Pleasure doing business with you." She kissed him on the cheek and strutted out of the garage. Despite the confidence, she was scared. She just wouldn't allow us to exploit it.

TWENTY-TWO

"Jen will be so proud you picked up a hooker last night,"
I murmured in Nick's ear.

"You paid for her."

"But she gave you a kiss."

His glance was searing. "It's not like that, and my wife
doesn't need to hear about it," he continued to glower,
"unless you want Martin to hear about the bar fight.
Doesn't he get back today? Perhaps I'll call him to say
hello."

"Fine." I pantomimed zipping my lip. "Mum's the
word." My eyes darted across the street to the gym where
Mrs. Wellington was taking a pilates class. "Did the PD
turn up anything on Ivy's story? Do we know who wants to
take control of the neighborhood, or why she's so freaked
out?"

"The gang's not talking."

"What about the clinic? Sparrow said she was going
through their records. If what Ivy said is true, there has to
be proof somewhere. The Seven Rooks would only protect
the clinic if they're getting something out of the deal. Do we
know what that might be? Since they're incarcerated, you
must have gotten search warrants for their cell phones. Do

any of the calls or numbers correspond to clinic personnel?"

"Alex, we're working on it." He poked at the cherry pie. Apparently, he didn't learn his lesson with yesterday's slice of blueberry. "Nothing telling has popped up yet. The calls link to unregistered burners. They're careful. So it'll take some time to trace everything. What about Cross Security? Shouldn't you know something about something? You people get paid enough. You should be fucking encyclopedias on every criminal enterprise in this city."

"We would be if the cars didn't cost so damn much." I drove the company car today, figuring I should get some use out of it while I could. "That's what's eating up our client fees. We're too busy dressing the part to actually know anything."

He raised an unbelieving eyebrow. "I doubt that very much." He scooped some whipped cream onto his fork. "Do you still think William beat the shit out of a hooker? Ivy didn't exactly deny it."

I thought about the look on Ivy's face when I showed her his photo. I didn't see any recognition in her eyes, but maybe after a few tricks, the johns just became faceless, nameless dicks in every sense of the word. "I don't know. If his porn preferences are any indication, it's possible."

"But you rather think the clinic is involved in Jessika's disappearance than her father."

"Yeah."

"That doesn't explain why Capshaw was attacked a few nights ago." He was playing devil's advocate.

"Maybe it does. Ivy said the clinic and the Seven Rooks have an arrangement, and the Rooks will retaliate against anyone who messes with the neighborhood. William hired me to look into his daughter's disappearance. Perhaps the attack was their dumbass way of getting him to back off."

O'Connell wasn't convinced. "I don't know."

"There's a lot of that going around." I fell silent, drinking my coffee and thinking about everything I didn't know. Bastian's words haunted me. "Janet said she knew nothing about Jessika working for that particular clinic. William denied signing the form, and when I spoke to him, it didn't seem like he knew anything about his daughter. That means Jessika must have forged the signature, but do you think her mother was really that clueless?"

"Her daughter was a good kid. She had no reason not to trust her. Her husband is a different story. Their marriage hasn't been functional for some time. They probably went through the motions, but she must have felt the distance. Whenever he started to pull away, she noticed. Her attention was probably focused on him and not the kid. I bet that's why they're separated now. She blames him, even if she doesn't realize it."

"You don't think it has anything to do with his infidelity?"

"That's a symptom of an underlying problem, not the cause."

I assessed him for a moment. "You spoke to their marriage counselor."

He shrugged, picking up his mug and taking a sip. "Maybe we happened to be eating breakfast at the same place this morning and got to talking. Purely off the record, hypothetical situations only. Y'know, the way most of our conversations go."

"Did he say anything about William's sexual fantasies?"

O'Connell worked his jaw for a moment. "As long as he expresses them in a healthy manner, it doesn't mean he's a deviant or violent. He might just be curious."

"Did you ask about the possibility he might have beaten a hooker?"

"I did. He didn't think it was likely."

Snorting, I shook my head. "Sixty hours of videos featuring violent hate sex with barely legal women saved on his laptop begs to differ. I'd say that's more than curiosity or a passing fascination." I rested my head in my hands. "What if he molested Jessika? That might explain why she disappeared."

His lips formed a grim line. "Nothing indicates that was the case. When Jessika disappeared, Sparrow went through her medical records. We even had a psychological profile drawn up. Jessika didn't have the victim mentality. You read her texts and messages. She was a little introverted, not secretive or withdrawn. She was just driven. That's probably why she forged her mom's name on the application. She wanted to volunteer at the clinic. Face it, she was too young and naïve to realize the kinds of dangers a place like that might conceal, and her yutz advisor was way too gung-ho about encouraging it. As a teacher, she should have known better."

We fell silent for a time, and I glanced around the nearly empty diner. It was the middle of the afternoon. The slump of the day. Skye was hanging out in the kitchen, avoiding us. She looked bored and checked the time every few minutes. Her jet black hair was pulled back in a ponytail with long side swept bangs practically covering her right eye. It made it impossible to tell if the dozen piercings in her left eyebrow matched the ones on the other side. She had a bull ring in her nose, and studs all around her ears. No one could tell me that didn't hurt.

Sighing loudly, she maneuvered around the counter to refill our coffee cups. "Anything else, I can get for you?"

A glance at Nick told me one piece of pie was his limit today, and he had to move as soon as Mrs. Wellington emerged from the gym. "Just the check."

"Yep." She went around the counter, pressed a few buttons on the cash register, and came back. "You can leave it on the table. I'm going on break."

It wasn't our normal semi-hostile banter. "Is everything okay?"

"It's fine." She glanced uncertainly at Nick. "You don't need me to stand around and talk to you, do you? Isn't that what you have him for?"

"Jealous?" I teased, but she didn't respond with a comeback.

"Like I said, I'm going on break." Without waiting for a response, she walked away.

"Sure thing, Skye," I replied. She didn't even acknowledge me. Skye. What kind of name was that? She didn't look like a bottle of vodka or even old enough to drink vodka, not that the spelling was the same, but frequent intoxication might explain the pierced goth look. "Damn, I'm old."

O'Connell chuckled, clearly having read my thoughts. "It's the thing now. Piercings, tattoos, it's about personal expression. It's artistic. It doesn't mean she has or will be incarcerated at any point in the future. It's just a look. It's cool."

"If I was into that look, half of my face would have been torn off in a fight."

"Yeah," he said slowly, dragging the word out. "That's the price you pay for artistic expression."

I dug some cash out of my wallet to cover the bill and a decent tip. I didn't want Skye to get more annoyed with me than she already was. Maybe it wasn't me. She did seem pretty hostile toward O'Connell. Deciding it was his fault, I relaxed in the seat. Next time I stopped by, I'd make sure he wasn't with me. And maybe I'd order a salad or some soup, just to mix it up and keep her on her toes. For a moment, I wasn't even sure why I cared so much. But there was something about her. She seemed like a lost soul with sad eyes, alone in a sea of millions of people. Perhaps I recognized her as a kindred spirit. Ten years ago, I felt the same. My adopted parents abandoned me, and I had nothing except my college courses and the desire to join the FBI. It was insane to think how so much changed in a decade. I wasn't the same person. Hell, I wasn't even the same person I had been a few years ago. Meeting Martin changed everything.

"What are you thinking about?" Nick asked.

"Life." I took a deep breath. "Until we find some dirt on the clinic, I should focus on Julian Mercer's case."

"He saved my niece. If there's anything I can do to help, name it."

"I can handle this on my own. After all, he did save my life. So it's time I do something to salvage what's left of his."

O'Connell looked uncertain. "You're sure? I've never known you to work an investigation entirely on your own. The fact that we're inside a crappy diner is an excellent example of case in point."

"I already called in every favor I had when I was at the OIO, and Cross said I can use his experts and state of the art equipment to recreate the crime scene. The rest is just a matter of putting the pieces together. And for the record, the last time I did this private security thing, I worked plenty of cases on my own."

He began ticking off examples to the contrary, and I slapped his hand. "Fine. But I haven't forgotten the role you played in rescuing my niece. It doesn't matter how many favors you ask for. I'll always owe you."

I didn't like the sentimentality. "You don't owe me a damn thing. So don't you dare help me or risk yourself out of some skewed sense of obligation, or I'll just have to stop calling you all together."

"Really? Shit, I should have said that a long time ago." He grinned, letting me know it was a joke, and I balled up a napkin and threw it at him. He picked it up and put on his jacket. It was time to go. Nick held the door as we exited. "I imagine once we get something that substantially links the clinic to the gang or some other illegal activity, things will pick up. Until then, Sparrow has a few more interviews with the board that certifies the clinic and some hospital staff who have assisted there a time or two. After that, she'll move on to rest of the volunteers. Since people come and go, practically on a daily basis, it's guaranteed to keep us busy. I'll let you know if anything turns up."

"Thanks."

*　　*　　*

Unwilling to accept another defeat, I scooped the crime scene photos from Michelle Mercer's murder off my desk and went upstairs. The police would find something, and as soon as I knew what that was, I'd move on it. But for now, sitting behind my desk and being frustrated and pissed wouldn't help anyone. At least this was a productive way to spend my time.

The thirty-first floor was incredible. The level was partitioned off into different sections and labs; each filled with whatever equipment was necessary for those specific tasks. The woman working reception smiled when I stepped foot out of the elevator, noticing the ID badge clipped to my white blouse.

"Miss Parker," she nodded, "Mr. Cross said you might be dropping by to see us." Her eyes went to the file in my hands. "What can we do for you?"

"Um..."

"We have the equipment and means necessary to conduct evidence analysis. Our computer experts are able to run traces, conduct surveillance, analyze footage." She waited, hoping I'd make a selection.

"I don't need any of that." I blew out a breath. "Mr. Cross mentioned a crime scene could be reconstructed."

"Ah, follow me." She led the way to an empty room that smelled faintly of bleach. "Is this a large enough area?" The right side of the room had a counter with cabinets, drawers, and a sink.

"It's actually bigger than I need."

She shook off the comment. "Our resident crime scene expert has left for the night. His protégé is here, but she's working on another investigation. You can help yourself or leave the information with me and someone will get this room ready for you in the next day or two."

"Help myself?"

Opening a drawer, she pulled out some masking tape. "Everything you need should be here. Everything's labeled. Is this a ballistics issue? To ensure laser point accuracy, you might want to have someone do it for you."

"No, I don't need anything that precise." I suddenly found myself wanting to be left alone with all the neat toys. Being a field agent meant analyzing the scenes in the field, not hanging around with the geniuses inside the federal building who handed us the information on a silver platter or collected it from the most disgusting and disturbing of places. "I think I can manage."

"Very good, ma'am. I'll make sure no one disturbs the room. Mr. Cross said you might need a few days. So set up whatever you like and take your time."

After I thanked her, I rummaged through the drawers. Taped to the wall behind the countertop were basic instructions on how to reconstruct a scene. Step one, mark the designated area. Step two, place markers where necessary. Step three, recreate the crime using props.

After an hour, Mercer's kitchen was represented by masking tape marking the white tile floor. I marked the counter, the doorway, the table, everything. Then I taped the photos to the wall so I could examine them to make sure it was accurate.

Next, I unrolled the plastic and covered the floor before I made a mess. They even had an assortment of dummies, but positioning one wouldn't help much. Mercer held his wife during her final moments. When the police arrived, they had to pry her out of his arms. I blinked back the emotion, remembering this wasn't for fun. This was nothing like the staged crime scenes we examined at Quantico. This was real.

Returning to the photos, I studied the bloodstains on the floor, the pool of red where Michelle bled out, the bloody footprints and smudges that surrounded the body. Something itched at the corners of my mind. It didn't look right. Stepping back, I examined my handiwork in relation to the photo. Even though the photos contained three-dimensional objects, I knew everything was in the right place, but something was missing.

Finding a dye pack meant to imitate real blood, I opened the pack and dribbled it onto the plastic sheet representing where her body lay. Using a sponge, I dabbed around it, creating a fairly reasonable facsimile of how the blood spread and smeared across the floor. I marked where it was tracked by shoeprints. Aside from a few bloody smudges on the counter, the rest of the carnage was contained to the place on the floor.

I sat back on my heels and stared at the room. Deciding I needed some three-dimensional representation, I found some disassembled boxes and foam boards in one of the cabinets and recreated the island and counters in Mercer's kitchen. Checking the photos again to determine blood patterns, I realized what was wrong. There was no spatter. Not in the pictures and not in the recreated scene.

After borrowing a knife, I grabbed a second dye pack from the drawer and placed it on the ground. Stabbing the bag, I left the knife inside while I checked the photos again.

Michelle was stabbed multiple times. From the coroner's report, any one of them would have been fatal. The police speculated whoever did this was a professional but wanted to make it look like a random act of violence. Of course, that went perfectly with their theory that Julian murdered his wife. But I wasn't buying it.

As slowly as possible, I yanked the knife out of the bag. The blood dripped onto the floor but didn't spray. Granted, if the killer hit an artery, blood would have sprayed from the wound, but the odd thing was there was no drip pattern from where the knife was removed and thrust into the victim again. The attack was slow and methodical. I also determined which wound he inflicted first. The first strike immobilized Michelle since there were no defensive wounds or evidence she fought back. It was too clean.

Closing my eyes, I cringed. It must have been terrifying and excruciating to stare into the eyes of her attacker, feeling the knife cut through her flesh, and not be able to do anything to stop it. Did she think about Julian? Did she believe he would save her? He got to her so fast. Perhaps thirty seconds or a minute sooner would have meant the difference between life and death. I blinked back the tears. No wonder he was tormented.

"Miss Parker," I jumped at the sound of my name, wiping away a wayward tear with the back of my hand, "downstairs just phoned. There's someone here to see you. He doesn't have an appointment. We can ask him to schedule one."

I shook my head, dazed and upset by my recent revelation. "Who's here?"

"James Martin."

"Have him wait in my office. I just need to wash up." I held up my palms which were caked in red food coloring and corn syrup.

After my hands were clean, I gave the room another glance. It didn't serve a purpose, but it forced me to analyze the photos in greater detail. How did we miss this? The blade was removed slowly, only far enough to be repositioned and thrust into Michelle again. The drip patterns were masked by the pooled blood. There was no rushed force. The killer wasn't hurrying. He was savoring. Wondering if Bastian also failed to notice this, I gnawed on that thought as I made my way downstairs and to my office. Like they said, no news was good news.

TWENTY-THREE

"Hey, handsome," my voice was shaky from the macabre epiphany, "what are you doing here?"

Martin was examining the bar cart and turned. The smile quickly evaporated from his face. "Jesus." His eyes darted into the hallway, and he strode to me, his cell phone already in hand. "Take it easy. I've got you. I'll get help. Who did this? Is he still here?" He eased one hand around my back, as if I might collapse.

"What?"

"Sit down, sweetheart." He reached for my nine millimeter, and I grabbed his hand. "Is he out there?"

"Martin, you're scaring me. What the hell's going on?"

His eyes dropped to my stomach, just as the 911 operator picked up. I looked down, seeing the front of my shirt covered in a thick layer of fake blood. Shaking my head, I yanked the hem of my shirt free from my pants and undid the bottom buttons. His fingers skimmed across my unmarred flesh while the operator asked him for the third time about the nature of his emergency.

"Hang up the phone," I urged. "It's dye. The bag dripped. I didn't notice it."

"I'm sorry. I was mistaken." He dropped the phone onto

the chair. His hand shook as he explored the rest of my abdomen in disbelief. He let out a ragged exhale, grasped my face, and kissed me. His hands tangled in my hair, tugging me closer. "Don't you ever scare me like that again."

"I'm sorry," I managed to say around his kisses. He pulled me even closer. "You're going to get dye on your shirt."

"I don't care." He hugged me tightly. "I stopped by to surprise you. It wasn't supposed to be the other way around."

"That's what you get for showing up unannounced." Gently, I pushed him away and moved to my office door. I glanced out, but no one was in the vicinity. Just to be on the safe side, I closed the door and flipped the blinds on the windows. As it was, I wasn't positive Cross didn't have the rooms bugged. "When did your flight land?"

"Three hours ago." He ran a hand down his face and dropped onto the sofa. "I just left the office and figured I'd stop by and see the new digs." He blinked a few times and looked around. "Fancy. Too bad you don't have a view."

"Do you want a drink?"

"God, yes." He let out an uneasy chuckle, leaning forward and running a hand through his hair and along the back of his neck. "How come I never knew you were a whiskey girl? You never touch the stuff at home."

"Kellan gave it to me as a welcome to the company." I poured three fingers and put it on the table in front of him. "This place will definitely drive a person to drink."

He reached for the glass and held it up. "So true." He closed his eyes for a moment and sipped deeply.

"How was your trip?"

He shook his head. "Let's not talk about it." His green irises went back to the blood red patch on my blouse, and he took another gulp. "That's some high-end imitation blood. Maybe you can score some for Halloween, and we can scare the neighbors."

Taking the hint, I crossed the room and opened the tiny closet, pulling out a fresh top. Ever since my night spent in the office, I stowed two wardrobe changes for easy access.

Apparently, I was in desperate need of one now.

"So what are you working on that involved fake blood? Is this about the missing girl? Did you find her?" His voice was filled with concern.

"Not yet. Nick's working on it." I balled up my shirt and tossed it into a trash bag. "I was determining how Michelle Mercer was murdered." Swallowing, I tried to shake it off. "It's bad. I didn't realize just how bad until five minutes ago."

He snorted, downing the rest of the drink and getting up to refill the glass. "Do you want one?"

"I shouldn't. I already had more than enough out of that bottle last week. Help yourself," I said, even though he already poured another three fingers. "You're not driving, are you?"

"Marcal's parked out front." He crossed the room and took my hand, leading me to the couch. He kissed my knuckles and ran his thumb over my cheek. "Do you want me to leave?" He blinked, realizing where we were. "Shit, you're working. I didn't think this through."

"It's okay. I just need to finish a few things." I glanced at him. "Have you eaten anything today?"

"Not since breakfast." Judging from the nearly empty glass, it wouldn't take long for the alcohol to hit him. "Do you want to get dinner? I can probably swing it. I have an early morning tomorrow, but I just..." His eyes hadn't left my body since I walked into the room. "Fuck it."

"How about you get something to eat and I'll meet you at our apartment? It's not the weekend, but it's our place. We can bend the rules."

"I can wait for you. I don't think I can stomach anything right now."

"I'll be right behind you. Just go."

He stared for the longest time until his gaze started to wander. "Yeah, okay. I need to shower after traveling all day." He grinned. "*Our place.* I'll meet you at *our* place."

Once he left my office, I watched him walk down the hallway to the elevator bank, waving at the receptionist. As soon as the doors closed, I sent a text message to his driver with instructions since I wasn't sure how long Martin would remain coherent. At least I knew Marcal would get him inside the car, get something in his stomach, and get him safely inside our apartment. The rest was up to me.

After checking to see if there were any updates from the precinct, I dialed Bastian. Our conversation was brief. He didn't remember any investigator pointing out the lack of arterial spray or blood drops, but he'd do some asking. The implication hung heavily over the line. Michelle was slaughtered by a professional. The killer was trained. He knew precisely where and how to strike to avoid making a mess and escape without detection. He also knew intimate details concerning Julian's gear and habits. This was personal, not a random act of violence.

Bastian agreed the killer was probably stalking them. He must have been right outside the home when Mercer left. The timing was too perfect. Too precise, especially since he took his time with the blade. The target must have been Michelle. We just didn't know why, but from what I'd seen so far, it was probably a safe bet the killer hoped Julian would take the fall for the murder. Bastian made me swear not to tell Mercer about this until we knew more. Julian was already tormented enough with grief, but to possibly be the reason behind his wife's murder would do nothing but increase that agony tenfold.

"I'll get back to you in a day or so, love. I need to ask Jules a few things," Bastian said.

"This was extremely personal. Someone had a vendetta. Someone close to him. Any idea who it might be?" I didn't know enough about Julian to even know where to begin looking for suspects. "Bas, are you sure it's not someone on your team?"

"Hans and Donovan would die for him. So would I. The good thing is Jules doesn't have many mates outside the team, so that should narrow things. Like I said, I'll get back to you."

"What else can I do in the meantime?"

"You're bloody brilliant, just stay the course."

Disconnecting, I jotted down a few notes concerning a broad range of possible suspects since I couldn't come up with any specifics, and then I gathered my things and left the office.

When I arrived at the apartment, Martin was slumped on the couch. A half-eaten burger and fries were on the coffee table in front of him. Between the alcohol and the jetlag, he was probably done for the night.

I ran a hand through his hair, and he let out a faint murmur. Moving into the kitchen, I filled a glass with water and put it on the table in front of him. Then I took a bite out of his burger and grabbed a handful of fries, seeing no reason to let the fast food go to waste. Leaving my shoulder holster and gun on the counter, I scanned our lonely little apartment. We didn't even have a TV. We barely spent four days in this place since we bought it. At least we had clothes and furniture.

He shifted on the couch. "Alex?" Spotting me, he sat up. "When did you get here?"

"A few minutes ago." I nudged my chin at the food and water. "If you're not careful, you're going to have one hell of a hangover."

He shook off my comment, taking another bite and sipping some water. "I gotta piss." When he was close enough, he snaked his arm around my waist and buried his face in my neck. "I missed you."

"You mentioned that."

"Did I tell you I love you? Because I do." He clung heavily to me for a moment, finally managing to right himself and head in the direction of the bathroom. A few minutes later, the shower turned on. Assuming he didn't drown, that might be one way to sober up.

When he came out, we didn't talk much. He drank more water, ate a banana, and headed to bed. Sleeping that night was a mess. Hell, it would have gone smoother if O'Connell called and told Martin about the bar fight instead of the things he thought when he found me covered in fake blood. He fidgeted and jerked in his sleep until it culminated in a deep growl that burst from his throat and jolted him awake. Neither of us slept afterward.

Instead, we talked about the shit we survived, our fears, and finding some way to go forward. My giving up a career in law enforcement didn't do much to alleviate the danger or the worry; it just meant a better paycheck and crappier benefits. But we were talking about it. That was new. It was different, and it was basically the entire reason we tried therapy in the first place. Hell, maybe it worked.

"You've been talking to Bastian again," he said, smirking. "Every time you do, you start using British slang. It's cute."

"I do not."

"Rubbish. Just promise me if things go tits up, you'll walk away alive. That's all I ask. That's all I've ever asked."

He ran a hand down my side.

I gave him a look. "I promise, and I did not say rubbish."

He grinned. "Rubbish. And don't think for a second I didn't notice the faded bruises. You were in a fight."

"I'm surprised you noticed anything with those whiskey goggles you were wearing."

He made a face. "Ugh. Starting right now, no more drinking."

"For how long?"

"We'll see." The phone rang, and he reached around to grab it. Answering, he held it to his ear. It was a little after five a.m. The office shouldn't be calling him now. "No. You're joking." He paused. "We set that in motion yesterday. What do you mean they backed out?" Pulling his arm free from beneath my pillow, he sat up and threw his legs over the side. "We did not negotiate in bad faith. The paperwork was signed." He waited for a response. "This is bullshit. They can't just break the contract we agreed to yesterday. If anyone negotiated in bad faith, it was them." He let out a sigh. "Of course, I want to reach an agreement. Is the original deal still on the table?" He glanced back at me, a bittersweet smile on his face. "Fine, get Luc up to speed. He'll have to handle my meetings for the rest of the week, so I can go back and get this straightened out. Have the jet prepped and ready. And I want the entire legal team to accompany me. I won't tolerate any more misunderstandings. If they think they're going to try something like this again, they're going to pay for it."

When he hung up, I said, "You probably shouldn't have

bothered coming home."

"Probably not." He went to the closet, pulling out a few suits to take with him. "I'm hoping to get back by this weekend, but I'll call and let you know." He swallowed. "I don't want you to be bloody when I get back. I don't care if it's real or fake. No blood. Understand?"

"Then don't surprise me. I might need a few minutes to clean up."

He pressed his lips together, contemplating saying something, but the words never materialized. Finally, he spoke again. "You have to help Mercer. A man can't survive like that."

"No pressure," I quipped.

He moved closer to the bed and kissed me. "So what does your day look like, sweetheart?"

Chewing on the inside of my lip, I checked my phone, but none of the detectives sent any messages. "I'm not sure yet. Perhaps I'll drop by the clinic for an unexpected inspection."

"That's where the missing girl volunteered?"

I nodded.

"Text me the name and address. I'll see if anyone from my charity foundation has donated to them in the past."

"Don't you have enough on your plate?"

"The way I see it, I have a long flight. I just said I wasn't drinking, so I'll probably be bored, unless you want to drop everything and come with me."

"Maybe next time."

TWENTY-FOUR

After Martin left, I debated texting him the information. I didn't like his involvement in my investigations, but he wouldn't let it go. Plus, if the clinic was corrupt, the last thing he needed was to donate to a shady organization. So despite my better judgment, I sent the text and drove to work. When I arrived, Detective Sparrow was waiting outside.

"Parker," she called, glancing around as if Cross might chase her away, "something's happened." Her eyes went hard. "It's been brought to my attention you and Detective O'Connell spoke to a possible witness in Wellington's disappearance."

"Witness is an exaggeration. We talked to a hooker two nights ago."

The differentiation was lost on her. "Where were you between midnight and four this morning?"

"What happened?"

"Answer the question." Sparrow waited, not willing to give an inch until I said something.

"I was at home with my boyfriend."

"I assume he can vouch for you."

"Yes. Now would you care to explain why I need an alibi?"

She looked around. "Ivy Greene was found dead this morning. The PD received an anonymous tip. We haven't determined the precise time of death yet. The body is at the ME's office, but evidence suggests she was killed elsewhere and dumped."

A cold chill traveled down my spine. "What do we know so far?"

She bit her lip, her eyes shifting around. "You didn't hear any of this from me, but she bled out. Her neck was pierced. The coroner found fresh track marks on the inside of her arm. We're running a toxicology report." She sighed. "The anonymous tipster didn't give us much to go on. He just said a woman was dead, and we should investigate. We have cadaver dogs sniffing around. It appears this could be a dumping ground. It's close to the Seven Rooks' turf. I'm guessing we might find Jessika's body near there."

I narrowed my eyes. "Where exactly?"

"That old construction site a few blocks from the clinic. That's where we found Ivy's body. Whoever dumped her didn't even waste time concealing her. They must have been in a rush."

"Why do you think Jessika is buried there?"

Sparrow didn't respond. Instead, she dragged the toe of her shoe across the sidewalk. The conversation replayed through my mind. I remembered Ivy's words clearly.

"Are you sure the drug dealer didn't do it? Ivy kept mentioning a Dario. She said if the Seven Rooks knew she spoke to us, she'd feel it."

"I don't know. O'Connell already filled me in on the conversation. We're searching the scene for clues. Clearly, she wanted to escape the neighborhood. She should have come to us. She should have let O'Connell bring her in. We didn't have a tail on her, so we don't know what happened. I thought there might have been a chance you or another of Cross's private eyes were there."

"Or you thought I beat the answers out of her."

She shrugged. "It might have crossed my mind. You have a stake in finding Jessika Wellington." She jerked her chin at the office building. "That is a condition for keeping your job, isn't it?"

"I didn't touch Ivy."

We stared at one another for a long moment. "I know," she finally admitted. "Aside from a dealer or pimp, do you have any idea who would?"

Only one name came to mind. "Do you have units watching the Wellingtons?"

"We do. I considered the possibility William might have decided to vent some of his anger or retaliate for the attack on his assistant, but he was at the hotel all night. It wasn't him. Maybe it was a john. Shit, it might be the anonymous tipster, calling to gloat. It's hard to say with these whack jobs. I really was hoping you or one of Cross's people were keeping tabs on the neighborhood. Are you certain you don't know what happened?"

I shook my head, but I knew someone who might. "Do you have units canvassing the area?"

"We do." She didn't say anything else. She just turned and headed back to her car. "Whoever did this is serious. This is murder, and we can't ignore it. The brass has created a task force. Homicide and gangs are taking over the investigation. The captain doesn't believe this is about a missing person. It's starting to look like a serial crime." She opened the car door. "I can't say it isn't. Five years is a long time to harbor a cover-up concerning a missing teenager. Whatever is going on goes a lot deeper than one missing girl. Be careful, Parker. These aren't the kinds of people a private dick should screw with. If you hear about anything else, let the police handle it."

"Yes, ma'am." I tapped my finger to my brow in a mock salute.

When I made it upstairs, I spoke to my boss about the investigation, the dynamic shift the police were taking, and asked what else I could do. Cross was working additional angles concerning the clinic and their staff. He was vague on the details, but he assured me he was thoroughly checking into each of their backgrounds. It sounded like he was on to something, but he didn't deem it necessary to share his knowledge.

Finding no reason to argue with a brick wall, I checked the time and drove across town to the neighborhood I was supposed to avoid. It wasn't even noon. The bar didn't open until four, and despite the background check on Jared Prince, I didn't have his home address memorized. But somehow, I suspected he'd be at work, and sure enough, I saw him through the glass door, seated at the bar and going through the books.

The door was locked, and I tapped against it. He turned, scowling when he saw me. The last time we met, he made it very clear I should go away and never come back, but the police were out in force this afternoon. It was the perfect opportunity to convince him he needed my help as much as I needed his.

Ambling to the door, he flipped the lock and pulled the door open six inches. "We're closed. Don't come back."

I slid my foot into the space before he could shut the door. "A hooker was killed last night. The cops are investigating how it happened."

"I didn't do it." He tried to shove me backward, but I put my hand on the door. "Did you forget what I told you last time?"

"No, but the longer the cops are hanging around, the worse it might be for you and your business. If you tell me what you know, I might be able to get them to back off. It's a quid pro quo. What do you say?"

The bartender stood in the doorway for several long moments. "Dense," he muttered. Yanking the door wide, he waited for me to step inside before locking it behind me. "Like I told the police officers who came knocking an hour ago, I don't know anything. I didn't kill the hooker. I was here until four, and then I closed up. Went home. Didn't see anything."

"The Seven Rooks hang out in your bar. Maybe you heard someone talking about it," I suggested.

"Do you want to know what I heard?" He stepped closer, his warm breath hitting my cheek. "I heard you and some cop picked her up and started asking questions. That's why she was killed, so if you're looking to blame someone, look in the damn mirror."

"I didn't do this," I spat, despite the guilt that was eating at me since Sparrow told me about the murder.

"You sure about that?" He stepped closer, and I took a step away, my back hitting the wall. "Didn't I make myself clear the last time you entered my bar? Do you really want to test me to see what happens?" His eyes were ablaze. "If they see me talking to you, I'll be the next casualty. I'm surprised they haven't done anything yet, considering I saved your ass."

The warning bells went off in my brain just from the way he was looking at me, but I pushed the fear aside. Intimidation wouldn't work. It was time someone told him so.

"They won't touch you. They know better. Tell me I'm wrong," I snapped, pushing away from the wall until my chest brushed against his. "You did time for cigarette smuggling, so you have a network. You know how to get things and move things. You aren't part of the Seven Rooks, but they frequent your bar. I'm guessing you do business with them. That's why they leave you the hell alone. It's also why no one pulled a piece on you the night I was here. You don't let them bring guns into your establishment. And they know to respect you. You're someone of value. Importance. They need you. If they didn't, they would have wasted you the second you stopped them from killing me. That means you must also be valuable to other people. And that value is why the ATF keeps tabs on your habits. They figure you'll slip up, so you keep to yourself. You use the bar for cover, and you keep your head down. Anyone who steps foot in this neighborhood is going to focus on the shit show outside and not what's going on in here. You need the Rooks as much as they need you, so why the hell did you tip off the police?" It was a guess, but the truth shone in his eyes.

He took a step back. "Why would I do that?"

"That's what I'm asking. Who killed Ivy?"

He didn't speak. He glowered, slamming his palm on the table beside us. I flinched at the unexpected sound, and he knew I was scared. "By your own acknowledgement, you know my threats are more than empty promises, so why are you still standing here?"

"I'm trying to figure something out." I stared at him.

"Why'd you let me live? Why did you call in the tip? What's going on that is so heinous you'd put yourself in jeopardy?"

"At the moment, I'm asking myself the same question."

"You're not a killer."

"You want to bet?"

I'd seen a lot of men like him before. Most were all bark and no bite. But I couldn't get a read on this guy. He was too careful. He stayed off the grid. Out of the way. Out of sight. He knew how to blend in and disappear, but he also commanded authority and didn't let anyone push him around.

"I want to know what happened to Ivy. Did the Rooks kill her?"

He blinked, backing away and heading for the bar. "Her pimp didn't touch her, and neither did anyone else in the gang." He glanced over his shoulder. "It wasn't a john either. I'm not the only one using the gang to stay below the radar. You're right. I've done business with them. I've earned their respect and the protection that comes with it. But my connection to them is nothing compared to what goes on inside the clinic. But you already know that. That's why you're asking for my help." He wet his lips. "I can't help you. I mind my business. I just know whatever it is has been happening for a long time, but I've made it a point not to stick my nose into it. It'd be bad for my health. And I have to watch out for number one."

"That's why Jessika disappeared, isn't it? She found out what was happening."

"I wouldn't know." He watched me uncertainly. "Now get out. I don't want to see you or any cops back in my bar again. And this time, I mean it."

I opened my mouth to ask another question, but he lifted the shotgun from behind the bar. And I wasn't certain he wouldn't use it. I backed away, reluctantly turning around to unlock the door before slipping outside. So much for my brilliant attempt to gain an ally in this mess. Now I just had more questions.

Detouring to the precinct, I spoke to O'Connell again. Despite the warning, I told him about my meeting with the bartender and everything he said. It was a stupid move on my part. The risk wasn't worth it, but I couldn't shake the thought Jared Prince might be the only one not afraid of defying the Rooks. Too bad he wouldn't help us.

Afterward, I stopped at the diner. Since major crimes was busy working the murder, a patrol unit was sitting on Janet Wellington. I thought I'd drop by and make sure they were doing a decent job. It was earlier than usual when I arrived. Janet wasn't due at the gym for another couple of hours, but I didn't know what else to do or where to go. I needed a quiet place to think, and if I returned to the office, I'd end up buried in research or hounded by Mercer's case. Neither of which was conducive to thinking through this clusterfuck of a cold case.

"You're early," Skye said, slamming down the coffeepot. "Where's your friend?" Obviously, she was in a mood. Unfortunately, so was I.

"It's just me today."

"Whatever." She stormed away, handing a check to the couple a few tables over. The place was actually crowded. Five minutes later, she returned to my table. "Do you know he's married? He wears a ring." Her eyes went to my left hand. "You don't."

"Who?" So much for finding a quiet place to think.

She stared at me like I was mentally challenged. "Your boyfriend. The guy who's been eating his way through our pie menu. The one you were being all cutesy and flirting with."

"Nick? He's not my boyfriend. He's like my brother." I studied her for a moment. "Is that why you've been so bitchy these last couple of days?"

"You looked awfully cozy for siblings."

"We're friends. What's your deal today? Did someone piss in your Cheerios?"

She rolled her eyes. "I don't like cheaters. Marriage should mean something. Finding a shitty diner away from wherever you normally hang out just so you two can cuddle up in the corner is sickening, and I don't want to see it."

"Seriously, you need to ease up."

"Then why have the two of you been coming here so much in the middle of the day? It's weird. And you don't usually eat a normal meal. Just coffee and pie. It doesn't make sense, and you almost always pay the check early, like you might have to rush away. Are you afraid his wife is going to catch you?" She narrowed her eyes. "You're both pretty fascinated by the gym across the street. Is that where his wife works out? Does he pick her up after he hangs out with you? Do you bang in the car?"

I didn't realize she was paying so much attention, but I wasn't about to compromise the case. "We're just friends. Don't you have any guy friends?"

"Not married ones."

I laughed, hoping to ease her suspicions. "I'd hope not. You're like eighteen."

"Try twenty-one," she snapped. "And you shouldn't fool around with married men. That's just wrong."

"Well, I'm not."

"Well, good." She let out a huff and picked up her pen and order pad. "What'll it be?"

I glanced uncertainly down at the coffee cup, wondering if she spit in it. I had no idea what triggered the hostility. Maybe her boyfriend cheated, or her parents went through a nasty divorce. I didn't need to figure out another mystery; I had enough of that at work.

"Nothing."

She looked at me over the pad. "Then you need to leave. We need the table."

"Seriously?"

"By the way, I'm not your charity case either. No one leaves a fifty percent tip every day. Are you trying to buy my silence or something?" She glanced at the company car. "I thought you didn't have a job. But now you have a fancy new ride, and you throw money around all the time. Who are you? What do you want from me?"

"Decent service and a friendly smile."

She glared.

"Nothing. I don't want anything from you, except a cup of coffee and maybe some lunch every now and again." Perplexed by the conversation, I scrutinized everything about her, trying to figure out what was going on. She looked different; her eyes were brown instead of blue. She must have been wearing colored contacts. Choosing not to mention it, I said, "I just needed a quiet place to hang out. I'm sorry if I offended you. I thought you might need some extra cash for college or rent or," I gestured at her face, "getting another metal bar shoved through your lip. I don't know."

"I can take care of myself. I don't need some weirdo watching out for me. I've been doing just fine on my own. If you really want to do me a favor, stop coming here. It freaks me out."

"Okay." I stood up. "That's not a problem."

With nowhere else to go, I headed for the office. Obviously, no one wanted me around. My presence was toxic. The cops warned me off. The bartender threatened to kill me. And the waitress thought I was a weirdo. Maybe I was.

At least I could spend the rest of the day working on Mercer's case while Cross looked into the oddities surrounding the clinic and its staff. There was more to Michelle's murder, and even though I didn't want to think about it, the thirty-first floor of the high-rise was probably the safest place to be right now.

I turned down another street, noticing a possible tail. A second quick turn verified it, and I tried to figure out who was following me or when it started. I'd been distracted by my argument with the waitress. I should have been paying more attention.

Thinking it might be the bartender sending some goons to follow through on his threat, it would be best to lose the follow car. As I raced through the streets, I dialed O'Connell. The phone was still ringing when my tail caught up to me.

These small side streets didn't provide various lanes of traffic to weave through. At an intersection, I darted to the right, slamming on my brakes when a large, silver SUV pulled diagonally in front of me. I flung the car into reverse, but my tail and a white sedan pulled up to my bumper, boxing me in. I opened my car door, just as men with ski masks and automatic machine pistols stepped out of the SUV. Men from the other two vehicles stepped out, equally armed, and surrounded my car.

"Lose the gun and phone," one of them said.

Knowing surrender was my only option, I tossed my nine millimeter and phone to the ground. The men moved closer, and I raised my hands. There were too many of them, but if they wanted me dead, they would have shot me by now.

"What do you want?" I asked.

"You're coming with us." Something sharp jabbed into my neck, and I collapsed into someone's arms as the world blinked out.

TWENTY-FIVE

I awoke with double-vision. My head pounded, and I tried to rub my forehead, only to find my wrists bound to a hospital bed. Shit. I blinked, hoping to clear away the blurry double-vision, but it didn't work. I twisted hard to the right, hoping to figure out where I was or what was happening. Something popped in my arm, followed by the sound of trickling water.

"Dammit," a man swore from the other side of the room, and instinctively, I shut my eyes and lay still. "The tubing came loose. This equipment is ridiculous. Why do we have to take care of her? I thought he wanted to work her over to see what the cops know."

"She's worth more than that. No reason we can't turn this into a paycheck while we're at it. We have to wait for the labs, but assuming her blood's clean, we'll drain a few more units, and depending on if she's a match, we might be able to sell off a few spare parts before the night is through. He has someone on the hook for a liver. That's a six figure payday."

"I already took two units and blew a few of her veins in the process. If there's something wrong with the line, it'll be hard to run another one for surgery."

"He'll start a central line. It'll just depend on how quickly she cooperates. When's he getting here? We might have to get more ice."

"Should I make a run now?"

"No. He'll tell us what he needs." I heard faint tapping, followed by a few muttered uh-huhs. Cautioning a glance, I saw one of the men conclude a phone call. "He's on his way. He said ten minutes. He'll want her awake, so just leave her be for now. There's no reason we need to pump more saline into her at this point."

The two men wore long sleeve t-shirts underneath light blue scrubs and were seated at a card table at the end of the room. Their identities were concealed by skull caps and surgeon masks. There were two doorways and no windows. Peeling, beige paint covered the walls, and the floor was a neutral tile. I was in a hospital bed, held in place by the thick restraints of a psych ward. An instrument tray was to my left, but I had no hope of reaching it.

Who was coming? Where were we? I remembered being surrounded and the prick of a needle in my neck, but that didn't provide any indication of where we were now or how long I was out.

Shivering, I realized I had been stripped to my bra and panties. I tested the restraints again, tugging at the thick belts in the hopes one of them wasn't properly secured. But I had no such luck. My muscles felt like jelly. My eyelids were heavy, and my screwed up sight was making my headache worse. But I continued to survey the room, aware of the surreal calm I couldn't shake. The sedative made me foggy but did nothing to numb the pain. These men knew what they were doing.

The door on the right opened, and a man stepped through. He was dressed like the others, except his scrubs were green. The rectangle around his eyes was the only visible part of his face. From the way he moved, it was apparent he was in charge. His attention went to the IV bag, dripping on the floor beside me, before his eyes settled on mine.

"She's awake." He ripped the needle out of my arm, and I hissed. My tongue felt thick and uncooperative. He turned to the men at the table and asked, "Did you do as I said?" Something about his voice didn't sound right.

"Yep," one of them responded.

He nodded. His gloved fingers pressed hard against my inner elbow, and I shuddered at the unexpected pain. "Good. Your pain receptors aren't dulled."

"What do you want?" I choked out, the words mangled.

"I want to know why you've been looking into Jessika's disappearance." He removed the topmost strap and continued unhooking each one as he worked his way down the bed. "What do the police know about last night's murder? How did they find the body so quickly?"

"I don't know."

He removed the final restraint, drawing his finger over the scars on my wrist. His focus shifted to the jagged scar on my thigh and the lengthy one along my clavicle. "These are superficial, but this one is precise. Did you cut yourself?"

I tried to sit up, but he pushed down on my chest. My left hand gripped his wrist, but I didn't have the strength to force him away. "Let me go."

"Answer the question." For some reason, this concept fascinated him. "Did you cut yourself? Are these wounds self-inflicted?"

"I'll show you self-inflicted," I growled.

When he spoke again, I realized his voice sounded odd because it was muffled by the surgical mask. I reached up to snag it so I could identify the son of a bitch, but he batted my hand away with ease. "We will have no more of that."

I struggled to sit up, but my muscles were sluggish and uncooperative. That only fueled my determination. "Where are we? Who are you? What did you do to Jessika?"

"She's been tortured before. I've seen similar injuries in POWs. Did you run films?" he asked the men. They didn't, which irritated Green Scrubs. "Did you at least make sure she's clean?"

"We took a sample. It's being run now," one of his subordinates responded. "I also took two units to save time later."

"Okay. Take her into the other room. I'll find out how much she knows, and by the time I'm finished, I expect to see the lab results." He looked at me. "Depending on how things go, we'll figure out how to dispose of you." He opened the door on the left and disappeared inside.

Now that my bindings were removed, I needed to fight my way out of here. The door on the right should lead out of the room. From what I gathered, we were probably in an abandoned medical facility. My only basis for that was the equipment and the bed, but it didn't matter. I needed to get out of here and away from these people. The men came toward me, but my limbs wouldn't respond to my commands.

"Stay back," I growled.

One of the men moved to the left to lower the railing, and I scurried to the bottom of the bed as quickly as I could, which was to say not very quickly. The second one was waiting at the foot of the bed. He grabbed my right arm, and I swung at him with my left. My reactions and movements were delayed on account of the drugs, and he grabbed my other arm before it made contact with his jaw.

"She's a fighter. Let's tie her wrists," he said. "We don't want any accidents."

The second guy grabbed a zip tie off the tray table, and they shoved my face into the mattress while they bound my arms behind my back. They dragged me off the bed and across the floor. No matter how hard I resisted, I was overpowered.

The next room was a bathroom, and my eyes took as much of it in as I could. Tub, sink, towel hook, a separate door for the toilet. Was this a motel? I scanned the room again, failing to locate a viable weapon. A metal framed pair of glasses caught my eye. I might be able to use the stem to free myself from the zip tie. That is, if I could reach them.

Green Scrubs emptied a large cooler into the tub. The ice cubes splashed, and a sick feeling grew in my stomach. Waking up in a tub of ice and missing a kidney was supposed to be an urban legend. This didn't look like a myth; it looked like I was an extra in a horror film. But I didn't remember being cast as naked brunette number three.

"Who are you?" I asked, the fear awakening my senses as my adrenaline combated the tranquilizer. "Why did you take me? Where are we?"

Green Scrubs snorted, jerking his chin down, and the men dropped me in front of the tub. My knees cracked against the tile. "Aren't you just full of questions? Those questions are the reason you're here. You should have backed off when you had the chance. It's been five years. She's gone. You should have let it go."

He moved behind me. I tried to turn, but he shoved me against the side of the tub and held me in place. I stared down into the fuzzy water, blinking desperately to clear the fog. His gloved hands traced the curve of my spine, coming to rest on more of my scars.

"You didn't notice these?" he snapped to the men. "This is why we needed films."

"That's a gunshot wound. We see those all the time," a voice said from the back left corner.

"Not that. This." He poked hard to the left of my spine. "This is surgical." He grabbed my hair and yanked my head back, even as he continued to push me forward. "Why did you have surgery?"

"Why do you care?" I retorted. "Do you work for my insurance company?"

"Answer me," he snapped.

"Fuck you."

The hand pulling my hair suddenly pushed my head down, and I was plunged face first into the ice cold water. He held my head under while I jerked side to side, hoping to get loose from his grip. When my lungs started to burn and panic took over, he yanked me up by the hair again. I coughed, my heart rate jump-started by the frigid assault. Blinking the tears from my eyes, I turned my head to the side and scowled at him.

"You will answer."

"Okay," I said, my eyes darting around the room in search of a weapon, "I'll let you in on a little secret." I took a deep breath. "You suck at torture."

Predictably, he shoved my head under the water again. I didn't fight or struggle this time. I remained still, conserving as much air as possible while I waited. I wasn't stupid enough to think I'd been abducted because of some emergency surgery. He wanted answers in regards to the Wellington case. The fact that these men were dressed like doctors made me think they were from the clinic, but I couldn't be sure. For all I knew, the reason for the long sleeves was to hide their ink. Most of the Seven Rooks had gang tattoos. But gangbangers didn't strike me as this smart or methodical. The men in scrubs had this down to an art, as if they'd done it a hundred times before. And I wasn't sure they hadn't. Jessika was probably one of their earliest victims.

The pressure against the back of my skull eased, but I didn't push back. I remained still. The plastic handcuffs were cutting into my wrists, but I continued to work my hands while my captor was preoccupied. I tried to pinch a piece of the plastic together. After fifteen more seconds in which I wasn't positive I wouldn't black out, he yanked my hair again and dropped me sideways onto the floor.

I gasped, sputtering as water ran down my face. I stopped fidgeting with the zip tie and waited. Green Scrubs spoke softly to one of the men, who promptly left the room. Whatever the reason, I was sure I wasn't going to like it. Then he grabbed my upper arm and sat me up against the tub. He slapped me across the cheek with his left hand. The burning sting was from the ice more than the smack, but I couldn't stop the wince.

"I'm not wasting any more time." He leaned back on his haunches. "What have you told the police about Jessika Wellington's disappearance?"

Dragging my eyes upward, I was relieved my vision was finally clear. I stared into his eyes, hoping to recognize him, but my mind was reeling. "Who?"

This time, he punched me, a left hook that rattled my teeth. He shook out his hand, as if he wasn't used to hitting people. Physical violence was something he didn't do. His assaults were controlled, methodical, surgical even. He dressed the part, and I scanned his attire for insignias that might give away his identity.

"You know who." His eyes went cold and hard, the yellow in them burning in hatred. "How much do the police know?"

I grinned, tasting blood. "They know everything. They found your dumping ground. They're coming for you."

"Bullshit. They would have arrested me if that were true." He watched as I shivered. "I can make you comfortable." He stepped toward the counter and filled a syringe. "This can be pleasant. But I have to know what you told them?" He was unpredictable. He never tortured anyone before and wasn't sure how to proceed. So he flip-flopped between hardass and nice guy too quickly. He was untethered and out of his element. That meant I could get the upper hand, unless he snapped and killed me on the spot.

"You must have seen the dogs. At this moment, they're digging up all your dirty little secrets. They'll identify your victims, and then they'll have everything they need on you. I suggest you take that needle and shove it up your ass."

"How'd they know about the body? Is the neighborhood under surveillance? The extra patrols stopped. Are the police using unmarked units?"

I smiled. He was more afraid than I was. That fear would keep me alive, at least for a little while.

He put the needle down and spun me around, shoving my head back into the freezing cold water. This time, he was angry. He was losing control. He shoved harder, forcing me deeper until my knees were off the ground. I inhaled some of the frigid water, igniting my lungs. The involuntary coughs and sputters made him realize if he didn't stop I'd drown, and he dropped me back to the ground. As I choked and coughed, he kicked me right below the ribs, expelling the water I inhaled up my throat and out of my mouth.

"Answer me," he screamed. When I refused, he shoved me under again. Over and over, he brought me to the brink of drowning, but he was careful not to go too far. He knew just how much the human body could take. "Answer the question."

"It was an anonymous tip. One of your people betrayed you. He wants to make a deal. They'll give him immunity if he flips." It was a lie but a damn good one. I curled into a ball, shaking from the cold while I fervently flexed my wrists, feeling the plastic start to bend at a point in the middle. If I could weaken it enough, I'd be able to break free. I just needed to buy more time.

"I don't believe you," he said, but I heard the uncertainty in his voice.

"It doesn't matter what you believe. It's true."

He took a step back and rested his hip against the sink. "Why'd you go into gang territory to look for Jessika?"

"The police have a file. They always have." I inhaled a few times, the burning in my lungs starting to ease. "It's just a matter of time until they find her. Everything is coming to an end."

"You're right about that." His eyes remained cold and distant.

I let out an ugly laugh. "You killed her. You killed Ivy Greene. And now you're going to kill me. You won't get away with it."

"I don't want to kill you, but I don't have a choice."

"You can let me go. I won't tell anyone anything. You kept your identity concealed. I can't hurt you. You can escape."

He narrowed his eyes. "I'm not an idiot. You've been watching the neighborhood. My guys didn't betray me. You told the cops where to find the dead skank. That's the only way they would have come across her body that quickly. You know more than you're letting on. Stop lying. What else do they know? Do they know about my operation?"

With a smug smile on my face, I said, "Wouldn't you like to know?"

He threw me into the tub and forced my head under the water. My skull hit the side, and I flailed. His hands were on my shoulders, holding me down. Instinctively, I fought, but I forced myself to stop, sinking deeper. My back hit the bottom, and I used that point of connection as leverage to kick him in the groin. I kicked again into his thigh and stomach until he lost his grip on my shoulders.

Tugging with all my might, I freed myself from the zip tie and surfaced, grasping the edge of the tub in order to heave myself out of the ice water. The cubes skittered across the bathroom floor, and I ran, my bare feet sliding on the wet surface. Green Scrubs underestimated my survival instinct. The adrenaline burned off whatever remained of the tranquilizer, and I was in fight or flight mode, emphasis on flight.

I tugged open the door just as the second man in blue scrubs returned. A tray of surgical instruments crashed to the floor as I pushed past him, racing down the hallway. It was narrow and dimly lit. A large window was at the very end, and I sprinted toward it. Someone tackled me to the ground in a blur of blue.

I twisted, clawing at his face and arms. His mask slipped, and he let go of me in order to cover his face before I could identify him. I drove the heel of my hand into his nose, hearing a satisfying pop followed by a howl. The mask he wore turned red with blood, and I knocked him off of me. Before I could get up, the other man in blue jumped on top of me, attempting to hold me down. He had a scalpel in his hand, and he put the blade against my throat. Grabbing his wrist with both my hands, I tried to force him back, but he was too strong. He was going to slice me open.

Thunderous footsteps raced down the hallway toward us. "Don't do it," Green Scrubs commanded. "Not here. Not like that. We need to keep this contained. Get her back in the room where cleanup is easier." Green Scrubs glanced at the man with the broken nose. "Get that taken care of. Nothing can trace back to us, so don't bleed on anything. Did she see you?"

He held his nose. "No."

The one with the scalpel jerked me upright, never allowing the blade to leave my throat. He wasn't falling for any more tricks. And I wasn't certain I had any left. He kept the blade against my jugular and dragged me back to the room.

I noticed a dozen other doors on the way. I should have tried one of them. I should have been faster. I needed to think. I was running out of time. How was I going to get out of this mess? I'd been in worse situations, right? I couldn't remember. I just remembered the stupid promise I made to Martin early this morning. I'd be damned if these goons made me break it. Think, Parker. Fucking think.

When we reached the door, I grasped the interior knob in my left hand. This would hurt, but hopefully, it'd hurt him more than it was going to hurt me. I pulled the doorknob as hard as I could, slamming the door into us. It glanced off his shoulder, and he threw up a hand out of reflex to block the door from colliding with his face. Taking that opportunity, I grabbed his wrist, twisting it upward and forcing the scalpel to drop. Scooping it up, I took a step back, realizing I was trapped.

Not seeing another way out, I knew I had to go through him. I sliced in the direction of Blue Scrubs. He held his palms up, edging to the side. I slashed at him again, and he dove out of the way. At least now he wasn't standing between me and the only way out.

Cautiously, I moved to the exit, but Green Scrubs blocked my path. He sidestepped when I slashed at him, carefully assessing my movements with a deep level of consternation. He reached for my arm, but my reflexes were faster now than they had been earlier. Still, I wasn't at a hundred percent and being practically naked didn't provide any protection from an attack. He grabbed one of the folding chairs from the table, closing it in one swift motion and using it as a shield to stop another slash of the scalpel. The sound of the blade against the metal was like nails on a chalkboard.

"Get away from the door," I snarled, but he didn't listen.

He stood between me and my means of escape. Intent on cutting his throat, I moved closer, slashing viciously. The scalpel sliced through his left forearm, and he dropped the chair, cursing. I advanced, but he blocked at the last possible second, letting the blade embed itself in the back of his bicep. He backhanded me with his other hand, and my bare feet slid on the wet floor.

"Now," Green Scrubs growled, and Blue Scrubs stabbed a syringe into my spine which instantly put me on the ground. I could feel everything, but I couldn't move.

Green Scrubs tied a tourniquet around his arm and retrieved a towel from the bathroom. He removed a phone from his pocket and made a call. After a few seconds, he hung up. "The police are looking for her. We need to clear out. Dump her in the tub for now and make sure everything is disinfected before you leave. I doubt they'll find this place, but we need to be careful. We'll come back later and dispose of her remains." He glanced at his arm. "I need to stitch this up."

He took care to wrap the wound and take anything with traces of blood with him. Then the ground moved away from my face as I was carried into the next room. For the briefest moment, I thought I heard the faint sound of sirens before I was dropped into the ice water bath. My body was paralyzed. I wasn't bound, but I didn't have the ability to lift my head out of the water. If I could just flip onto my back, I could float.

The sound of a door slamming echoed through the porcelain tub. I phoned Nick when I realized I had a tail. He'd find me. He had to. Holding on to that single thought, I held my breath as long as I could, ignoring the burning sting of the frigid water and the internal burning of my lungs. The cold was sobering, just not enough to counteract the effects of the paralytic. I had to think my way out of here.

My finger twitched. I was able to move my ring and pinkie fingers, but that wasn't much. Concentrating on turning one of these slight movements into a bigger movement wasn't working, and I was almost out of air. My palm sunk deeper into the ice water, hitting against something hard. It was the drain stopper.

Come on, just move one finger. You can do this. One finger. After three tries, I was able to hook the plug around my finger. Pulling it loose would be harder. I focused my attention entirely on lifting it up. When it budged half an inch, my body inhaled in preparation for another try, and I choked, my muscles jerking in response to the influx of water into my lungs. Apparently, I wasn't completely paralyzed. By some miracle, the drain plug popped, and the water level slowly sank.

I continued to choke in the draining tub to the point where I was clinging to consciousness, unsure if I was breathing or drowning. With the final slurp of the drain, I blacked out, my body cradled on a bed of ice.

TWENTY-SIX

The sound of slamming doors rattled the tub and ice. Another door slammed, and I assumed Blue Scrubs finished wiping down the room. He probably scrubbed the floor in the hallway too. No wonder we never found Jessika. These sinister shitheads were well-versed in covering their tracks. They probably binge-watched every episode of *CSI* and took notes.

My body was numb. I'd been out for a while. Maybe they were back to dispose of my carcass, probably in a lake or river in order to make the drowning appear accidental, except I didn't drown. Now they'd have to ship my corpse to Siberia or Alaska to make the hypothermia look like natural causes. Well, good. I wasn't going to make this easy for them.

A creepier thought entered my mind. Did they actually plan to harvest my organs? From the way they spoke, it was possible. It would also explain the tub of ice. Since I was still alive, they'd be able to cut me up into little pieces without a problem.

Shit. I struggled to move, finding my body responsive but too weak and wracked by shivers to get out of the tub. I managed to turn onto my side, hoping the less contact with the ice, the greater my chances of survival. My thoughts started to blur, and I fought to hold on to them. If I gave in to sleep, I would never wake up. I started to drift again, and I thought about Jessika. Why did they target her? They should have realized her disappearance wouldn't go unnoticed like the rest of their victims.

A door slammed, and I couldn't help but think this was it. I'd never know the answer to that question. Julian may never know who murdered his wife. And Martin, my insides clenched, he'd probably spend the next few years trying to find out what happened to me. Maybe I was wrong. Truth be told, I wasn't anything special. They'd be fine without me. The world would keep spinning.

Another door slammed, this time a lot closer. Heavy footsteps thundered into the bathroom, echoing off the tile. From the muffled rumble, it sounded like the entire floor was being searched. In a last ditch effort, I tried again to escape. This time, I was able to lift my arm out of the tub and grip the edge. I'd go down fighting. I wouldn't make this easy for them.

"Alex," a familiar voice said. He lifted me out of the tub, placing me on the tile floor. A hand brushed my hair out of my face, and I shivered uncontrollably. "I've got you. You're safe," O'Connell said. He draped his jacket over my naked and numb skin. "I need help in here." O'Connell held me in his arms on the bathroom floor, his jacket thrown over my body. "Come on, Parker, talk to me." He glanced over his shoulder. "Get the paramedics. She's alive."

After hearing the request repeated several times, another man entered the bathroom and knelt beside O'Connell. For the briefest moment, my gaze went to him. Lucien Cross was the last person I ever expected to see working with the police. Apparently, crisis makes for strange bedfellows.

"Detective," Cross said, and the curious nature of my boss's voice drew my attention, "it appears she was drugged."

He fished the syringe out of the tub, holding it up with a gloved hand. His gloves were black leather, thick and expensive, not like the white latex the assailants wore. Leaving the needle in the tub must have been an oversight. Then again, it would be impossible to pull a print anyway.

"That's why she wasn't bound," O'Connell surmised. He glanced into the other room. "Did the damn paramedic get lost? Someone go find him."

Cross went to check on the delay, and I squirmed in O'Connell's arms, my skin tingling from the sudden temperature change. Despite the discomfort, I felt nothing but relief. When my boss returned with a pair of EMTs in tow, my body tensed. O'Connell felt the shift, his eyes narrowing on my face.

"What is it?" he asked.

"The men who did this wore scrubs. One of them might have been a doctor. He could work in the hospital." I eyed the paramedics, staring at their purple gloves. "Or he could be a paramedic. Maybe even one of them."

Cross eyed the men with the ferocity of a mountain lion on the prowl. "Check her vitals, but I better not see a needle. Is that understood?"

One of the EMTs slipped my arm out from under Nick's jacket, noticing the bruises and puncture marks. He took my pulse, checked my blood pressure, and shined a light in my eyes. O'Connell and Cross exchanged a look I didn't quite understand.

"Is she stable enough to transport?" Cross asked. When his question was met with an affirmative, he barked at someone for dry blankets. He handed them to O'Connell, who pulled his jacket free from beneath the blanket only after I was covered.

"Thanks, Nick," I said, relieved he did his best to maintain my modesty. The last thing I needed was to add insult to injury. I struggled to stand, but my legs were shaky. The shivering didn't help either.

Left with few choices, O'Connell allowed the EMTs to put me on a stretcher and carry me down the stairs. He remained glued to my side, responding to a few questions from the dozen police officers we passed. The entire floor was being searched. Every room and door was filled with police personnel. I wondered where we were.

When we made it outside, I looked up at the sign. At least I was right about something. It was an abandoned medical facility. It used to be a collection of offices and specialties, but they moved to a new building. Idly, I wondered if any outdated diagnostic equipment remained. Surely, the police would find it and determine the reason the three men were using this building for their abductions. Green Scrubs must have been a doctor, probably a surgeon. It was the only thing that made any sense. I thought about his eyes and mannerisms, everything I could recall, even his speech patterns. But it didn't feel like enough. I didn't know who he was.

The EMTs hoisted me into the back of the rig, and Cross stood at the opened door. "I wasn't joking about the needles, gentlemen," he reminded them, his voice as cold as I felt.

"Sir, she needs warmed saline. Given the condition in which you found her, dehydration and hypothermia are likely," one of the men responded.

"Miss Parker," Cross asked, "how are you feeling?"

I blinked. How was I supposed to answer that question? "Tired. Overwhelmed. Pissed off." Scared.

He placed a reassuring hand on my shoulder, pulled out his cell phone and dialed a number. Dropping his hand, he spoke quietly. "Have a team prepped. From what we've seen, it looks like some type of paralytic agent. I'm guessing it was administered over an hour ago. Her vitals are stable." He turned back to me. "Squeeze my hand."

I did as Cross asked. My attempt to grasp didn't go so well. He relayed his observation to the caller, and I sunk deeper into the blankets. Hopefully, he wasn't keeping a tally of all the ways I failed him today.

After a few uh-huhs, he hung up the phone. "A medical team is on the way. In the meantime, keep her warm." He glared at the EMTs.

"Sir?" one of them asked, ignoring Cross and focusing on O'Connell. A badge meant a lot more to first responders than a nice suit. "We should take her to the hospital. It's protocol."

O'Connell stepped into the rig, pushing them aside.

"She said no hospital. The men who did this are medical professionals. Since her life isn't in any immediate danger, it'd be best not to put her at risk." He gestured to a few uniformed officers. "My colleagues have a few questions to ask. Once they're done, she'll sign the forms stating she refused treatment, and you can get back to work."

The two paramedics exchanged looks. This wasn't something they typically encountered, but they were suspects. The senior one radioed for advice, and after a few minutes of back and forth with dispatch which appeared to be patched through to the police frequencies, they agreed to step away. O'Connell waited for the men to finish hooking me up to a few monitors before willingly vacating the back of the rig.

"Hey, you." He rubbed his thumb against the swollen red band around my wrist from the broken zip tie. "You scared me shitless. What the hell happened?"

Cross leaned into the rig, interested in the conversation. I swallowed, unsure if I should speak, but O'Connell urged me on. So I told them everything from the moment I spotted the tail until they arrived.

"It sounds like they were prepping you for surgery. They would need to type you to determine if you were a match. But that's basic. Organ donation requires much more thorough testing," Cross surmised, "unless they didn't care. Black market sales aren't exactly regulated."

I didn't want to think about what could have happened. "If that's even what they were planning. Things are fuzzy. I just wish I knew who they were and what they wanted."

"Don't worry about what they wanted." Nick licked his lips. "Do you remember any identifying marks? Tattoos, scars, jewelry, accents? Anything?"

My memories were hazy. "The one in charge, his eyes burned yellow. I think he was left-handed. He hit with his left, but if he is a surgeon, maybe he was afraid of busting his dominant hand. He wasn't accustomed to throwing punches. He hit wrong, and he didn't expect his hand to hurt afterward."

Nick leaned closer. "What else?"

"He knew he needed stitches. He also didn't try to stop

the scalpel from cutting into him the second time. It's like he figured out the best place for it to strike and stick. It was weird." I blew out a breath, angry at myself. "I wanted to cut his throat, but I missed."

"What about the other two?" O'Connell pressed.

"One of them has a broken nose. The other seemed pretty excited over the prospect of killing me. I'm guessing he might have a previous record or be part of the gang, assuming any of this has to do with them." Something about the two men in blue scrubs stuck out in my mind. "I feel like I know them. I can't explain it. I just... I don't know."

"It's okay. It'll come back to you," Nick assured.

A large white van pulled up, and Cross waved them over. While he did that, O'Connell stepped down from the rig and spoke briefly to an officer. A second later, she returned with a pair of sweats.

"You might want to get dressed," he said. "We're about to take this show on the road."

He lifted one of the blankets off of me and held it up like a curtain while I slipped out from beneath the other blanket and fumbled to put on the drawstring pants and zippered sweatshirt. Luckily, I was able to slip it over my head and avoid the zipper. Then O'Connell helped me down. I scribbled something illegible on the paperwork, barely able to keep the pen in my hand.

Another set of medics were waiting just outside the white van. They didn't have uniforms or city insignias. The interior was state of the art. Diagnostic equipment, beds, medicines, bandages, it was like a mobile clinic. Cross made the introductions, but I wasn't paying attention. My heart rate skyrocketed, but O'Connell assured me it was safe and he wasn't going anywhere.

After I was hooked up to a warmed saline bag and placed beneath a heated blanket, they took a blood sample. A few officers entered the back of the van. I answered their questions, gave a statement, and went through the entire ordeal again. By the time I was finished, the shivers were gone.

"Is that it, Detective?" Cross asked. "I believe Parker's

been through enough."

Nick nodded. "I agree. Since we questioned her here, there's no need to take her to the station to finish this. Right now, we need to clear out and maintain eyes on this building." O'Connell fielded a few radio calls, requesting additional units. He wanted eyes surrounding the building. As soon as it was swept, the police would pull back and wait. With any luck, my attackers would return. O'Connell saw the exasperation on my face and hid his chuckle. "You know this is what I do."

"Yeah, yeah," I replied, my eyelids drooping as the adrenaline surge wore off.

"Relax, Alex. I can handle this," Nick insisted.

*   *   *

When I opened my eyes again, I was in an unfamiliar room beneath a layer of blankets. I was dressed in sweats with the police department's insignia, and an IV was in my arm. Not again. Fear and dread ripped through me until I spotted Nick just beyond the doorway. Someone stepped in front of him, and my eyes traveled from the Italian leather shoes to the tailored designer pants. By the time I made it to his belt, I knew it was Cross. He wore thicker, more practical belts to support his holster, unlike Martin who always coordinated his accessories.

"Miss Parker," Cross said, his voice soft and gentle, "did you have a nice nap? Are you feeling any better?"

"Much. Thank you." I exhaled, lifting my hand and brushing my now dry hair out of my face. "How did you find me? God, I'm so glad you did."

His eyes went to the nearly empty IV bag pumping into my veins. "That was a long four hours." Realizing I didn't understand his comment, he clarified, "You were missing for four hours. The GPS in the car gave us your last known location. Given the circumstances, Detective O'Connell was able to obtain traffic cam footage. It took time, but we tracked the cars to your location." He looked away. "I should put a bell around your neck to keep from losing you." He cleared his throat. "We have a matter to discuss."

"What is it?"

"You went back to the neighborhood after I specifically told you to stay away. What were you thinking? That's probably how those assholes found you. If you listened to me, this wouldn't have happened."

"You're probably right."

That admission surprised him. "Remember that in the future." He stood and went to the door. "I'll find a medic to disconnect the IV. The police assigned a protection detail, but this is a security firm. I've already enlisted our best security team to ensure your safety. Whatever you need to do, they will accompany you."

"What if I refuse?"

"Why would you?" He left the room, tapping O'Connell on the back.

Nick returned with my nine millimeter and cell phone. "I found these next to your car. We dusted them for prints, but nothing came back. They aren't evidence, so you might as well hold on to them." I took the items from his hands. "Your phone's been buzzing like crazy. Martin sent you a few texts. You should tell him what happened."

"I don't even know what happened."

While I unlocked my phone and read through the details Martin managed to gain about the clinic from his various charity connections, a medic disconnected the IV. At least I was free to go, but I didn't know what to do. I looked to Nick for answers, but instead, he plopped down in a chair. I pushed the covers away and sat on the edge of the bed.

"Where are we?" I finally asked.

"The thirty-first floor of your office building."

"Why did you bring me here?"

"I didn't. Cross did." He shrugged. "You didn't want to go to the hospital. The possibility doctors or surgeons did this to you was enough of a deterrent, and aside from being hopped up on some serious tranquilizers and having a few scrapes, you seemed fine. Cross said his medical team could handle it, and since he was instrumental in locating you, I gave him the benefit of the doubt. I just stuck around to make sure it wasn't a mistake."

"Great."

"Seriously, Alex, you were lucky. Things could have been a lot worse. Do you think the bartender sent those men after you?"

"No, but he called in the tip about Ivy's murder. He didn't exactly provide details, but he did say whoever's using the clinic for unscrupulous things is controlling the gang."

O'Connell let the thought roll around for a few moments. "I don't think it fits, but I do believe your statement is enough to get a warrant to bust down the doors of the clinic and tear the place apart." He studied me for a long moment. "Is there anything else I should know?"

"Probably, but everything's jumbled in my head right now. Once I process it, I'll fill you in on the dirty details." Slowly, I climbed off the cot. "Martin did some digging for us. The clinic relies on charity. Henry Brandt and Dr. Dalton made it sound like a lot of their funding depends on donations, even though from what Cross and I gather it's largely paid for by a private corporation. I'll look through the info Martin found and what Cross has and forward it to you. When in doubt, follow the money." I led the way out of the room, contemplating what I needed to do first. Lucien probably had a list of things waiting in my office.

We made our way to the elevator, and Nick pushed the button. "Truthfully, if it weren't for your boss, I don't think we would have found you in time. The man might have a reputation at the precinct, but he didn't live up to it today. As soon as we get everything straightened out, you'll need to come in and answer more questions, but it can wait until tomorrow. A cruiser is parked outside. If you want to go anywhere, they'll take you. Whoever you screwed with isn't messing around. You need to be careful. Once they realize you aren't face down in the bathtub, they'll come looking."

"Not if I find them first."

TWENTY-SEVEN

Spending a couple of hours drugged in an abandoned medical building wasn't exactly how I thought the afternoon would go, but it might have provided the greatest chance of figuring out what happened to Jessika Wellington five years ago and what was continuing to happen in or around that neighborhood now. I was close to finding the truth. That's why they came for me, but they didn't expect the police or Cross to interfere. Now the men in scrubs had bigger problems. If they were smart, they'd scramble. But they probably thought they had too much to lose by abandoning whatever twisted endeavor they'd been pursuing for half a decade or longer.

At the moment, the police were staking out the abandoned medical facility. They had visuals on every possible route leading to the building. If anyone so much as came within sneezing distance, he'd be apprehended. The three vehicles involved in my abduction vanished. From the traffic cam footage, they didn't have plates, and no one ever got a close enough shot to check their VIN numbers. And since there were thousands of them in the city, it proved to be a dead end. For all we knew, they were stolen. O'Connell was checking, but so far, we didn't have any bites.

The police found a functioning lab and a refrigerator full of blood packs. Apparently, I wasn't the only donor, but it would take months to test all the samples for DNA in the hopes of linking them to anyone reported missing or dead. The only small comfort was we didn't find any ice chests full of body parts. At least we weren't chasing Hannibal Lecter.

A knock sounded at the door, and I glanced up. Cross leaned into the doorjamb, his arms folded over his chest. I gave him a questioning look, and he stepped inside.

"You're still here?" he asked, despite the obvious answer. He exhaled slowly. "Have the police made any arrests?"

"Not yet. I don't know if or when the men in scrubs might return. If they had some type of camera or security system in place, they know they've been compromised." The obvious question entered my mind again. "Do you believe they followed me from the bar? I did make a stop in between."

"I know. If you remember, I tracked your car." He took a step closer. "I don't think those men just happened to pick you up outside Mrs. Wellington's gym. And if that is the case, then they've been keeping tabs on the Wellingtons and fortuitously spotted you."

"That might explain why Capshaw was assaulted. Jessika's family could be in danger."

"I'm aware. I've assigned security teams to protect them." An amused smile found its way to his face. "New investigators are supposed to bring in revenue, not incur additional costs."

"Sorry."

He grinned playfully. "No, you're not."

My eyes went back to the reports on my computer screen, and he stepped behind my desk to read over my shoulder. This wasn't an isolated incident, which had been the premise surrounding Jessika's disappearance up until this point. The police found a possible dumping ground. The blood packs came from multiple donors. We were dealing with a spree of some sort.

I was researching suspicious deaths and missing persons reports for the last five years. The problem with most of these cases was they remained unsolved. No arrests were made, and the authorities never considered them in relation to one another.

"You think this is a serial crime?" Cross asked.

"Maybe. We don't know how the victims are selected. It might be purely accidental or opportunistic. We also don't know if these are victims." I gestured to the column of photos. "I was hoping to find some type of commonality or connection, but nothing stands out."

He picked up a manila folder from the edge of my desk, containing detailed financial information on the clinic and its benefactors. "Did you already look into this?"

"I just started. On the surface, it doesn't say much. Everyone has a charity these days. A contact of mine offered to help. He's expressed an interest in making a substantial donation, but before doing so, he asked to see how charitable contributions are spent. Once we have that information, maybe we can follow the money."

"Who was contacted from the charity?" Cross asked.

"I believe the request was made directly to Henry Brandt's office."

Cross nodded, flipping through the pages. "I wanted to do that but was afraid Brandt would become suspicious since I'd already shown an unhealthy obsession with his medical holdings."

I swiveled around to face him. "Did anything surface?"

"I don't have any proof, and William denies it. But Brandt was a client of William's investment firm prior to Jessika's disappearance. I tried to suss out an actual connection between the two, but William didn't work for Brandt. And if he did, there's no record. If William invested for Brandt, it was under the table, possibly through a shell company or an alias. I have a team of accountants digging through the paperwork. Brandt's portfolio is exceptionally diversified. The medical holdings he has are highly profitable, even the free clinic."

"Doesn't that strike you as odd, particularly since everyone says the free clinic is struggling?"

"It should be struggling. But it isn't presented that way to the board. Either Henry's lying to them, or he's lying to us. From what I've been told, the reason the clinic is so profitable is because of the donations they receive on top of the government grants. That allows the excess funding to be used for other sanctioned things like research."

"What kind of research?"

Cross rubbed a hand down his face. "It wasn't specified, but Brandt has amassed most of his wealth through ties to pharmaceutical companies. Drugs are big business in this country. The more donations he receives, the more he can invest in research."

"And the deeper his pockets become." Donations were a simple thing nowadays. "Any idea if they have some kind of crowd-funding campaign running?"

"I'll look into it. What are you thinking?" Cross asked curiously.

"They might have an online donation to pull in funding with unscrupulous incentives, or they could have some kind of dark web ad we haven't found. The blood and abandoned medical facility could be used to conduct unethical or unreported procedures. One of them said a liver was worth six figures." I shrugged, feeling myself tumbling down the rabbit hole. "Or Brandt could be clean, and the reason my abductors did what they did was nothing more than a really great misdirect."

Cross worked his jaw for a moment, flipping through the papers. "Why don't you go home, Miss Parker? You've had a difficult day."

I swallowed and looked away. "It's not over yet."

He touched my shoulder, and I cringed at the unexpected contact. "Think about calling it a night. I assure you it won't reflect negatively on your performance."

"I'm not leaving until I find out who these assholes are. I don't scare easy. I just get angry. And then I get even."

"Okay." He tapped the folder to his chest. "I'll look into this while you continue to work on that. I have some charity connections that might know more about what types of events and methods the clinic uses. If they have a whale on the hook, we need to check into that. Whenever your contact provides those records, send them up to my office. We'll go over them together."

My eyes went to the phone which hadn't rung since I'd been back in the office. "Just so we're on the same page, this is a police matter, right? Doesn't that mean we aren't supposed to interfere?"

"Yes, but when they took you, it became personal. I doubt the police are opposed to any assistance we can provide to them. Perhaps your presence at my company will pave the way for a better working relationship with the badges in the future."

I didn't think that was something Lucien Cross wanted, but he didn't give me enough time to question it before he left my office with the leads Martin provided in hand. At the moment, we were all on the same team. I just hoped we'd win.

The reports I read weren't helpful. Nothing was. Getting out of the chair, I walked around my office. After feeling helpless, I needed to move under my own power. Sure, I told Lucien I wasn't scared, but that was a lie. Not having control over my own body or my own safety was unacceptable. I wouldn't let it happen again. Grabbing a pen and paper, I paced the office, writing every thought that came to mind regarding the men in scrubs, the room, the set-up, and the things they said. Somewhere in this mess was the truth behind their identities.

"Knock, knock," Renner said from the doorway.

My back was to him. My eyes were closed as I struggled to remember something telling about Green Scrubs. His eyes. There was something about his eyes. What was it?

"Yo, Alex, I started thinking about that teacher again, the one who mentored Jessika. She seemed really close to some of her students. She probably friends them on social media. We checked out Jessika's friends and contacts when she disappeared, and no one knew anything. But maybe she had a connection to someone else like a networking business thing. We never explored that possibility because Jess was just a kid, but there could be something there."

"Huh," I muttered, my eyes still closed. Maybe it wasn't the eyes. Could it be his voice? There was something familiar about him. About all three of them, actually. I just couldn't figure out what it was.

"Parker, are you even listening?" Renner asked, his voice a lot closer now.

He grabbed my shoulder. Surprised by the sudden contact, I spun and shoved him backward, ready for a fight. His nose was bandaged, and he had two black eyes. My hand went to my nine millimeter. Jablonsky taught me coincidences don't happen. And this was a big coincidence.

"Whoa," Renner threw up his palms, "didn't mean to sneak up on you. Take it easy."

Narrowing my eyes, I focused on what I could see. He was about the same height and build as one of the men in blue scrubs. Did he tackle me to the ground? Was that why he panicked when his mask almost came undone? Did any of the men in scrubs walk with a limp? I didn't think so, but I could be wrong. Something was familiar about them. Why couldn't I figure out what it was? Drawing my weapon, I pointed it at the floor near his left foot, unsure of what I was doing.

"The next words out of your mouth are very important. How did you break your nose?" I asked.

Startled, Renner took a step back while his eyes darted around the room, an obvious reflex as he evaluated the situation. "What is this about?"

"Stop stalling. Answer the damn question."

He took half a step backward, slowly edging toward safety. "I got sucker-punched by a client."

"When?"

"A little after twelve."

"Why'd he punch you?"

Renner was getting annoyed with the twenty questions, but the sight of my nine millimeter kept him playing along. "It was a divorce case. He wanted photographic proof of her infidelity. I showed him some pictures. In hindsight, I probably shouldn't have used myself as a honey trap." He made it to the doorway; escape was just in sight. "Now do you want to tell me why the fuck you're holding me at gunpoint?" he said loud enough to attract the attention of everyone nearby.

"Can you prove your client hit you?"

"Jesus. We were in a restaurant. The waitress brought ice and tossed in a free dessert. I probably have the receipt in my pocket. Now are you going to put the gun away, or do we have a problem?"

Exhaling a long breath, I deflated, tucking my gun into my holster. Before I could ask if I could see the receipt, a security team came down the hallway. Renner remained in the doorway, an incredulous look on his face. Apparently, he wasn't used to his co-workers threatening to shoot him.

The security team pushed into my office, taking up the space between us. "Ma'am," one of the four men asked, "is everything okay? Do you need assistance?"

"What the fuck is going on around here?" Renner asked, flabbergasted. "She pulled a gun on me. Talk about some sexist bullshit. We don't even know her. She's been here for two weeks. I've been here for years. What is going on today?"

"Mr. Renner," Cross's cold tone stopped the tirade, "what happened to your nose?"

"Oh my god." Renner threw up his hands. "What do you think happened? I got punched in the face."

"By whom?" Cross asked, which only infuriated Renner.

"Stop," I said, "he has a receipt."

"A receipt?" Cross asked skeptically.

As I listened to the same conversation play out again, I couldn't help but think that nothing had ever sounded more ridiculous, and I burst into a fit of giggles. Dropping onto the couch, I tried to stop laughing, but that only made it worse. It was official. I lost it.

Once I regained my composure and Renner's story was verified with a quick call to the restaurant, Cross told him what occurred. Shaking his head, Renner poured a glass of whiskey and took a seat beside me. The security team left us alone, and Renner downed the drink. After a few moments, he nodded as if he reached an internal agreement.

"Sir, I want back on this case. Parker could use a hand, especially now that she's been targeted. We can't let this stand," Renner said. "They mess with one of us, they mess with all of us."

"The police are investigating," Cross replied.

"That's not enough. I just wrapped up a case. The other two need more research, but I can make time for them. This is more important."

"I don't need help," I interjected.

Renner snickered. "The fact that you almost shot me five minutes ago says otherwise."

After a moment, Cross came to a decision. "Actually, I think this situation warrants the entire firm's attention. I'll give a briefing in the morning and divide up duty assignments. In the meantime, pull backgrounds on every male who volunteered at the clinic in the last decade. I want photos and current addresses on my desk by seven a.m. The briefing will be at eight. You volunteered, so get to it, Mr. Renner."

"I can handle this. Once the police have a lead, everything will be straightened out," I said, not sure if I believed it. "You don't need to waste your resources or money on me."

Cross's expression turned stern. "I can't have you threatening my employees. Grab your things. I'm taking you home. No arguments. You're done for the day."

"I can take myself home."

"That sounds like an argument." He glared. "Need I remind you that your car is in police impound right now?"

"And there's a unit outside to take me wherever I want to go. It's like having my own driver, kinda like you." I regretted saying it the moment the words left my lips. This was my boss. The same man who saved my life earlier today. "Sorry, I just..."

"It's okay. You need time. Trauma affects everyone, regardless of training. Let's go." He waited at the door while I grabbed some files and whatever else I thought I might need since I'd be working from home.

When we arrived at my apartment, Cross walked me to my door, insisting he needed to relay the lay of the land to his security team. The patrol car stationed out front was monitoring the area for any suspicious activity. They gave me a radio to use in the event someone slipped past and made it inside. Since we didn't know who the three men were who abducted me, the odds of that were pretty high.

"Not what I expected," Cross said, staring out the fire escape. This is the only other entry point?"

"Yep."

"And the building itself just has the front door. Nothing around back?"

"Nope, unless someone knocked down a wall when I wasn't looking."

"That seems like a building code violation." He nodded more to himself than to me. "Okay. I'll have the team split. Two will cover the fire escape. The other two will maintain eyes on the front door. The police are also guarding the front, but we can't be too careful."

"Do you really think they'll try again?" I asked, feeling like these measures were a tad extreme.

"Why wouldn't they? They had no qualms about snatching you in broad daylight in the middle of traffic. I doubt they'd think twice about coming here to finish the job."

"It's different," I insisted.

He cocked an eyebrow. "How?" When I didn't provide an answer, he went to my front door. "You don't need to attend the briefing in the morning. And if you aren't up to coming to work, just let one of the assistants know."

"Don't get too excited. I'll be there."

TWENTY-EIGHT

When I exhausted the research materials and my eyes were strained to the point that I couldn't look at the computer screen for another moment, I went to bed. Sleep came easily, probably due to whatever sedatives lingered and my lowered blood count, but the nightmares followed. I'd been plagued by them for years. And tonight was brutal.

I woke up screaming, a combination of what happened, the horrors my mind conjured, and memories I spent years attempting to repress. I wiped the layer of sweat off my face and flipped on the light. My mind raced almost as fast as my pulse, and I struggled to cling to the few fleeting thoughts I had only moments ago. When my heart calmed and the shaking abated, I climbed out of bed and went into the kitchen. The files were open on the table, and I glanced at them. It was late. I was exhausted, but thoughts of Renner's broken nose came to mind. He said he was meeting a client. He had a receipt. But the whole thing could be bogus.

Cross checked his alibi, but that didn't mean my boss wasn't a part of this. Sure, he helped O'Connell find me. But was that too convenient? My boss had been spying on me since the get-go. That was weird. Why didn't he want me at the morning briefing? Why was he suddenly letting the police take over? Why did he tell me to stay out of the neighborhood? He hindered my investigation several times. Could he be a part of this? He might be covering for someone, or maybe he was afraid I was getting too close.

And what about the bartender? Jared Prince was dangerous. He warned me away, and when I came back, he definitely wasn't happy. He could have followed me. He could have asked some of his goons or whatever members of the Seven Rooks that remained to abduct me. He could have been one of the men in scrubs, just not the one in green. His eyes were the wrong color, and he would know how to throw a punch. He'd been in prison. He would have picked up some skills. He might have been the one with the scalpel, but it didn't sound like his voice.

Aware that these theories were nothing but the result of sleep deprivation and fear, I closed the files, grabbed the necessities from my bedroom, and curled up on the couch. After channel surfing for twenty minutes, I found some family-friendly programming that didn't seem violent or deranged and stared at the screen until I couldn't hold my eyes open any longer.

Something buzzed, and I jumped, grabbing my handgun and pointing it at the source of the sound. "Shit." Reaching over, I grabbed my phone. "Parker," I said.

"We made an arrest." Nick sounded drained. "We've been grilling him for the better part of two hours. We haven't gotten a thing out of him."

"Do you want me to take a crack?" I asked.

He sighed. "No. His lawyer's here. We're going to put him in a lineup and see if you can identify him."

"How the hell am I supposed to do that?"

"I don't know," he replied glumly. "The thing is we don't have anything on him except trespassing. Just come down here, listen to his voice, look at his eyes, watch the way he walks, whatever it is you need to do in order to figure out if he's one of the men who attacked you."

"Does he have a broken nose?"

"No."

"Maybe you could break it."

Rubbing the back of my neck, I untangled myself from the blanket and found the remote. Turning off the TV, I checked the time. It was a little after seven. Cross's briefing would be underway soon. Good thing he didn't expect me to be there. My paranoid theories from last night resurfaced, and I realized I didn't trust anyone at the office. I didn't know them. Therefore, how could I trust them? They didn't know me either, which might explain why someone was constantly looking over my shoulder. Still, it left an unsettling feeling in my gut. And I learned long ago to trust my instincts. Something wasn't right, but I didn't know what it was. All I knew was I couldn't shake the feeling I previously encountered my attackers.

After a quick shower and a liquid breakfast of caffeine topped with more caffeine, I drove to the station. The patrol car followed with the Cross security team a few car lengths behind. When our little caravan arrived at the precinct, I went upstairs to find Detective O'Connell.

The lineup didn't take long. Out of the six men, I had no idea which one they arrested, but I did have a sneaking suspicion numbers two and six were cops pulled in to fill out the room. Then again, I might be wrong. The man's counsel lingered behind me, practically jumping with joy at my inability to make a proper identification.

"Asshole," I muttered under my breath.

"I expect my client will be released. Trespassing is a misdemeanor offense. He should be free to go," the lawyer insisted.

O'Connell rolled his eyes. "Yeah, we'll get him out of here in a few minutes. Why don't you go with the officer and wait with your client in the interrogation room? We'll bring the paperwork to you."

As soon as we were alone, I slumped against the desk. "Do you think he was involved?" I gestured vaguely at the now empty room where the six men had stood.

"I'm not sure what other reason he'd have for entering the abandoned medical building." O'Connell sighed and opened the door. "You really didn't recognize him?"

I shook my head. It was barely eight a.m., and I was already a failure. I should probably go back to bed before the day could get worse. "Did you find anything damning on him? Latex gloves? Syringes? A face mask?"

"Nope. I don't know this for a fact, but since those things were already inside the building, the men who grabbed you probably shed the ski masks and put on their doctor disguises after they entered the medical facility."

"Unless it's a different group of guys."

"Which is also a possibility."

A thought gnawed at the corners of my mind. "When did they take them off?"

"What?"

"The gloves. They were latex. Did you find any discarded latex gloves inside the building? If you can flip them inside out, you might be able to get a usable print."

"CSU didn't find any used gloves or masks. They must have disposed of them elsewhere."

I stared at Nick for the longest time. "What interrogation room is he in?"

"I can't let you go in there. You're not law enforcement. You're a victim."

"I don't want to go in there. I want to wait outside. Is that a problem?"

"You're playing a dangerous game, Parker."

"What else is new?"

He didn't bother to mask his annoyance. "Stay here," he pointed to a row of chairs. "I'll come back for you when I'm finished."

I took a seat near the front desk and watched O'Connell go down the hallway. The interrogation rooms were down the next corridor, but since the perp was free to go, he and his counsel would have to go past me to get out of the building. They weren't special enough to sneak out the back.

Fifteen minutes later, I recognized the defense attorney as he moved through the precinct. His eyes were focused on his phone. Judging by his age and dress, he was probably a junior partner for some ambulance chasers. He didn't give a shit about his client any more than the man on the moon. He was probably relieved that without a reliable eyewitness, the cops couldn't pressure the DA to file felony charges. His day just got a lot easier, and mine got a lot harder.

Behind him was an unremarkable man. He carried the telltale police envelope containing his personal belongings from the time he was booked. I studied him. He was number three in the lineup. As he walked through the police station, he emptied the envelope and put the items into his pockets. The attorney turned at the door, said something, and shook his hand. Their business was concluded.

The perp didn't notice me, or he did a good job making sure he didn't. The men went outside, and I followed several steps behind them. The attorney didn't waste any time getting into his car and driving away. Without having to worry about someone interfering, I followed the perp down the front steps. The first thing I noticed was he didn't have a phone. That was rare, almost as if he expected to get picked up by the police.

"Excuse me," I called. He spun around, but I didn't see the slightest bit of recognition on his face. "Oh, I'm sorry. I thought you were someone else."

He offered a slight smile. "That's okay." He turned back around and went down the remaining steps to the sidewalk. Even his voice didn't sound familiar. I watched as he continued on a path toward the bus stop.

My eyes scanned the area, and I spotted an unmarked car on the street. At least the police were following him. He was our only lead, even though it appeared to be another dead end. Trudging back inside, I found O'Connell waiting near the vending machine. He pressed a button, waiting for a bag of chocolate candies to fall from the second shelf. After retrieving the treat, he tore off the top and popped a handful into his mouth. Then he offered me the rest.

"It wasn't him." I poured a couple of pieces into my palm and bit into one thoughtfully. "It's weird he didn't have a phone."

"Cell phones are expensive," O'Connell retorted, playing devil's advocate.

"True, but how many guys have you arrested who don't have a phone?"

"Well, last night made one."

"Yeah, that's what I thought. Is that why you're shadowing him?"

Nick shrugged, making it clear we weren't discussing an ongoing investigation. For all intents and purposes, I was a victim, even though my investigation is what led to the incident in the first place. Unsure of what else to do but knowing there was more to discuss, I followed him upstairs.

Detective Sparrow was huddled around Thompson's desk, sorting through the medical examiner's report. Apparently, the ME identified Ivy's cause of death. From a quick glance at the scattered paperwork, the blood work came back clean. That was odd, particularly for a hooker. Drugs were often how the women got into the life or how they dealt with the life. The other strange thing was the cause of death.

"Anything interesting?" I asked, wondering if the papers were from another victim's file instead of the hooker's.

Thompson let out a disgruntled snort, and Sparrow glanced in my direction. She didn't say anything, but she picked through some pages and handed them to Thompson. O'Connell didn't even bother to ask what had their interest. Knowing Nick, he already knew.

After five minutes of awkward silence, Thompson took the file into the lieutenant's office, and Sparrow dropped into his chair. She studied me for a moment, taking in the previous day's injuries. Her eyes shifted to O'Connell who was typing up a report regarding the perp's release. Deciding she might as well spill the beans, she glanced around again to make sure no one was nearby.

"The hooker was killed elsewhere. We didn't find any defensive wounds or any indication she put up a fight. Of course, there were indications of recent sexual activity, but given her profession, that's to be expected. What isn't expected is the lack of narcotics."

"What killed her?" I asked.

Sparrow glanced down at the papers again, as if the answer couldn't possibly be correct. "I already told you she bled out." She flipped through the photos. "Do you believe in vampires?"

"Nosferatu or sparkly ones with feelings?"

"Either." She flipped the image around to show me a close-up photo of Ivy's neck. Two deep puncture marks marred the side. They were large, almost as if someone stuck a spile in her.

Subconsciously, my hand went to the side of my own neck where I'd been pricked yesterday afternoon. "Any idea what caused that?"

"Not yet. Someone speculated a nail gun." She examined the photo again. "Except we didn't find any nails. Perhaps they were pulled out and left at the murder scene."

"Shouldn't her clothing be bloody? If someone pulled two nails out of her neck, she would have gushed blood." For a moment, my mind went back to Michelle Mercer's murder, and I physically had to shake the images away. This was the second case where the lack of blood spatter didn't match the crime.

"It's possible someone changed her clothes," O'Connell surmised. "We did find a few splotches on her shoulder but nothing to warrant the bloodshed those wounds would have inflicted." He glanced at me. "She didn't fight back. If it was a nail gun, it happened at a distance, and it was over before she could get a hand on her attacker or even on her own neck. It's also possible she didn't fight back because she couldn't." He pushed a chair closer, suggesting I sit. "Perhaps she was given the same type of paralytic you were. That's why we're running another tox report to scan for similarities to what we found inside you. The preliminary one only checked for common narcotics."

"You wanted me to see this?" I asked.

He scratched at the stubble on his cheek. "As far as I'm aware, you haven't seen any of it. You're a victim. I can't share details like this with you. Frankly, you shouldn't even be here. Shouldn't you be at work? Or did you call in sick?"

"Do I look sick?"

"Actually," O'Connell said, critically judging my appearance, "you have looked better."

"Thanks." Turning, I nodded to Sparrow. "Should anything else surface, maybe a little bird can fill me in."

She rolled her eyes in annoyance. "That's the one and only time you get to say that. I'll stop by to see you once we know more. Missing persons is all over this."

"I thought major crimes and gangs took over," I replied.

"They did," she narrowed her eyes at Nick, "but they're looking to make arrests for the murder and attempted murder. In the unlikely event they aren't connected, solving Jessika Wellington's disappearance reverts back to me."

"Wow, those guys sound like such bastards." I winked at Nick. "I'll be at work if you need me."

His eyes fixed in a warning stare. "You better be. No more disappearing or getting into cars with strangers."

"Believe me, that will never happen again."

TWENTY-NINE

Before I made it out of the precinct, I was asked to provide another statement. The police were being thorough. It was possible I remembered something else now that the shock wore off. The things I remembered weren't helpful; at least I didn't think they were. After a few photographs of the darkened bruises from the failed attempts to put a needle in my arm and the physical altercation with the three men, I was free to go. I'd just taken a seat behind the wheel when I remembered Sparrow saying Ivy had fresh track marks but no narcotics in her system. The men who killed her were the same ones who tried to kill me. There was no doubt about that.

We needed Jared Prince to answer some questions. He was the tipster. He knew who was behind this. But a healthy dose of fear discouraged me from going back to the bar alone. Instead, I returned to the office, the police escort and Cross Security's bodyguards trailing behind.

When I made it to the thirtieth floor, everyone was congregated in the large conference room. Cross was speaking when I barged inside. He stopped talking, studying the way I looked as I took a seat in the nearest empty chair at the end of the table. A few of the other investigators glanced in my direction, eyeing the deep red marks along my wrists and the bruises on my face. Kellan shifted, catching my eye and offering a reassuring nod.

"Are there any questions?" Cross asked, commanding their attention. No one spoke, and his eyes fixed on mine. "Is there something you'd like to say, Miss Parker?"

"Ivy Greene was murdered two nights ago. Whoever killed her came after me yesterday. There is no proof, but it's my understanding Jared Prince is the anonymous tipster. The police don't know this, and even if I told them," I licked my lips, "it's complicated."

"I'll find out what's what with Prince," Kellan declared, glancing at Cross who must have already doled out the assignments.

"Did the police disclose anything else this morning?" Cross asked.

I shook my head.

"Do they have a lead?"

"Possibly." My gaze drifted as more thoughts entered my mind. "We'll see where it goes."

Cross nodded, dismissed the room, and took a seat beside me. "You should be at home."

"I'm fine."

"You're agitated."

"Damn right. The only thing that will cure it is work. So tell me what to do. I'm guessing you already handed off the entire investigation to everyone else."

"That isn't a reflection on you. This is a big case. Hell, this isn't even our case."

"Then why are you wasting your time?" I spat, getting up and circling the table.

"It might be great publicity." Even though he sounded sincere, I wasn't sure I bought his answer. "Take the morning to get your shit together and meet me in my office in two hours. We'll decide how to proceed from there." He went to the door. "And Miss Parker, don't draw your gun on any more of your colleagues."

I dropped into a chair and stared into the hallway. My brain was in overdrive. There were so many avenues to pursue. I had to believe Cross already sent his army to tackle those obstacles. But I had the answers. I just wasn't sure how to sort through the noise to find them.

The shrill ring of my phone broke the silence of the empty conference room, and I jumped. Damn, my nerves were shot. A check of the caller ID showed it was Martin. Striding out of the room, I locked myself inside my office before hitting answer.

"Hello?"

"Listen, sweetheart, my accounts manager phoned this morning. We received the breakdown on the charitable distributions. He's looking over it for any obvious discrepancies or inconsistencies. I asked him to forward the original document and his analysis to your inbox. Is that okay?"

"That's great."

As usual, Martin had a sixth sense. "Is everything okay?"

For a moment, I fought the impulse to lie. We were in this together. He would want to know. "Actually, something happened yesterday." I downplayed the situation, giving him just enough so he wouldn't be freaked out when he saw my new bruises.

"I can fly back."

"Martin, don't be ridiculous. That's entirely unnecessary. Right now, work is crazy. O'Connell and the rest of the department are on top of this."

"What's Lucien doing?"

I filed the oddity of Martin using my boss's first name in the back of my mind for later contemplation. "Everyone at Cross Security is on it. Is there any way your inquiry could lead these men to target you?"

"I don't see how. You've always guarded our connection, and the inquiry was just a boilerplate we send to every charitable organization we are considering for a donation or joint venture. I don't think anyone in Henry Brandt's office will give it a second thought."

"Just be careful."

"I am." I could practically hear the muscles in his jaw clenching as he thought what to say. "Alexis, ask me to come home. I can be back in a matter of hours."

"I'm okay."

"Promise?"

"Yes."

"Make sure you stay that way."

After we hung up, I checked my e-mail, but the information hadn't arrived yet. Knowing Martin, he probably had his entire charity foundation reviewing the information before I received their expert assessment. Frankly, I was sure Cross had people who could do it, but since I had another ninety minutes before our meeting, it could wait. I needed answers. Marching back to the conference room, I found it empty. I glanced both ways, watching as investigators and assistants scurried to perform their tasks.

"Can I set some things up in here?"

An assistant turned at my words. She clicked a button on her headset, repeated my question, and nodded. "Go ahead."

Scrubbing a hand down my face, I grabbed some things and returned to the conference room. Honestly, there was no reason to do this here. My office was spacious enough to house what I needed, but it was something about a community workspace and a task force that made the conference room seem like the best option. Perhaps I was homesick for the federal building, or I just didn't want to be alone. Either way, I set to work.

When I was finished, I leaned against the table and stared at my handiwork. The various panes of glass that composed the interior wall of the room were now covered in photos and notations. Every suspect and potential lead in Jessika's disappearance was visually displayed, along with possible connections. I mapped it out, drawing lines and connecting people.

I just stared, thinking through everyone and everything. Lines connected Jared Prince to his unknown "drunk" associate and Josh and Victor. Henry Brandt connected to the various clinic staff, including Dr. Dalton. His investments connected him to William Wellington. The Wellington family connected to Capshaw, Cleese, Dylan, and every other friend and teacher we knew about. I went back and drew a line connecting Capshaw to the Seven Rooks. They connected to the clinic and the neighborhood and Ivy, who connected to the dumping ground. After taking it in, my head started to pound. I drew a few more lines with question marks to label the unknowns, like the man who attacked Capshaw.

"Is that what it looks like inside your head?" Renner asked, entering the conference room.

"That's just scratching the surface. I owe you an apology for yesterday. I had no right to accuse you."

He crossed the room to stand beside me. His limp, while not a great impediment, was hard to miss. If one of the men in scrubs limped, I would have remembered. "Who would have thought a broken nose almost got me killed?" He folded his arms over his chest while he stared at the photos and notes. When I glanced at him, I realized his gaze had shifted to me. "Those assholes roughed you up pretty bad, huh?"

"I've had worse."

"And you really don't know who they are? That's pretty fucked up." He pulled out one of the chairs and took a seat, dropping a file on the table. "Lucien wanted you to look at some photos and see if anyone rings a bell. Why don't you sit down?" After flipping through a few dozen photos, I stopped on one. Renner smiled. "Do we have a winner?"

"This man, Josh Addai, he and his pal Victor attacked me at the bar." My eyes narrowed as I studied Josh's eyes. I didn't trust my memory. I had flashes from the attack inside the bar, seeing him close-up and prepared to drag me out from beneath the pool table. He might have been the man whose nose I broke. I just wasn't sure. "Where did you get these?"

"Clinic records."

"I went through the clinic's records. He didn't pop up."

"He isn't a steady volunteer. They keep those records separate. You can't access them online. The police department received copies of everything when Detective Sparrow got a warrant for their records. Intrigued yet?"

I dove back through the photos, intent on finding Victor, but he wasn't in the mix. "I need to make a call." I dialed

O'Connell and gave him the name. Oddly enough, he didn't ask for anything else in conjunction with it. Instead, he told me he'd let me know if and when they needed me.

Renner tapped the stack of photographs against the table. "Are they going to bring Addai in for questioning?"

"I think so."

"You might have to press charges. If they don't have something solid, he'll walk."

"Don't worry. He's not going anywhere."

Before I could say anything else, Cross's personal assistant appeared in the doorway. "Pardon the interruption, but Mr. Cross is waiting."

"Duty calls." I brushed my hand against Renner's shoulder. "Thanks for digging through the records. I'm glad I didn't shoot you."

"That makes two of us."

Before taking the elevator to Cross's office, I ducked into mine and printed the documents Martin's accounts manager forwarded, tearing off the e-mail address from the top so Cross wouldn't know more than was necessary. We might be on the same side, but I intended for my personal life to remain personal.

Documents in hand, I entered through the open office door and took a seat on the sofa across from where he was seated. Since Cross wasn't behind his desk, this meeting was meant to be less formal. Perhaps he wanted me to feel at ease. Oddly enough, he took my abduction a lot harder than I thought he would. Maybe he wasn't a heartless, tyrannical douche. He did help save my life. That counted for a hell of a lot in my book.

He held out his hand for the documents, glancing at them before putting them on the table. After clearing his throat, he rested his forearms on his thighs. "Henry Brandt might be a genius. He's in charge of an entire umbrella corporation which encompasses a million different aspects of healthcare. He runs several free clinics in the city. Those fall under the nonprofit label. In addition to that, he's the money man behind several medical facilities, a local private hospital, three nursing homes, a psychiatric center, and a women's shelter."

"How does the shelter fit with the rest?"

Cross shrugged. "It's categorized as a charity. He must have deemed it necessary for tax incentives." His eyes went to the breakdown. "This should reinforce the assumptions my financial experts reached. You see, aside from the day-to-day expenses, doctors, equipment, upkeep, etcetera, Brandt's umbrella has a branch that assists in clinical trials and pharmaceutical studies. The medical offices and hospitals they control provide the patients, the locations, and kick back a good portion of funding for further research. And it's entirely privatized."

"What about the FDA and certifications? Things like that are closely monitored," I argued.

"They are. And I'm sure his paperwork is in order. The issue isn't with the studies. The issue is with where he's getting this extra income to throw back into research. His overhead cancels out a good deal of profit. The free clinics and women's shelter should be operating in the red. That's basically what he said when we spoke, and from the records I've seen," again he looked at the documents I handed him, "that fact couldn't be further from the truth."

"How does he explain the discrepancy?"

"Highly efficient fundraisers. Allegedly, the charitable donations are so far beyond anyone's expectations the clinic could be constructed out of gold. Instead, the fine print stipulates donations may be used for research into cutting-edge medical advancements."

That clause rubbed me the wrong way, particularly since everyone affiliated with the clinic claimed they didn't have enough supplies or help. "So you think he's cutting operating costs to fund more research?" I picked up a few sheets with a breakdown of Brandt's personal accounts. "You did say his personal portfolio centered on pharmaceuticals and biotech."

"I don't know what he's doing, but he's doing something shady."

"Do you think it involves butchering people for spare parts and forcing blood donations?"

Cross sighed, knowing whatever this was it didn't fit with the problems we were facing. "I'm not sure how it connects."

"Janet Wellington works for a nonprofit, and William works at an investment firm. Are we certain there isn't overlap?"

"Nothing hard and fast." He slid another sheet toward me. "That abandoned medical facility where we found you used to be leased by the company Brandt represents."

THIRTY

The intercom chirped. "Mr. Cross, the police are here to see you."

"Send them in," he replied. I moved to stand, but Cross held up a hand. "I'm sure they want to speak to both of us." A moment later, the door opened, and Detectives O'Connell and Thompson stepped into the office. Cross gestured to the L-shaped sofa. "Have a seat, gentlemen."

"Thanks." Nick offered a slight smile while Thompson took in the room. "We just wanted to touch base."

"Have you made any progress since this morning?" I asked, my eyes darting from O'Connell to Thompson.

"Yeah, some." O'Connell eyed Cross. "Is our agreement from yesterday still in effect?"

Cross nodded. "My resources are at your disposal."

"Okay." O'Connell gave Thompson the floor.

"We unearthed twelve bodies in various states of decay. Presently, dental records are being used to identify the victims. We've matched three to other missing persons cases and one to a former clinic worker." He handed Cross a sheet of paper.

"It's the former employee we were unable to locate," Cross clarified.

"Did you find Jessika?" My stomach churned.

"Not yet." O'Connell stood and paced the room. "There

might be more bodies down deeper. We aren't sure, and not all the remains have been identified yet. If we find her, we'll let you know. In the meantime, we arrested three men in conjunction with your abduction yesterday. Jared Prince is a material witness."

I closed my eyes and took a breath. "Do you think he's involved?"

Thompson shook his head. "He volunteered to help."

"What?" My eyes went wide. "He threatened to kill me if the police questioned him."

"It appears he's changed his tune. It might have something to do with the ATF agent who hauled him into the precinct two hours ago," O'Connell said. "Apparently, they received a call from someone inside this building and realized their confidential informant might be involved in a killing spree. They apparently talked to Prince, and he had a come-to-Jesus moment. He's been talking up a storm, but it's mostly hearsay. He hasn't given us proof of anything, but he did identify the men who attacked you inside his bar."

"That's why you were indifferent when I told you to pick up Josh Addai." Things were starting to make some sense.

O'Connell shrugged noncommittally.

"You should probably know the man we released this morning led us to another of your assailants, Victor Harrendale. We need you to come down and identify him as the man from the bar brawl," Thompson said, something sparking in his eyes told me it was more than just that.

"I'm ready when you are," I said, standing.

"Not so fast." O'Connell turned his focus back to Cross. "Show us yours."

So my boss spent the next forty minutes speculating as to the financial connections we previously discussed. "The abandoned medical facility is no longer part of Brandt's holdings. It's owned by the bank and available for purchase. We contacted the real estate agency in charge of selling it, but they failed to comment as to why no one has visited the property or cleared out the remaining items. Maybe your people could see if someone is getting paid under the table to keep interested buyers away. If this is where these murders are being committed, then whoever is abducting these individuals wants the building to remain vacant."

"We'll look into it," O'Connell declared. "Thanks for the heads up." He jerked his chin at the door, waiting for me to lead the way out.

*   *   *

I stared through the two-way glass at Josh Addai. His nose was broken. Flashes of my failed escape attempt played through my mind on a loop. He was on top of me, scrambling. His mask slipped in the fracas, and he covered his face. I knew it was him. Everything indicated it. The problem was I never actually saw his face, making the entire case circumstantial at best.

Closing my eyes, I tried to remember if there was anything definitively telling, but there wasn't. We couldn't even get him for aggravated assault because he never took up a weapon to use against me at the bar. Hell, he never even hit me. That led to a thought, and I turned to Thompson who was standing beside me.

"He's your weak link. He wasn't thrilled by the prospect of killing me." I turned away from the glass and left the room, entering another room two doors down. The man who waited on the other side of this mirror was another story.

Thompson pulled O'Connell out of the interrogation room, shared my tidbit, and then joined me. "Are you okay, Parker?"

Ignoring the question, I pointed an accusatory finger at Victor Harrendale. "This man wanted to kill me. He tried. Twice. He should have a stab wound right here." I indicated the place I knifed him on my own body.

"Did that happen during the bar fight or yesterday?" Thompson asked.

A part of me wanted to lie. A lie might be the only way I could prove these men abducted me, and it might be the only way to find out what the clinic was doing and what they did with Jessika. I didn't speak for several moments, realizing the stab wound would have already healed to a certain degree. A lie would have the entire case thrown out of court, and the stakes were too high to risk on a gamble.

"You know when it happened," I replied. "But he was there yesterday. He had the scalpel. He stabbed the syringe into my back. He tossed me into the tub and left me to drown. That's attempted murder."

Thompson touched my arm, and I jerked backward. "Easy. We have him. He can't hurt you."

"He can't, but what about the man in Green Scrubs? We have no idea who he is." I pointed emphatically at the glass. "One of these bastards has to tell us."

"We're working on it."

"Work faster." I didn't like feeling as if I were unraveling. This case wasn't about me. It shouldn't be personal, but it sure felt that way, especially as I stared into Victor's cold eyes. My only solace was he couldn't see me. "Where's Prince?"

"He's upstairs, speaking to Brooke," Thompson said. "Did you know he was an ATF informant?"

"No. It makes sense, but I didn't know. Is his handler with him?"

Thompson nodded. "Do you want to talk to them? Since he isn't implicated in your abduction and has an alibi for the time of Ivy Greene's murder, I don't think it's a conflict of interest."

"No conflict," I repeated, wondering if any of what Prince said was true or if his involvement was being swept under the rug by the federal government in exchange for whatever big fish they were chasing. "I just want to stop by and say hi."

Sure, I was damn woozy after getting clocked in the back of the head, but I still recognized Prince's drunk friend as the same man carrying ATF credentials. Glaring at him, I waited for Sparrow to make the formal introduction.

"We've met." I cocked an eyebrow. "Pretty convincing undercover work, Agent Ivers. Would you mind providing the name of your supervisor and agency contact?"

"Not at all." He gave us a name and phone number, and I looked expectantly at Sparrow to verify those details. After she hung up, Ivers smiled. "Happy?"

"No. What interest does the ATF have in that neighborhood?"

"I'm not at liberty to share that information."

"You are supposed to notify local law enforcement of ongoing operations."

"This is sensitive. It's information gathering only. There is no active op," Ivers insisted.

"Does this have to do with the murders or the missing girl?" Sparrow asked, diving into the questioning since I got the ball rolling.

"Neither, ma'am." He looked at her. "Jared has nothing to do with the clinic or the bodies that surfaced. His usefulness to us is in regards to an unrelated matter."

"How can you be sure it's unrelated?" Sparrow asked before I could get the question out.

"It just is," Ivers said. He glanced at Prince who'd been eyeing me throughout the conversation. "I didn't want to risk interfering in police matters but helping out would be proper; even though it could jeopardize my informant and our operation."

Prince's words were meant for me when he said, "I told you to walk away. I told you what I knew and warned you to stay out of the neighborhood. When you came back, they must have seen you in my bar and tracked you."

"So you came forward because you were afraid they'd come after you next," I surmised.

"Detective, are we done?" Ivers asked. "If you need any further elaboration, you can have someone from the ATF contact me, and I will get in touch."

Even if she didn't agree, someone with enough pull would make a few calls and force her to comply. That's how things were done. I had half a mind to call Jablonsky and see if he could force the ATF to read the OIO in on the situation, but I walked away from that job and those resources. Asking for a favor now wasn't the answer.

"Yeah, you can go. But don't go far. We might need you to testify," she said.

"I didn't see anything. I heard some guys talking about the dead hooker. I don't know who they were, and I don't remember what they looked like. It was a long night," Prince declared. He gave me another look. "And I don't know anything more about the missing girl. And for the record, I don't know who took you yesterday either."

"Did you hear anyone talking about it?" I asked.

Prince spun. "Only that they lost another one." He shrugged. "Whatever that means."

"Dammit," I growled.

"Hold that thought," Thompson said, looking behind me. "The DA's here, and from the look on Nick's face, things are about to get worse."

It was rare the district attorney made an appearance in the precinct. Most cases were handled by ADAs. The big ones, the ones that would lead to plenty of positive publicity, were the ones he chose to tackle. It was no secret he had political aspirations, and a win on a major case could pave the way to something grand.

"Alexis Parker," he said, nodding. We'd met a few times in the past.

"Sir," my eyes darted to O'Connell who was standing a polite two steps behind the DA, "where do we stand?"

"I won't lie to you. The circumstances are not optimal. I've reviewed your statement, Mr. Cross's statement, and the police reports concerning the unfortunate events that transpired yesterday. If we prosecute, the defense will shred your testimony on the stand. We have no physical evidence linking either of those men to where you were held. Sure, we could argue they have a motive based on what occurred a week ago in a bar, but it could be construed that you're holding a grudge or your mind has combined the two events."

"She used to be a federal agent," O'Connell snarled, "doesn't that lend itself to her credibility? She's been trained to recall faces and events."

The DA swallowed. "In the event we were to pursue that route, the defense would delve into the reason for your resignation. I don't know any agent who resigns just for the hell of it. There's always dirt or some facts they can twist.

Pursuing this without hard evidence is not something my office is willing to do at this time." His eyes went to Sparrow and Thompson. "That being said, as soon as you have solid evidence linking those twelve bodies to someone, I will be more than happy to prosecute."

"This is bullshit," Thompson said. "We know they're involved. The more charges and accusations we can make, the more likely they are to open up and roll on whoever's orchestrating this."

"Then get me some hard evidence. A confession out of either of them would go a long way. Without it, I need something irrefutable or even a reliable eyewitness." With a grim look on his face, the DA excused himself and walked away.

"At least we have them for assault and battery," Sparrow muttered. "We can keep on them until we uncover something useful."

"You searched them, right?"

"We searched everything and everyone. Homes, vehicles, work. We didn't find anything to indicate they were involved in your abduction. We'll keep looking until we find something."

"You won't, but they don't know that." I contemplated our options before deciding on a convincing bluff. "They wore gloves and masks. It muffled their voices and concealed their faces. Josh's mask came loose. That's when I broke his nose and made a run for it. Victor caught me then. He had the scalpel."

"Several scalpels were on the premises," Sparrow offered, unfamiliar with the dynamics of the fight.

"The one he planned to use to cut my throat didn't remain in the building." I bit my lip, trying to think through the dilemma.

"What about the syringe?" O'Connell asked. "We have it in evidence. We analyzed it to determine what type of paralytic they gave you. It was run-of-the-mill, readily available at most medical facilities."

"Yeah, and he was holding it pretty tightly to jab it into my back." My face contorted at the word, and I sucked in my cheek to hide the sudden surge of emotions. "He only wore latex gloves."

"They were thick enough to prevent leaving any prints," Thompson said, earning a searing glance.

"Victor doesn't know that." O'Connell focused on me. "We do this right, he might be willing to make a deal. Are you okay with that?"

"I have to be."

THIRTY-ONE

Since O'Connell just finished grilling Victor, it was best to let the perp stew. If not, he might realize it was a ploy. The detective would have shown his hand if he had an ace up his sleeve. So now, it was important to wait. Victor knew the techs were scouring the scene for evidence. He knew they were determined to find a link, so it'd be easier to convince Victor he left a print in a few hours when presented with a different syringe with a blatantly obvious fingerprint on the stopper. Nick would convince him he fucked up. After all, Victor left the syringe in the tub, and it was his responsibility to make sure nothing was left at the crime scene. However, my gut said Josh would be easier to manipulate.

"I want to talk to him. I'm aware of the possible ramifications, but I think it's worth it," I insisted. "I'm just a civilian. What harm can it do? I promise not to threaten or coerce him. Just keep the camera on and the mic turned up. Anything he says outside an interrogation room is fair game."

Sparrow was edgy with my plan. Unlike the boys in major crimes who were used to the way I did things, she was iffy. She was a good cop. They were too. This wasn't illegal. It was just a conversation between two acquaintances which happened to occur in front of a webcam.

"The district attorney isn't going to like this," she warned.

"He doesn't like much," I retorted, offering a grin, "but if it leads to Josh flipping on his associates and offering up valuable intel regarding the clinic's involvement and the twelve bodies, he'll be damn impressed. And if he ever makes it to mayor, maybe he'll appoint you as commissioner."

Her eyes shot skyward. "Puh-lease. Like that would ever happen."

"Would you want it to?" Thompson asked, his tone gave away the fact he didn't want to think about his girlfriend in a command position.

Sensing this might turn into a lover's quarrel, O'Connell intervened. "Look, I'll haul him out of interrogation and bring him to my desk to fill out some forms we misplaced during booking. I'll tell him we need the room for something else. When I go to check on the papers, you and Thompson keep your distance but keep an eye on him in the event he tries to make a break for it. Alex will come through those doors, take a seat, and confront him. We'll see what we get."

"For the record, I don't like it," Sparrow replied.

"You don't have to," I said. "Get out of here. Go check on something somewhere else."

She nodded. "Yeah, okay."

After she left, I glanced at the boys. "Let's not waste too much time." My eyes went to the lieutenant's office door. "Do you think Lt. Moretti will have a problem with this?"

"Not really," Thompson said, "but he likes you. He might be the only one, besides Nick."

While I waited for our plan to commence, I drank coffee and looked around the major crimes unit for some friendly faces. Detectives Heathcliff and Jacobs were out on a call. The other few officers I recognized by face only. They had seen me around enough when I consulted for the police on a case or two and when I was a federal agent that my presence didn't strike them as odd. It was a relief since they'd probably be seeing a lot more of me in the future.

After Nick left a handcuffed Josh Addai at his desk, telling Thompson to keep an eye on the prisoner, I sauntered over and took a seat behind the computer. Clicking the record button, I minimized the window and swiveled to face Josh. His hands were bound behind his back which seemed fitting given that was the position he forced me into twenty-four hours ago.

"Remember me?" A wicked smile pinned my lips back.

His eyes moved from the tile floor to my face, and he nodded. "Pinball girl."

"Cute. I have a nickname."

"I didn't know you were a cop." The way he said the words let me know he knew exactly who I was.

"That's because I'm not. They asked me to identify the men who attacked me." I pointed a finger at him. "Found you."

His Adam's apple bobbed. "Things got out of hand at the bar. You should have let me escort you from the neighborhood."

"Really? Where would you have taken me?"

He didn't say anything. He might be scared, but he wasn't stupid. Frankly, I would have taken stupid any day of the week. But stupid people didn't get away with crimes for half a decade.

"Look, Josh, I might be naïve to think this or even say it, but I believe you didn't want to hurt me." I let the words sink in. His eyes met mine for a moment and darted away. "I can't say the same about Victor or your other pals."

"You stabbed Victor," Josh hissed, showing the first hint of anger since I sat down. "What did you think was going to happen after you pull a shit move like that?"

"Well, I thought he might bleed out." The matter-of-fact way I said those words surprised him. "I'm sorry about your nose. I had to do something to get away. You should have let me go." His eyes widened ever so slightly, and I smiled. "Oh, you didn't realize I knew it was you yesterday. Blue really isn't your color. Victor's either." I leaned back in O'Connell's chair, gripping the edge of the desk and stretching my arms out so he could see the painful bruises he caused. "You should be better with an IV since you've been doing this for years." I pulled the chair closer. "Did you strip me or was that Victor?"

His jaw muscles clenched. He inhaled sharply, glancing around before leaning close. "I didn't do anything to you."

"So it was you." I nodded sagely. "Figured it must have been. I'm guessing Victor is the type to take a few liberties when the ladies are unconscious. That guy has some serious issues when it comes to anger and control. Is that why you do what he says?"

"I don't do what he says." That touched a nerve.

I shrugged. "I'd probably be afraid of Victor if it weren't for the man in charge. He's the real sicko in the bunch. He calls the shots, and Victor listens to him. You do too." I gauged his reaction carefully. "Most of the time."

"Whatever. Since you act like you know so damn much, why haven't you told the police any of this?"

"How do you know I haven't?" I grinned. "The thing is whoever talks first gets a deal. I'd like it to be you. After all, you offered to take me to bed. Hell, in another life, we might have even had some fun. And from what I remember, you never hit me. Tackled me to the ground, abducted me, drugged me, and handcuffed me, yes. But you didn't hit me, so you get a few brownie points for that."

"Thanks," he said sarcastically.

"What'd you do with my clothes anyway? I just bought that blazer, and those were my favorite pair of shoes."

He didn't speak. He was too smart to answer the question.

I exhaled. "Yeah, well, those brownie points won't go far when you're implicated in a dozen murders. How long has this been going on?" I didn't want to admit we didn't know what this was. The more he thought we had, the more likely he was to cave. "Based on my best guess, it started at least five years ago. That's why you made Jessika Wellington disappear. She caught on to your scheme. She saw what was happening, didn't she?"

Josh didn't say a word, but he twitched, pushing up from the chair. I shoved his shoulders down before he could stand. The handcuffs made it easier.

"The medical examiner is sorting the remains through dental records. Every time I turn around, another cadaver pops up. We haven't IDed Jessika yet, but it's just a matter of time, isn't it? You realize once that happens everything will crumble. Her disappearance made national news. Finding her body and prosecuting the people responsible will be even bigger. You and your buddies will fry for this. That's why I'm giving you the chance to come clean. Tell the cops what you know, and they'll give you a deal. If you have a good enough attorney, you might even get immunity. Think about it."

A smug look crossed Josh's face. "That's not going to happen."

"Why not?"

"They won't find Jessika's body."

"I wouldn't be so sure. It's amazing the scientific advancements that have been made in identifying remains."

He smiled, so self-assured I wanted to punch him in the face again. "You can't find a body when the person isn't dead."

"How would you know that? Did Victor or Mr. Green Scrubs tell you she's alive?"

Josh laughed at my stupidity. "I helped her escape."

"Wow. You're a knight in shining armor. How'd you help her escape?"

He shook his head, shutting down my questions.

I glanced at Thompson who was watching the exchange from a desk across the aisle. "You get that?"

"Yep." He shot me a thumbs up. "It looks like we have a lot more to discuss, Mr. Addai." He hauled him out of the chair and back to the interrogation room.

*   *   *

"He was playing you, Miss Parker," Cross said. "Addai is smart. They all are. If they weren't, Jessika would have been found five years ago and there wouldn't be a dozen bodies buried at an abandoned construction site. You want to believe it's true, but it just isn't. I'm sorry."

I rolled my eyes. "Share your condolences with someone who cares."

"Fine." His voice took on an edge. "But you are not disclosing this nonsense to the Wellingtons. They don't need false hope. We've already given them enough of that."

"I agree," I said, remembering Janet's begging. "Are you sure we can't get anything solid from the property records?"

"The medical building is vacant. No one wants to move in. It would take extensive renovations in order to comply with the most recent standards, and it would be more costly than buying or leasing a new space. Brandt's umbrella company doesn't hold the title on it. They never did. They leased it from the bank which acquired it when the original owner defaulted." He sighed. "This was a dead end, and it wasted an entire day. Have you made any headway on determining the identity of the man in green?"

In response, I sneezed.

He pressed the intercom. "Get me some orange juice and a cup of herbal tea with honey and lemon. Also, see if medical has any of those zinc lozenges."

"Right away, Mr. Cross," the assistant chirped.

"Wow, someone's a germaphobe."

"It's for you."

"I'm fine."

"You've sneezed ten times in just as many minutes. You're coming down with a cold. An afternoon in an ice bath will do that to a person. And the last thing I need is my newest investigator out sick with pneumonia for a few weeks. We can't afford to lose that kind of time."

He selected a few folders from the pile and moved to the couch. After O'Connell dropped me off, I spent the rest of the day in my boss's office. I couldn't shake the feeling he wanted to keep an eye on me.

We searched extensively for something useful to convince Josh to talk. The police were hoping to bluff their way with Victor, but as the hours passed, that felt like less and less of a certainty. The clinic was temporarily shut down while the police conducted their investigation, and everyone who volunteered was under surveillance by either the PD or Cross Security. We were desperate for answers.

I picked up the file on Brandt's charitable endeavors. He had a charity gala scheduled for Saturday evening. The guest list included several hospital administrators, as well as some of the current and former staff from the clinic. It was the perfect opportunity to catch these men off guard and determine who was involved.

It didn't look like the police would have much of a presence. The event was being held at a private estate. Without an invitation, warrants would be required, but that didn't mean I couldn't crash the party. Lucien placed several calls, finally being granted an invitation and a plus one.

I sneezed again which brought about an uncomfortable pressure in my head. Cross cocked an eyebrow in my direction. "Allergies," I insisted, reaching for another folder.

With the tip of his pen, he slid the teacup closer. "Let me ask you a question," Cross said, his expression encouraging me to take a sip. "What do you think would have happened if the men who took you yesterday succeeded?"

"I don't think I'd care because I'd be dead."

Cross made a face. "Be serious."

"I am." I swallowed a mouthful of tea and picked up one of the lozenges, unwrapping it while I thought through the question. "Victor would have cleaned up the mess. The lookout they sent would have reported back an all clear, and at least one of the men would have returned to dispose of my body."

"The police already discovered their dumping grounds."

"Maybe they have more than one." I didn't like that thought, but it wasn't beyond the realm of possibility, particularly since we didn't find Jessika's remains yet. "You really don't believe it's possible Josh is telling the truth?"

"Let's look at the facts," Cross said. "She hasn't been seen since that day. If she escaped, wouldn't she go to the police?"

"Maybe she was scared."

"Okay." Cross leaned back. "These men are killers. The

motivation behind their killing spree remains unclear. We're assuming it's for organ harvesting, but we can't be certain. We are certain they've murdered at least twelve people. Until two days ago, no one had any idea what was going on. You really think they wouldn't eliminate one of their own if he betrayed them?"

He was right. If Josh stepped out of line, Green Scrubs would have taken care of him or asked Victor or someone else to do it. No one's hands were clean. That's why they weren't talking. They were all involved. All guilty. It was the only way to guarantee a certain level of trust. Mutually assured destruction.

"They must have another dump site," I declared. "How many people have these assholes murdered?"

Cross went behind his desk. "I'll look through the missing persons reports again. It can't hurt. I'm sure the police are doing the same since they dropped the ball on this."

"What can I do?" I asked, hating the overwhelming feeling of being powerless.

"Drink your juice."

THIRTY-TWO

I bolted upright, sending a flurry of files to the floor. Blinking, I took in the unfamiliar surroundings and knelt to pick up the papers. "What time is it?" I asked.

Cross clicked away at the keys, pausing momentarily due to my abrupt wake-up. "It's after midnight." It was unlikely he failed to realize I had fallen asleep, but he didn't mention it. "The security team is waiting downstairs. They'll take you home."

"I'm all right."

He stopped typing and picked up the phone. "Miss Parker is ready to leave. Have the car waiting out front." He put the receiver down and looked at me. "You probably don't want to think about this, but Josh and Victor aren't the only men involved. Someone will be back to finish what they started. They'll attack when you're at your weakest and most vulnerable. Right now, you're sick and exhausted. Go home. Get some sleep. We have a long day of planning and preparation ahead of us. Saturday is our one shot at this. After that, I'm pulling my resources, and the police will handle the investigation on their own." He jerked his chin at the door. "Now go."

It didn't take long to arrive home. I was glad someone

else was driving. I probably would have fallen asleep at the wheel. The security team dropped me off at the door, and I gave the exterior of my apartment a thorough examination. The police cruiser parked a moment later, and I waved at the officers before making my way inside. Vulnerable or not, six armed men were watching my back. Green Scrubs wasn't stupid enough to try something under those conditions. He only took me to get answers and solve his problems, not cause more. Coming at me again would be his undoing, and he was smart enough to know it.

After changing for bed, I crawled under the covers and fell asleep instantly. My mind sent me back to two days ago. I was strapped down, unable to move. I jerked from side to side, unable to get free. This time, there were several other beds in the room. A woman was screaming. I turned to see Victor Harrendale drag Michelle Mercer into the center of the room before plunging the scalpel into her body. She went limp, blood pooling and turning the floor crimson. It took a steady hand and a lot of strength to extricate the blade without flinging the blood backward during the removal. Harrendale's hand was slow and steady, and he grinned evilly at me.

"Who's next?" he asked.

My eyes remained fixated on Michelle, her body forced into that macabre position, surrounded by a sea of blood. Someone else screamed, and I jerked my head to the side. Jessika Wellington was strapped to a bed beside mine. Josh Addai was standing over her. She wouldn't stop screaming. She was dressed in a pair of scrubs, similar to our captors.

"Get away from her," I growled.

Josh looked at me with a level of disinterest. "Don't you want me to set her free?"

Frantic, I tugged harder at the straps cutting into my wrists. "Jessika, look at me. You're going to be okay. They'll find us."

She continued to screech, thrashing against the bindings, until Josh stuck a needle in her arm, and she went limp.

"No," I screamed.

"She's free now. I saved her," he declared.

Muffled sounds came from the other side, and I twisted to see Green Scrubs plunge a stake into Ivy Greene's neck. The hooker dropped, her blood mixing with Michelle's and spreading to the very corners of the room. The bathroom door opened, and two men in blue scrubs dragged Samantha Capshaw and Skye into the center of the room.

"They have nothing to do with this. Let them go." I broke free from one of the restraints.

"It's your fault," Skye said. "You can't stop them. You caused this. All of this. I told you to leave me alone."

I screamed as they were slaughtered, and I bucked and fought until Green Scrubs plunged the dagger into my neck.

Waking in a cold sweat with tears streaming down my face, I clutched my throat, feeling the blade's sting even though it was a fabrication of my mind. I wiped my face and pulled my knees to my chest. It wasn't real. None of it was real. Still, I couldn't shake the images from my mind's eye.

Loud knocking sounded, and I darted to a cover position, my gun in hand. Did they come for me?

"Parker, it's the police. Open up."

Silently, I crept to the door. Clutching the nine millimeter, I glanced through the peephole and unlatched the lock. Slowly, I opened the door, remaining behind it for safety.

"Is everything okay?" the cop asked, giving me one look and deciding it wasn't. He signaled to his partner who entered with his gun raised to sweep the apartment. "We received a call about a disturbance. Are you okay? Is anyone here?"

I tugged on the hem of my pajama shorts. "No one's here. Everything's fine."

"Are you sure?"

His partner finished checking the bedroom and went into the bathroom. "All clear." He looked at me. "What happened?"

"Nothing." Before I could say anything else, two men from Cross Security stepped through the doorway, and I aimed my weapon before I realized who they were. "Shit." I put my gun on the table, raising my palms and dropping shakily onto the couch.

"We were listening to the police frequencies. Is everything okay in here?" one of my security team asked.

"Yeah, everything is fine. I had a nightmare. It must have freaked out the neighbors. Thin walls. I'm sorry about this."

The cops nodded. "We'll check the rest of the building to make sure there aren't any actual problems. Try to get some sleep." The officers went to the door, nodding to the security team on their way out.

"Anything we can do?" one of the security guys asked.

I shook my head. "Do you want something to drink?"

They declined, swept my apartment a second time, made sure the fire escape was secure, and left me alone with my treacherous thoughts. The first thing I did was call O'Connell's work number. It was three a.m. He wasn't at the precinct. I didn't expect him to be, but I wouldn't have minded hearing a friendly voice. I left a message, begging him to check on Skye and make sure she was okay. The men who took me probably saw me at the diner. I didn't want to be responsible for handing them another victim, as my nightmare suggested.

After that was done, I left a message for Kellan, asking if anyone at Cross Security was still monitoring Samantha Capshaw. I knew the police had beefed up security on the Wellingtons in light of recent events, so I didn't have to worry about Janet or William. But Capshaw was a different story.

Ivy was dead. I didn't know what fate would befall the other hookers or gangbangers. Honestly, the ones arrested might be safer behind bars. The police had several blocks under heavy surveillance. We might not know what was going on, but we knew where it would happen. Hopefully, that would be enough to stop it.

After convincing myself I'd taken appropriate steps to safeguard the few remaining individuals I put in danger, I went back to the bedroom. My sheets were soaked in sweat and tangled in a heap. I was afraid to go back to sleep. I didn't have the strength to fight off the torment from another nightmare.

Scrolling through the contacts in my phone, I resisted the urge to call Martin. He always made me feel better, but I told him I was okay. Calling in the middle of the night would prove I wasn't, and he'd be on his way to the airport before we even hung up. I didn't want that. Regardless of how much I might want his company, I didn't want to depend on him or anyone. It's how I learned to survive. The more he was around, the more I'd lean on him until I freaked and pulled away. We'd done that dance too many times. We weren't doing it again.

I could call Mark. He'd let me crash on his couch. He was like the father I never had, and he'd do anything for me. But the price I'd pay for that would be a lecture and a guilt trip, and I didn't want either of those things. I felt guilty enough.

Instead, I dialed someone who I was supposed to be helping. Bastian answered on the fourth ring.

"I'm sorry to call so early," I said.

"It's earlier for you, love. Isn't it the middle of the bloody night?"

I cringed at the prophetic word use. "It is the middle of the bloody night," I agreed.

"All right?"

"I guess." Letting out an uneasy laugh, I added, "My mind was working overtime with the nightmares it conjured. I just need to talk it out with someone."

"Consider me someone. How's it coming?"

"Not good." And then I unloaded everything that occurred since the last time we spoke.

"Shite." The sound of a lighter being flicked came through the earpiece, followed by a lengthy exhale. "Anything I can do?"

"That's not why I called." I waited a beat. "I thought you quit smoking." He didn't comment. "Whoever murdered Michelle is strong and has steady hands. It's hard to remove a knife without tugging it backward, but that would lead to a spatter pattern. From the crime scene photos, there wasn't any spatter. He took care to take his time. It is possible he wiped up afterward, but I'd have no way of knowing that."

"The bastard didn't rush. He knew how long it'd take for Jules to get to the market and back. He had the time." From the conviction in Bastian's tone, he had a few suspects in mind.

"You never sent any additional details on the intel you were rounding up concerning the plate numbers or possible leads. What's going on? Do you know who killed Michelle?"

"Are you positive you want to discuss this now?"

"I could use the distraction."

For the next two hours, I listened as Bastian went through his suspicions, serving as a sounding board for the revelations he made. By the end, it was apparent whoever killed Michelle Mercer knew Julian intimately. It was someone he trusted. The killer was familiar with everything, including the neighborhood, in order to blend in so seamlessly. He might have even been on the footage, and we missed it.

"I'm going to watch everything again and see if I recognize anyone," Bastian said. "If I don't, I'll ask Jules to do it. I don't know everyone from his past or who he served with before I was assigned to his command, but based on your impressive skills, I'm certain it's someone who trained with him. That would explain the skills and the strength. Plus, if it's one of Jules' former mates, Michelle probably knew him and didn't realize she was in danger. If a strange man entered her home, she would have fought back. She was a scrapper. Had to be to put up with Jules." Bastian's sadness was undeniable. "Don't concern yourself with this, love. Your debt has been repaid. I'll take it from here. I'm sure Jules will ring you at some point to ask questions or express gratitude."

"I didn't do much."

"You did plenty." Bastian sighed. "The rest is up to him."

"How do you think he'll take the news? It isn't much of a lead. If you want to send a list of possible suspects to review, I can do it. I promised him I would."

"No, darling. This isn't your fight. Jules wouldn't want

you involved. You have enough nutters gunning for you. Take care." His voice took on a teasing tone. "We might need you again."

"I'll be here."

It was after five in the morning. Talking to Bastian calmed my nerves, but my unconscious mind was a dangerous thing. Apparently, I was a masochist, determined to torment myself to the brink of insanity whenever I faced a perceived failure. No wonder I always had so many nightmares. I was definitely fallible and had proven it over and over again. But that was going to stop right now.

THIRTY-THREE

The first thing I did when I made it to the office was go to the thirty-first floor to clear out the recreated crime scene. In my absence, the experts used the photos I taped to the wall to complete the scene and left a report on the counter. I leafed through it, finding the conclusions to be similar to mine. They speculated someone tampered with the crime scene and cleaned away the spatter patterns before the police arrived. That was also a possibility Bastian and I discussed.

Glad to put something behind me, even though it wasn't nearly as satisfying as identifying the murderer, I knew why the former SAS wanted me to step away. Mercer wasn't looking for justice. He wanted vengeance, and Bastian knew I didn't need more blood on my hands. This was their fight, not mine.

I just stepped foot in my office when Kellan knocked on the doorframe. "A security detail is assigned to Capshaw. They took over when I dropped my surveillance. I asked Lucien about it earlier."

"He's already here?" It was just before seven.

Kellan snorted. "He never left." He must have spotted the look on my face because he said, "Whenever we have a big case, he works through the night. Don't worry. He doesn't expect us to do the same. Although it appears you worked through the night too. Any progress?"

"Not on the Wellington case."

A funny look came over him. "You're working on something else?"

"Not anymore. Any word from the police?"

"I'm sure we'll hear about it at the morning briefing." He looked at the time. "We should go."

I followed Kellan to the conference room and took a seat beside him. Renner stepped in a minute later, taking a seat across from me. Lancaster, Darwin, and a few other investigators I didn't know by name filed into the room. Everyone was silent. A moment later, Cross entered with a portfolio in hand. He went to the front of the table, meeting my eye for half a second before launching into the latest updates from the police department.

The clinic and its employees were still under surveillance. Any remaining members of the Seven Rooks were questioned and also being followed. If anyone so much as jaywalked, they would be taken to the station. As of yet, Josh Addai and Victor Harrendale refused to cooperate. The police hoped someone at our office found something damning to loosen their lips, but no one had anything to add.

"Keep searching," Cross insisted. "Mr. Renner, have you finished interviewing Wellington's contacts to see if any of the names ring a bell?"

"I'm almost done. I've made several calls to Jessika's friends, but they don't remember anything. I'm waiting to hear back from the boyfriend," Renner replied. "I've also been going through their social media profiles. Even though Jessika's is defunct, I've been tracking the visitors to see if there is any crossover between them and the clinic workers or Victor Harrendale. Upstairs is running IP addresses."

"Very good." Cross waited a beat and dismissed the room. I didn't move. When we were alone, he said, "I heard about the disturbance last night. Anything you failed to mention?"

"I had a nightmare. It must have rattled my neighbors."

He fought back a scowl. "Are you certain you're up to the tasks required of a Cross Security investigator?"

"I'm here, aren't I?"

Resisting the urge to berate, Cross cleared his throat. "I spoke to Lieutenant Moretti of major crimes a few minutes ago. He knows we are going to Brandt's charity function tomorrow evening, and since he can't post officers inside, he wants us wired. The police are operating under the assumption the unidentified third assailant will be at this event. Nothing is indicative of it, but I tend to agree. Brandt runs a large portion of the local medical industry, and the people who support his charity are involved with his clinics. It's reasonable to assume whoever is using the clinic to commit these murders will want to have some say in what happens to it and its funding."

"You think it's Brandt?"

"It's possible. Even though Brandt isn't a doctor, he's spent his life around them. He also spent a few semesters in med school before flunking out. He might know how to perform a few dissections. Plus, he's made his millions off of other people's pain and suffering. He's a tycoon and possibly a sociopath." Cross flipped through some pages. "It could be him." He pushed a large photo of Brandt toward me. "What do you think?"

"I'm not sure. But I think they're all dirty. The ones who aren't, are dead."

"That's also a possibility. The police will have units posted outside, prepared to render assistance should we find ourselves in a pickle. It'd be advantageous if you take the rest of the day to familiarize yourself with everyone on Brandt's staff and payroll in addition to the current and former clinic workers. Should you recognize any of them as being the man in green, we will notify the police."

I didn't bother to say I already went through the IDs and photos. I just nodded. "There's one other thing," I said. "I don't want a security team following me around."

"They are assigned for your protection while the man remains at large."

"I'm aware, but you're making it too hard for him to

finish the job."

"That's the point."

"Unless someone comes back to finish me off, we may never figure out who he is. He needs to think it's safe. We need him to try again."

"Discuss this matter with the police. If you are comfortable enough with their protection and your friends have no problem with it, then I'll reassign the team."

"Thanks."

He eyed me for a long moment. "Don't be stupid, Parker. If this is about your embarrassment, get over it."

My face heated. "We don't have any other options. And I can take care of myself."

"I've yet to see that." Cross stormed out of the conference room, and I pushed back in the chair, angry that his words rang true.

The rest of the day was a blur of intel and calls back and forth to the police. O'Connell assured me Skye was safe. He and every other detective assigned to the case were doing their best to work over Josh and Victor. The ploy with the syringe softened Victor's resolve, but he didn't break. O'Connell was sure they could get him there if they just had something else. Until then, Josh and Victor remained isolated from one another.

"We'll get them," O'Connell insisted. "We have everyone and everything under surveillance. If anyone steps out of line, we'll notice. Something will pan out. Have faith."

"I'm sure Jessika's parents heard the same pep talk." I shook away the annoyance. "I told Cross to pull the detail. If we apply enough pressure, the unsub will make a move. My protection detail needs to be invisible. Can you get some plainclothes in an unmarked car to keep an eye out instead? A personal vehicle would be even better. Or something from impound."

"Okay, but I better not have to frantically search the entire city to find you again. Are you planning on taking any other precautions?"

"I have a few thoughts in mind."

By the end of the day, I was no closer to determining who murdered those twelve people. The victims were mostly transients. A few popped up as having ties to rival gangs, but none of them died from gunshots or stab wounds. They died because a few men were playing doctor. Based on the coroner's report, four of the victims were missing vital organs. That led to two possibilities, ritual killings and black market organ sales. My money was on the latter.

Instead of going home, I went to the apartment I shared with Martin. He was flying home tomorrow, so the place was empty. I didn't know if anyone was waiting to strike, but this building was secure. The measures in place were the biggest selling point as far as I was concerned. The best part was, aside from the doorman and twenty-four hour concierge, the security wasn't overt. Someone might make an attempt, and they'd be stopped.

Despite this knowledge, I slept in short bursts throughout the night. I'd wake every hour or two and dig through more of the original case file until I couldn't see straight and then grab another few minutes of sleep. Jessika must have said something to someone before she disappeared. After her shift at the clinic, she went home and to school the next day before vanishing. In those hours, she must have confided in someone. I just had no idea who.

Dylan remained my best guess, but he swore he didn't know anything. Instead of calling him in the middle of the night, I found myself searching the internet for his online presence and Jessika's. Finding dated material on the internet was about as easy as locating a needle in a haystack, but Jessika never posted anything indicating she feared for her life. I even tried tracking the IP address, figuring she might have searched online for advice, but that search was equally pointless.

By morning, I was wrecked. My cold was full-blown, and my entire body ached. I sent a text to Cross to ask what time we were meeting at the precinct. After he responded that I had twelve hours until our rendezvous, I grabbed a pillow off the bed and a blanket, made some tea, poured a large glass of orange juice, and stocked up on tissues before settling on the sofa.

Around three, my phone buzzed. Martin just landed. I told him I was sick and asked for a rain check for the weekend before rolling over and going back to sleep. I hoped the fear Cross would bust my balls for being sick was enough to will my body to get better in the next few hours. Of course, the juice and tea didn't hurt either.

I was dead asleep, curled around the pillow, when I heard a familiar voice. "Sweetheart, I'm here." I let out a tired moan and curled into a tighter ball. This was a pleasant dream, one where Martin pulled my pillow into his lap and was stroking my hair. "Go back to sleep."

The next thing I knew, the alarm was buzzing. With bleary eyes, I turned it off and put my phone back on the table. It was six. I needed to shower and dress. My throat hurt, but at least I was able to breathe through my nose. A hand touched my side, and I jumped.

"Whoa, easy. It's me, Alex. It's just me." Martin removed his hand instantly.

When I tried to speak, my voice came out hoarse. I reached for the glass and swallowed whatever juice was left. "I forgot you were here."

"I'll try not to take it personally." He pressed into the corner of the couch, doing his best to give me space. His eyes went to the faint red marks on the outer edges of my wrists. "Y'know, for a second, when I got your text, I thought maybe you were avoiding me."

"I wouldn't have stayed here if I was avoiding you," I croaked.

"Why are you here?" he asked, the concern clear on his face. "I don't mind. I was just surprised to find you when I opened the door."

"It's a long story." I stretched and moved toward the bathroom. "The short answer is building security." After reaching in and turning on the shower, I turned around to find Martin lingering in the doorway.

"Are you in danger?"

"I sure hope so." I coughed a few times. "You might want to head home. I'm sick, and with any luck, I'll find a doctor who makes house calls."

Martin reached for his phone. "I can get someone."

I laughed. "No, that's not what I meant." I shivered, quickly stripping down and stepping underneath the steaming water. "The men who abducted me were dressed like doctors. Given the limited details we have, one of them might be a physician or had some training. Cross and I are going to a charity function tonight in the hopes we'll get lucky, but in the event we don't, maybe the unsub will follow me home to finish the job. You should make yourself scarce."

"The hell I will." Martin rested his hips against the vanity and waited for me to get out of the shower. "I'm not leaving."

I wrapped the towel tighter around my body before reaching for the hairdryer. "I didn't think you would." I poked him in the chest. "And I didn't ask you to go. It was just a suggestion, but since you're staying, you'll need to take precautions."

His fingers gently brushed against the back of my hand. "It was bad, wasn't it?"

"We might be dealing with the fallout for a while."

"Okay." He leaned down to kiss me, and I turned my face away. "Alex, I'm going to kiss you. Not even the plague could stop me." His second attempt was a success. "I'll let you get ready." He left the bathroom. "How late do you think you'll be tonight?"

"It depends on what happens. If it's a bust, not more than a few hours. So I'm hoping for a long night."

"In that case, I'll make some soup. It's my mom's recipe. I can almost guarantee it'll knock that cold right out of you." He opened the fridge and peered inside. "Is it safe to ask Marcal to make a grocery run, or are we in lockdown?"

"It should be okay, I think."

"Are you sure you're feeling well enough to work. You sound delirious," Martin teased. "You must be sick to be this blasé."

"They're too smart to make another move on me."

"If they were that smart, they never would have messed with you in the first place."

Ignoring him, I dried my hair, put on my makeup, and grabbed the black evening gown from the closet. It was either that or the black cocktail dress, and Cross said this was a formal event. I stepped into the kitchen to find Martin chopping vegetables.

"Zip me up." I spun, pulling my hair over one shoulder to give him better access.

"You're wearing this to go out with Lucien?" He tugged the zipper up. "And you aren't certain what time you'll be back?" He let out a growl and nipped at my earlobe. "You tell your boss to watch where he puts his hands."

"It's probably not his hands you should worry about." I turned, seeing just the slightest hint of anger in Martin's green eyes. This was new. "Hey, I was just joking."

He shook his head to clear his thoughts. "Yeah, I know. I was just thinking this job was supposed to be safer." He hugged me, burying his face in my neck. "We'll talk about this later."

"We will." I picked up my nine millimeter, double-checked the clip, chambered a round, and put it on the counter. "Anyone comes through the door you don't recognize, shoot first, then call for help. You got it?"

He searched my eyes for a moment. "Is this really what it's come to?"

"I don't know. This building is supposed to be secure. It's why I slept here, but I guess we'll see. I'm not taking any chances with your safety." I went into the living room and grabbed my back-up from the end table and stuffed it into my evening bag, along with a handful of tissues. "I would tell you don't wait up, but we both know there's no point."

He smiled. "I'll be waiting."

THIRTY-FOUR

"Let's do another sound check," O'Connell said, pointing to the technician. Cross Security was providing the surveillance equipment for the evening, and one of Cross's guys was on standby in case we encountered compatibility issues. "I guess that's it." O'Connell gave me an uncertain look. "Are you sure you want to do this?"

"It's our last shot."

"We approached Brandt this afternoon since you were taken to one of his old facilities and Josh Addai volunteers at his clinic. He claimed ignorance, and his legal counsel stonewalled us. We've threatened to leak it to the press if he doesn't cooperate, but that didn't do anything but raise his hackles. I don't imagine you'll have a warm welcome tonight," O'Connell surmised.

"I brought my checkbook," Cross declared. "Money speaks volumes. A man like Henry Brandt wouldn't dare toss out possible donors."

"Either way, watch yourselves. You need help, you know the safe word."

"Argentina," I said.

Cross opened the rear doors of the surveillance van and stepped down, offering a hand to help me out. We were parked behind a gas station a half mile from Brandt's estate. The surveillance van would remain here. Additional units were positioned just slightly closer.

Cross opened the door to his Porsche. "Are you positive you want to arrive separately?"

"I want to make it easier for someone to follow me home," I replied.

"You know what they say about playing with fire, Miss Parker."

I shrugged and slid behind the wheel of my car. The drive only took two minutes, and we pulled to a stop at the top of the circular path. Brandt hired parking attendants, and Cross tossed the kid his keys and flashed his invitation at the bouncer before jerking his thumb at me.

Stepping out of my car, I took a breath. Joining Cross at the door, he put his hand at the small of my back and waited for the man to check his name off the list. Then we were ushered inside. The place was spectacular with an open floor plan and at least two hundred people. It was catered with a large spread near the back and an open bar on the side. A quartet was playing live music on the patio. The doors were open, and tables and chairs were set up beneath a tent. A podium was at the center.

"Charity my ass," I mumbled. This was nicer than most weddings.

Cross snickered. "Up to five percent can be used for fundraising events. Just imagine how much he rakes in to afford this. And don't forget, the nicer the function, the more money he'll raise." He nodded to an ice sculpture in the center of a champagne fountain. "I should speak to the event planner and find out how much went into this." His eyes darted around, honing in on the caterers and the security. "Can I leave you on your own for a few minutes?"

"I'm fine."

"You better be."

Cross disappeared into the throng of people, and I maneuvered to the far corner. This provided the best vantage point to see who was in attendance. A large group congregated near the bar, and I watched the men exchange handshakes. Some of the faces looked familiar, and I recalled a name or two from the hospital's board of trustees. It didn't take long to rule the men out as suspects. Two had beards which extended well beyond the range of a surgical mask. One was Asian. Two were Middle Eastern. And the rest were either too short or too fat to fit the description of Green Scrubs. My eyes continued to scan the room. Several women were standing near the buffet.

One of the women caught my eye and excused herself. She crossed the room, and I took a deep breath, tucking my left arm tightly against my body so she wouldn't see the black bruises at the inside of my elbow. I chose not to hide the damage from the abduction in the hopes it might serve to lure out our suspect.

"Miss Parker, what are you doing here?" Janet Wellington asked, leaning in to exchange air kisses.

"Mr. Cross needed a plus one." I made a show of looking around. "I have no idea where he went. What are you doing here?"

She smiled with just her mouth. "Bill was invited. Henry used to be one of his company's biggest clients."

"Did your husband handle Mr. Brandt's account?" I asked.

Janet dismissed the question with a wave of her hand. "I have no idea. It's not like he ever spoke to me about much of anything." I heard the anger and betrayal in her voice. "He's around here somewhere." She turned on her heel, surveying the room. "There he is." She pointed to him. "That's his boss and a few of his work buddies. Did you ever get a chance to speak with him?"

"I did." My eyes continued to roam the room. "He wasn't particularly fond of me."

Something crossed over her, and her eyes narrowed. "You're here because of my daughter."

"This is a charitable function meant to raise money for Mr. Brandt's free clinics. That was something Jessika was passionate about."

"I never knew until the police asked about it." She looked sad. "It's good you're here. If you'll excuse me." She stepped to the bar and took her drink across the room to stand beside her husband.

I wondered if everyone was playing a part. Another large group congregated in front of me, blocking my view. I moved around the perimeter, glancing at the closed doors and the roped off staircase. Obviously, Brandt didn't want anyone snooping around his house, which instantly made me curious if the med school failure turned business mogul had something to hide.

"Did I miss anything?" Cross asked, sidling up beside me.

"The Wellingtons are here." I jerked my gaze to the side. "Did you know about that?"

"No." His voice was tight. "Did he see you?"

"Janet did. She wanted to know why I was here."

"What did you say?"

"I told her this charity was something Jessika was passionate about."

The aggravation was evident in Cross's annoyed growl. "I'll speak to them."

Lucien grabbed a drink off a tray and walked up to the Wellingtons, shook hands with William, and kissed Janet on the cheek. Then he introduced himself to the other investment bankers, shaking their hands and clasping each one on the left shoulder. He was checking to see if anyone sustained an injury recently.

After a few moments, I lost interest in my boss's schmoozing. He would find out why the Wellingtons were really here and if they were involved in whatever nefarious scheme the clinic was running. What did O'Connell say? I had to have faith.

Snorting, I moved to the buffet at the back corner and grabbed a dessert plate and skewered a few orange slices. Standing around casing the place wasn't a great move, and I could use a bit more vitamin C. A man walked up beside me, using the tongs to drop some fruit into his cocktail.

"Have we met?" he asked, smiling. "I'm Henry Brandt." He held out his hand, and when I went to shake it, he noticed the bruises on my arm. The marks from the restraints weren't lost on him either, but he didn't comment. Instead, he dropped my hand.

"We met before," I said.

"You're Lucien's plus one." Something registered on his face. "You look lovely this evening."

"Thank you."

He waved to someone across the room. "I must mingle. Enjoy yourself."

I watched him walk away. Could he be the man who attacked me? So far, two men in this room weren't happy to see me. Frankly, the only man who wanted to see me tonight was home alone with a loaded nine millimeter and a pot of soup. That sure as hell said a lot about this situation.

I made my way through the clusters of people, hoping to spot some familiar faces from the clinic roster. As of yet, I didn't recognize anyone from the clinic. The nurses and staff didn't have blood rich enough for this type of crowd, but the doctors did. Several served on a rotation at Brandt's various clinics, and I wondered if the other locations were also involved in the killing spree. Digging out my phone, I shot a text to O'Connell, asking if he looked into it.

It was a bust. Why do you want to make this problem bigger than it is? he replied.

I tucked my phone back into the side pocket of my bag and rested against the end of the bar. Someone brushed against my arm.

"Let me guess," a familiar voice teased, "you're stalking me." I turned, surprised to see Dr. Dalton. He motioned to the bartender for another.

"I'm not stalking you."

"That's a shame. Should I assume you're here on business?" He raised an eyebrow, silently asking if I wanted a drink. I declined, and he drained half of his glass. "I probably owe you an apology for being such an asshole the other night."

"Don't worry about it."

"Well, if you ever want to get an actual drink sometime and not talk shop, I'm game." He signaled for another drink and tipped the remaining contents into his mouth. "Brandt expects me to give a speech, and just the thought of it breaks me out in hives."

"I'm sure you'll be fine." My eyes went to the expensive watch on his right hand and the silver reading glasses peeking out of his inner jacket pocket. "Just imagine everyone in their underwear."

His eyes raked over me. "I probably don't need to imagine it." His gaze stopped on my arm. "Wow, whoever did that needs to go back for training. Blood draws shouldn't bruise that badly. It looks like you have a nasty hematoma. I bet it hurts like a bitch. Have you tried icing it?"

"Who said I had my blood taken?"

He laughed. "You don't strike me as an intravenous drug user. Hell, I doubt you ever even drink."

A woman came up to us, an earpiece in her ear. "Ridley, we're going to ask everyone to move outside in the next three minutes. We need you at the podium to kick things off."

"I'll be right there." He looked at me. "Wish me luck."

"Sure."

I watched the way he carried himself, certain of a simple fact that made little sense. Dalton provided the data that led our investigation to the clinic. If he was the man in green scrubs, why would he jeopardize himself and his operation? He could have denied Jessika's presence at the clinic, and we would have never been able to prove it. Now, every word out of his mouth was like a taunt, meant to goad me into acting. He wanted me to know it was him. He started this game of cat and mouse, and I intended to end it.

A moment later, someone clinked a spoon against a glass and called for everyone to head outside. Cross found me a moment later. Reading the expression on my face, he scanned the area for danger. As everyone moved outside, we followed behind the crowd, taking an unobtrusive spot on the patio, opposite the quartet.

"It's Dalton," I whispered. "He tortured me, and he wants to make sure I know it."

"What did he say?" Cross asked, and I filled him in as the woman gave a brief introduction, followed by a round of applause, and then Dalton took center stage. "He might just be observant. He noticed your bruised ribs the first time you met."

"That's because his guys inflicted them." I covered my mouth and sneezed.

"All right, as soon as he shuts up, I'll find out what's what." Cross took his jacket off and draped it over my shoulders. "In the meantime, you're going to catch your death out here."

"Only if that psycho is lying in wait." I stopped talking and listened to Dalton's speech, growing even more certain by the second that he was the man in green scrubs.

I listened to Martin give several speeches at functions similar to this, so I knew what to expect. Dalton spoke about Henry Brandt's company and mission statement. Someone at the rear was working a projector, tossing slides of cutting-edge medical research and happy, healthy patients onto the back wall of the tent. The next image caught me by surprise. Dalton was wearing fatigues and was kneeling next to a cot.

"My education was paid for by the military. It wasn't until I began working with POWs that I found my true calling. After my time in the service, I spent several years working with Doctors Without Borders. And even now, that same siren song calls me to volunteer at Brandt's free clinics. We forget there are neighborhoods right here that face the same difficulties those in third world countries and actual war zones face. Poverty and gang violence run rampant. People can't get the care they need. Please help us put a stop to this and bring much needed healthcare to those in our own backyards."

The blood drained from my face as more applause erupted. "The man in green said he worked with POWs. That's how he knew I'd been tortured. Dalton's our guy."

"We need to prove it," Cross replied.

THIRTY-FIVE

"Dr. Dalton," Cross called, jogging to catch up, "may I have a moment of your time? This won't take long, I promise. I find your work fascinating, and I just wanted to ask you a few questions about your speech." He put a hand on Dalton's elbow and led him inside while Henry Brandt droned on about the many ways a donor could contribute. He gripped Dalton's left bicep firmly and held out his hand. "Lucien Cross, I don't believe we met."

Dalton didn't flinch. He shook Lucien's hand, catching my intrigued gaze from where I remained on the patio. "What can I do for you, Mr. Cross?"

"You worked with POWs. That must have been very rewarding. Do you find your work at the clinic just as beneficial?"

"It can be."

Cross cocked his head. "That's a fine timepiece. I wouldn't imagine volunteer work would cover a twenty thousand dollar watch."

"I'm an attending physician at the hospital." His eyes narrowed. "I don't see how that is any of your concern." He smirked. "Why don't you just ask if I know anything about Jessika Wellington's disappearance and save us both some time?" His gaze went to me. "She already asked, and I'll tell you the same thing I told her. The clinic had nothing to do with it."

Cross smiled as if he knew something no one else did. "Unlike my associate, I believe you're correct. The clinic didn't have anything to do with Jessika's disappearance, but some people who work there did."

"Really?"

"Josh Addai is currently in police custody. It's my understanding he's been volunteering at the clinic for years. He's an EMT by trade, right?"

Dalton worked his jaw. "I think so. Did he say anything about Jessika or her disappearance?"

"Plenty."

"Oh, really?" Dalton looked amused. "This is the first time I'm hearing about it."

"Why would you have heard about it? Do you moonlight as a cop when you're not saving the world and treating the sick?"

Dalton's look was disconcerting, and I strode into the house, my heels clacking against the floor. It was just the three of us alone in the main room. The caterers were outside, and the rest of the staff was in the kitchen.

"Are you afraid we're getting too close?" Cross asked. "Is that why you panicked and kidnapped Miss Parker?"

Dalton's jaw twitched, the muscle at the joint jumping. "I have no idea what you're talking about."

"You fucked up. You trusted your people to clean up your mess, but they didn't. They left evidence behind," Cross smiled wickedly, "and a witness."

"Listen, buddy, I don't know what crazy things you've been told, but I'm in the business of saving lives, not ending them."

Cross leaned in, practically nose to nose with Dalton. "Say it again, and this time, make it sound convincing."

Dalton shoved Cross backward. "Get out of my face." The doctor's hate-filled gaze focused on me. "Say something. You can't honestly believe this shit."

"Take off your jacket and roll up your sleeves," I insisted.

Dalton's eyes grew wide. "I don't know what game you're playing, but I'm out. I have nothing to do with any of this. You have the wrong guy."

"No, we don't," I hissed.

He held out his wrists. "Then slap on the cuffs." He looked around. "Oh wait, you're not the police. And if you had anything besides some bullshit theory, they would have already come knocking. You're trying to bait me, but I'm not biting. Are you wearing a wire? Is that what this is? You're hoping to trick a confession out of me?" He glanced at Cross. "Your company must be pretty hard up if you're stooping to coercing confessions out of innocent bystanders in the hopes of cashing in on a big payday from a wealthy client like William Wellington. But there's nothing for you to find." His eyes went back to my wrists and then to the visible scar at my collarbone. "It looks like you've had a hard life, but how do we know those recent injuries weren't self-inflicted? It looks like you people will do just about anything to get paid, and I won't stand for it. If either of you attempts to discredit me or muddy my good name, I'll sue you. And as you pointed out, Mr. Cross, I have ample resources. Now I think it's time you leave, or I'll have a word with Mr. Brandt's security and maybe the Wellingtons."

"You son of a bitch," I snarled. "You couldn't finish the job yourself, and you're terrified to try again. You wanted me to fear you, but even dazed and out of my mind, I knew you were nothing but a joke. You just proved it. And your boys know it too. Josh and Victor had no problem defying your orders, and it's just a matter of time before they turn on you. Enjoy your resources while you can."

Something I said hit a nerve, and Dalton's eyes blazed, the yellow flecks igniting the same way they did before he lost control the last time. I would gladly take a few punches if it meant we could arrest him for assault.

Dalton grasped my sore elbow and leaned down until his lips were against my ear. "I am sorry for whatever happened to you. You should take care to make sure it doesn't happen again."

Cross grabbed Dalton by the upper arm, pulling him

away from me. "We're leaving," Cross said, positioning himself between me and Dalton. "The police will deal with you."

"Maybe you're the one who should be restrained," Dalton retorted.

I turned. The only thing keeping me from going for his throat was the unyielding grip Cross had on my back. We exited the mansion just as security entered through the patio doors. My boss handed the valet our parking slips. Once the cars were brought around, he did a quick sweep of each of them.

"Get in and don't stop until you reach the rendezvous point," Cross insisted. "You're not going home straightaway. We need to speak to the authorities."

Unfortunately, he was right.

*　　*　　*

"You're home early," Martin said when I stepped through the doorway. "I take it things didn't go well."

"We made them worse." I coughed a few times and dropped onto one of the stools at the counter. "Did anything happen while I was gone?"

"No." He slid the gun toward me.

"Good."

Dragging myself off the stool, I let out a plaintive whine, and Martin unzipped my dress. I went into the bedroom and slipped into a t-shirt and pajama pants. Then I scrubbed my face at the bathroom sink and returned to the kitchenette, trying to think of something that would cinch Dalton's involvement.

Now that I knew who the third assailant was I just had to convince the police. Dalton's denial of the claims did nothing to help our case. Also, his lack of a pain response when being manhandled by Cross worked against us. I stabbed the man in green scrubs, so it was reasonable to assume contact with the affected area should result in at least a wince. But Dalton acted like he didn't feel a thing.

At least O'Connell believed me. He intended to toss out Dalton's name as a bluff against Josh and Victor. Since

Victor already thought we found his prints at the scene, self-preservation might kick in, and he'd throw Dalton under the bus.

"Sweetheart, I'm trying my best to be patient, but what is going on?" Martin asked, concern and exasperation competing for dominance in the timbre of his voice.

I sighed and sat up straight, eyeing the bowl he slid in front of me. "I told you I wasn't able to identify the men who took me. With Nick's help, two of them are in custody, but the third remains at large. Tonight, I identified him. I'm sure I did. I remember some things, like his eyes and being left-handed. His reading glasses were in the bathroom." I shook my head, trying to figure out what the problem was. "His reaction tonight said it all, but the evidence isn't on our side."

Martin took a seat beside me, his hand resting on my thigh. "What happened?"

"Cross grabbed him where he'd been stabbed. The guy should have howled. He should have bled, but he didn't flinch." I rubbed my eyes. "Fuck. I seriously thought it was him. I don't know. I just don't understand how he could have healed so quickly."

"Are you sure he did?" Martin asked. I cocked my head to look at him. "It was a black tie affair. The only way you'd know if he was bleeding beneath his jacket is if the blood trickled down his fingertips."

My boss and I had a lengthy debate about Dalton's lack of reaction. It was possible the doctor was on painkillers or was drunk enough not to feel anything. Dalton did drink a lot tonight.

"We left too soon to find out," I admitted. "Nick's taking me at my word, but the police department can't do much without hard evidence. Given the circumstances, they have Dalton under tight surveillance. They searched the entire clinic, but they didn't find anything inside. They're going to start questioning the staff again. The problem with that is more of them could be involved. It's a gamble."

"Can't the police force him to disrobe since he's a person of interest?"

"They can if they get a search warrant. At the moment,

they don't have anything solid."

"What about your word? You were attacked. You're the only person on this planet who can identify him."

I exhaled. "I discredited myself with the statements I gave. I can't identify the men. I never saw them. Even the two in custody aren't being held for the abduction, just the bar fight. The stab wound is the only way to identify him."

Martin's face contorted, but he fought to tamp down his rage. "If this bastard is injured, the police will find out. He can't hide it. At some point, he'll have to take off his jacket."

"Yeah. Eventually. And if he tries to take another victim, I'm hoping the police will be there to stop it."

His lips thinned, but he didn't say anything. I finished my soup in silence, and Martin refilled the bowl when I was done. Truth be told, I was famished, even though eating was the last thing on my mind. When I was done, he rinsed my bowl in the sink and put it in the dishwasher.

"How was your trip?" I asked, hoping for a lighter topic.

"We renegotiated the entire contract from scratch. Those douches decided since Martin Technologies is so successful, we should pay more to acquire their product line and specs. They were acting in bad faith, but it was easier and cheaper to haggle over the price than to take action and spend a year in litigation over their shitty contract negotiation. But if they do it again, my legal team will tear them apart, and I made sure they knew it."

"It might have been easier if you took my nine millimeter with you," I joked.

He chuckled. "You're probably right." He studied my bruises and blown veins. "I would have come home, but you said you were all right."

"You needed to be there, and physically, I'm fine," I said, and he gave me a skeptical look. "My arm hurts a little, and I have a cold. Big deal. Dalton's other victims weren't so lucky." Climbing off the stool, I circled the kitchen. "The police found twelve bodies. That doesn't include the hooker I questioned. And they haven't found Jessika yet, so I'm guessing there's more than one dump site."

"Jesus."

"He's killing for spare parts. We know he's been draining blood from his victims. From what I gather, I'm two pints short at the moment. When Nick found me, they found dozens of blood packs in the fridge. The police have surveillance units everywhere. They've questioned people, canvassed the neighborhoods, talked to the gang members, the bartender, the ATF, and every Tom, Dick, and Harry they can find, but people are scared to talk. And with the level of decomp, the ME isn't even finished sorting through the remains. The police know there's a murderer on the loose. They're hoping the most recent victim will provide a trail for them to follow. But no one wants to come forward. They're afraid."

"Shouldn't they be?" Martin asked. "Whatever these men are doing, they've taken dozens of lives."

"But no one reported it until now. They only victimized people on the fringe." That reminded me of Josh's question inside the bar about whether or not someone would miss me. I grabbed my phone and shot O'Connell another text. It probably wouldn't help, but I had to do something. "At least we have some idea what they're doing, so it'll make it harder for them to strike again."

He paled. "This doctor was going to cut out your organs? How would he even know if you were a match?"

"He wouldn't. He wanted to run tests, but if his other victims were former patients, he would already know their test results." I looked at Martin. "You might have just figured out how he selects his targets."

"See, I'm not just sexy muscles and a pretty face."

Rolling my eyes, I remembered Mrs. Wellington saying Jessika had a rare blood type. Maybe she didn't witness anything. Maybe they needed her because she was a match. Dialing Cross, I knew he would answer.

"Are you okay?" he asked.

I filled him in on my recent revelations, even though I felt as if I'd been toying with these concepts for a while and they hadn't exactly coalesced like they should have. "Did our team find any under the table surgeries that link to Dalton, Brandt, or the clinic?"

"Not yet. I'll double our efforts. In the meantime, get some sleep. I don't want to see you again until Monday morning. Is that understood?"

"Yes, sir."

"Good night."

Tapping my phone against my lips, I thought about calling Janet Wellington, but Martin crossed the room and put his hands on my shoulders. "It's late, Alex. There's nothing else you can do tonight."

"It's not fair. Jessika's parents were at the event. They stood there listening to the man who probably murdered their daughter give a speech about doing good and helping those in need. It makes me sick." I sat on the couch, hugging the pillow to my chest. "I wish he would have hit me. I tried to provoke him, but he turned the tables. Maybe if Lucien didn't push him away." I shrugged. "I don't know."

"You'll figure it out. You just need to sleep on it."

"I haven't been sleeping. The nightmares are back."

"I figured. Why don't you go lie in bed? I have a surprise for you."

Leaning forward, I rested my cheek against his chest. "I know you just got home, but I'm really not feeling great. Lefty will have to suffice if you're hoping to score."

"That's not the surprise." He pressed his lips to my forehead. "And you should know that's the last thing on my mind right now. Get in bed. I'll make some tea and join you in a sec."

THIRTY-SIX

"Alexis, wake up." Martin nudged me again, and I gasped, opening my eyes to the eerie shadows cast by the glow of the phone charger. "You're okay. It's okay. It was just a dream."

Truthfully, I didn't recall any of it, except the paralyzing fear. He woke me before my subconscious became too invested, and I was grateful. Reaching for his hand, I placed it on my hip, needing to feel safe without being smothered. That's why he was doing his best to remain hands off. But that wasn't going to cut it at the moment.

"Can you turn the TV back on?" I asked.

"Sure." He reached for the remote and powered on the set before clicking on the blu-ray player. A sitcom from the nineties continued where we left off, and he lowered the volume until it was barely audible. "Is that better?"

"Uh-huh."

"At least it was a useful surprise."

"I wish it wasn't." I put my head on his chest and closed my eyes, listening to the laugh track. When the theme music played through the credits, I spoke again. "You're a saint for putting up with me and this shit. We've done this too many times already. And we shouldn't have to. You shouldn't have to. It's stupid. So stupid."

"Alex."

"No. It is. I know it is." I sat up and rubbed my eyes with one hand. "It's work. It shouldn't be like this. It should stay at the office. This is our bubble. Work isn't supposed to invade our bubble. These assholes aren't supposed to get inside my head. I shouldn't let them screw with me like this."

"Sweetheart, you can't control your dreams." The light from the television flickered, showing something disconcerting in his eyes. "This isn't like all the other times. It's different. You're different. And I'm so tired of this." He gestured wildly around the room. "We don't need the distance. I want you to know I am all in. I don't want to keep you at arm's length. Not anymore. Not after this week. Especially not after tonight. When we got back together, you swore it'd be different. That you'd try to change, and you have. You talked to me. Trusted me. Confided in me. And you trusted that we would come to an understanding. That's why I didn't come home, and why when I did, you didn't send me to hide inside my compound all alone. You came to this apartment because you perceived it to be safe, but you knew I'd show up. And you didn't push me away when I did."

"Maybe I was being selfish. Maybe I wanted to see you." I snorted. "I do need you more than I care to admit."

"You weren't being selfish. You let me be part of the team. And that's what we are. A team." He turned on his side, brushing the hair out of my face. "I want you to come home. And I want you to stay for good. What's mine is yours. It's time."

I closed my eyes and sunk into the pillow. "I'm not ready. I'm on shaky ground. I have a new job, which I might lose next week. My sanity is questionable, and my nightmares are back. I can't handle any other life changes right now. My foundation needs to stabilize, or there could be a catastrophic backslide. And I do not want to risk losing you when it happens."

"I get it, but you won't lose me. I'm all in."

"Don't say it when you can't predict the future."

"Then let's stay here until things settle down," he

suggested.

"You're okay with that?"

"I'm okay with anything that means I get to be with you."

"Even under the current conditions? I don't want to push you away, but if I get spooked, I might. This is neutral territory. You can go home, and I can go back to my place if it gets to be too much. You can't hold that against me, agreed?"

"There's something I should tell you." He scooted closer. "It's my fault. I'm the reason you're in this situation and the reason you were taken." He swallowed. "I got you the job at Cross Security."

"The headhunter, right?"

He shook his head. "No, sweetheart. Lucien called. He was checking your references. I dealt with him before. Hell, I almost hired Cross Security to deal with my death threats, but I didn't like the way they handled things."

"So you picked me instead, and his firm lost a potential client."

A sad smile lined his face. "Yeah. We've spoken a few times since then. Lucien claims he values my opinion and wanted to know my thoughts on your qualifications. After I gave you a glowing recommendation, he hired you."

"Temporarily." I sighed. "It's not like he'll let me stay on after the mess I made."

"He might."

I blew out a breath and focused on him. "Why? Because you said so?"

"Alex, I don't know. I was just trying to help. I didn't realize how dangerous this would be. I thought it'd be corporate work."

"You mean the stuff I hate?"

He looked guilty. "It's safer."

"Are you saying the only reason I got this job is because Cross hopes you'll put his firm on retainer?"

"I don't know."

"Dammit."

"I'm sorry. I don't know if that's why he hired you. He just asked for a recommendation, but he's difficult to gauge. He just kept asking if I had plans to rehire you now that you returned to the private sector."

"What did you say? Does he know we're together?"

"I kept it professional. I told him I have my own team, but I wouldn't be opposed to working with you in the future. That seemed like the right thing to say, but now I wish I said something else."

"Don't blame yourself for anything that happens to me. I make my own decisions. If you want to be part of this team, you have to respect that. Just like I have to respect your decision to put yourself in the crosshairs to be with me." I sighed. "I don't want to think about this now. My brain is already over capacity. I can't deal with anything else."

"Okay." He played with a strand of my hair. "Are we okay?"

I snuggled against him. "I guess so."

*　　*　　*

"We haven't located any other body dumps. None of the victims' dental records match Jessika Wellington's. They probably have another method of disposing of the remains," O'Connell surmised.

"Was the construction site abandoned five years ago?" I asked.

"I'm not sure. I don't think so."

"Then she wouldn't be there."

"Unless they moved the bodies," Thompson muttered.

I gave him a look. "Rule number one, never move the bodies."

Thompson narrowed his eyes. "Speaking from experience?"

"Wouldn't you like to know?" I turned to O'Connell. "Did you find anything that will help identify the killer? My money's on Dalton."

O'Connell shrugged and glanced at Thompson, who said, "We checked, and of the victims we have already identified, all of them were patients at the free clinic. Aside from that, we haven't found anything to tie them together.

They're different races, genders, and ages. The murders don't follow typical victimology. The killings aren't in any specific pattern. They appear random, which coincides with the theory you floated last night. It makes sense the killer works at the clinic."

"Great, I'm brilliant."

Thompson scoffed. "I never said you were brilliant. The entire department reached the same conclusion, and several of them couldn't find their way out of a paper bag."

O'Connell drummed his pen against the top of his desk. "I listened to the recordings you and Cross made. Ridley Dalton was pretty convincing, but he's still our prime suspect. You put him on tilt the moment you stepped foot in that neighborhood, and he's lashing out. He isn't making plans to escape. He's figuring out how to retaliate and get away with it. When I speak to him, I want him off balance. I heard the change in his tone on the recording. You push his buttons to the point of unpredictability. Last night, he shut you down. I don't need him to shut down inside the interrogation room, so I'm asking you to back off."

"Fine, I'll keep my distance. Any progress on the other fronts?"

"We're hoping one of the twerps in holding will cave," Thompson volunteered. "We have to interview every member of the gang again in lieu of recent discoveries."

"Did anyone bite?" I asked.

"We just started. If we get enough for a warrant, we'll be in business, but even if we don't, we'll bring Dalton in tomorrow morning to have a chat. He's under surveillance. At some point, he'll slip up," O'Connell said.

"Nick," I began, but he held up his palm to silence me.

"I already spoke to your boss. He's on board. You need to get there. I know this is personal after what they did to you, but you have to trust me on this. Let me do my job."

Before I even got out of the chair, O'Connell received a notification. Opening the attachment, he clicked through the surveillance photos, cocking an interested eyebrow. He forwarded the documents to Thompson and printed hard copies. When he returned with a stack of glossies, he tossed them on the desk.

"Hold up a sec. Where did you say you stabbed the man in green?" Thompson asked.

"Upper left arm."

Thompson studied the photos. "And you slashed his forearm. Am I remembering that correctly?"

"Uh-huh." I leaned forward and reached for the photographs. "Shit. I didn't do that. What the hell happened to him?"

The police surveillance footage showed several stills of Dalton running shirtless. The left side of his body was marred in extensive scars and what appeared to be recent lacerations, making it nearly impossible to see if he was stabbed or cut. He had jagged red scars and several healed sutures. Most of the damage appeared to be from burns, and I wondered if he had nerve damage. That might explain why he didn't show pain and why he allowed the scalpel to cut into him. It might have just been another calculated move by the psychopath to throw us off the scent.

"Do you think he made sure we saw this just to taunt us?" I pointed at the image.

"It isn't clear, but he stayed on his property. I'm not sure he knows we're watching him. But I will ask him about it as soon as I get the chance," O'Connell assured me. "If we have any other questions, we'll give you a call."

Nodding, I climbed out of the chair. This changed things. I wasn't exactly sure how, but it did. Deciding I needed to do more research on the good doctor, I left the precinct with Cross Security as my intended destination. Five minutes into the drive, my phone rang. It was Janet Wellington. She wanted to meet in person to talk about last night.

When I parked in her driveway, I recognized her husband's vehicle. Oh boy. Lucien was not going to be happy about this.

Deciding there was no reason to give my boss the heads up, I went up the walkway and rang the doorbell. Janet answered the door, a tight smile on her face. She stepped backward, and I entered her home. It looked exactly the same as it did during my previous visit. The throw pillows and glassware were probably even in the same positions.

She swallowed and led me into the kitchen. William was seated at the table, a cup of coffee and the newspaper in front of him. He looked up at the sound of our footfalls, nodding slightly. Janet took a seat at the other end of the table. The silence was deafening.

Finally, William tilted his head back and looked up at me. "You caused quite the scene last night."

"Sorry, if I ruined your evening."

"What are you going to do about it?" he replied.

"Bill," Janet hissed, "manners."

He glanced briefly at his wife. When his gaze went back to me, I saw the slightest hint of fear. "Lucien said removing you from my daughter's case was a mistake. So tell me, what does Ridley Dalton have to do with my little girl's disappearance?"

"You should speak to my boss."

"I'm speaking to you," William said matter-of-factly.

"Mr. Cross wouldn't comment," Janet mumbled. "I thought you might. You actually give a damn, unlike everyone else we hired."

"Have you spoken to the police?" I asked, hoping to deflect their questions.

"They spoke to us this morning. They asked more questions about Jessika's volunteer work. We didn't know she worked with Dr. Dalton. When she went missing, he denied she volunteered at the clinic." William leaned back in his chair. "Janet, can you get the blue file out of the safe in the bedroom? I want to show Miss Parker something."

Obediently, she stood and went down the hallway. William patted the chair and waited for me to take a seat. He glanced into the hallway to make sure she was gone before he said, "I know you've been looking into me. The police have some pretty interesting ideas and intel, and I'm guessing it came from you."

"I go where the investigation leads."

He glared. "My marriage counselor had something to say about that too. Do you want to know why I have so many adult videos on my hard drive? It's because I was told this is what becomes of runaways. Girls get desperate and are preyed upon by sex traffickers and pornographers. The first firm I hired turned me on to some locally filmed videos. I've been watching them for research."

"Okay." I didn't believe him, but that was irrelevant.

"It's also the reason I regularly pick up escorts. You've seen my credit card expenses. The girls provide better answers when they are given nice gifts. I've been asking around in the hopes of finding Jessika, but no one's ever seen her. She's not turning tricks, at least not here."

"Did you ever go into the Seven Rooks' territory?" I gave him the street names, but he shook his head.

"Ever pick up a girl named Ivy?"

He blinked. "I don't know."

"Did you ever beat a hooker?"

That question made him angry. "What kind of man do you think I am?"

"What kind of man are you?"

"One who's spent years doing whatever he can to find his daughter."

"So you thought she decided to become a high-end call girl." Admittedly, I considered that also. "You realize girls that do are usually repeating abuse patterns." My eyes went hard. "Did you molest your daughter?"

"Fuck no. I'm not a monster."

"You didn't know a damn thing about her or what she was doing. You admitted that when we first met."

"Just because I was never father of the year doesn't mean I touched her or hurt her. I would never do that. I love her."

"What about the assistant you're banging? Any idea why Samantha Capshaw was attacked? Or who attacked her?"

He bit the inside of his lip and waited for his wife to return with the folder. When she placed it on the table, he removed a tattered envelope and held it out. "Read it."

Carefully, I slid the paper out of the envelope. Type-written in red ink were the words *Tell Cross Security to back off, or you'll lose someone else you love.*

"I showed that to Lucien the morning after Samantha was attacked. He said it meant we were on the right track. This morning, he phones and says he's dropping the case.

It's a police matter. I don't know what happened, but given the exchange the two of you had with Ridley Dalton last night, I have to assume the doctor is involved. We want answers, Miss Parker. We deserve them."

THIRTY-SEVEN

After my meeting with the Wellingtons, I went back to Cross Security with every intention of giving Lucien a piece of my mind, but he wasn't there. Instead, I found a manila envelope in my mail tray. Tearing it open, I shook out the contents and stared at the surveillance photos. Apparently, Agent Ivers actually wanted to help.

From what I could tell, the ATF had the Seven Rooks under surveillance for some time. The timestamp on the images was dated five years ago, just a few months before Jessika's disappearance. Victor was standing at the rear of a SUV. I couldn't identify the other men, but they were probably part of the gang. The crates in the back contained firearms. Without context, I could only speculate what was happening, but like they say, a picture is worth a thousand words.

When I arrived back at the precinct, O'Connell wasn't at his desk. Most of the floor was busy. There had been a shooting at a mall, but it wasn't related to my investigation. Thompson materialized a few moments later, a wary look on his face.

"Didn't you just say you weren't going to interfere?" he asked.

"Things change." I handed him the photo. "Agent Ivers delivered that to my office. Victor was a gun runner. He's probably what links the killings to the gang."

"Yeah, okay." Thompson put the photo on the edge of his desk. "In case you haven't noticed, we're in the middle of something."

"Put me in a room with Victor. I'll help out."

"Parker," he growled.

"It'd be faster to just agree." I gave him a look. "We'll keep the recording equipment on. I'll tell him I'm acting on behalf of the police and remind him of his rights. It'll be fine. Everything's copacetic."

Grumbling, Thompson got up from his chair. "Clear it with Moretti, and just remember if this asshole gets kicked, it's your fault." Then he disappeared down the stairwell, and I went to the lieutenant's office and knocked.

After some cajoling, Victor Harrendale was delivered to an interrogation room. A uniform came with me to keep things official. Victor snorted, a smirk plastered on his face. He leaned back in the chair, his hands cuffed in his lap.

"I thought I'd see you again," he said.

"Funny, so did I." I placed the surveillance photo on the table in front of him. "We ran your name, but nothing pinged. It's weird you're not in the system. Maybe you have a new identity, but you still have the same fingers. Dr. Dalton didn't do a finger transplant, did he?"

The mention of Dalton's name caused a shift in Victor. He knew we had him. And he was worried.

"I'm guessing you made a deal last time. From what I'm seeing, you were a middleman, brokering deals between your supplier and the gang. Let me guess, you handed over your gun connection, and the ATF made your problems go away, except you found a new racket."

Victor bit his upper lip. "You don't know anything."

"Agent Ivers does." I grinned. "And let's not forget, you're the idiot who left the syringe. You had no problem stabbing me with it. Hell, you held it in your sweaty palms so long the oils from your skin bled through the thin latex and left a nice usable print. So my only question is why aren't you willing to roll this time? You did it before. What happened? Did Dalton take your balls?"

Victor lurched forward. "Why don't you find out?"

I sighed and dropped into a chair. "Josh gave us Dalton. He gave us the location of the dump site. He also said it's your job to put the victims out of their misery. Dalton says he was coerced to perform the procedures. You forced him with constant threats and violence. Everyone is saying you did this. They'll serve time, but it'll be nothing compared to you, especially when your previous activities come to light."

"It wasn't like that." He looked at the cop. "I want a deal in writing before I say another word."

Harrendale's attorney was not happy I questioned him without counsel present, but Victor just wanted a deal. The district attorney agreed to drop the murder charges if Victor testified against his accomplices and fleshed out the gang connection to the clinic. Frankly, the deal was too good for that prick, but until now, everything was circumstantial.

Victor originally ran guns, but when the ATF used him to bust his supplier, Victor found himself in a tough position. The Seven Rooks didn't know he was a snitch, but if the wrong person talked, he'd be in trouble. So Victor looked for the next biggest player as a means of protecting himself. He and Josh met at Prince's bar. One night after getting totally shitfaced, Josh said he was tired of getting shafted with low wages and shit work. He saw so many dealers driving luxury cars that he wanted a piece of the action. Victor said he could line up some buyers and bridge the gap between the gang and the clinic, if Josh could get him a steady supply.

At first, it was just drugs. Pharmaceutical reps loved to hock product, and since the clinic had a steady supply and the hospital and doctors' offices had an oversupply, it wasn't hard to steal the extras or pocket some of the expired pills before they could be returned or destroyed. When Dalton found out about their scheme, he threatened to report them, but when he didn't, Victor got curious. That's when he discovered the doctor was performing surgeries on the side.

The hospital's rich patients needed faster alternatives

than being at the bottom of some transplant waiting list, and the Seven Rooks were in need of a creative way to dispose of their rivals. Some of the men they shot or beat were taken to the clinic. Most were users, but the few who weren't made excellent donors. And so it continued. Now the potential donor pool grew to include rival gang members as well as clinic patients.

Victor worked the trenches, brokering peace with the Rooks by supplying them pharmaceutical grade narcotics and an easy way to dispose of their victims while Dalton performed the surgeries, saving the lives of the wealthy at the cost of society's throwaways. According to Victor, Dalton rationalized the murders as ending suffering. It was just another way of assigning worth to a person based on socioeconomic status, and the thought was infuriating and sickening.

Victor never mentioned any other names besides the ones I gave him, and he didn't have any hard evidence to corroborate anything he said. It would be the word of a dealer against a respected doctor who served his country and his community. It wasn't enough for an arrest, but it was enough for a warrant.

*   *   *

The judge granted a sweeping search of Dalton's home, his various offices, his finances, phone records, and online activity. The police had a lot to process. Dalton was livid and fought tooth and nail to have the warrant rescinded, but that didn't happen. Unfortunately, no one found any hard evidence. The doctor owned several pairs of green scrubs, none of which were cut or torn at the sleeve.

His finances showed he amassed quite a fortune, but his funds came from reputable sources. There was no way to disprove the bonuses he received were compensation for illicit surgeries. Aside from interest payments and investments, every deposit into his account came from Brandt's corporation. And on top of that, the bulk of his investments were brokered by the same firm that employed William Wellington. Everyone was inextricably linked to the point I couldn't help but think every bit of information on Jessika could be easily accessed by Dalton. Even if her father wasn't involved, the men who took Jessika knew enough to hurt William and the Wellington family should anything ever come to light.

When Ridley Dalton stepped out of the interrogation room, free to go, he spotted me in the hallway. Putting a business smile on his face, he approached. "It's nice to see you again."

"You really think so?" I asked.

He grinned. "The police said I can leave. They searched everything. I didn't hurt you, Alex. I'm a doctor. The Hippocratic Oath means something. I've dedicated my life to putting an end to suffering, not to causing it."

"Is that how you justify ending one life in order to save another?"

"I don't know what you mean, but that is the nature of triage."

"Jessika didn't fit the typical profile. She wasn't living on the fringe. She came from a good family. She had a future and a lot of people in her life that gave a damn. She also had money. So why did you take her? Was it because she had a rare blood type? Or was it because she found out what you were doing?"

He didn't answer.

THIRTY-EIGHT

Monday morning, I barged into Cross's office despite his assistant's protests. Cross looked up, his expression unreadable.

"Would you like me to call security?" his assistant asked.

"That won't be necessary. I'm sure Miss Parker has her reasons for intruding." His eyes flicked to the assistant. "Close the door." Cross leaned back in his chair. "What's the problem?"

"The problem is you told the Wellingtons we're done."

"Aren't we?" Cross cocked an eyebrow. "I made it clear we do not involve ourselves in murder investigations. Our interference could taint evidence and prevent a conviction, not to mention the potential obstruction of justice charges. This isn't new news."

Exasperated, I paced in front of his desk. "The police aren't looking for Jessika. They are trying to stop Dalton from abducting and killing people."

"And you don't think they are one and the same?"

"Of course, I do."

"Then we need to back off. I won't jeopardize this firm or my people. That includes you. However," he flipped through the calendar on his desk, "you have a week left to find out what happened to the girl. We aren't going into the field. We aren't questioning suspects. And we sure as hell aren't stepping foot inside the clinic or near Dalton or his associates. Whatever work we can do remotely is still being done, but I wanted the Wellingtons to know we aren't actively looking for Jessika. This is a police matter now. The answers they seek will have to come from the authorities."

"This is bullshit."

"No, Miss Parker, this is the life of a private investigator. Get used to it or go back to your government job." He jerked his chin at the door. "You're dismissed."

Angry and irritated, I stopped on the thirty-first floor to see if the computer techs uncovered any online activity indicative of the killing spree. As predicted, the dark web was full of illicit dealings — murder for hire, traffickers, and a fair amount of people looking to buy or sell body parts. As of yet, they didn't find anything conclusive. Perhaps Dalton did everything the old-fashioned way. He worked at a hospital. He knew what patients were in need and who could pay through the nose. Everything could be kept quiet and off the radar. It's probably why he was never caught.

Returning to the thirtieth floor, I realized I couldn't decide if my priority was nailing Dalton or finding Jessika. I wanted both. I didn't want anyone else to fall prey to that sadist, but this began with Jessika. It needed to end with finding out what happened to her.

"Hey," I said, knocking gently on Renner's open door, "what are you doing?"

Bennett pushed back from his desk, the skin around his eyes a sickly greenish yellow. "Looking for a new angle on Jessika's disappearance. I heard you and Lucien had one hell of a Saturday night. What are the cops doing about it?"

"I don't know. They didn't want me to stick around and find out."

He chuckled. "Yeah, that's how I would have played it too. Don't take it personally." Pressing a button, he sent the display from his computer to the large screen on the wall. "Before you threatened to shoot me, I told you I was looking into possible networking or business connections. I've gone through every group Jessika was a part of and checked into every member of those groups. Now, I'm working my way through Dylan Hart's contacts. He and Jessika traveled in the same circles. If she reached out to someone about the happenings at the clinic, it could have been someone close to him." He read the skeptical look on my face. "I know it's grasping at straws, but we're out of leads. My gut says Jess vanished because she saw something she wasn't supposed to. She had over twelve hours to seek help, and she was a smart girl. I bet she reached out to someone. We need to find that someone."

"All right. Let me grab my laptop, and you can tell me where to start."

The hours turned into days. Dylan Hart had over five thousand friends across his various social media accounts. Most of them came into the picture after Jessika's disappearance, but we wanted to be thorough. Plus, every other avenue was barred.

O'Connell phoned constantly with updates. Since I was willing to back away from the investigation, he was keeping me looped in. He probably hoped I'd be able to turn something around.

The second interview with Dalton didn't go well. When asked why he lied about Jessika working at the clinic, he stuck to the story he told me. He allegedly had an alibi for the time of my abduction, saying he was in his office. However, no one saw him during a two hour time span, and the hospital cameras didn't cover that particular area. It was his word against mine, and I was unable to positively identify him, which meant everything was circumstantial.

The next day, Dalton filed a TRO against Cross Security in general and me specifically. It was a bullshit move, aimed to discredit any testimony I would theoretically be able to provide in the event the police ever found something damning against the murderer. Dalton was smart. He knew how the game was played, or he had enough sense to hire an attorney that did. It also painted him as guilty in my book. And his scar tissue did nothing but add to my suspicions.

Dalton had several recent skin grafts. He had these procedures done periodically to repair the damage done from being too close to an explosion. It made it nearly impossible to tell if he was stabbed or cut, particularly since the blade I used was a surgical instrument. However, O'Connell managed to get access to his military record and medical reports, so we knew a lot of the nerves were damaged due to the third degree burns. It was likely Dalton couldn't feel pain in that part of his body, making it even harder to prove he was the man in green scrubs.

"We need a credible witness," O'Connell surmised, "preferably someone who saw him committing murder or hacking up a body and who wasn't involved in the scheme. Unless that happens, everything we have is circumstantial."

"What about Victor?"

"We've hit another snag. We found something at Harrendale's apartment during a second walkthrough that makes his statement questionable."

"What?" I asked, fearing whatever he was about to say.

"The weapon used to kill the hooker. We discovered a metal tube with jagged edges that tested positive for Ivy's blood. The medical examiner determined it fit the punctures in her neck. The strange thing is we didn't find it during our first search of Victor's apartment, and I can't help but think Dalton planted it."

"Don't you have him under surveillance?"

"We do," O'Connell insisted, "but he could have asked someone else to do it. He knows we have Addai and Harrendale in custody, and he might know Victor talked. Dalton would want to discredit him, and this was the best way possible. It's pure manipulation. It would definitely confuse a jury. Hell, if I didn't know better, I might be convinced."

"So what's it going to take to get Dalton dead to rights?"

"A miracle."

"I'll see what I can do. In the meantime, maybe you should check back with the ATF and Mr. Prince. They might have something useful."

"Been there, done that." He sighed. "Let me know if

something pops."

"Didn't you tell me to stay away from this?"

"Like you ever listen to a word I say." Nick hung up, and I went back to endlessly searching through every single one of Dylan Hart's online acquaintances to see if any of them knew Jessika or what happened to her.

It'd been four days. Renner and I had gone through nearly three thousand individuals. It was pointless. We ruled out most of them simply based on when and how Dylan met them. Getting up, I rubbed my eyes and lifted my empty coffee cup. At least my cold cleared up. Too bad time didn't heal everything.

"You want a refill, Bennett?" I asked.

He held up his mug. "Thanks."

Returning with fresh coffee, I placed Renner's beside him and went back to my spot. We needed to find a connection. "Did you ever run across Josh Addai in relation to Jessika Wellington?"

"Why? What are you thinking?"

"He volunteered at the clinic the same time she did. When I spoke to him, he said he let Jessika go. O'Connell figured he'd say just about anything to save his own ass, but the way he said it was like he knew her. I thought maybe they had some kind of online connection."

Renner raised a single brow. "You know that would have been one of the first things the PD checked."

"Yeah, but I doubt they're being this thorough."

"Actually, they have software that runs through connections and algorithms. They probably did a better job in a fraction of the time. Upstairs has it too. And I know they looked."

"Then why are we doing this?"

"There's something to be said for the human element, particularly when someone could make a fake profile, use a fake name, or post a bogus image. It screws with the software. The parameters are too finicky to compensate. Plus, you're out of a job in two days. It's not like you have anything better to do. Maybe I'm auditioning you to be my assistant."

"Assist this." I held up my middle finger.

"I'd love to."

I laughed. "Screw you."

"That is kind of the point." He winked. "You know, you're not so bad when you're not pointing a gun at me. And you know just how I like my coffee. That makes you okay in my book. So what do you say to the assistant thing?"

"Shut up and get back to work." I tossed a playful smile in his direction and settled behind the computer.

After a half hour of silence, Renner leaned back in his chair, throwing his screen onto the large monitor. He shrunk Dylan's social media page and opened a blank document. "More people have to know what Dalton's doing. Most of the Seven Rooks are in custody, including dealers, bangers, and hookers. Then we have the allegedly upstanding clinic workers. We have those bastards who roughed you up, which weren't affiliated with the Rooks but think they're tough guys anyway. And there's the actual hospital staff who basically alibied Dalton out." He typed up the categories and stared at the screen.

"You forgot the bartender and ATF agent."

He added those to the list. "Yeah, I don't get it. What could this guy possibly have on all of these people?"

I shrugged, placing my laptop on the table. "He has money and obvious connections to pharmaceuticals."

"So he's supplying the Seven Rooks with product, and they know snitches get stitches. All right." He crossed off that category.

I stood and pointed to the next category. "The rest of the clinic could be involved, or he made sure to fly below the radar. They're clueless, or they're part of it. So they can't talk because they'll be implicated."

"It goes back to Henry Brandt. He controls everything."

"Yeah, that's the thing. He invested with the firm where William Wellington works. He knows things about the Wellingtons. Janet works at a nonprofit, which has hosted joint functions with his nonprofit. There's so much overlap it's sickening. Even Dalton has an account with the same firm."

Renner narrowed his eyes. "Brandt's behind this. It's his

hospital. His clinic. His funding. And he's lining his pockets with ill-gotten gains and paying Dalton to perform the surgeries."

"We can't even prove Dalton's involved. How the hell do you think we're going to make the connection to Brandt?"

Renner sighed and marked off that category. "Okay, that makes two. The same might be true for the rest of his colleagues." He slashed off the last category. "That leaves us with his two known and identified accomplices. They're already implicated. They have nothing left to lose. Why isn't Addai backing Victor's story?"

"That's what I've been wondering. When I spoke to Addai, he was afraid. He was afraid of what they were doing and who would be targeted next. Maybe Dalton threatened someone he loved."

"Like he did with the Wellingtons to try to get us to back off." Renner bit his lip and let out a growl. "Do you think Harrendale murdered the whore?"

"I don't doubt he's a killer." I glanced up at Renner. "What if he's the triggerman?"

He snorted, shaking his head with disgust. "That would explain a lot. Assuming Henry Brandt's in charge, maybe the doctor is just upper management. Dalton selects the victims based on some perverse criteria, has someone else do the snatch and grab, does the dissection himself, and has Victor finish the job and clean up. The more people involved, the less likely anyone is to talk." He stood and stretched. "We need to cross-reference the clinic's records with hospital patients to see who was a match and who might have benefitted. It's the only way we're going to connect this."

"Except we don't have that kind of access," I said. "And even if we did, why would someone who's been saved from a death sentence give up their doctor?"

"The police can get access. The threat of years in prison might get someone with a new lease on life to come forward." He picked up his phone and dialed. "Just in case the PD forgot how to function without me, I'll give them a little reminder."

While he was on the phone, he played with the mouse,

minimizing the list and going back to Dylan's social media page. One image stuck out like a sore thumb. I'd recognize those piercings anywhere.

"I need to check on something," I said. My subconscious had seen it. Why didn't I?

THIRTY-NINE

"Nick, I need you to drop everything and meet me at the diner. If I'm right, I just made your case. But we need pie. Now."

I sat inside my car, staring through the window at the two waitresses. There were so many little things I should have picked up on, but I wasn't paying attention. Even now, I wasn't entirely sure my assumption was correct. A lot was different. But like Renner said, I'd be out of a job in two days, so it was now or never.

O'Connell pulled up behind me, thankfully in an unmarked cruiser. He got out of the car, narrowing his eyes. "This better be fucking good. I was in the middle of working over some of the Seven Rooks. One of them is willing to testify the clinic supplied them with narcotics to sell."

"That's great. Did they point the finger at Dalton?"

"Not yet. So what's this about?"

"You'll see. First, I have to make sure I'm right. Take a seat near the rear exit and order whatever you like. It's on me."

"What are you going to do?"

"You'll see." I pushed him toward the door, and he went

inside and did what I asked.

The chiming of the bell drew the attention of Delores, who smiled. "I'll be right with you, dear."

She disappeared into the kitchen to grab someone else's order, and I went to the front counter, leaning over to see if I could catch a glimpse of Skye. She was emptying a tray of dirty dishes into the machine. She finished what she was doing, her eyes focused on the floor as she left the kitchen and headed for the register.

"I need to talk to you," I said.

She looked up, anger in her eyes. "Dammit, I thought I finally got rid of you." Her gaze darted to where Delores was taking Nick's order. "And you brought your boyfriend back. Didn't I tell you messing around with married guys isn't cool?"

"Your dad cheated on your mom, huh?"

She looked at me. Her bright unnatural blue eyes were piercing. Everything about her was so different now, not at all like the old photographs. She shrugged with one shoulder. "It happens, right?"

"When did you find out?"

"This isn't some daytime talk show. What the hell do you want?"

I licked my lips. If I was wrong, Dalton wouldn't be the only one filing a restraining order. "Skye Bleu, interesting name. Did you pick it out from a box of crayons? I would have gone with something else. Burnt sienna has a nice ring or maybe mandarin orange. Then again, I knew a woman named Ivy Greene, so colors are just popping up everywhere nowadays."

"Who are you?" she growled. I saw the fear in her eyes. She was five seconds from bolting.

I took a step back and held up my palms, appearing as nonthreatening as possible. "Dylan misses you. You took one hell of risk friending him, but it's not like you ever spoke directly to him. I checked. No private messages. No communications. Not a single like. It's okay. It's natural to wonder what an ex is up to."

She blinked, her lips pressed so tightly together I wondered if her mouth was glued shut.

"When I broke up with my boyfriend, I left town, but I still found myself drawn to things that reminded me of him. I needed to feel a connection. For what it's worth, Dylan wonders what would have happened if you stuck around."

"Who the fuck is Dylan?"

"Tell me I'm wrong." I rolled up my sleeves and turned my arms to show her the barely faded bruises. "The same thing happened to you, didn't it? It's happened to a lot of people. And it's going to keep happening unless you come forward. I can protect you."

She snorted. "Clearly, you can't even protect yourself."

"Fair enough, but I survived, just like you. Twelve people didn't, and I'm guessing there are more we haven't found yet. Don't you want to go home? Don't you want to be free from the constant fear they'll find you?" Slowly, I reached into my pocket and pulled out my Cross Security identification.

She looked down at it. "I don't know who you think I am, but you have the wrong girl."

"Did your dad hurt you? Is he part of this? Is that why you ran away?" I narrowed my eyes, watching her. "If you're afraid to go home, I won't make you. I will walk out that door and not say a thing to anyone. I'll keep your secret safe."

"Like I said, you have the wrong person."

"I guess I do." I glanced behind me and across the street at the gym. "You miss your mom. Isn't that why you work here? So you can see her every day. Can I at least tell her you're okay, Jessika?"

She bit her lip as tears rolled down her cheek. "They'll kill them. Josh said if I ever went home they'd kill my entire family."

"I won't let that happen."

"You can't stop it. The gang does their bidding. These people are everywhere. They know things about my mom and my dad." She sneered. "This was the only way I could keep them safe, unless I let them kill me."

"Jessika, we can stop them."

"No." She shook her head vehemently. "I had to

disappear. I thought it was safe, but I guess I didn't do a good enough job. You found me. Now I have to leave again." She angrily brushed at her tears. "I'm so sick of starting over. This is your fault."

"Wait," I implored, "Nick's a cop. He pulled me out of a tub of ice water where those men left me to die. He arrested two of them, Josh and Victor. Dr. Dalton isn't in custody yet, but Victor will testify against him. I will testify against him." Dalton's name sent shivers through her and drained what little blood remained in her face. "But we need to make a stronger case. You can do that. You're the only one who can stop him. Everyone else is dead."

"Why can't you? You're an investigator. Shouldn't they listen to you?"

"Dalton wore a mask. I can't positively identify him. I promise if you come forward, we'll lock him and everyone else away for good. They won't be able to hurt you or your family. You can have your life back. You had a ten year plan. I know you didn't expect the first five to go like this. Don't let those shitheads take any more time from you. Don't let them get away with this. You wanted to be a doctor in order to help people. I know you're scared. But you can help now. You're a survivor. You will survive this. You have my word."

"I don't know."

I had one trick left up my sleeve, but it was a gamble. "The hiding isn't working. Your parents won't stop looking for you. No matter what, they'll keep searching. And if they keep it up, one of these days, someone will put a stop to that. I know you're trying to protect them." I placed the threat on the counter. "You can put an end to this. We just need your cooperation. The police will protect you. I promise."

She glanced uncertainly across the diner at Nick and back at me. Then she came around the counter, tossing her apron and order pad onto a stool before breaking down in my arms. She changed everything, gained twenty pounds, colored her hair, altered her eye color, and covered her face in so much makeup and so many rings the only thing anyone saw was the piercings and not the face behind them.

"You're safe now," I said, hugging her as she sobbed. "You're going home."

*   *   *

It didn't take long for O'Connell to move the Wellingtons into protective custody with their daughter. Jessika overheard a conversation at the clinic and saw Dr. Dalton sedate a patient and load him into the back of a van. The doctor thought the clinic was empty, but Jessika was taking inventory in the storage room. Dalton cornered her and tried to convince her what she saw wasn't accurate. But Jessika was a smart girl. She didn't believe him, so he tossed her into the back of the van with his latest victim.

She was taken to another facility. Her description was eerily similar to the room I described. He left her bound and gagged. When he realized she had a rare blood type, he planned to drain her and dispose of her like the others. Josh was supposed to have done the deed, except he couldn't. He waited until they were alone, put her in his car, and dropped her off at a bus station. He told her to run and never come back. If she didn't listen, her entire family would be slaughtered.

Jessika emptied out the secret stash of cash her father kept, probably to sneak around with his mistress. It was nearly a thousand dollars. She already had a fake ID for going to bars and listening to music with her friends. Her plan was in motion. The problem was she didn't want to go too far in case Dalton or Josh decided to end her family anyway.

She brought a change of clothes to school, and during the pep rally, she switched outfits. She left her phone, purse, and other belongings at school and took off. A rideshare was waiting to pick her up a few blocks away. She had the driver go across town. After buying a box of black hair dye, she paid cash at a motor inn, one of the less scrupulous establishments that made a point not to pay attention to its customers. She changed her hair and started wearing goth makeup. Eventually, she convinced the manager to let her clean the rooms in exchange for a place to stay until she found somewhere else to go.

After a couple of years working odd jobs and keeping tabs on her mom and dad, she noticed the diner across from her mom's gym had an opening. She took the job, added a few more piercings, and bought colored contacts on the off chance her mother ever came inside. Janet didn't, but even if she did, I doubted she would have recognized her own daughter.

Now the police just had to sort through the mess. They were building a case against Henry Brandt with the help of the Wellingtons. It would take time, but given the things William and Janet knew, they'd get there, particularly since Jessika's parents lost five years with their daughter because of that son of a bitch. At least Dalton was locked up, and bail was denied. Jessika's testimony would ensure he never got out. But it'd be a long, hard road ahead before life returned to normal. She'd been surviving and running for so long it'd take time before she ever felt safe again.

"It looks like I was right to give you a shot," Cross said. We were seated opposite each other at the conference table. "I'm curious. Do you always let things go down to the wire?"

"Only when my hands are tied," I said pointedly, which Cross ignored. "If it wasn't for Renner, I wouldn't have made the connection. You ought to give that man a raise. I hear he's in the market for an assistant."

Cross gestured at the contract. "Are you planning on renegotiating that into the terms of your deal?"

"No." I looked down at the document. Two years with the option to renew based on performance. "I got lucky. If I'd just gone to the coffee shop on the corner instead of the diner, we never would have found her. Dr. Dalton would still be performing unsanctioned surgeries and grabbing donors off the free clinic's patient roster or from the victims the Seven Rooks dropped off."

"Now it sounds like you're hoping to renegotiate your salary," he said.

"I'm not." I gave the contract another glance.

He leaned back, scrutinizing me. "Have you decided to

go back to a federal position? Are murder cases the only ones you want to work because the police department might have a few openings in homicide division? I can make a call."

Linking my hands together, I put my elbows on the table and rested my chin on top of my thumbs. "For most of this month, I've had the distinct impression you don't particularly care for the way I do things. I won't tolerate the micromanaging and oversight. I want case autonomy. Actual case autonomy." I flipped pages. "And I want you to waive the non-compete."

He rubbed his chin, finding a spot he missed when he shaved this morning. "It sounds like you plan to freelance."

"Is that a problem?"

He waited half a beat and reached for a pen, marking out a few lines and altering some stipulations. "It will decrease your starting salary by half."

"I can live with that."

"And James Martin becomes a client of Cross Security."

"Excuse me?"

"Your relationship with him isn't a secret, Miss Parker. He's the reason you were moved to the top of my list. A few years ago, you stole him away from Cross Security. Now that you're back in the game, I imagine he'll want to rehire you as a consultant. That won't be freelance. He's a whale, and I want him. You might work for him, but he'll be invoiced by me."

"What if he doesn't hire me?"

Cross cocked his head slightly to the side as if the question didn't compute. "Why wouldn't he? He's already dropped by these offices once to speak to you."

Unsure if Cross knew of my personal relationship, I decided not to volunteer anything extra. "Like you said, it's been a few years. He might have found someone better. I hear he has in-house security."

"Which you helped establish. If he needs something in the future, he'll come to you. I'm sure of it."

"Is that why you hired me?"

Cross leaned back, knowing he had me where he wanted me. "At this point, the reason for your hiring is irrelevant.

You found a missing girl after five years. You unearthed unscrupulous medical practices, brought a local gang to its knees, and at last count helped the police arrest Dr. Dalton and several of his associates. Like I said, murder investigations aren't our thing, but that's impressive work for a single month. I'd like to see what you do in six months or a year."

Picking up the pen, I toyed with the idea of signing on the dotted line. "I want full access to your resources for all of my cases. Is that a problem?"

"Not in the least. By the way, did you ever figure out what you were missing on that other matter?"

"It's being handled."

He nodded, watching as I signed my name. "Welcome to the team, Alex."

"That's the first time you've called me Alex."

"I know your type. You hate authority. You don't like to follow orders, least of all from someone who has never been on the job. You think you know better. I like to make the boundaries clear from the beginning. I'm hoping after the shit we just went through respect won't be an issue between us. Maybe I'll loosen the reins a little." He pushed away from the table. "You have a client meeting in ten minutes. I suggest you prepare."

ALEXIS PARKER WILL BE BACK IN 2019

BUT YOU CAN CONTINUE THE
INVESTIGATION INTO MICHELLE
MERCER'S MURDER WITH REPARATION
(JULIAN MERCER #4) NOW AVAILABLE IN
PRINT AND AS AN E-BOOK

ABOUT THE AUTHOR

G.K. Parks is the author of the Alexis Parker series. The first novel, *Likely Suspects,* tells the story of Alexis' first foray into the private sector.

G.K. Parks received a Bachelor of Arts in Political Science and History. After spending some time in law school, G.K. changed paths and earned a Master of Arts in Criminology/Criminal Justice. Now all that education is being put to use creating a fictional world based upon years of study and research.

You can find additional information on G.K. Parks and the Alexis Parker series by visiting our website at
www.alexisparkerseries.com

Made in the USA
Middletown, DE
14 January 2021